THE FEAST

"Come forward where we may see you."

His mouth watering in anticipation, Hamish walked into the firelight. He bowed.

The nobleman and his lady smiled.

The fire blazed up, larger than before, and Hamish saw the source of the delectable odor that had drawn him.

It was a human torso with the head still attached. It had been skewered by a metal rod supported by a tripod at either end. The underside was charred and the top was raw.

The remains of half a dozen other corpses were scattered around under the trees.

Books by Ken Hood

Demon Sword
Demon Rider
*Demon Knight**

Published by HarperPrism

*coming soon

I am most grateful to Clélie Rich, without whose help the spells would have been quite incomprehensible, even to demons, and thus the ending would have been very different.

BAY OF
BISCAY

BORDEAUX

CASTILE

AQUITAINE

NAVARRE

ARAGON

ZARAGOZA   LERIDA

MONTSERRAT

BARCELONA

R. EBRO

TOLEDO

TORTOSA

VALENCIA

MEDITERRANEAN
SEA

CASTILE

CONTENTS

[In August 1522] Queen Caterina fled and Barcelona opened its gates. . . . After a merciless wasting of Aragon and Navarre, Nevil invaded Castile. When his guns began bombarding Toledo and his hexers rained down thunderbolts, King Pedro surrendered. Although the Fiend had never granted quarter to any foe in the past, he allowed Pedro to retain his throne after doing homage for it and renouncing his allegiance to the Khan. Caterina and her sons were handed over in chains and never heard of again, but the usual gruesome rumors were probably well founded. . . .

Undoubtedly the most surprising clause in the treaty was the second, which dealt with a matter seemingly too trivial to mention in a document so weighty—it must have puzzled contemporaries as much as it intrigues modern historians. King Pedro agreed to hunt down an insignificant outlaw identified as "Tobias Strangerson, otherwise known as Longdirk." He was to be put to death "in a fashion appropriate to those possessed by demons," and his body, clothes, and possessions were to be handed over promptly to the Fiend's agents. . . . Nevil himself then withdrew from Spain. . . .

The Fall of the Khanate in Europe
Jeremiah Hammer,
Oxford, 1932

ONE

JOURNEY'S END

The door of the crypt swung open with a long creak of rusty hinges that echoed through the black interior like a groan of despair. Iron-bound timber thundered against stonework and stopped; the booming reverberation faded into a tread of boots as a soldier entered, wearing the scarlet sash and gold-hilted sword of an officer. He carried a lantern, but after a few paces he had to stop and hold it motionless in the fetid air until its flame burned up more brightly. Then the darkness crept away behind pillars and back into corners, going grudgingly, as if unwilling to expose the horrors it had been concealing—chains and manacles and intricate machinery for inflicting pain.

When he could see adequately he walked the full length of the chamber and played his light over the fetters and pulleys. He confirmed that the staples were securely anchored in the ancient stonework and that two wooden buckets had been provided, as he had ordered. He set the lantern in an iron sconce on the nearest pillar and waited, impassively ignoring both the pervasive stench and the gruesome furnishings lurking in the shadows.

Soon marching footsteps approached the door. A dozen soldiers entered, clanking mail and weapons and chains, clumping boots, raising the echo again. They herded their solitary captive as if he were some fiercely dangerous monster. Admittedly, he towered a head taller than almost any of them and had shoulders like battlements, but he was unarmed and four men held chains from the fetters on his wrists and ankles. He offered no resistance as he was hustled along to the end of the crypt, being intent on keeping his unshod toes away from all the heavy boots around him.

He wore only a short doublet, faded until its original checkered pattern was barely visible, and hose so ragged that they ended at his ankles. His brown hair was thick and curly, although the relentless Spanish sun that had burned his face to walnut had perversely bleached his beard almost to gold. His face was more notable for strength than beauty—square-jawed and heavy-browed, stubborn and self-willed—yet the steady hazel eyes were surprisingly unhostile, even as he was being manhandled. He seemed quite resigned to what was happening.

His captors turned him. Four of them thrust him back against the wall and held him there. Under the captain's watchful eye his fetters were secured to staples near the floor and the chain joining his wrists to one above his head. Only then did the men holding him relax and step back. As a final indignity, the captain himself came forward and drew his dagger to sever the laces that attached the prisoner's hose to his doublet and then cut the hose themselves in half so that they fell as useless rags around his ankles, leaving him naked below the waist. One of the soldiers placed the empty bucket midway between his outspread feet.

The officer dismissed the squad. They marched out, leaving the door open. Silence and relative darkness returned, with only the single lantern burning in its sconce. Captain and captive looked at each other without expression.

"I do hope you are not frightened to be left alone with me." The large young man spoke in an awkward mixture of Catalan and Castilian, and his accent for both was atrocious.

"I do what I am told, senor. Do you wish a drink of water?"

"Thank you." The young man seemed surprised by the offer. He drank greedily when the captain took a dipper from the second bucket and held it to his lips. The water would be fresh, for it had been drawn from the well less than an hour ago. He spilled some as the dipper was removed, and shivered.

"You are cold, senor," the officer said tactfully.

"Just frightened."

"I think not, senor. I can recognize fear. In Queen Caterina's day, we did not treat men so." He turned away, ashamed. Even the Inquisition allowed a prisoner to keep his private parts covered—except when he was actually being tortured, of course.

Obviously waiting for something, the soldier began to pace from left to right and right to left, never going very far away. The prisoner had no such option. He could only stand there against the slimy stones of the wall, shivering from time to time as the damp bit through to his bones. Then steel links would clink and the captain's head jerk around.

After twenty minutes or so a faint glow beyond the door announced the arrival of two men in civilian clothes, who advanced along the crypt, their cork-soled shoes making little sound. The first was a flunky carrying a lantern and a stool, the second a man of ample girth, which was emphasized almost to absurdity by the sumptuous, many-colored garments of a noble. His shoulders were padded out to twice their natural width, his features upholstered with rolls of fat. He walked with an affected, mincing sway, wielding a jewel-topped cane and sniffing a posy of flowers. When they reached the end the servant put down the stool and departed, taking the lantern with him.

The soldier drew his sword in salute. "Your Excellency, the prisoner has been secured as you instructed."

"Knowing you, I do not doubt it, Captain Diaz. There is a lot of him, isn't there?"

"He is a fine-looking man, your Excellency."

"Did he cause any trouble?"

"None at all. He displays commendable courage."

The nobleman frowned at this blatant admiration. "Close the door when you leave. I will knock when I am ready. See that it is guarded by six men at all times. The prisoner is to be inspected every two hours and given water if he wishes it. See he is well fed. He is a large man, and we must keep his strength up, you understand?"

"Oh, I understand completely, Excellency." The captain's tone was perilously close to insolence. He saluted again and marched out. The door groaned and slammed, filling the crypt with echoes.

The newcomer turned his back on the prisoner

and strutted away until he reached about the middle of the chamber, where he raised a hand to his mouth, spoke softly, turned around once to the right and twice to the left, and said something else. Thereupon the blocks of the barrel-vaulted ceiling began to glow with a pale, gentle lavender light that grew rapidly brighter until the entire cellar was clearly illuminated. That was gramarye.

The change was no improvement, for it revealed the fungus and rat droppings in the corners, the glint of moisture on walls and floor, the meager barred slits that admitted little air and no light. Worse, the macabre furnishings that had hitherto been mercifully invisible were now in plain view. Most obvious was the notorious rack, a table of massive timbers with a windlass at one end, but the vises, braziers, and metal boots were every bit as ominous—as were the mysterious metallic contraptions that had no obvious purpose and therefore challenged the imagination to supply one. Walls and pillars were festooned with chains, whips, rods, pincers, branding irons, knives, and pulleys. No known means of generating unbearable agony seemed to have been overlooked.

The visitor paraded back with his finery now displayed in glory: a knee-length cloak of crimson velvet lined with sable over a hugely inflated jerkin of blue and gold satin, whose sleeves were puffed, slashed, and embroidered, and which gaped at the front to display a decorated and padded codpiece. The hose above his buskins were crimson, bulging over his fat calves. His hat was flat and wide, shadowing his features, and his hair was gathered in a cowl of golden net. He settled on the stool, sniffing his posy to avoid the stench of the room. In a plump face of indiscernible age, smoothly shaven and powdered with flour, his eyes were barely visible, lost in slits between pads of fat, but he smiled with thick scarlet lips.

"So we meet at last, Tobias Strangerson, known as Longdirk."

"Oh, thank the spirits!" said the prisoner. "Someone who speaks English! My lord—your Excellency, I mean—there has been a terrible mistake. My name is William of Crieff, a sailor from Scotland, and I don't know how—"

His Excellency laughed with what sounded like genuine amusement. "Still you do not give up? Master Longdirk, I am honored to meet you. There is an old saying that journeys end in lovers' meetings, but sometimes they can end in enemies' meeting, also. It has been a long time, has it not?" His voice had a guttural, Germanic rasp.

The young man shrugged to concede defeat, rattling chains. "Yes it has, Excellency." His expression gave away nothing.

"I am, of course, Karl Fischart, Baron Oreste of Utrecht, currently King Nevil's viceroy for Aragon."

"I know you," the prisoner said simply. Possibly his eyes glinted a little.

"Indeed?" Oreste spoke more softly than before. "You continue to surprise me, Toby, even now. How do you know me?"

"You were pointed out to me in Bordeaux."

"I was that close? Astonishing! Yes, it has been a long chase, but I have you now, and I do not think you will escape this time." Sequins sparkled on his hat as he looked around the crypt. "I apologize for the accommodation—this odious cellar belongs to the Inquisition, of course, and I regret to say that they use it. Please understand that I do not intend to apply any of those revolting instruments to your flesh, young man. I have other ways to obtain what I need. I put you in here because this chamber happens to be very carefully warded, and in an unusual way. As you saw, it will permit one to use gramarye with immured demons." He spread out his fingers, and the rings flashed in spears of red and blue and green. "But it suppresses the weaker powers of incarnates. I hope this interests you. I am not boring you, am I?" If he was gloating, at least he was being polite. He might have been at home on his estate, speaking graciously to one of his retainers.

"Not at all, Excellency. I welcome the company." The prisoner was responding with suitable deference, neither defiant nor groveling. He shifted his weight from his right leg to his left. He had been given enough slack that he could bend his knees a little or move his hips, but the cold was his worst torment at the moment. The cramps and exhaustion were still to come.

"Ah, be careful, Toby! You may regret my presence soon enough and find solitude preferable. I always enjoy a worthy opponent. I admit I underestimated you at first, of course—a lowborn bastard from some remote Highland glen, ignorant, barely literate, never been away from the cows before. When the Scottish Parliament rushed through a special act condemning this unknown boy to death without trial on the grounds that he was possessed by a demon, I really thought your eggs were scrambled. Who could blame me?"

"It was your doing."

"Parliament? Yes, I did use a little influence there, I admit. But the possession was Lady Valda's fault, wasn't it?" The fat man chuckled. "I congratulate you sincerely on besting her. She had eluded me for ten years."

The prisoner shrugged.

Oreste smiled, amused by something. "So the big, dumb Highland lad is hunted by the full majesty of the law and two of the finest hexers in Europe. What odds would you give on his chances? Yet he escapes! Your companion, by the way, the boy who sailed with you—Hamish Campbell, wasn't it? He can hardly be a boy now, any more than you are. He is well?"

"The last I saw him he was, Excellency. He must be eighteen now."

That remark amused the baron even more. He laughed until his paunch shook. "I am supposed to infer that you haven't seen him for a long time? No matter. Let us get back to you and your demon."

"It isn't a demon. What happened was an accident."

"Not a demon, no. It's the local elemental from Strath Fillan, a partially domesticated sprite, or hob as you call them. But it is dangerous, isn't it, Toby? Even more dangerous than a demon in some ways. A demon always has a conjuration to control it, but the hob is a free spirit, untrained, childlike. It doesn't know good from evil. It is liable to do anything, ja?"

The young man nodded. "It scares me sometimes."

"Scares *you*, Toby? Oh, I don't think so, I really

don't. Not you! No matter. You also had another spiritual companion, even more unusual. Lady Valda had stolen the soul of King Nevil of England. During her bungled efforts to conjure with it, that soul was translated into a jewel, an uncut amethyst. I want that soul. I want that amethyst! Where is it, Toby?"

"How do you know all this?"

"From your former companion, Father Lachlan. He was very forthcoming. He had no choice, of course."

"What did you do to him?" For the first time anger flashed in the prisoner's deep-set dark eyes.

Oreste sighed. "Killed him. I had to, Toby. He was a pleasant old man, although rather ineffectual. He was muddled on the details, but he had learned—learned from you, I'm afraid—that the soul in the king is a demon. Anyone who knows that must die."

The prisoner ground his teeth. Suddenly he looked almost dangerous enough to explain the severity with which he was being restrained.

"Ah, Toby, Toby! You also told Fergan, the pretender to the Scottish throne. He was useful to us as bait for the unruly, but after he learned that truth, he had to go, too. You must have heard that he was caught and executed?"

"Murdered!"

"Oh, come! You weren't one of his foolish rebels. You knew he would never sit on his throne again—not with Nevil wanting to keep it, he wouldn't! It doesn't matter. Anyone who knows, dies. Only you and Hamish Campbell are left. And you have the genuine king's soul hidden somewhere. I want it, Toby. I will have the amethyst no matter what it

costs . . . costs you, of course. I will do anything to
get it."

The prisoner licked his lips. The thick muscles of
his neck were tense. "I think you're mistaken,
Excellency. Valda couldn't find any trace of Nevil's
soul. I think it was lost somewhere in all that hexing. So the amethyst's only a piece of shiny stone as
far as I'm concerned. It has sentimental value for
me, but if you want it so much, you can have it. You
ought to be willing to perform a small favor in
return, yes? You're a great hexer, and I admit I find
the hob troublesome at times. You could remove it
from me, exorcize it. Do that and let me go, and I'll
give you the amethyst gladly. That's a fair bargain,
isn't it?"

"Bargain? Bargain, Toby?" The baron shook with
mirth. "You stand there, chained up like a side of
beef, and talk of bargaining? Oh, dear me no! You
won't be bargaining. And you find the hob *troublesome* you say? When the *Maid of Arran* was
wrecked on the coast of Brittany, only three people
survived: you, Campbell, and a sailor, Derek
McGonagall. McGonagall blamed you for that
wreck and all those unfortunate men lost at sea."

Longdirk swallowed but did not speak. His
cheeks above his beard were visibly paler than they
had been a moment before.

The baron shook his head sadly. His jowls wob-
bled. "But it was the hob's fault, wasn't it? I don't
suppose it meant any harm, but it drove the ship on
the rocks and killed all those men. So what did you
do? At Vannes, in Brittany, just a few days after the
wreck, you tried to go to the local shrine. You were
convulsed by cramps before you even reached the

door. Your friend, young Hamish, helped you back to your lodgings. The keeper insisted that Vannes had never hurt a suppliant like that before, so it wasn't the spirit that was keeping you away. The culprit was the hob, yes?"

Receiving no answer, he smiled again, obviously enjoying the game. "So you tried once more in Nantes, where there was a full sanctuary and a powerful tutelary that would surely not tolerate any insolence from a trespassing hob. As before, you did not even reach the building. Halfway across the courtyard, you fell to the cobbles in convulsions, choking and vomiting blood. Young Campbell was forced to hire porters to carry you home. I was told you writhed in pain for some hours, until the hob forgot why it was mad at you. I can see why you might find it a little *troublesome*."

The prisoner glared angrily but did not comment.

As if he were growing stiff with sitting, Baron Oreste rose and flexed his back, smiling apologetically at the prisoner. He strolled off to inspect the rack, still talking.

"You tried again when you reached Bordeaux. A great city like that must have a great tutelary, a wise and powerful spirit to protect and guide it. The sanctuary there is enormous and splendid, although somewhat too ornate for my own taste, I admit.

"And there you took an acolyte into your confidence. That was very rash of you. You risked denunciation and a blade through the heart, Toby, but I expect you were becoming desperate. Father Verne was disbelieving at first. After all, who ever heard of voluntary exorcism? An incarnate does not ask to be dispossessed and will certainly not allow its husk

enough free will to do so for himself. But you convinced him eventually, and he agreed to provide an
escort of novices for the deluded foreign youth.
Thus you went to the sanctuary that time in the
company of Hamish and three brawny young men,
all instructed to get you inside the holy premises at
any cost, yes?"

The baron took a vicious-looking hook down
from an array of implements and hefted it in his
hand, frowning as if trying to decide what it was
used for.

"Again you collapsed in a heap of agony, but this
time your henchmen picked you up bodily. It still
didn't work, did it? The hob countered instantly with
a local whirlwind. Horses panicked, carts were overturned, chimneys toppled, three women killed." The
baron shook his head sadly.

"So you never did manage to get the hob exorcized. You could never be rid of it. And those three
women were not the first nor the last innocent
bystanders to die around Tobias Longdirk. At La
Rochelle—"

"What did you do to Father Verne?"

"Killed him also. Quite painlessly, I assure you. I
am not a creature, Toby. I have no demon inside me.
I work for a demon, yes, and I am hexed to obey
him utterly, but I am allowed to choose my own
methods—most of the time." His eyes were still
hidden behind slits, and his smile did not crinkle the
pudgy flesh around them.

"Did you choose your own methods at Zaragoza?
Did you enjoy wasting Navarre, burning, torturing,
public—"

"Be silent!" the baron snapped. "Or I will make

you silent. My only purpose was to track you down. But the hob defended you. Without the hob you would have died a dozen times, and I would have caught you a dozen times. I nearly had you in Bordeaux, although I admit I did not realize how near that was until you told me just now. Ah, but you were a wily quarry! In Brittany and Aquitaine you were within Nevil's realm, so I could get at you easily, given just a little more time. But then you slipped away south, over the borders, into Navarre and then Castile, and there you were in lands still loyal to the Khan. That presented a problem for me. Of course you did leave quite a trail.

"Two able-bodied young men wandering a continent at war . . . There were attempts to recruit you, weren't there? You were conscripted more than once. But loud noises make the hob excited, don't they? And when guns went off around it, terrible things happened. No army could hold you. There were other stories. . . ." His tone sharpened. "What did happen at Mezquiriz?"

The prisoner shivered, chain tinkling, but he did not answer.

"How many people has this *troublesome* hob killed since you left Dumbarton, Toby?"

"I don't know. Lots."

"Thousands. Tens of thousands."

"No! Maybe a hundred. That's bad enough, but not thousands!"

Oreste shook his jowls. "The only way to get at you in Spain was to come and get you. You seriously inconvenienced his Universal Majesty."

"You mean the Fiend."

"Guard your tongue, Toby!" The baron waggled a

fat finger. "The penalty for using that name is five hundred lashes. Nevil has been fighting the Khan for twelve years now. Because of you he had to break off his war in Saxony and march his army down here to invade Aragon, Navarre, and even Castile."

"For me? You're telling me it's my fault the two of you turned half of Spain into a desert?"

"Absolutely, dear boy. You have the soul of the genuine King Nevil, and Rhym will never rest until he can destroy it." The baron came wandering back, still clutching the hook. "I don't think you are a callous man, Toby. Not like King Nevil, whose favorite occupation is watching children being tortured to death, preferably by their own mothers. You seem to have a conscience. A nice young man like you must be very tired of leaving a trail of dead and dying wherever he goes." Oreste smiled up at the prisoner.

For the first time the big man raised his voice. "All right!" he shouted. "Yes, I would do anything to be rid of the hob! I detest the damage it does, the deaths and injuries. Take the hob from me, let me go, and I'll give you the amethyst."

Baron Oreste shook his head pityingly. "I warned you there would be no bargains, Toby. Your purse is empty. The hob is powerless in this chamber, so it cannot save you this time. The amethyst is mine to take." He raised the hook in front of the prisoner's face. "With this!"

"What do you mean? You said you weren't going to torture me!"

"I said I wouldn't torture you with anything as crude as this. That's not quite the same. But watch."

Oreste slipped the point into the neck of the prisoner's doublet and with one long pull ripped it away.

Another rip and his shirt followed, leaving him effectively wearing only a small leather locket—a rough-made, ugly thing hung on a thong around his neck.

"That's a very impressive chest, Toby, but this is what I want, isn't it?" The baron lifted the locket on the hook and broke the thong with a quick jerk. Chuckling, he minced back to sit on his stool and peer at his prize. He picked carefully at the stiff flap. "That wasn't so difficult, was it?"

The prisoner was breathing harder than before, shifting his stance more often, perhaps feeling the cramps starting. "So now will you kill me?"

"Hmm?" Wary of breaking a nail, Oreste was now trying to push the point of the hook under the locket's flap. "Seems the Inquisition does not believe in sharp edges. I wonder if that's a matter of policy? Kill you? No, I don't think so. Not yet, anyway. Think of yourself as a trophy of the hunt, dear boy, mounted above a fireplace." Inside all the grandiose garments his blubbery form shook with quiet laughter.

The prisoner eased his shoulders and hips in a clink of chain. Drained of blood, the hands over his head shone unnaturally pale, like white bats clinging to the stonework. "Mounted how long?"

"As long as I please, dear boy. You and your resident hob are an interesting problem in gramarye. I used no less than eight demons to ward it on the way here, but it is powerless inside this chamber, as I told you, so we shall leave it—and you—until I have time to think about it. I may try to extract the hob, because it could be useful if properly trained, but the operation is likely to rip out large parts of your mind as well. I may decide to leave the hob in you and hex both of you to obey me. We shall see. All I really needed, and what I have now obtained thanks to your generosity, is the amethyst containing the soul of . . ."

He had worked the packet open. The stone that fell out was a smooth black pebble, nothing at all like an amethyst. He looked up and stared hard at his prisoner, who smiled mockingly back at him. It was a smile that said the game was not quite over yet, however hopeless it might seem.

"Where is it, Toby?"

"Are you sure we cannot bargain, Excellency?"

Oreste bit at his bottom lip with small white teeth. He might reasonably be seething with fury at this absurd defiance, but if he was, he concealed the fact admirably. He laid the hook on the floor beside him so gently that it did not even clink. He tucked the pebble and locket inside his cloak; then he crossed his legs and folded his hands.

"You have nothing to bargain with, Toby. Not now. Granted, you managed to escape from Castile, although King Pedro swore on his mother's eyes that he would catch you and hand you over to us. I expected you to head for Portugal, or even Africa, but I knew you might try doubling back, as you have before. So I set up a few trip-wires for you in Aragon and Navarre—I do rule those countries now, useless as they are. One of the groups I had looking out for you was the Inquisition, specifically a group of Black Friars led by Father Vespianaso. You eluded him, too, which really surprised me, I admit. How did you manage that?"

The prisoner shrugged. "Ask him."

Oreste smiled. "I have. Father Vespianaso is extremely indignant. He feels you insulted him—all Castilians are excessively prickly, as I'm sure you know, even their preachers. He feels you, um, *belong* to him, you understand? Were I to mention to him that you are chained up here in the Inquisition's own dungeon, your life would at once become nasty, brutal, and much too long. Sometimes the Inquisition holds prisoners for years, Toby. I am sure you have heard stories of its methods, hmm?"

The young man just glowered defiantly. He had discovered the Sway already, moving his right foot and left hand as far as possible, then left foot and right hand, then back again.... *clink—clink—clink*—right—left—right—left . . . They all discovered the Sway sooner or later. It could not do very much to help his circulation, but now he had started, he would keep it up for hours, until his wrists and ankles were bloody and torn by the fetters. Only exhaustion would stop him. That might take a long time in his case.

Oreste seemed peeved by the lack of response. "That's just one possibility, you understand. His Majesty has expressed admiration for your abilities and may well take you into his service, with or without the hob. You will be hexed to absolute loyalty as I am, but you will be a man of authority and power, respected and obeyed. You will have a team of demons of your own to serve you. This is a glittering future you have earned, Toby!"

"I'd rather go to Father Vespianaso."

Absurd defiance! Oreste rose to his feet and strolled over to him. "That decision is not yours to make. Now, little Toby, listen well. The chase has ended. You lost. Don't be a sore loser, lad. Let bygones be bygones, ja? I need that amethyst. I also want Hamish Campbell. You will give me both of them."

"You can hex me into doing anything you want."

"Yes, I can. Anything. So why struggle? We may be working together for many years, serving his Majesty. It would be a pity to have unhappy memories stand between us."

The young man stared at him without expression, just swaying: right—left—right—left—*clink—clink—clink—*

"Tell me what really happened at Mezquiriz."

No response. *Clink—clink—clink—*

Oreste clenched a fat fist. "Toby, Toby! I only put you in here because of the warding. Just answer my questions and I will let you have enough chain to sit down, even lie down. I will get you some blankets and leave you a light."

No one in the prisoner's position could refuse that offer, and yet somehow the baron knew it was not going to be accepted this time. He might not keep his side of the bargain if it were.

It wasn't. Nothing, absolutely nothing except that steady, heavy-browed stare and the animal Sway. *Clink—clink—clink—*

"How curious!" the baron said softly. "Why is the sweetness of victory soured when the vanquished refuses to concede? It should be even sweeter. No, I shall not hex you, boy. Having spent three years hooking you and landing you, my foolish pride wants to gut you by hand. Gramarye is a battleaxe, and in such cases I still prefer the stiletto. I can break you easily enough without it." He ran his tongue over his scarlet lips. "I have lost a lot of sleep over you in the past, Tobias Longdirk. Tonight I shall sleep soundly, knowing I have you safe. Tomorrow, unfortunately, I believe I have other business to attend to. I hope I will be able to spare some time to drop in and see you later in the week."

Simpering, he patted the prisoner's cheek. "Sleep well, Toby."

He took the guttering lantern and walked to the center of the cellar. There, safely out of earshot, he issued orders to one of the demon gems on his fingers and repeated his little dance. The supernatural light died away. When the door closed behind him, the crypt returned to total darkness.

Clink—clink—clink—clink—clink—

TWO

THE ROAD TO BARCELONA

1

On their second night out of Valencia, Hamish said, "I am still not certain that going by way of Barcelona is a wise move. It will take us a month to get there at this rate, and we're going to starve to death first. Supposing Oreste is there? He'll detect you with gramarye. You'll never slip past him."

Toby did not answer. He might be asleep already, or else just not want to repeat an argument they had rubbed raw several times. He insisted that the best way to escape from Spain was to tiptoe past the monster's lair. All other ways out would be more heavily guarded, he said, and once Toby made up his mind nothing would ever change it.

"We ought to head inland," Hamish muttered. "Back to Navarre."

Still no reply. Toby must be asleep. It had been a hard day. The walking was not so bad—they were seasoned walkers—but the heat was absurd. This was September, after all, or perhaps even October, and weather like this was ridiculous. Every night Hamish dreamed of fine misty rain blowing down the glen, wet moss under his toes and shaggy, long-horned cattle wallowing in the bog. How wonderful it would be to shiver again! Spain was just sweat, sweat, sweat.

Hamish sighed and went back to his book. He was stretched out on his belly in the ruins of a cellar with the stars above him and too many ants and sharp pebbles underneath. The ruin was ancient, not part of the recent devastation, and although it was a zitty uncomfortable place to camp, it provided shelter for the fire—a very small fire, just enough to cast a little light on the pages of the book. No one would see it down in this hole, and in Aragon these days the wise traveler did not attract attention to himself.

The book was excessively dull for even his omnivorous tastes—everything he did not need to know about designing a formal garden for a chateau. Being written in langue d'oïl, northern French, it had no market value here, or he would have traded it away for food a long time ago, like everything else. His worldly possessions were down to the minimum needed for survival: tattered hose (if they tattered any more there would be very little point in wearing them at all), one equally ragged doublet, a shirt in quite disgusting condition, the remains of a straw hat that a donkey had chewed, buskins almost ready to fall apart, one thin blanket and a piece of rope to tie it, one leather water bottle with two leaks, one very small knife, a quarter staff, and a book. He owned a half share in a whetstone, a tinderbox, and a copper cup; everything else had been stolen or traded away for food. Toby still had the steel helmet he had won in Navarre, but only because it wouldn't fit anyone else's head—much like the book. They did not have a sword between them, or even a dagger, just staves, here in a land where strangers, especially foreigners, were liable to be shot on sight.

His stomach rumbled. Steak. Suet pudding with cream. A bowl of steaming oatmeal, well salted. Or roast pork? He had not seen a pig or a cow or a goat or even a habitable house for days. The rebels had burned crops and vineyards and cut down trees by the thousand, but even they could not reduce a fertile land to a total desert, so there were still pickings to be had. He had been living on onions and fruit. He hated oranges.

Back to the book. In his father's house were many books. Zits, but he was homesick! Homesick for books, for Ma and Pa, for Eric and Elsie, for soft rain and soft, peaty drinking water, and brown soil. Anything but this red, burned wilderness. He had left home to see the world. He had wanted to see life but had witnessed too much death. For three years he and Toby had been hunted by the Fiend's agents—Brittany, France, Aquitaine, Navarre, Castile, and now Aragon.

The puny fire shot up a few sparks. Having nothing to cook, Hamish had claimed a fire would be a defense against the feral dogs prowling around. Toby had agreed solemnly, although he had known perfectly well that Hamish just wanted to read. Somewhere not too far away, a dog howled. He shivered. Nasty noise! Those brutes hunted in packs. They were dangerous. His stomach rumbled a surly reply. Back to the book.

Then a man cried out. Hamish was on his feet in

an instant with his staff in his hand and no recollection of picking it up.

"Toby! *Toby?*"

Toby wasn't there. His blanket was, and his staff, so he could not have gone far.

Hamish scrambled over the wall, out of the cellar. The moan came again. He headed toward the sound, feeling his way carefully with his staff until his eyes adjusted to the starlight. Another groan . . .

Toby was a few yards off—flat on his back with his hands above his head and his eyes shut—not asleep, then, because he always slept facedown, which he claimed was all Hamish's father had ever taught him in school. He appeared to be unconscious. Again?

Demons! For three years Hamish's recurring nightmare had been to wonder what he would do if anything ever happened to Toby—anything permanent. Normally the big lunk seemed indestructible, but twice in the last few days he had passed out for no apparent reason.

"Toby! Wake up! Toby!" Sick with alarm, Hamish grabbed a shoulder and tried to shake him. Easier to shake an oak tree. He lay down and put an ear on the big man's chest and was reassured to hear a steady *Dum . . . Dum . . . Dum . . .* He was alive, anyway.

"Uh?" Toby said. A huge shiver ran through him. His eyes opened. "Hamish?"

"Who d'you expect, you big ape—Baron Oreste?"

Toby frowned and did not answer.

"What's wrong?"

He winced. "Cramps. Can you move my arms?" He grunted with pain as Hamish took his arms and rotated them to a normal position at his sides. "Now help me up." That was easier asked than done, for he weighed tons, and he gasped a few more times as Hamish heaved him into a sitting position.

"What by all the spirits is wrong?"

"Told you—cramps."

"Why? Why cramps? What happened?"

Gingerly Toby raised one knee. "I just spent a night in a dungeon."

Hamish discovered that his fingers were wet. There was blood on them.

It made no sense at all. Back at the fire they inspected Toby's scraped and bleeding wrists. The blood had run *up* his arms to the elbows. His hose were bloody, too, and when he removed them, he displayed ankles almost as bad. Worse, though, the cloth was only blood-soaked, not shredded like the skin underneath. How had he managed that? It had to be gramarye.

"It's the hob's doing!" Hamish said, and was annoyed at the shrillness in his voice. "Why is it mad at you now?"

"Don't think it is. Tell you in a minute. I was going to the spring. I had the water bottles."

Hamish went back out to find the water bottles. He took them to the spring beside the burned cottage. As he was filling them he raised his head and sniffed. Roast pork? Impossible! He went back to the cellar and watched in frustration as Toby washed the blood from his wounds.

"We should bandage those!" But they had nothing to use for bandages. They could tear up a shirt, but

their doublets were made of coarse hessian that
would scrape intolerably in the heat of the day.

"They'll be all right," Toby said. "Just scrapes.
Better to leave them uncovered. Then I can pick the
maggots off. I told you these visions were more
vivid than your average daydream."

Hamish did not believe in the visions. He thought
they were delusions. "What did you see this time?"
He added more twigs to the sputtering little fire.

For a dawdling moment it seemed he would get
no answer, then Toby said, "Barcelona. The water
there tastes terrible."

"What happened to your wrists?"

"Manacles. I was in jail." He peered up at the
stars. "How long was I gone? How many pages?"

"Not many. I wasn't reading much. Ten minutes at
most."

"I was in jail a lot longer than that. Look, I'd better wash these clothes before the blood dries any
more."

Hamish took the hose from him. "I'll do it. And
your shirt, too."

Normally any hint of mothering provoked the big
man to bull-headed stubbornness, but this time he
muttered thanks and meekly stripped. Still moving
as if every joint hurt, he stretched out on his blanket
and covered himself. "I'll tell you when you get
back." He must be in much worse shape than he was
admitting.

Hamish headed off to the spring. Three times in a
week Toby had passed out cold and wakened up
babbling about visions. The first time he had talked
of a tent in the woods, a knight, and beautiful lady.
Then a man in a city street. Now what? He thought

the visions were prophetic, but that was plain impossible. Since leaving Scotland Hamish had read every book about spirits, demons, gramarye, and hexing he had been able to lay his hands on. He had spoken with every acolyte who would spare him a minute. He knew as much about spiritual powers as anyone except a true adept could ever know, and one of the things he had learned was that seeing the future was impossible. Not even the greatest tutelary could ever foresee the future.

Not visions—delusions! Madness.

As he was rinsing the garments, his belly rumbled again, louder than ever. A month to Barcelona? How many oranges could a man eat in another month? Oranges and sometimes dates, although most of the palms had been cut down, and onions, and . . . and roast pork?

Demons! His mouth was watering like the Fillan in spate. He scrambled all the way to his feet and sniffed. He was *not* imagining it. Someone *was* roasting pork somewhere upwind, and not very far away, either.

He went back to the cellar, laid the wet shirt and hose on a prickly bush to dry, and then sat down cross legged. "Tell me. They hung you up by your hands?"

Toby was sitting up, wearing his doublet, wrapped in his blanket. "Nothing so crude. Baron Oreste has more subtle methods." He grinned more surely this time, more like his own self.

"*Oreste?* He's in Barcelona?"

"He was in my dream."

"That was no dream!" Hamish squeaked. "You mustn't go to Barcelona if he's there!"

Toby frowned and looked mulish, which he did

very well. "I suppose that would be charging the bull, wouldn't it? Does this mean that you believe in my visions now?"

Oh, demons! "No, I don't believe in visions, not yours, not anyone's." The only thing Toby's visions might mean was that the hob was finally driving him out of his mind, and Father Lachlan had warned him of that years ago. Or the hob itself was going crazy, locked up in his mind. It wouldn't make much difference, would it?

"Then there's no problem!" Toby smirked at outwitting Hamish Campbell. "No reason not to go to Barcelona? We can talk about it in the morning. Nice town, Barcelona. Roomy dungeons, all the latest torturing machines. I didn't see you there. You didn't miss much."

"Tell me about the second vision."

"I've told you a dozen times."

"Tell me again!"

"You sound just like your father. You want me to pull down my britches and bend over, domine?"

"Is that the only way to get your attention?"

Toby smiled ruefully. "Sorry. We were walking along that street in Valencia, the one I pointed out to you the next day. It wasn't much of a street, because all the houses had all been burned. You saw that. What you saw in reality was just what I saw in the vision, except there was a ragged old man there. We talked with him."

"You don't remember what we said?"

"No. He seemed friendly enough. After a while we went off with him, and he led us through a doorway. That was all. Then I was sitting on the trail feeling giddy, and you were asking if I was all right."

"And when we reached Valencia, you found that street, but there was no one there."

"Yes."

"So these . . . these dreams you're having . . . they're not real, Toby! They don't show you the future. They can't. That isn't possible! What you're having are fits of *déjà vu*. It's not uncommon to see a place and think you've been there before. Everyone does, sometimes. I do."

"Not like this." Toby held out a thick wrist, torn and scabbed with blood.

"It's the hob playing tricks on you."

"Then I wish it would stop. Now I'm going to go to sleep. So should you." He eased himself down, moving like a very old man. He rolled over.

"Toby. Someone's roasting pork. I could smell it. Upwind. Not far."

Longdirk heaved himself up on one elbow, grunting at the pain. He fixed Hamish with a dangerous stare. "I smelled it too."

"Well?" Hamish pleaded. "They might share?" Zits, but he was hungry for a decent meal!

"Not me. That's what I saw in my first vision, Hamish. Or smelled, I should say. There was a fire in an orange grove with something being roasted on a spit. I'm not going near it!"

"What?" Hamish swallowed a mouthful of drool. "Why not? I know it's a risk, but if we warn them we're coming and we're not armed—"

"I did. Last time. Listen, I'll tell you again exactly what I saw. There's a fire, obviously, and a tent. Made of cloth, blue and gold. I think there were horses, but I'm not quite sure about that. You were with me, and it was a night just like this one:

warm, starry, very little wind. In the vision I shouted to warn whoever was there, and they came out of the tent, two of them, a gentleman and a lady, very well dressed. He had a green and gold jerkin on, she was in red and white. The man called to us to come forward. We walked forward, me in the lead, and just as I neared the fire, something frightened me."

"What?"

"I don't remember! All I know is that I shouted and turned to run. Then I ran into you, and that was all. I woke up." He grinned menacingly. "You go and explore if you want to. You don't believe in my visions, so you've got no reason not to, right? I'm in no state to go anywhere, but if you feel like bringing me back a juicy rib or two, I won't refuse."

Hamish glared back at him suspiciously. "How far did you go tonight?"

"Just to where you found me, I'm sure. I wouldn't have gone on without my staff, would I? Go and see if my vision was true."

Tobias Longdirk was not the only man who could be stubborn. "Very well!" Hamish said. "I'm going."

"Wind's from the northwest. Take your bearings from the stars. *Bon appétit!*" Toby smirked and lay down again.

Hamish took his staff and went to the wall.

"Hamish?"

"What?"

"Be careful!"

"I can look after myself," Hamish snapped. So he could, by most men's standards, because Toby had taught him. Toby was in a class by himself when it

came to fighting, but that didn't mean Hamish
Campbell was a pushover.

2

Beyond the spring Hamish came to the start of an
orange grove, just as Toby had predicted. Toby could
have seen that in daylight.

The trees made things tricky, and there was no
clear path. He went slowly, being extra cautious.
Creeping up on anyone was dangerous in war-
ravaged Aragon. People slept with their bows strung
nowadays. He was a little surprised that Longdirk
was letting him do this—not exactly an unwelcome
surprise, but an uneasy-making surprise. Toby was
treating him as an equal now, no longer the boy he
had been when they began their adventuring
together. Although he was full-sized, or almost so,
and a seasoned traveler with smatterings of five or
six languages, he was still a little disbelieving every
time he drank from a pool and saw the fuzzy fringe
of beard around his face. He would never admit it to
anyone, of course.

Nor would he admit that he was now scared spit-
less. Creeping up on strangers in the dark like this
was not prudent. Normally he would have tried
to talk Toby out of trying it. He would certainly
never have volunteered to do it himself, alone. He
couldn't go back now, of course. But if something
jumped out at him, he knew he would head for
Longdirk fast as prunes through a goose.

There were other things moving in the woods. He
paused a couple of times to listen, but when he
stopped they stopped, and all he achieved was a

higher level of funk. They were probably those feral
dogs, attracted by the smell, just as he was. Feral
dogs and feral Scotsmen . . .

There was no way to go quickly in the dark, even
knowing that the roast pork might be all eaten
before he arrived. The ground was littered with dead
branches, the air full of live ones at head-height.
Don't trip in the tangle of weeds, which . . . *ouch!*
. . . included thistles.

Yes, a faint light twinkling in the darkness ahead!
The mouth-watering odor was stronger. Not very far
at all, and Hamish had a nervy vision of the men who
had built *that* fire creeping around in the trees to find
his fire at the same time as *he* was creeping . . . no,
his was downwind and it didn't have any pork on it.

He began planning what he would say. He
would start by telling whoever was there that they
were in no danger, of course, so that they didn't
start banging away with muskets. Then admit to
being a foreigner but not part of the Fiend's army.
The delicious aroma of roasting meat was making
him slaver like a dog. He eased through the grove
toward the yellow flicker, keeping eyes peeled for
guards or sentries, but the fire was a small one,
and there was only the one. He couldn't see any
people near it, only trees. The smoke stung his
eyes.

Time to warn them he was coming.

"Friends! Friends! Good evening! I am alone. I
come in peace. I mean no harm!" He used Castilian,
because his Valencian and Catalan were still as thin
as the seat of his hose.

Nothing happened.

He clattered his staff on branches and marched

forward, shouting out the same message, over and over, with variations, adding a few words in Valencian. "Friends! I come in peace. I seek only charity and companionship."

The fire was quite close now. It still seemed deserted, but campfires did not build themselves. His scalp prickled. He shouted again.

Suddenly he saw the tent beyond it, exactly as Toby had described, gold and blue stripes. He stopped dead. How could he reconcile that with prophecy not being possible? The flap lifted. They came out, a man and a woman, young and handsome, both beautifully dressed. The man wore green hose, a green and gold jerkin padded wide at the shoulders, a shining cloth-of-gold cloak with fur trim. A sword dangled at his belt. The lady's gown was snowy white, slashed with crimson on the full skirts and puffed sleeves, cut low at the neck over a sheer chemise. Her hair was hidden by a red and black *mantellina* trimmed with braid and velvet that hung to her shoulders. What were a prince and princess doing here in the woods with no attendants?

At least Hamish couldn't see any attendants. Perhaps there were other people or even horses in the darkness beyond the tent. Hard to say—he was too fascinated by these gracious nobles.

"Who approaches?" shouted the man in Castilian. He had a hand on his sword.

"One hungry traveler, senor! I am unarmed and come in peace."

"Come forward so we may see you." The man gestured to his lady to keep back while he advanced to meet the stranger.

Hamish walked forward until he entered the firelight. He bowed.

The nobleman smiled.

Then the fire roared up, much larger than before.
Hamish jumped and looked toward it. The source of
the delectable odor was a human torso with the
remains of a head still attached. It had been skewered lengthwise by a rod about eight feet long, supported on a metal tripod at each end. The underside
was charred and the top raw. There were remains of
half a dozen other corpses scattered around under
the trees.

Hamish turned back to the handsome *caballero*,
but he had gone. The tent and the beautiful maiden
had vanished also. The thing standing in front of
him, leering at him, was a demon.

3

During his last few hours in the baron's dungeon—
they might have been around midday or midnight
for all he had been able to tell—Toby had started
falling asleep, and for once *falling* had been the
appropriate word. Time and again he had awakened
with a sickening jar, tearing his wrists on the manacles and bruising his back against the wall. His
shoulders still ached as if his arms had been pulled
from their sockets.

Nevertheless, the moment Hamish disappeared
over the wall he lurched up and grabbed his hose
from the bush. He hauled them on, and fortunately
the wet cloth clung to him well enough that he
could trust them not to fall off, so he left his doublet
where it lay. He pushed his feet into his buskins,

grabbed up his staff, and followed Hamish, veering
to the left to move parallel to him and confident that
he was making a lot less noise.

Hamish could argue all he liked that there was no
such thing as prophecy, but those three visions had
been utterly convincing. Three times Toby had
found himself somewhere he could not possibly be,
and yet sights, sounds, smells, and in the last case
sheer agony, had all compelled belief. The hob used
him as a mount to ride around and see the world,
and it cared for him much less than a man would
care for his horse. It was stupid, childlike, and
treacherous, but it had never played this sort of joke
on him before.

Certainly the visions were not exact prophecies.
The street in Valencia had turned out as he had
foreseen it, a litter of rubble between burned out
buildings, but the man he had expected was absent.
Hamish seemed to be constitutionally incapable of
disbelieving anything he had read in a book, but if
he now stumbled upon the tent and its occupants as
Toby had described them, then even he might have
to change his mind. Then he might be able to think
up an explanation, for the teacher's son was a lot
smarter than big, dumb Toby Longdirk.

Hamish was still creeping gently along through
the trees like a stampeding herd of buffalo, although
Toby could see a twinkle of firelight ahead already.
Be fair! Not many men would make less noise.
Hamish spent every spare minute reading and thus
was an invaluable source of information. Toby
never read. He preferred to practice useful skills like
fencing, marksmanship, wrestling—and stalking. In
the middle of this smug self-praise he stepped on

something squishy and recoiled so fast he almost
fell.

The revolting stench told him it must be a corpse.
Too small to be a horse or cow. Goat? Sheep? He
was about to move around it when something
reflected the starlight. He poked with his staff and
concluded it was a steel helmet. Gagging, he
stooped and forced himself to explore further.
Slime, maggots . . . The man must have been dead
for weeks. He found the prize he was hoping for, a
sword. He wondered if the hob had guided him to it,
then dismissed the idea as absurd. Any stray dog
was smarter than the hob. Still, a sword would be
very useful if he was about to encounter what he
feared.

He wiped his hands on the grass and rose.
Hamish was shouting in Castilian, hailing the
camp. Trailing his quarterstaff and carrying the
sword, Toby moved faster, heading straight for
the fire. Even without the vision he would have
been suspicious of this lonely campfire. Only a
strong, well-armed group would advertise its presence in this lawless, starving land, and there was no
sign of such a camp here. In a few moments he was
close enough to see Hamish through the trees, and
his worst fears were realized.

Hamish stood near the blaze, apparently quite
oblivious of the revolting object suspended above it.
He was smiling and talking, but the creature stalking
him was obviously a demonic husk. Once it had
been a woman, and there was probably some life left
in it even yet, but when demons managed to possess
people, few of them could resist the temptation to
torture their hosts and enjoy their pain. The thing

that had lured Hamish into its trap was naked and scarred with burns. It had torn out most of its hair and chewed on its own limbs. Its eyes were empty bloody sockets, but the demon would be able to see without them. Hamish Campbell was a dead man.

Any army employed hexers, so it was not surprising that a war demon had escaped its controller and remained behind to add to the miseries of Aragon. But it had not yet detected Toby. With luck, he might be able to slip away unseen. His legs trembled with the urge to flee.

It lifted its web of illusion from Hamish. He screamed, flailed his arms, and tried to run, but his feet did not move. He swung his staff. The demon cackled shrilly and wrested it out of his grip as if he were a child, then tossed it away. Then it clasped his face in the ravaged claws that were all it had left of its hands.

"Pretty, pretty!" it gibbered. "The pretty man is welcome. You will find happiness here—food and love, yes?" It pulled Hamish's head down to its breast in mock affection.

Hamish was doomed. It would take possession of this new victim and torture him also until he died and someone else walked into the trap—which happened first would matter little. In theory a creature and its resident demon could be slain with a blade through the heart, but that was only in theory. In practice the demon would freeze an attacker to the spot or throw lightning bolts at him or pick up a tree and hit him with it. No one except a hexer could creep up on a demon undetected, or evade its powers.

Or possibly the hob. Capricious and unpredictable

though it was, it did hate demons. Toby could not abandon his friend. If the hob would let him, he must try to do something.

Hamish was squirming in the creature's grasp, retching at its stench, but powerless to avoid that odious mouth approaching his. The horror was about to kiss him, and even Toby's stomach turned over at the sight.

"Stop!"

The husk released Hamish and spun around, staring with festering blind sockets toward the sound.

Toby took a step forward, and neither the demon nor the hob blocked him. "Stop, monster! Here is a larger, stronger body for you to claim. Let the boy go and take me." He blundered forward.

"Idiot!" Hamish screamed. "Get out of here!"

"Come!" the husk shrilled gleefully. It jiggled and waved its arms. Its torn dugs flapped up and down. "Two of you to play with! Much feasting and loving and pain! Come to my embrace, lover!"

Toby felt it take control of his feet, rushing him forward to his doom. Hamish was still rooted to the spot, still cursing Toby's folly.

The ghoul spread its arms to embrace its new victim. At the last moment Toby's arm brought up the sword. The hob must have revealed itself then, for the demon screamed, but it was too late to stop the blade. It slammed into the woman's chest, straight through the heart. Corpse and Hamish collapsed at the same moment. Toby felt his limbs returned to his own control and staggered, grabbing a branch to support himself.

His hose dropped around his knees, and he started to laugh.

Even after he had managed to choke down the laughter it was a few moments before he could do more than just shake. Then he pulled up his hose and retrieved both sword and staff.

Hamish had scrambled away from the dead husk. His face was chalky in the firelight. "You flaming fool! That was crazy!"

"Don't thank me, friend. Thank the hob."

Apparently not yet trusting his legs to support him, Hamish sat where he was and stared up incredulously. "I didn't know you could control it that well!"

"I didn't control anything," Toby said. "I just remembered how it hates demons."

"You knew there was a demon here, and yet you let me come?"

"I thought there might be, because of the vision. I didn't suggest it, because you don't believe in visions."

Hamish said something in langue d'oïl that did not sound polite.

4

Toby wakened with the sun blazing down on his right ear. He had overslept, which was annoying but also confirmation that his sleepless night in the dungeon had not been pure hallucination. Not that he needed more evidence than his arms, which still ached all the way from wrenched shoulders to bruised wrists. And now was the moment to wonder what might have crept into bed with him: spiders, snakes, scorpions? He rolled over and heaved himself upright.

Hamish was reading, of course. Beside him lay a heap of oranges and two swords. He smirked with the smugness of the earlier riser. "Sleep well?"

"A few nightmares. You?"

"No. I had my nightmares before I went to bed. There aren't any more demons around. If there were, your snoring would have brought them running."

Since he was wearing nothing but his locket, Toby reached first for his clothes. "You found another sword."

Hamish nodded, closing the book. "I found eight bodies, too. There's other stuff on them, but I couldn'a bear to touch any of it. Yours is a demon sword, you realize?"

Of course. They were conventional, single-edged military swords, with simple L-shaped guards, probably of Spanish make, but one of them had slain a demon and so would have power against demons. That might be useful, for although incarnates were not exactly commonplace he seemed to have a knack for running into them.

Dressed, he reached for the oranges. "Any thoughts on my visions now?"

Hamish scowled. "No. That hob of yours breaks all the rules. And your prophecies aren't accurate— but they do seem to come close," he conceded.

Toby thought of Baron Oreste's dungeon and shivered.

As soon as he had eaten they set off northward, still carrying their staves. Having no scabbards, they tucked the swords in their bundles, hilts ready to hand in case they were needed. Westward lay the scrubby hills, and eastward the brilliant sea.

Amazingly, Hamish seemed none the worse for his horrifying experience with the ghoul. For a while he indulged in aimless chatter, explaining that the Mediterranean had been named by the Romans and meant Middle of the World but the Moors called it Bahr al-Rumi, the sea of Rome; that from the south coast of Castile you could see Africa; that it was only thirty years since the king of Castile had conquered Granada for the Khan; and that a tigress could outrun a horse, but the rider could escape it by throwing down a glass ball, which the tigress, seeing her own reflection in it, would think was one of her cubs and stop to suckle.

"What do you do about the tiger?" Toby asked. "Can't it run too?"

Hamish frowned. "The book didn't say. You suppose no one ever came back to tell them?" Then his eyes twinkled. It was never possible to tell how serious he was when he recounted a tale like that. He usually seemed to accept anything he read in a book without question, but he might have just been having fun with his big, stupid friend. Although his dark coloring made him look like a native, he was tall by Spanish standards and still gangly, so recently come to his full height that he had much filling out left to do. Fine-boned and yet firm, his features combined a pair of very solemn dark eyes with a mouth ever ready to smile. Dress him as a gentleman instead of a beggar and those long lashes would quicken every female heart in the land. If they didn't, it would not be for want of fluttering.

Suddenly he went to business. "What exactly did you foresee last night?"

Toby told what he could remember of the vision. "It's odd, but I don't recall much of what we said. Everything else was as vivid as real life, but the conversation's all fuzzy and patchy."

"Like the meeting in Valencia. You didn't remember what was said then, either." Hamish was wearing his smug expression.

"So?"

"This sounds to me like the hob's doing. It wouldn't care much about words, would it?"

"No it wouldn't. So, yes, you're right." Trust Hamish to work that out.

"Then what?"

"That's all. Oreste just went away and left me in the dark." For how long? All night? The soldiers had checked on him several times.

"Standing up? Chained?"

"Yes. Now you know everything. You're the scholar. Explain it."

Hamish scowled down at the trail. "I can't. It makes no sense. *Déjà vu* isn't usually so dangerous. If you're seeing the future—and you can't be—then how can you change it? But you mustn't go to Barcelona now. Even you can't be that pigheaded!"

Toby grunted.

"Well?" Hamish demanded. "We've got no reason to go to Barcelona. There are other ways out of Spain!"

Barcelona was the shortest, but the real reason Toby wanted to go there was to find a ship for Hamish. He had hoped to find one in Valencia, but the city was a graveyard and no ships came to El

Grao. Hamish, although he hated to admit it, was bitterly homesick for Scotland. Hamish had done nothing to earn this endless, dangerous life as a fugitive except be loyal to his friend. It was time to repay the debt by sending him home. Scotland was a poor land with troubles of its own, but he had friends and family there, which Toby had not, and the sooner he was shipped back there the sooner he could start living the sane, ordinary life he deserved.

So Barcelona it must be, but that argument would not sway him, so think up another reason:

"You know I want more than anything to be rid of the hob. Didn't you tell me that Barcelona has one of the greatest tutelaries in Europe?"

"Montserrat? Its sanctuary is near Barcelona, yes. But the hob won't let you go near a tutelary. You know that."

"A hexer could exorcize it," Toby said çautiously.

"I expect so, but all hexers are evil, and how do you find one anyway? How do you bribe him or pay him?"

"The Khan must have hexers. He'd help."

Hamish groaned. "And how do you get to Sarois?"

That was certainly the problem and always had been. Ozbeg Khan was a thousand leagues away, beyond the Caspian Sea. He would love to have the amethyst, because that would give him the real Nevil's soul, and Nevil had known Rhym's true name, so the Khan could then conjure the Fiend and regain the half of Europe Nevil had conquered. That was why the Fiend had been chasing Toby so relentlessly for the last three years.

"I know a hexer in Barcelona—Oreste himself."

"What?" Hamish howled.

"He has dozens of trained demons. I'll offer to give him the amethyst if he'll take the hob off me."

"You have the brains of a field mouse!" Hamish yelled. "Oreste would hex you or turn you into a creature or just torture you to death out of spite. There is no way you can bargain with Oreste! How could you trust a man so evil? He won't deal, he'll throw you in jail and torture what he wants out of you, or just hex you to obey him. You're joking, Toby, aren't you?"

"Suppose I send him a letter, offering him the amethyst in—"

"He'll trace it back to you by gramarye."

"Well, think about it," Toby said complacently. "I'm sure you'll find a way." And he would see Hamish safely on a ship before he tried it.

"You are deliberately being stupid!" Hamish said, sounding very much like his father had when little Toby Strangerson insisted that three and three made five. "Look at this country!" He waved at the desolate landscape, the burned houses and ravaged orchards. "Nevil marched half his army down this coast to Valencia and Toledo and back the same way. Oreste took the rest to Navarre. They destroyed everything. But somewhere in between there must be lands they never reached. There will still be people there, and food. I am sick to death of living on oranges and onions. I want to cut across country to Navarre. We have friends there, even if Nevil does rule it now."

Toby eyed the hills. "Cutting across country in Spain is like going through a city without using the streets."

"It's worth a try. Over there is a valley leading inland. Let's try it. Please, Toby?"

This was serious. Hamish never begged.

"If we go to Barcelona, I might be able to get my hands around Oreste's neck and strangle him."

"That's a beautiful idea. He certainly deserves it. When you have a vision of yourself doing it, let me know."

Toby shrugged. "All right! We'll head for Navarre."

Hamish looked at him incredulously and whistled. "Truly? Spirits! I'm going to write home and tell Pa that I managed to change your mind about something."

"He won't believe you."

"No. He certainly won't."

5

At first the valley seemed as barren of life as the coastal plain. Towards noon, though, they sighted a little town on a hillside ahead, a speck of promise amid desolation, although the odds were that it had been sacked and burned like everywhere else. The trail led to it, so they pushed on, dispensing with a siesta. Toby's buskins were rubbing painfully on his raw ankles, but he saw no reason to mention it.

Hamish did not notice his limp. Mostly he prattled about things he had read, often years before, as he so often did. Toby listened in silence as usual. Only once did they return to the prophecy problem.

"Toby?"

"Hmm?"

"No spirit can see the future. The books all say the same—not even great tutelaries ever prophesy. All they can do is assess a person's potential, and they're not much better at it than mortals are. Remember back in Tyndrum? Everyone knew Vik Tanner was a no-good that would never amount to a heap of horse dung while Will Donaldson was a promising lad who would go far. But Will Donaldson fell off a roof and broke his neck. When we went to the shrine at Shira, the spirit said you showed signs of greatness. It didn't say you would live to achieve it. Bordeaux said much the same. It thought you might do remarkable things."

"Like seeing the future, you mean?"

Hamish growled angrily. "I still think the hob is playing tricks on you somehow. Let's just hope that it doesn't play any of them around the Black Friars, or you'll find yourself explaining things to the Inquisition."

Although the hob had no mind, no concept of right and wrong, and little akin to any human sense of purpose, it certainly had strong likes and dislikes. It would reduce a military band to screaming chaos in seconds, usually inflicting serious injuries, and it adored pretty things, which were liable to turn up later in Toby's pockets. When it got angry, people died. But none of that explained the visions.

"Ha!" Hamish peered down at horse droppings in the road as intently as Dougal the gamekeeper tracking the laird's deer.

"Not very recent," Toby said. "Two weeks?" He was guessing wildly. Dung had never been one of his most pressing interests.

"Hard to say in this heat. But it's on top of the tracks." Hamish looked up with his angular face twisted in a pout. "Don't think we're going to find anyone home."

"Let's go and make sure."

The town was larger than Toby had expected. It had no freestanding fortifications, but the outer houses faced inward and their backs presented an unbroken wall of masonry to visitors. The road led to a gate, which had been reduced to charred scraps of timber on half-melted iron hinges—obviously by gramarye, not cannon. Clutching his staff and peering around warily, he limped in behind Hamish, who strutted forward, all eagerness to explore.

No dogs came yapping, no chickens scurried, no goats bleated. The country trail became a steep and rutted mud-floored alley winding between tight-packed stone houses, two or three stories under red-tiled roofs. Most doorways stood open on dark interiors; most of the barred windows were shuttered. The ground was littered as if the contents of the houses had been thrown out into the street: broken furniture, smashed pots, rags, dead cats, shattered rain barrels. Seemingly the place had not been put to the torch, for the usual reek of ashes was missing. In its place was a sickly scent of decay that grew steadily stronger as the visitors advanced. They passed the remains of a body, then another, both far enough decayed for the bones to be visible. When they reached a fork, with neither branch providing a view of anything except another bend and flights of steps,

Toby veered right and Hamish followed his lead
as usual.

"May be able to find food here," Hamish whispered, "real food, not just zitty oranges."

The idea was mouth-watering. "If it's fit to eat.
What's that noise?"

Hamish cocked his head and then shrugged
blankly. "Starlings?"

Together they rounded a corner and reached a little open place, a cobbled plaza where four or five
alleys met. Arcades of gloomy arches surrounded it,
and on the far side stood the grandest building of all,
the sanctuary, with a tiled facade, marble steps, and
a little minaret. The jumble of litter was even thicker,
comprised of broken casks, furniture, merchants'
stalls, and general rubbish—and a heap of corpses in
the center. Here the people had been rounded up and
massacred. Bodies were piled head-high, distended
like barrels by the sun, swarming with grotesque
black shapes that were the source of the puzzling
noise—crows and bigger things that might be kites
or vultures. They squabbled and shrieked, crawling
over their feast in search of juicy titbits.

The visitors' arrival sent them aloft in a wild flapping. Scores or hundreds of black birds whirled
upward, raising dust, darkening the sky. Others, so
bloated by their feast that they could not fly, flopped
around amid the carnage, trying to escape, while a
tide of rats swirled across the cobbles and disappeared into the arches and buildings. The airborne
flock gradually settled on rooftops to scream at
intruders like living gargoyles, nightmare guardians
in a town of the dead.

Toby closed his eyes until he could breathe again

and his stomach writhed less urgently. Then he risked another look. The carrion feeders had ripped the uppermost bodies to shreds of meat on white bone, but there were many layers underneath. He wondered if King Nevil himself had been here in this plaza, supervising the slaughter.

"Throats cut, mostly. It would be quick. We've seen worse." Impalements were worse—people left to die on posts. In some villages they had been burned alive, or hung up by their feet, or staked out along the road for miles, and there were other ways to inflict slow and painful death.

"Don't be so sure," Hamish mumbled through the hand he held over his mouth and nose. "Women on top, see? Children next, men at the bottom. How long do you think the women lived after they saw their children die? Hours? Days?"

"Too long, I'm sure."

Yes, the women were bad, but the children were worse—children with rotting green faces, eyes missing, teeth grinning maniacally where the lips had been torn away. There were dead animals in the heap, also, mostly dogs and cats, of course, because the victors would have driven off the livestock or just eaten it.

That thought of eating made his insides lurch again. This was the first settlement they had seen in weeks that had not been burned to the ground. He turned his back on the atrocity and spun Hamish around also, to face the alley.

"Let's explore." His legs were still stiff from his hours in Oreste's dungeon. He needed a rest from walking, even if it must be in these nightmare surroundings.

"As long as we're away before dark!"

"Obviously. I hate looting, but I'm going to take anything I can use."

"They have no more use for it," Hamish agreed.

"Let's start by seeing if we can find water and something to eat."

Hamish choked. "I'll eat outside the gate."

"If you want. We do need food. And clothes. Why don't you start hunting?"

"What are you going to do?" Hamish peered at him suspiciously.

"I'm going to visit the sanctuary."

"It won't be there!"

No matter what Toby ever suggested he could rely on Hamish to shoot back objections, usually very logical objections. Sometimes they were wonderfully sensible and he had to overrule them anyway, although he hated doing that. Hamish was an equal partner now, but he had always been senior deputy in charge of objections. Sure enough:

"The tutelary won't be there, and even if it is, what's happened to its town may have driven it completely insane, so it'll attack any stranger on sight, and even if it isn't, you know what the hob will do to you if you try this, but we can't risk having you injured here, so there's no reason to go there at all; its pointless and dangerous, so I'm going to come with you, and why are you laughing?" He pouted, hurt and resentful.

"Just nerves," Toby said, for it seemed inhuman to be amused by anything in this terrible place. "Yes, it's a long shot, but worth a try. If there is still a spirit to tend the souls of the dead, then we can spend a night undercover for a change. I don't think there's any real danger. And if the hob gives me trouble, I'd rather you were out of it so you can come and pick up the pieces afterward."

He strode off around the plaza, holding a hand over his nose and trying not to look directly at the hill of rotting corpses. Soon he had to slow down, because the piled junk made treacherous going for a man whose buskins sported more holes than a lace shawl. He stepped between timbers with nails in them, broken glass, broken crockery, scrap iron. If the hob reacted to the spirit as it had in Bordeaux and other places, he would soon find himself rolling in all that. But even before he started he had been about as close as he had ever come to a sanctuary and the hob had raised no objection. Sometimes he could tell when the hob knew a spirit was nearby, although that did not always work—he had felt no premonition of the demon in the orange grove. He certainly felt none now. Almost certainly, Hamish was right and the tutelary was gone.

Birds fluttered and shrieked. The stench made his head swim, but he came at last into the cool shadow of the archway. He almost turned to see if Hamish was still there, watching over him, and decided not to. If he was, it would embarrass him to know that his intentions were so transparent; if he wasn't, there was no point.

Toby stepped through the space where the doors had once hung, then waited until his eyes adjusted to the dim, cool light of the high-vaulted chamber. So this was a sanctuary, was it? Before the rebels came it might have been very beautiful, although in an ornate Spanish style that would have seemed alien to an ignorant Scottish Highlander. Now it was a ruin, a singularly repellent one. The invading army had smashed everything breakable and then used the place as a latrine, leaving a deep layer of excrement on the floor and splattered over the walls. Stained glass, frescoes, and carvings had all been smashed. At the far end, where there would have been an altar and probably a throne, there remained only bare stonework above a heap of ruins.

No, the tutelary had gone, for no spirit except a demon would tolerate this ugliness and filth. Furthermore, since no spirit ever left its own haunt willingly, it must have been raped away by a hexer and perverted into a demon itself. Tutelaries made the worst demons of all, Father Lachlan had said, because they were wise in the ways of men. It need not have been Nevil himself who worked this abomination—he had many hexers in his service— but it might well have been. Doubtless the former benevolent guardian of this sad little town now resided in a jewel somewhere, perhaps on the rebel king's own finger. A spirit once dedicated to the welfare of its people was now given over to hate and destruction.

Obviously Toby's harebrained plan to rid himself of the hob was even less likely to work than he had expected. Had he found the sanctuary bereft of its tutelary but intact, then he would have shown all its beauty to the hob and tried to persuade it to remain there. He did not know if it could voluntarily quit him without killing him, but it would have been worth a try. It still was.

"Hob? Fillan! I'm talking to you." Could it even hear him or understand? Probably not. "This is a sanctuary. People lived in this town once, many people. Others would like to come and live in the houses, but they cannot if the place lacks a spirit to care for them. If you choose to remain here, then people will come and repair it and make it beautiful again. You see on the walls and the ceiling? They will repair all the pretty pictures for you. They will bring offerings and praise you for helping them."

He heard nothing, felt nothing. He said what had to be said:

"If you can only leave me by stopping my heart, then I will pay that price. Let me die and you will remain here. This will be your house."

No response. The hob either did not hear or did not understand. Or else it wanted to continue traveling the world, because it was peculiarly crazy, even for a hob.

With a sigh, Toby turned away from the desolation and walked out into the brightness. Hamish had not moved from his place in shadows at the far side of the plaza, keeping watch. The birds were back at their feasting.

6

The first houses they investigated had been thoroughly looted, the furnishings broken or deliberately fouled, including the water casks, which had long since dried out anyway. Whether demons or mortals led by a demon, the invaders could have destroyed everything more easily with fire, so they must have taken pride in their work and wanted to leave evidence of their thoroughness.

Toby's canteen was long empty. A town must have a supply of water, and the rain barrels could not possibly be adequate. There would be a spring or a cistern of some sort, but would the demons have poisoned it?

Moving together in ever-grimmer silence, they turned a corner into a tiny yard and almost knocked over a girl coming out. She leaped back with a scream and then continued to retreat. She was short and slight, dressed all in black: a long skirt and a sleeved blouse. Her cloth bonnet was tied under her chin to conceal her hair and ears, leaving only her terrified face exposed. Incongruously, she had a bright-colored pottery bottle hung around her neck on a cord, and this she clasped to her with both arms as she backed away, staring at them in horror

"Senores! Do not hurt me." Her voice rang shrill and cracking with terror. "I will submit! I will do anything you say, and I can cook for you, too, or wash your clothes. Anything, senores! There is a bed upstairs, senores, and I will not resist, if you promise not to hurt me and not to tell your friends. I will be just yours, yes? Just the two of you. And you will not—"

"Stop!" Toby howled, turning his back. "Hamish, speak to her."

Hamish went down on one knee. "Senorita!" he said, speaking Castilian, as she had. "We mean you no harm, no harm at all. We have no friends with us. We are foreigners, but we are loyal subjects of the Khan, not the Fiend. There are just the two of us, and we do not molest women. We will not touch you. Please do not be alarmed."

How could she not be alarmed in this place,

trapped by two strange men, and one of them a giant? What horrors had she experienced to make her react so? She had expected to be raped before she even knew they were foreigners.

"I will do anything you want, senores, but please do not hurt me."

"We shall not touch you, senorita. We are honorable men. You have nothing to fear from us."

"You are not soldiers?"

"No, we are merely travelers, men who honor and respect women."

Cautiously, Toby looked around. She had backed against the wall, very small and vulnerable, arms crossed across her breasts and that inexplicable bottle. Her face was sickly with fright. She was scarcely more than a child.

Hamish rose and bowed. "I am Diego Campbell Campbell. We are visitors from a faraway land. We will not harm you, I promise."

"I am Gracia Arnalt Arias de Gomez."

"Senora de Gomez, I am at your service. May I have the honor of presenting my friend Tobias Longdirk Campbell?"

Toby bowed also. "Your servant, senora." She did not look old enough to be married, and her black garments implied mourning—a widow? He did not know what to say next.

Hamish came to the rescue, more proficient with words in any language and especially words to women—not that he was much of a ladies' man, although he tried hard enough, but Toby was most certainly less of one. "You also are a stranger here, I think?"

She nodded, staring at him with the huge dark eyes

of a cornered rabbit. Why was she wearing a bottle?
It was ornamental, not practical everyday ware,
glazed in whorls of red and green, fitted with a handle through which the thong was strung. The mouth
was corked, but the way it lay on her breast and the
way it moved when she did suggested that it was
empty.

"Then we may have interesting tales to exchange.
Senora, my friend and I are very thirsty. May two
weary travelers beg the mercy of a cup of water?"

She nodded, shooting a hasty glance at a dark
doorway.

"We shall wait out here." He strolled over to a flight
of stone steps leading up to another house and sat
down. By the time Toby had joined him Gracia had
vanished indoors.

"She probably has fourteen brothers and three
uncles in there," Hamish growled, watching the
door. "Women don't travel alone."

"Unless she's the last survivor."

"She's from Castile."

"She's been here for some time, though." The little yard was the first clean place Toby had seen in
the town, sunlight and shadows on ancient
stonework, barred windows, two weathered doors
broken off their hinges and one whole. It had been
tidied and swept. "I wonder why the wraiths haven't
driven her away?"

"If she offers you roast pork, refuse politely."

"Don't be obscene!" To compare that sweet child
and the creature in the orange grove was utterly
repugnant. "She may have jumped out the back
window and run away already."

Hamish shrugged cynically. "She's from somewhere near Toledo, I think. Not a great lady, more than a peasant."

Toby could not have guessed that much, but Hamish had an ear for languages. He had known Latin as well as Scots and Gaelic before he left Scotland. Since then he had picked up a working fluency in Breton, langue d'oïl, langue d'oc, and Castilian, although even he had been stumped by Euskara. Soon he would be jabbering away in Catalan like a native. They were all variants of either Gaelic or Latin, he would explain solemnly, as if that were obvious. He was Diego now because he enjoyed translating his name into the local tongue: Hamish, James, Seamus, Jakez, Jacques—Diego.

Gracia reappeared, struggling two-handed with a bucket. She set it down in front of the men and retreated quickly. She was no longer wearing the bottle. Without rising, Hamish slid to his knees and reached for the cup under the water. He drank, refilled it and passed it to Toby, both of them being elaborately courteous, making no sudden moves. The water was sweet and fresh.

"You are wounded, senor." The girl was staring at Toby's swollen wrists, which had been bleeding again. Anyone could guess those wounds had been made by manacles.

"Just, um . . . How do you say 'scrapes,' Hamish? They are nothing, senora. But I should clean them if you will tell us how we may refill your, um, fetch more water for you."

"There is a cistern. If the senor will permit me to tend his injuries?"

That hint that she was regaining her confidence

was welcome and must be encouraged, however much Toby disliked being mothered. "They are only scratches, senora. You are very kind." He held out his hands.

Gracia approached as warily as a deer, producing a rag she must have brought for this purpose. She barely took her eyes off his face as she washed away the blood, and he felt her fingers shaking, but she was more deft than Hamish would have been.

He thanked her and insisted he did not need bandages.

"The senor was also limping?"

Hamish had not noticed that! It was true that Toby's ankles were in worse shape than his wrists now, but he could not reveal those without removing his hose.

"My buskins do not fit well," he said. "We have walked a long way." His buskins were falling apart. What chance did he have of finding a pair to fit him in this ruin of a town?

Gracia seemed to accept the explanation, and she was gaining more confidence by the minute. "I can find the senor a new pair!" she said eagerly.

"To fit me?"

"I believe so. If the senor will excuse me a moment?" She hurried off into the house again.

"You know," Hamish said thoughtfully, "if you can get hurt in these visions of yours, then one day you may come back dead!"

Oh, he had just realized that, had he?

"If they're the hob's doing, then it won't kill me." It had never worried about hurting him, though.

Gracia returned with a black cape trailing from her shoulders. She carried an empty bucket, but she also had the bottle hung around her neck again. "If the senor will be so kind as to follow me?"

Toby took the bucket and moved to her side, leaving Hamish to empty the first bucket and follow behind. She was ignoring Hamish completely, but she seemed to have lost her fear of Toby, for she shot a few hesitant smiles up at him, which he returned. He felt overwhelmed by her softness, her femininity. He admired the slight bulge in the front of her blouse and thought he could detect a scent of roses from her. A single dark curl had escaped from under the edge of her bonnet, but most of her hair was tied in a long braid, encased in a tube of black cloth that hung down her back. She was a reminder that there were still decent, honest people in this terrible world, vulnerable people.

Hamish, meanwhile, kept trying to flank the lady on the other side but was balked by the narrowness of the road. That did not stop him from talking. He explained dramatically how he and Toby were refugees from the war and had never been part of the Fiend's army. That was not quite true, but true enough. Gracia responded by telling her story. Toby missed much of it, but he gathered that she had lived in a little village called Madrid, two days' walk north of Toledo, where her husband, Hernan Gomez Ruiz, had been keeper of the shrine. The rebel army had sacked the village and stolen the spirit away. Her husband and brothers had died. She did not mention what had happened to her.

"My sons also died in the war," she said. "They died bravely."

The men exchanged puzzled glances. Admittedly a woman could be a wife and mother at fourteen, but Gracia was not much more than that even now. Could babies die bravely?

She led her new friends directly to a shoemaker's dingy workshop, which was in predictable disarray, with heaps of old boots and buskins covering the floor. Obviously the invaders had helped themselves to whatever they could use and left their own footwear behind, and most of it was as disreputable as Toby's. Gracia, though, headed straight to a back corner and produced a brand new buskin of greater size than the rest, an adequate fit for his right foot. Its mate proved elusive. They had almost concluded that it had never existed and the cordwainer had died before completing a special order, when Hamish uttered a whoop of triumph and dragged the missing partner from under the ruins of the workbench. It was a little snug, but it would do.

"I feel guilty robbing the dead," Toby complained, although he knew he was going to.

"Oh, you must not care about that!" the girl said excitedly. "He does not grudge them to me, and I give them to you. So that is all right! Now we must find some better clothes for the senor. And the boy, also." She headed out of the shop, apparently unaware of Hamish's outraged glare or Toby's smirk. She was enjoying herself now. "This way! There are some garments that I believe will fit you. The senor is a very striking man!"

She blushed at her own temerity and moved off quickly. Hamish made a snorting noise and rolled his eyes.

This time she had to investigate several houses before she found the one she wanted. It had been home to someone almost Toby-sized, and no one

had bothered to loot the clothes he had left behind
in his tiny attic room. Even Gracia could not stand
erect under the roof.

"Obviously servants' quarters," Hamish remarked
acidly.

"A child's, a growing lad," Toby retorted. He
found green-and-brown hose that fit when he cut the
toes off, although they were uncomfortably snug
around his calves and thighs, baggy at his hips and
waist. The anonymous donor must have been wearing his jerkin the last time he went out, but he had
left two shirts and a shabby brown doublet that
could just close around Toby with gaps at the lac-
ings. Even with the cuffs dangling above his wrists
they were a big improvement on his previous rags,
and Gracia was as thrilled as a child when he
appeared in his new splendor. She wanted him to
accept a flat cap of black velvet with a red feather in
it, but he perversely insisted on retaining his steel
helmet.

"Now the boy," she said as they emerged into the
evening light. "He will be harder to fit because he is
so ordinary."

Fortunately Hamish had his nose in a book by
then and was so busy trying to walk and read at the
same time that he did not hear.

"What is the name of this place, senora?" Toby
inquired.

"Name?" She hesitated, looking up and down the
street. "I believe the house we need is this way,
senor."

So she did not know the town's name, and that
probably meant she could not read, because a little
later in the looting expedition Hamish located some

letters and announced that it was Onda. Gracia was
also very vague as to how long she had lived there,
but she had obviously explored it from cellars to
chimneys, and her memory for what she had discovered was astonishing. Most clothes that would
fit Hamish had already been looted, but she had
noted and remembered a few shirts, hose, doublets,
and even cloaks, and was able to lead the men to
them.

So they trailed around Onda after her, carrying the
buckets, and she picked out the garments. None of
them matched any other, some were bloodstained or
impossibly soiled, but eventually Hamish was outfitted.

"I feel like a court jester in this motley," he whispered as they followed their guide down a narrow
staircase.

"You look more like a looter," Toby responded
glumly. Looters were hanged. Stealing made him
feel guilty, even stealing from the dead.

Gracia puzzled him. She made him think of a
songbird in an invisible cage. Her attitude had
changed from abject terror to absurd airs, so that she
was issuing orders as if she expected to be obeyed
without question, yet next moment she would be
laughing and chattering like an excited child. She
ignored the bodies in the streets except to lift her
skirts when she stepped over them. At times she
made nonsensical remarks about how much easier
the senor's journey would be if he would just obtain
some horses, and a moment later she would comment perceptively on the difficulty of finding anything to eat in the hills.

When she had her new retainers outfitted to her

satisfaction, she led them to little caches of food the looters had overlooked: beans, meal, onions, dried fruit, jars of oil, and a sack of hard wheat—most precious of all, because it would keep indefinitely. She had been dipping into it for her own use, but she expected Toby to carry off the whole bag, as well as all the other things she had loaded onto him. He was already feeling like a pack mule, but that did not stop her from detouring on the road home to top him up with bottles of wine and some firewood. Then she took her porters to the cistern so they could fill the buckets. Hamish was too laden with books to be much help.

"The senor is perhaps hungry?"

"The senora has not spoken a truer word since her naming day."

"I am an excellent cook."

"I hope you are also a speedy one, or I shall eat the firewood raw."

Laughing at this brilliant wit, Senora de Gomez hitched up her hems and stepped over a dead child without seeming to notice it.

Her little kitchen was clean, tidy, and cosily cramped with three of them in it, a bizarre oasis of domesticity in a city of death. She set half a bushel of beans to boil and rapidly peeled about a hundred onions. She put Toby to grinding the grain in a hand mill and Hamish to opening a wine bottle. By the time they had passed that around several times and he had opened another, the party became jolly. Toby's mouth watered copiously as the scents of food wafted around him—he could not remember his last good meal. Gracia bustled merrily, clattering pans while the fire crackled in the grate and her guests sat on their stools, awkward in their mismatched, ill-fitting finery.

She put another stool between them, set a bowl on it, and began tipping food in. The men reached for it, burning their fingers and not caring. As soon as they emptied it, she would add more and they would start all over again. More wine bottles went around. She was as good a cook as she had said she was, considering the material she had to work with, and she had the sense to realize that her companions needed large portions. She helped herself to a few handfuls without ever sitting down.

"It grows late." Hamish frowned at the little barred window. "We must be gone from here before sunset."

Gracia's spoon paused in its vigorous beating of batter. "There is a room upstairs where the senores may sleep." She did not look at them. "There are no neighbors to gossip. Besides, it will be perfectly proper, because I shall be out." The spoon walloped against the bowl again.

The senores exchanged glances.

"I am concerned about the wraiths," Hamish said. "There are many unburied dead here and no spirit to care for them."

"You need not worry about wraiths, senor. They have been attended to." She thundered her spoon in the batter.

"I do worry about the wraiths. Wraiths drive men insane."

"I have lived here for several nights, and they have not harmed me."

Hamish looked skeptical.

"What have you done for them, senora?" Toby asked quietly.

Gracia flipped a drop of oil onto the griddle to test its temperature. "I have collected them." She added more oil and spooned out some batter.

More glances. Women could be driven insane as easily as men, but Toby had been expecting something along these lines.

"In the bottle?" The bottle was never far from her.

Hesitation. "Of course."

"Is this gramarye, senora? It is not a custom familiar to us in our homeland."

"Have you had so much war and death in your homeland? No, it is not gramarye! How dare you suggest that I would stoop to such evil?" But she still did not look at her guests.

"Will you tell us the way of it, then?"

She tipped more beans into the communal bowl. "Eat!"

They ate in silence, while she plied them with tortillas and beans and onions, helping after helping. Toby felt as if he were filling an empty barrel. When at last they could eat no more, the light in the alley outside showed that the sun must be very close to setting.

"Tell us about the wraiths, senora," said Hamish.

"It is of no importance."

He opened his mouth to protest—probably to point out that he regarded his sanity as of considerable importance—and Toby silenced him with a shake of his head. She responded better to him.

"You are taking your sons' souls somewhere, senora? And these other souls also?"

She promptly filled her mouth so she could not answer, but then she nodded.

"This is a noble mercy, although I never heard of it being done before. Who taught you this skill?"

After a moment she said, "My sons."

Hamish rolled his eyes and looked around for his staff and bundle.

"Where are you taking them?" Toby asked gently.

She bit her lip, staring at him, and then seemed to decide to trust him. "To Montserrat, senor. There is a great tutelary there, just north of Barcelona. My sons asked me to deliver them to the spirit in the monastery at Montserrat."

"You are traveling alone?" he asked incredulously.

With a little more hesitation, she said that, yes, she was traveling alone.

"This is a most fortunate coincidence. We are going to Montserrat. Will the senora permit us to escort her?"

She gave him a smile as warming as a blazing fire on a winter night. "So that is why they told me to wait!"

"Who told you, senora?"

"My sons, of course!"

"Toby!" Hamish was glowering.

Toby shrugged apologetically. He could not possibly let this poor child go wandering off alone again! It was a miracle she had managed to come this far without being molested.

But Hamish's practical soul was much less impressed by this damsel in distress. "Tell us how you work this conjuration with the wraiths."

"It is not your concern!"

Toby said, "It should not be, senora, but if we are

to be traveling together, then it might become so. The Inquisition, for example, might—"

She froze, staring at him. The color drained from her cheeks.

"We disapprove of the Inquisition," he added hastily and sensed Hamish shuddering at this indiscretion.

"I have no dealings with demons!" Gracia cried.

"Nor we, I assure you, but it takes only a whisper to start the Inquisition asking questions, and we all know how they ask questions."

She looked down at the floor and spoke very quietly. "After the soldiers left Madrid . . . I was the only one left, senor. They overlooked me at the end, when they slew the women. I hid under the bed where . . . it was not my bed. I was the only one left, the houses were burning. I went to the shrine, and the spirit did not answer, so I knew they had taken it. I hunted everywhere for my husband and my sons, to bury them. All day I searched and could not find them. But that night my sons came to me. Their wraiths stood beside me—not as I had known them but as the men they would have been, tall and strong and handsome. They wept because their lives had been so short and they would never grow to that manhood. They wept more because they must evermore remain wraiths with no spirit to cherish them. They told me to take a bottle and gather up the souls, theirs and all the others, and carry them to the tutelary at Montserrat, for it would take them in and care for them always as if they had been its own people. That is what I have done, senor. There and anywhere else I found death. Is this a wickedness?"

"No, indeed. It is a virtuous thing." He did not know if what she claimed was possible, but he certainly did not know that it was not. He dared not look at Hamish. No doubt Hamish could quote books on the subject.

Gracia was relieved to have his approval. She smiled wistfully, her eyelashes glistening. "They still speak to me sometimes. Here I found much death, and it was hard for me to make the wraiths understand, because of the language. My sons told me to keep trying, to stay here for a while. They must have known you were coming, senor, a strong man to escort me through the troubled lands. But I think I have gathered all the souls in this town now. I shall go out again tonight to make sure. There may still be a few of the very little ones, I fear, who find it difficult to understand. They will not trouble you." She looked at him like a wounded plover.

"I believe you. I shall sleep here tonight, then, with your permission." The hob would defend him, but it might not worry about Hamish. He stole a quick glance at his friend.

"And I," Hamish croaked loyally, although he looked as if he could see the room full of ghosts already.

7

He had a lot more to say later, when the two of them were alone in the poky bedroom Gracia had appropriated for her use during her stay in Onda. The bed was too short for Toby and would not be wide enough for both of them anyway. He spread his blanket on the floor.

"Toby, I thought you agreed we would not going to go to Barcelona?"

"We can't abandon that child!"

"Child? She's borne two children—or thinks she has. She's crazy!"

"All the more reason to be kind."

"Ha!" Hamish hurled the last of his clothes down and scrambled into the bed. "Kind? Child? She was dropping broad hints that she didn't really have to go out if *the senor* needed her and *the boy* could sleep in the dog kennel."

"You're imagining things!" Toby stretched out on the floor and rolled himself up.

"She wanted you to share her bed, and you weren't exactly ignoring her yourself. This is no time to start falling in love with a demented—"

"You are being ridiculous and evil-minded!" Toby sneezed several times as his efforts to get comfortable raised dust from the ancient boards. "I am certainly not falling in love! I'm sorry for her, that's all." Memories of last spring . . . Jeanne in the springtime . . . disaster at Mezquiriz . . . Agony in his throat. Never, never fall in love! Love was not for a man possessed. The dust was making his eyes water.

"And you promised we wouldn't go near Barcelona." Hamish sounded aggrieved.

"We can go around it. We'll cut overland, avoid the coast. That'll be just as safe as heading for Navarre. And if we find a convent, we'll leave her there, all right? Or some town with a tutelary that will care for her. Besides, I'm not convinced she's crazy at all. The wraiths don't seem to have molested her."

"How could they?" Hamish said glumly, moving the candle closer and balancing a huge leather bound tome on his chest, a history of Aragon. "She was crazy before she arrived."

"Is what she thinks she is doing possible?"

"Not without gramarye, I shouldn't think. Ah, me! Demons last night, ghosts tonight? You won't mind if I read awhile?"

"Not as long as you don't laugh too loudly."

"If I cut your throat in the night, don't blame me for it." It would take more than a few hundred wraiths to distract him from a good, meaty book, but after a moment he said, "Toby? I realize that your vision, or whatever it was . . . that your vision of Barcelona was pretty bad. I know you suffered. That doesn't mean you have to prove anything."

"Prove what?" Toby asked his blanket.

"Prove that you're not scared, I mean. I know you're brave."

"Huh?" He could still smell that odious cellar, see the barbarous implements of torture, feel those cold manacles scraping his flesh. How long could a man endure being chained to a wall like that? How long survive in the cold and the dark? How long endure without sleep? And what happened after he broke, when he begged for release, telling everything, promising anything at all . . . ? "What do you mean? That's an absurd backward way of thinking! Why would a frightening vision make me *want* to go to Barcelona? That's nonsense. Bloody demons! That's just as crazy as anything Gracia has said."

Hamish grunted. "You needn't shout. Go to sleep, you big ox."

•   •   •

Toby was awakened in the morning by a delectable odor of fresh-baked bread. Gracia was clattering pots downstairs. The candle had burned itself out, and Hamish lay fast asleep, the book pitched over him like a Gothic roof.

Soon after that, the three of them walked out of Onda and headed north, over the hills.

THREE

THE HIRED GUARD

1

Toby closed the door carefully. This dim, poky room was Master's workshop, where he did his hexing, and it held far too many fragile things that a big clumsy oaf like him might knock over—balances, mortars, brass instruments, bright-hued glass bottles, and a bewildering clutter of other mysteries, including a mummified cat. Dozens of books were heaped in disorder on shelves above the benches, but they did not look like the sort of books that would have pictures in them. The baron was stooped over a bench under the window. Rain streamed down the little leaded panes, and he had several candles burning, even in daytime.

"Toby?" he said without looking around.

"Yes, Master."

"Come and see this."

Toby moved gingerly between a chair piled high with books and a globe of the world bigger than a wine cask.

Master was poking a metal rod in a tiny brazier. "See this gem?"

"Looks like glass, Master." It was hard to see at all on the bright-glowing coals.

"It's rock crystal. But what matters is that the hob is inside that glass. That's where I put the hob, Toby. Immured, we call it."

"Thank you for taking the hob out of me, Master. The hob was bad."

"Yes, well we're making it badder." The baron chuckled. Perhaps he had made a joke. "It shows promise of being a truly vicious demon. At the moment I'm teaching it respect. A few hours' roasting should get its attention, wouldn't you say?"

"I don't know, Master."

"No. Well, sit down. Ah! Your new outfit. Turn around and let me see. Yes, very fair. Continue to dress like that, dear boy, and the annoying crackling noise you hear will be the breaking of innumerable hearts."

Toby wasn't sure what that meant either, but he seemed to have pleased Master, and that made him happy, so he smiled anyway.

"Sit down, Toby."

There was nothing to sit on, for all the chairs were piled with books or bundles of scrolls, so he sat down on the floor with his knees up like a grasshopper—green silk hose, very soft buskins. His fancy new outfit had cost a very big amount of money, bigger than he could count. He had never owned clothes like these before—not that he could remember—and he had three more outfits as grand upstairs in a big cupboard. He felt a fool in all of them, with his shoulders barely able to fit through doors and his feathered bonnet brushing the lintels. He knew people laughed at him behind his back and sometimes he caught them smirking at his codpiece. Every man wore a codpiece, but why did his have to be padded and embroidered with gold thread? The baron said this was the new fashion, but it was very embarrassing, and his layered, slashed jerkin was cut to gape in front and make it as conspicuous as possible. He was quite big enough already without padding, there or anywhere else. But this was how Master wanted him to dress, so of course he must.

Master began speaking, but not in a language Toby knew.

While he waited to hear why he had been summoned, he gazed proudly at the ring on his left hand, a bright yellow jewel in a thick gold setting. He breathed on it and rubbed it on his sleeve. He couldn't take it off, but that was good, because that meant he wouldn't ever lose it. (He lost things quite often.) There was a demon in that jewel! It kept him loyal, meaning he would do whatever Master told him to do, although he couldn't imagine why he would ever not do what Master told him to do.

"Tonight, Toby, you will be my guest at dinner again."

"Oh, thank you, Master!" He smiled so he would look pleased, but he wasn't really. It was wrong to be so disloyal and ungrateful, but he felt more than usually stupid at the viceroy's grand dinner parties—servants and musicians, chilled wine, raw oysters and stuffed peacock, twenty separate courses on gold plates, one plate for each guest instead of everyone sharing from a bowl. He didn't know how to talk to the sort of people he met there. Sometimes he got stuck in the wrong language. He didn't even know how to look at the ladies, because their gowns showed the tops of their breasts and he kept wanting to stare down the gap, although Master had told him not to. He didn't *really* slobber! Or not much. He rubbed his chin to make sure it was dry and he had remembered to shave.

"I hear your dancing lessons are going well."

The praise brought a prickle of tears to his eyes. "I try, Master. I am trying as hard as I can!"

"I know you are, Toby. And you are very nimble for a big man. At least you didn't lose that. There are two ladies who have especially asked to meet you. They want to sit next to you at dinner."

His naked face felt very hot. He bent his head between his knees. "I don't know why. I'm not witty or clever or any of those things. They ask me questions I should be able to answer and I can't." Sometimes he would cry, which was terrible.

Oreste laughed. "It is not your table talk they are interested in! Now listen, Toby, I'm giving you orders. There will be one lady on your right and one on your left. They are both older than you, but well preserved. After dinner, you will choose one of them, whichever one you like best. Invite her—or both of them, if you can't decide—up to your room."

"They wouldn't do that!"

"Oh yes, they will! And you know what happens then, don't you?"

"We take our clothes off and get into bed together?" He squirmed and bit his lip. I don't think I've ever done that with a woman, Master. I'm not sure, but I don't think so."

"Yes, you did once. And don't worry, because she will certainly know what to do, even if you don't. It will be all right, and you will enjoy what happens. Just be gentle."

"Be gentle. Yes, Master."

"But you will pleasure her most manfully."

"If she'll tell me what she wants. I'll ask both, Master." He thought that was what Master wanted him to do.

"Please yourself. I'm sure you'll manage. You don't have the hob to worry about now."

The hob was gone. The hob was roasting in that brazier. The hob didn't matter any more. "No, Master. Thank you for taking the hob out of me, Master."

"Enter!" The baron turned to a knock on the door.

Captain Diaz opened it and stamped his feet without coming inside. As usual, his face bore as much expression as a tree stump. "I have the honor to inform your Excellency that the judgment has been handed down and can be carried out at your Excellency's pleasure."

"Very good. We shall be out shortly. Send Ludwig in."

Diaz stamped again and closed the door.

"Toby?"

"Yes, Master?"

"I want you to do something for me."

"Anything I can, Master!"

"You're a big, strong lad. Can you use an ax?"

"Oh, yes! I use to chop down trees often back home in . . . when I was a boy, I mean." What was that place called?

"I want you to chop off two men's heads. They will lay their heads on a block of wood and you will cut them off."

"Um . . . Won't that kill them?"

"That's right. I want them dead, so you'll do that for me. You mustn't talk to them. Just cut off their heads. You'll have a mask over your face."

"Yes, Master. I'll make them dead for you."

That was something he could do. That would be more fun than trying to talk with men who curled their lips at his accent or dancing with ladies who showed that gap between their breasts.

Ludwig came in carrying Master's fur-lined cloak across his outstretched arms. Ludwig was the baron's valet, a blond, sullen, square-faced man. He never spoke to Toby at all. He laid the precious thing over a chair and turned to the baron, who waved a plump hand at Toby in a flash of jewels.

"Toby, Ludwig will help you. You have to strip for this. You need freedom of movement."

Toby jumped up and submitted in silence, letting Ludwig remove his jerkin and doublet, leaving only him his cap and shirt and hose. His hose were very well tailored, snug around his waist, so he wasn't afraid that they would fall off, but his awful codpiece showed even more than before. He took off his shirt as well. "I can keep my hose on, can't I, Master?"

The baron smiled. "Yes. You are very impressive-looking executioner, Toby! Hit as hard as you can, so you cut off their heads with one stroke."

"Yes, Master! I'm strong!" Toby grinned and bulged the muscle in his arm. "Bang! No head!"

"That's the way! Show that muscle to the ladies tonight—in your chamber, though, not in the dining room. One of these men is named Hamish Campbell, Toby."

Hamish Campbell? Hamish? Campbell? He ought to know that name! His memory was very patchy. He could remember some things clearly, and others not at all. He knew exactly how to load and prime a musket, but one night someone had asked him if he had any brothers or sisters and he was still wondering about that. One day he would ask the baron if he knew the answer.

Ludwig wrapped a cloak around him and laced cork-soled shoes over his buskins, then did the same for the baron. Toby hurried to the door so he could open it for Master.

Captain Diaz and an honor guard were waiting in the corridor. Not knowing where to go, Toby stayed close to Ludwig, and that seemed to be what was expected of him. The innumerable servants and flunkies who infested the palace cleared a path, bowing low as the viceroy and his escort marched down the stairs and across the hallway.

Then they were out in the courtyard with a flunky holding an umbrella over the baron. Ludwig tapped Toby's shoulder to stop him, beckoned him to a corner, and took away his cap, putting a black hood on him instead. Toby adjusted it until he could see through the eye holes. The cloak was lifted from his shoulders, letting cold rain beat down on his skin.

The world had shrunk to a keyhole framed in darkness. He scanned the court awkwardly, wondering where he was supposed to go. Master was already installed on a chair under a canopy, attended by a crowd of dignitaries, but his place must be on the platform, because he could see an ax waiting there. Pleased to have worked that out for himself, he stalked across to it and mounted the steps with

care, aware of lots of eyes watching him. Everyone
would laugh if the executioner tripped and fell flat
on his face.

The block was a massive knee-high chunk of
timber. He took up the great curved-blade ax, wishing Master had told him about this job sooner, so he
could have tried a few practice strokes. It was a
very heavy ax and necks must be easier to cut than
trees. He stood it upright on its blade, rested his
forearms on the end of the long handle, and smiled
at Master to say he was ready. But of course his
head was covered, so Master wouldn't see his
smile.

Those must be his victims there, standing in a circle of guards with their heads raised defiantly—two
boys stripped to their doublets and hose, feet shack-
led and arms bound behind them. A gowned acolyte
stood with them, giving last-minute comfort. From
their bedraggled appearance it seemed they had all
been standing in the rain for some time. They both
looked familiar.

The first one was led forward, clanking up the
steps with the soldiers behind him and shuffled forward to stand before the block. Why, it was Don
Ramon! Toby smiled at him, pleased to have
remembered his name.

The don stared back at him with a disdainful
expression, but he didn't speak. He couldn't,
because his mouth was held wide open by a wooden
gag. That must be very uncomfortable. Poor don!
His auburn hair had been hacked off short to expose
his neck. The ginger mustache that used to curve up
in twisted points hung limply over his mouth.

Why wasn't he putting his head down for Toby to

chop? A clerk began reading out a long thing about Don Ramon de Nuñez y Pardo being a Castilian spy. Toby fingered the ax impatiently. The rain was cold on his bare chest.

Poor, mad Don Ramon, with his fancy airs! He didn't look frightened. His face had always been pale and was no paler now, while the startlingly blue eyes were as haughty and contemptuous as ever. When the clerk's drone ended, he shrugged scornfully and sank to his knees. He laid his shoulders on the block, turning his head sideways, away from the headsman. Good!

Quickly Toby took a step backward and raised the ax. Master wanted one stroke, one stroke it would be. He brought his foot forward and his arms down with all the power he could summon. He felt the impact as much through his feet as in his hands. Don Ramon's head hit the planks with a thud and rolled. One stroke it was! Master would be pleased with him.

The explosion of blood took him by surprise, although he should have remembered how pigs bled when their throats were cut. At first it sprayed out against the ax in a red fan, but as the corpse slid back it hosed from the severed neck in high jets— two, three, and a weak fourth before the heart stopped beating. Ax, block, and scaffold were drenched. Nasty! He must remember to wash it off his arms and chest before he undressed with the pretty ladies tonight. He worked the ax blade free of the wood, a soldier picked up the head, and two more dragged away the body. The redness was seeringly bright in the drabness of the day.

The next one must be Hamish Campbell. His face

was sort of familiar. Toby smiled at him, but he couldn't smile back because of the gag. He clattered forward in his fetters less proudly than Don Ramon had, but not slowly enough to make the soldiers push him. His eyes were as wide as his gaping mouth.

The clerk began reading about spying again. The Hamish boy just kept staring at Toby and shaking his head wildly. What did that mean? Was he doing something wrong? Was his hood not on straight?

When the clerk fell silent, the prisoner did not seem to notice. A guard laid a hand on his shoulder. He squirmed away. Two men grabbed him and pushed him down to his knees. Still he struggled, making protesting animal noises in his throat— poor, foolish fellow! He might make Toby miss if he didn't stop doing that, or miss partly and have to hit again. But Master had told him not to speak, so he couldn't warn him.

Two more soldiers lifted the victim's feet. With four of them holding him level, his chest resting on the block, he could do nothing except twist his head around and wail. Squirreling like a worm on a hook was still not going to make things easy. Toby began to lift the ax and then put it down again.

The soldiers were unhappy, too, waiting for that whistling blade and the shower of blood. Fortunately Captain Diaz was nearby. "Keep still, you fool!" he roared. "You want him to botch this? You want to be hacked in pieces?"

The prisoner went rigid. Toby raised and swung, and again the scaffold trembled under the impact. The head jumped free. One stroke again! Master would be pleased. This time the body could not fall back, so the hot blood squirted in all directions off the ax blade, soaking even Toby's hood. That really was not nice. Some of the soldiers gagged and coughed, and they had gotten off much lighter than he had.

Duty done, he pulled the ax free and leaned it against the block, where he had found it. He turned his head for a glance at Master who smiled and nodded a welcome approval. Glad to have done a good job, Toby headed for the steps. A quick bath to clean off the blood, then back into his fine clothes and he would be ready for the dinner and the well-preserved ladies. He just hoped he could do as well for them as he had for the two spies, so Master would be pleased with him.

2

The wind was a restless silence in the night, quieter than the whisper of the sentry's tread on dry grass and rubbly soil. The first glimmerings of daylight were creeping in over the stony hills, not even bright enough yet to mark a horizon or distinguish a white thread from a black thread, which was how the Moors defined morning. Although he was wrapped in both his blanket and his cloak, the sentry shivered as he paced back and forth, forcing himself to stay awake. His legs ached already, and they must walk a weary way before sunset. More than anything in the world he wished he could just lie down and catch a few more hours' sleep, because three half-nights in a row had left him permanently bleary-eyed and yawning. No, more than anything else, he would like to be smelling the peaty scents of home and watching the sun come up on Ben More. . . .

When the scream burst forth almost at his toes, he jumped a foot in the air. It was diabolical, bestial scream, louder than a cannon barrage. Echoes answered from the steepness on the far side of the valley, and a couple of heartbeats later came a wild barking of dogs at the distant *casa*. Gracia wakened with shrills of alarm. By that time Toby had leaped from his bedding with his sword in his hand and was peering around to see where the noise had come from.

It had come from him.

Hamish said, "What's wrong?"

The big man dropped the sword with a clatter and grabbed him in a bear hug that seemed likely to crush his ribs. "Hamish, Hamish! You're all right! You're alive!" His hand pawed at Hamish's throat.

He fought back. "I was! Let me go, you maniac. What happened?"

Longdirk groaned and released him. "Demons!" he muttered. "Oh, spirits!" He flopped back down on the ground and put his head in his hands.

The dogs were falling silent and did not seem to be coming closer. Gracia was twittering questions.

"Senor Longdirk had a bad dream," Hamish explained. He knelt down. Toby was sobbing, heaving dry, soundless gasps of grief. He? Sooner would Ben More weep. "What's wrong? Another vision?"

"Umph." That sounded like agreement. He nodded and gulped through his tortured breathing.

Hamish put arms around him, but awkwardly, because it was the sort of thing an excitable, demonstrative Spaniard would do—Scotsmen never hugged each other. "You're all right, though? Not injured?"

"Not me, no. Hamish, I cut your head off!"

"You did?" That ought to be funny and wasn't. Nasty shivers ran down his back. "Well, it didn't work. I mean, I'm glad it's you who comes back hurt from these things and not me. Are you sure this one wasn't just a dream?"

"It is very impolite of the senores to talk so I cannot comprehend." Gracia had begun the morning ritual of combing out her long black hair, sitting with her back to the two crazy foreigners.

Toby shuddered and seemed to realize that he was being held like a child. Instead of trying to break free, he wrapped a thick arm around Hamish and squeezed. He was still shaking. "No, it was no dream. Oreste had me. He'd hexed me, enslaved me with gramarye, and he made me chop your head off, and another man's—ax and block and black hood and everything. Oh, Hamish, I did it! I didn't even protest. I was eager to do it, just to please him!"

Gooseflesh! "I'm sure you were. Anyone can be hexed—remember King Fergan . . . anyone. It wouldn't be your fault. But it could still have been a dream, Toby. You're worried about the baron and you remember the time Valda hexed you. The two got mixed up in a dream. Happens all the time."

"You had an awful lot of blood in you, friend!"

"What was this terrible dream, senor?" Gracia demanded, piqued as a child at being excluded. "I am very good at telling the meaning of dreams."

"The dream told," Toby said in his butchered Castilian, "that I was royal executioner in Barcelona and I cut off Senor Diego's head."

"How tragic! Why?"

"Because he had been flirting with you and I was jealous."

Gracia squealed at this outrage to her honor, barely managing to conceal her delight.

Hamish shivered and broke free. "We may as well be on our way." The skyline had come into view. "You're all right? You weren't tortured again?"

"No. In fact . . ." He peered at his wrists. "All better. No bruises, see? Not a hair out of place. When I took hold of the ax my arms were bare, and I'm sure there were no marks on my wrists."

"So Oreste cured you? After he'd tortured you and then hexed you."

"Must have done. Must be going to. Hamish, this is insane!" Toby's voice quavered, and that was not like him. None of this was like him. His eyes were round as birds' eggs in the gloom. "It wasn't just a dream!"

"No, it wasn't," Hamish said nervously. "Because where did your beard go? You had it on when you went to bed."

Of course Toby put a hand to his chin then, and of course Senora de Gomez noticed the absence of the beard. She squealed in astonishment and came hurrying over to see, and then she noticed his wrists also—she had joked about their purple and yellow colors at supper. It should have been funny to listen to him trying to convince her that he had shaved in the night and was a very quick healer. It wasn't.

Hamish left the two of them in heated conversation and wandered off to attend to necessary morning functions. As far as Gracia was concerned, he did not exist. To her he was merely *the boy*, although he was older than she was. He kept telling himself that it didn't matter because he would never let himself become involved with her even if she begged him. She was crazy. She collected wraiths in a bottle and heard voices. Oh, she was pretty enough with her dark Spanish eyes, and when she unbound her thick black hair it hung to her hips like a sable cloak, but she would flutter her lashes at Toby till the stars fell before he responded.

Toby had been attracting women's attention since he topped six feet, when he was about thirteen. It was well known back in Tyndrum that some of them had done everything short of stripping naked and crawling into his bed, and even that would probably not have met with any success. Toby never even noticed. He was oblivious to every hint or signal. If he ever did fall in love, then it would be a lifetime commitment, never a passing fancy, because he could not forgive what the Sassenach soldiers had done to his mother, although that was how he had been conceived. Hamish was quite certain that the big lad was just as much a virgin as he was, alas! The only girl who had ever won his interest had been Jeanne, last spring, in Mezquiriz. Yes, he had shown some reaction to her, and he had wept copiously when she died in the tragedy. Of course his lack of interest just made him more interesting to women. Unfortunately, it also made any other man in his vicinity even less interesting. With a sigh at the unfairness of things, *the boy* unlaced his codpiece and irrigated the desert.

By the time the sun flamed on the horizon, the three of them were on their way, heading down the narrow little valley, which must lead to the coast. Its sides were stony and rough, and the stream bed was dry as tinder, without a single tree in sight. Mostly there was nothing to see except the next bend, but almost certainly the travelers were being watched from afar.

The hills had been a mistake. There were no roads and few crops. The rebels had not ravaged this wild, barren landscape because there was nothing to loot except goats and sheep, but multitudes of refugees had swarmed through the area and made the inhabitants distinctly inhospitable. Every *casa* had become a fortress and every outsider a target. Fortunately none of the shots fired at them had been loud enough to rouse the hob, and the dogs had never come within tooth range.

At sunset they had all agreed that they must return to the coast, even Toby, who had hitherto led the way across country with his usual bull stubbornness, storming up and down those bare-bone hills, bent under three times the load Hamish could manage. Gracia with her grand airs carried only her precious bottle and expected her two henchmen to take care of everything else. Now that their food was running low, they had agreed that they must go back to the plain.

By the time Gracia had finished chattering about famous dreams in her family, Hamish had decided that Barcelona was the city of dreams. He secretly dreamed of boarding a ship home to Scotland there, although he knew he could never abandon Toby. Gracia's dreams of delivering a bottleful of wraiths to Montserrat were as crazy as Toby's nightmares of Oreste. But it seemed that they would have to pass very close by Barcelona, if not go right to it.

From the scrunch of his brows, Toby was doing some thinking of his own, and he suddenly said, "Hamish?"

"Hmm?"

"How close would a hexer have to be to hex me like this?"

"Depends on his demons, how strong they are, how well trained, whether they're immured or incarnate. Depends what the hexer's trying to do. Giving you dreams might not take much power, I suppose, but to rip skin off your wrists and then put it back again, or shave off your beard without you knowing it . . ." His voice withered under Long-dirk's glare. "I don't know." Books were always maddeningly vague about such things.

"Maybe it's Oreste doing this to me!"

"I still think it's the hob. Oreste would try to lure you to him, not scare you away." Except that Toby was the most bullheaded man alive. Flash a threat at him and he put down his bull head and charged—in Bordeaux only violent objections from Hamish had stopped him trying to go after Oreste with a cross-bow. Could Oreste have guessed that about him, or learned it from his demons?

"It has to be the hob, Toby. I know you don't think it's smart enough, but suppose it's learned to read your dreams, or fears, or thoughts? It could be reflecting them back at you like a mirror. . . ." Mirror . . . shaving . . . A fit of nervous laughter took him unaware. Toby's puzzled scowl only made it worse. He howled.

"What is the boy laughing about?" Gracia demanded angrily.

"He suffers from a looseness of the wits."

Hamish coughed himself back to self-control and wiped away tears. "I just thought—if your next attack of augury brings your beard back again, we'll know for certain that it's the hob doing it."

Toby looked startled, then his big mouth twisted into a smile. "Yes, I'd have to agree with you on that."

He walked on for a moment in silence, hitched his load higher on his back, and said, "I promised our companion, whose name I shan't mention, that I would see her to where she wants to go, which is not far away from the city I shan't mention either. Then I'm going to put you on a ship. I don't care what lies you have to tell or what sort of rat-infested leaky basket it is, nor whether it's bound for Scotland or Karakorum, if we can find a master willing to take you on, you go. Far away from this accursed land."

Hamish said, "Um." Nice thought but not possible. Can't desert a friend in need. But Toby would insist he try. No need to equivocate, though. "That's a promise! I'll try." If he was to be allowed to lie to the seamen, he would explain that he wanted to leave Barcelona because his mistress had just died of plague. That would reduce his employability to much less than zero.

He was still savoring a mental image of this mistress in her days of health and lust—naked on a bed, of course, with a rose in her teeth and a flush of desire spreading over her plump, red-tipped breasts—when Toby said:

"If these visions are Oreste's doing, would he find me harder to get at it if I had more company?"

Hamish riffled through all the books he had read

and stored away in his mind. "I have no idea. Where are you thinking of finding more company?"

"Right there." Toby pointed.

Their little valley had joined a larger valley, equally desolate, but not deserted. A party of travelers was proceeding down the larger way, heading in the same direction as themselves—a dozen or so, men and women both, some on horseback and some on foot. Two of the riders had already seen the trio and were coming to investigate.

"There are friars!" Gracia moaned. "You will not betray me to the Inquisition, senor?"

"Not all friars are Inquisition, senora. And we wouldn't. Why should we? You are not possessed by a demon. It would be wise if you will not tell them about my wrists healing, either."

Sunlight flashed off a metal helmet. The two horsemen were soldiers, or at least the one in front certainly was—indeed he was a knight, for he carried a lance and rode a huge warhorse. The other was probably his squire, for he was thumping his heels on a pony, trying to keep up.

Then Toby said, "Oh, demons!"

"What?" cried Gracia. "You turn pale, senor! What is wrong?"

He answered in Gaelic, to Hamish.

"I know him. His name is Don Ramon de Nuñez y Pardo. About an hour ago I cut off his head."

3

The images in the visions remained sharp as crystals, the sounds and scents and pains and tastes no less so; only the words spoken and heard lay blurred in Toby's memory. As Hamish insisted, that was a strong argument that the hob was behind the visions, for a human hexer would have more interest in conversation. But names were different. Ludwig, Captain Diaz, Don Ramon . . . those he remembered. This, without question, was Don Ramon cantering up on that gigantic horse.

Although the lance was presently being held high, it could mean death if it were couched.

"Cover me!" Toby hurled down his pack and grasped his staff in both hands, fading to the right. Hamish jumped to the left, preparing to make a fight of it. If the rider went for either of them, the other could smash the horse's legs.

Whatever his intentions might have been, Don Ramon reined in about a dozen paces away and stared down at the peasants with a hauteur that would have seemed pretentious on the face of Ozbeg, Khan of the Golden Horde.

He was as lean as Hamish and certainly no older than Toby, probably younger. His face was of an unusual pallor and bore a high-beaked nose over a slender ginger mustache curved up in twisted points like bull horns. Its expression of sublime arrogance was sadly out of keeping with his armor, for his helmet had come from some Castilian foot-soldier, the polished cuirass from one of Nevil's German mercenaries, and the great two-handed broadsword hanging from his saddle belonged in a museum. So did his lance and the shield on his back, for who fought with those any more? His breeches had a patch on one knee, his boots did not match, and even his shabby bay mount was notable only for its size and age. It looked old enough to be a veteran of the Granada conquest.

Toby was not accustomed to looking up to other men. He also felt he had a perfect right to raise his staff when an armed man charging him on horse-back, although the likes of Don Ramon would see the move as open rebellion. In the resulting silence, he heard only the steady thump of his own heart, and saw only those haughty, unwinking eyes so much higher than his own. Eventually the obvious contempt made him feel ridiculous, so he lowered his staff and bowed to the *hidalgo*.

Don Ramon turned his gaze on Hamish, who bowed also. Then the chubby little squire arrived on his panting pony.

"Francisco," declaimed the knight, "inquire what manner of men these be who contest our progress, whether they be persons of quality with whom one may seek honorable passage of arms, or common rabble that need be taught respect for their betters." Even Toby could recognize the lisping accents of Toledo in that arrogant voice.

The squire clambered down stiffly from his pony, which had seen many better years. So had his ragged jerkin and hose, and he himself was well past his best, for his round, pink face was sagged in many wrinkles and when he doffed his pie-shaped leather cap, he released a wild straggle of white hair. He advanced a couple of steps toward Toby and then spoke out in an unexpectedly high-pitched voice: "Sirs, my noble master seeks to learn what manner of men you may be."

Toby drew a deep breath, but Hamish forestalled him:

"Sir Squire, pray inform the gracious *hidalgo* that we are humble but honest men who have pledged our arms to defend the honor and person of a lady of virtue and quality traveling on pilgrimage, and that although we ourselves are foreigners in this country, we are not and never have been servants of the rebel armies which have so grievously wreaked havoc upon it. Furthermore, pray inform the dauntless and esteemed caballero that even in our distant homeland, far away across the boundless ocean, we have heard tell of his innumerable deeds of valor, superlative breeding, and legendary prestige among knights and thus we are honored beyond measure to find ourselves in the awesome presence of Don Ramon de Nuñez y Pardo."

The squire's eyes bulged and his jaw fell open.

Even Don Ramon raised a coppery eyebrow.

Beautifully done, Master Campbell! Taking his cue from Hamish, Toby bowed very low.

"The wench, Francisco?" Don Ramon murmured. Then louder: "Inquire of what sort is yonder fair damsel, so that, if she be worthy, a gentleman may pay homage to her beauty."

"Sirs—"

"Pray inform his magnificence," said Hamish, "that he is in the presence of the exalted and matchless but most unfortunate Doña Gracia de Gomez." (Who uttered a most un-exalted gulp at hearing herself thus promoted to the nobility.) "The noble lady, racked by innumerable misfortunes, is currently on pilgrimage to the monastery of Montserrat."

Don Ramon raised the other eyebrow also. For a moment he stared dubiously at the bottle hung around the damsel's neck, then he grounded the butt of his lance. Francisco hobbled over to hold it and take the destrier's reins, as if that ancient lump would ever move of its own volition.

Don Ramon dismounted in a bold leap and strode across to Gracia with the litheness of a stag, ignoring Toby and Hamish, although they were still armed and he was not. When he had gone past, they could see the heraldry on his shield, which depicted many quarterings, mostly white butterflies on red and blue, daisies on yellow. He sank to his knees and swept off his infantryman's helmet to uncover rich auburn locks reaching to his shoulders.

"Most noble lady, I am enraptured to behold this wilderness enriched by your unparalleled beauty, a loveliness such as I have encountered before only in the songs of the greater poets, and which must certainly be coupled with great elevation of birth and perfect nobility of soul. Reassure me, I beg you, that these yokels who seemingly attend you are indeed thralls in your service and not wayfaring ruffians who have in any way caused you distress. Tell me that they as much as brought a blush to your cheek by a crude word, and I shall instantly perform justice upon their bodies with my sword."

He would have to get to his sword first, Toby thought, fingering his staff.

Gracia shook her head violently, being apparently beyond speech as she stared down at the handsome young caballero. Her silence did not perturb him in the slightest.

"If you so implore mercy for them, sweet lady, then I can refuse you nothing. But surely the good spirits have blessed me today, because I myself am on my way to Montserrat, accompanied as you may see by a modest train of a hundred or so retainers. I beg you that you will consent to let me escort you, so that you may travel in more safety, greater comfort, and company considerably more appropriate to your noble station and personal beauty."

Toby looked again at the straggle of pilgrims trailing down the valley. Then he looked at Hamish, Hamish at Toby, both of them at the squire, and all three shrugged together. Doña Gracia managed to mumble some words of consent.

"Then, most dear lady, it is my dearest hope that you will agree to sup with us tonight in my pavilion, where my attendants will spread a table proper to your genteel taste, my bards and entertainers will seek to amuse you with music, and you will regale our courtly company with your lovely presence and delicate conversation."

"But, senor . . . I have nothing to wear!"

"A trifle, honored lady! My mistress of the wardrobe will see that you are provided with fitting raiment. You will not refuse me, else surely I must die of a broken heart!"

"No! I mean, yes. I mean I shall be honored beyond words."

"Till tonight then. Ah, how slowly the minutes will drag!" Don Ramon kissed her fingers, flowed upright, and withdrew backward, bowing three times. Having paid his respects to the newly ennobled Doña Gracia, he spun around and paced back to his horse, which had not moved a muscle except to continue its strident breathing. He took his lance from his squire and—despite his heavy cuirass and shield—vaulted into the high saddle as smoothly as any professional acrobat.

Hamish whistled softly and shot a wondering glance at Toby.

"Francisco," the don declaimed, "the superlative Doña Gracia will be joining our train. See that she is properly furnished with attendants and suitable quarters. As for her retainers . . ." He eyed the retainers with distaste. "Question them straightly and establish whether they are honest men or no better than they appear. If they are mere vagabonds, then slit their ears, administer a sound beating, and let them go. However, if they do have some merit, you may enroll them in our retinue with whatever standings their experience and abilities may justify. Have them clad in our livery, outfitted with proper equipage and weapons, and issued the customary rations. I shall accept their oaths of fealty later."

Hamish whispered, "Steady!" and Toby unclenched his fists on his staff.

Turning his horse and spurring it to a lumbering walk, Don Ramon headed for the rest of his companions, who had continued on down the valley. The others watched him go until he was safely out of earshot.

"Did he by any chance," Toby inquired, "recently fall off that mountain of dog food and land on his head?"

The old squire chuckled and shook his head. "Not at all. Will you accompany me, senora, senores?" He set off on foot, leading his pony. Gracia moved close to Toby as the men took up their packs and followed. She seemed understandably bewildered, so he smiled at her and she brightened.

"You mean he has always been like that?" asked

Hamish, wearing the owlish expression he displayed when faced with a knotty problem.

"I am Francisco. You have the advantage of me, senor."

"Sorry. I am Jaume Campbell i Campbell. My large friend is Tobias Longdirk i Campbell . . . and Senora de Gomez. Everything else was true." Jaume? Diego had translated himself again, this time into Catalan.

"I am honored to make your acquaintances. Let me put it this way, Senor Jaume. If you had a friend with a distressing disfigurement—a cast in one eye, for example would you draw attention to it by commenting?"

"Of course not."

The old man chuckled, high-pitched. "Then you would likewise be reluctant to mention any temporary misfortune he might be revealing—a lapse in the quality of his attire, for example?"

"I suppose so."

"Nor would you expect him to discuss it. So you understand! And surely I need not mention that a nobleman of impeccable ancestry, who can trace his line back to the later Caesars, will naturally be touchy on such matters. It would be extremely dangerous to emphasize any trifling discrepancies between what you may falsely perceive to be Don Ramon's current circumstances and the conditions to which he is entitled by his birthright."

Hamish walked on in silence, staring fixedly ahead, looking as if he had just met a dragon selling souvenirs.

"You are bound for Montserrat, though?" Toby asked.

The old man beamed up at him. "To Barcelona, which is very close. And if certain persons in our company are so deluded as to believe that they hired a strong young man with a sword to defend them on their journey, that may not be how everyone views the same arrangement."

Paid guard . . . mercenary soldier . . . wages?

"A nobleman could never stoop to a crass commercial arrangement of that sort!"

"Of course not. I see you are a man of discernment, Senior Tobias."

"The weapons and livery you are to issue to us?"

"They look very splendid on you, senor."

This was madness. Why, therefore, should Baron Oreste want Don Ramon's muddled aristocratic head chopped off? Unfortunately, that might become clear in due course.

4

The valley was wider now, affording some glimpses of rocky, scrubby hills, and seeming a little less barren than before, but the war had reached it. A *casa* on the far side had been burned, as had its surrounding crops and vineyard. While Don Ramon had been interviewing his new retainers, his charges had spread out in a dangerously extended line. Even in this bare landscape, Toby could see innumerable stone walls, patches of shrubbery, and rocky knolls that could provide cover for any evil-intentioned persons who wanted to lie in ambush. Whether or not the deluded don recognized the problem, he was heading for the front of the group as fast as he could move his antediluvian knacker.

Francisco was moving no faster, hobbling along beside his pony and stabbing nosy little questions in his squeaky voice.

Hamish gave an abbreviated account of his wanderings with Toby. Gracia recovered her tongue and began asking about the real live don who had invited her to dinner—Toby would be much in favor of this new interest if it would stop her making calf eyes at him. But Francisco was a quick-witted old rascal and proved more expert at prying than she, displaying a dry cynicism in total contrast to his master's grandiose posturing. He soon learned the lady's true status and what she had been in her former home, but even his skill failed to elicit an explanation of the bottle hung around her neck.

After a while the old man apologized for the state of his feet and mounted his pony so they could all go faster. "May I inquire, Senor Jaume, how you knew my master's name? While he will understand that his fame should have reached as far afield as you said, I myself—being cursed with a deplorably skeptical disposition—have some trouble with the notion."

"Oh, he was pointed out to us in Toledo."

"When?"

"Um . . . about a month ago."

"I am quite positive that he was not there then."

Hamish frowned in exasperation, for his guess had been a reasonable one. "Then it was a man who looked very like him, wouldn't you say, Toby?"

"Astonishingly so, and he looks even more like the man. But who are all these pilgrims? I trust those friars are not servants of the Inquisition, for I confess, being a stranger, I consider the Inquisition an institution of doubtful merit."

This heretical sentiment made the squire roll his eyes in alarm. "Do remember the wise old saying, Senor Tobias: *When in Rome, keep your mouth shut.* And you must not confuse the Black Friars, who are Dominicans, with the Black Monks, who are Benedictines. We have preachers of many sub-orders of Galileans in Spain—possibly even too many for our own good," he conceded. "The Mosaic and Arabic philosophies have been suppressed of late, as you probably know. We do have a friar, Brother Bernat, but he is a Franciscan, and the other learned scholar is Father Guillem, a Benedictine monk. I shall introduce all these fine people to you as we go by. Now these first, or perhaps it would more accurate to call them these last, are natives of Catalonia who fled before the invaders and now seek to return."

The four to which he referred were trailing some distance behind the main body of the pilgrims, having trouble moving a well-laden mule. The two men were dragging it along on a rope, and the two women driving it, whacking its rump vigorously with sticks. All of them wore the dark, monotonous dress of peasants and looked bent, weathered, and hopeless, prematurely aged by toil. Francisco introduced Senora de Gomez and her two fine guards, who would henceforth put their strong arms at the disposal of the company. The men regarded the strangers with glowering suspicion.

"Miguel and Rafael," Francisco explained, without distinguishing which was which or mentioning their wives' names.

Toby and Hamish expressed their honor and happiness at the meeting. The women paid no attention at all, one keeping her eyes on the ground, and the other redoubling her efforts to wallop the mule into faster motion. The men grunted and scowled. Then the taller spat. "Foreigners!"

Toby spat also. "Idiot peasants! Your mule will go faster if you take some of its load on your own backs."

Whether they understood the words or not, the men reacted with incomprehensible patois and very comprehensible gestures. The newcomers walked on.

"You will have to excuse them," the squire said. "Their homes have been destroyed, and they lost dear ones. The mule, whose name I am pleased to recount is Thunderbolt, carries all that they possess in the world—most of which they will have eaten before we reach our destination."

"They can have no cause to like or trust foreigners," Toby agreed. Their pleasure would be even less if they knew that he was the reason King Nevil had invaded Aragon at all. Miguel and Rafael each carried a stout staff. He wondered if they could use them, because he was already making mental notes about defense. If he was to assist the don in his task of guarding the pilgrims—as unpaid assistant, obviously—then he would see it was done properly. Taking orders of any sort was never his strong point, and he had endured floggings rather than obey foolish ones. To keep the party together, the slowest members should be put at the front.

Any marauder who tried to drive off Thunderbolt would not have a profitable outing, but the next two pilgrims were of a different sort, a large and well-gowned lady on a gray palfrey, and a more-simply dressed girl on a piebald pony, both of them riding on cumbersome sidesaddles. A roan packhorse trailed behind them on a tether. Here was wealth worth guarding, because people could be murdered in Aragon at the moment for a horse.

"Senora Collel," Francisco declaimed in a Catalan so mixed with Castilian that even Toby could follow it, "may I have the inestimable honor of presenting the charming Senora de Gomez, who travels like ourselves to Barcelona? And her stalwart companions, who will aid the don in guarding us?"

The two women exchanged polite words and penetrating inspections, Senora Collel being obviously intrigued by the bottle. She was a large lady of middle years, with a buxom figure and a coarse, mannish face bearing a visible mustache. Her imperious manner, while it would not match Don Ramon's, left no doubt that she was a person of considerable importance in her own eyes, and she was dressed accordingly, in a red and green gown with lavishly embroidered hooped skirt, puffed sleeves like strings of sausages, and an ornate neckline displaying an elaborate chemise beneath. The roundlet on her head and the long casing enclosing her braid were embellished with pearls and gold thread. Her wisdom in wearing such finery under the present circumstances could be doubted.

Her younger companion was not introduced, but the predatory way she looked Toby up and down gave him gooseflesh. He felt his bare-shaved face color under her calculating smile and averted his gaze quickly. She would doubtless be pleased to have won such a quick response.

Senora Collel's features stiffened when the new guards were named. "Foreigners?"

"But nothing to do with the rebels, senora," Francisco said hastily. "Wandering scholars who have had the misfortune to become caught up in this terrible war like ourselves."

"Scholars?" She ran a frown over Toby from his helmet and oversized pack to his already-battered buskins, and then back again, all the way. "And what do you study, Senor, er, Long . . . senor?"

"Civilization, senora," he said blandly. "I believe my own poor land of Scotland has much to learn from the more cultured ways of Aragon, and from Catalonia in particular."

"Indeed? Perhaps you are not quite so barbaric as you appear, then. I trust you have brought your own rations, because we have none to spare."

"You expect me to bleed for you without pay, senora?"

She glared. "The don has guaranteed our security. How he provides it is his concern. Senora de Gomez, will you not ride with me for a while? Dismount, Eulalia. A walk will do you good. You will, however, stay close to us." She reined in her horse and the others halted also.

Gracia viewed the saddles with alarm. "Oh, that is most kind of you, but I have no experience on the *silla*, only the *angarillas*."

"Then it is time you learned. If this halfwit girl can manage it, I am sure you can. Eulalia, you heard me."

The maid seemed unconcerned at losing her place, but she was waiting for Toby, holding out her hands so he could help her down. When her hopeful smile failed to produce the desired result and Hamish moved forward in his place, she refused his aid and slid easily to the ground on her own, contriving to reveal most of two very shapely legs in the process. Toby promptly lifted Gracia to the seat, which was a sort of chair mounted on a packsaddle. She blushed crimson, while all the others pretended not to notice.

Rafael and Miguel and the rest had almost caught up by then, so the horses were chevied into motion, and the three men set off once more toward the front of the procession, leaving the two senoras chattering like parrots.

"Senora Collel is going home to more than Miguel and Rafael are?" Toby inquired.

"I would presume so, senor." Francisco's manner was guarded, so he might have the same suspicions about the packhorse that Toby did. It seemed to be making heavy work of carrying a very compact, unassuming load.

"A formidable lady!" remarked Hamish, although he had spent the whole time ogling Eulalia.

"Indeed," Francisco agreed. "And a very well informed one. Senora Collel is the person to ask if you want to know anything at all about anyone in our party, Senor Jaume. That will shortly include your own life story, I am sure. Or else that will be the price required for the answers you seek."

"Is gossip a weakness of the fair sex, do you think?" asked Toby.

The squire quirked a puckish smile. "And of the old, senor. Now we come to our learned clerics. Father Guillem is from Montserrat, and is not merely a learned monk but also a holy acolyte of the sanctuary. I am not sure where Brother Bernat came from originally."

"And whose is the child?" Toby asked, for a skinny girl of about seven was bouncing along between the preachers, holding a hand of each and periodically lifting her legs so they had to swing her. As each man was laden with a bulky pack, this was probably not easy for them. "Are not friars and monks expected to be celibate in Spain?"

"Most are celibate, senor. A certain number are even chaste. The girl's name is Pepita. She is Brother Bernat's ward. I suspect her parents died in the war, but . . . but Senora Collel may be better informed on the matter than I am."

Hearing the three men and one pony advancing on them, the two robed men halted and turned. Little Pepita frowned with a child's frank distrust, moving closer to the taller and older of the two, who wore the gray and must therefore be Brother Bernat, the Franciscan.

The other spoke first, in a voice with the rumble of thunder. "Good spirits bless you, my sons!" Father Guillem was a monolith of a man in his forties, solid and square-cut—square his jaw, square his shoulders, and his sandaled feet seemed set too far apart. Even his black tonsure appeared somehow angled instead of round. In a large and hairy fist he clutched a staff almost as massive as Toby's own, much heavier than was needed for walking, so he could be added to the list of the company's defenders. He frowned as he listened to Francisco's introductions. "And whose men are you?"

The questioned burned, as it always did, and Toby

bristled. "We appear to have become Don Ramon's, Father. For the time being."

The cleric disapproved. "Laws in all lands require a freeman to have a lord. No land, no lord, no guild?"

"Only honesty and a strong right arm."

"The strong arm I can see. I trust you will demonstrate the honesty."

"I also try to be civil, unless I am given cause not to be."

"A civil reply in the circumstances," said Brother Bernat mildly.

Grateful for that remark, Toby turned to him. He was tall and spare, a willow. His face was lined and aged, even his eyebrows silvered, and his tonsure had shrunk to a trace of swansdown around a naturally bald pink scalp. He seemed absurdly ancient to be walking the length of Aragon with a pack on his back, but his wizened lips were smiling.

"Thank you, Brother." Toby bowed. He normally disapproved of friars, men who ought to find themselves honest labor instead of wandering around the country telling other people how to behave. Even monks were a cut above friars, if they performed useful functions like caring for the sick or providing hospitality to travelers. However, this old man was the first of the pilgrims he thought he might be able to like.

Then he noticed that Brother Bernat's eyes were surprisingly clear and dark for so old a face, and they were appraising him with more than normal curiosity. "So you are truly your own man, are you?"

He almost seemed to be hinting at something, and

Toby felt a shiver of unease. All these pilgrims were infested with curiosity.

"I answer to no one!" he snapped. The friar frowned.

"He's very big!" Pepita said accusingly. She was pretty, elfin, and probably undernourished. She was also a welcome distraction from the friar's disconcerting inspection.

Toby went down on one knee. "I can't help it. You're very small, but you will grow bigger. I don't know how to grow smaller."

She giggled. "I want to ride on your shoulders!"

"Child," Brother Bernat said reprovingly, "remember your manners!"

"I don't see why she shouldn't," Toby said, glad of a chance to demonstrate some civility for a change. He cupped his hands for her. "Mount!"

Instantly she scrambled up to sit on his pack and clasp her skinny legs around his neck. He stood up, making her squeal in delight. Her grip on his helmet tilted it to an uncomfortable angle, but her weight was trivial.

"You should not encourage her, my son," Brother Bernat said, but he was smiling again, sunshine on an ancient mountain.

"She's no burden. Pepita, you are our lookout. Watch for bandits and shout if you see any. I'll send her back in a day or two, Brother."

"You also travel to Montserrat, Tobias of the strong arm?" Father Guillem rumbled. "For what purpose?"

More nosiness! "We agreed to escort a lady there, Father. While I'm there, I shall ask the tutelary to foretell my future."

A frown seemed to be the monk's natural expression. "Spirits are not oracles. Seek out some fairground huckster if you want your fortune told—but waste only money you do not need."

"I have never known such money, Father. Is the tutelary unable to see the future or merely unwilling to reveal it?"

Father Guillem's manner chilled even more. "You raise heavy matters for a social chat, Tobias. A private discussion when we are camped would be a more appropriate setting."

"Why do you ask, Tobias?" Brother Bernat inquired softly. "Does your future seem especially clouded?"

The dark eyes were rummaging through Toby's soul again. He decided he was outmatched—which Hamish would certainly have told him must be the case, had he asked before he started this absurd fencing. He had not intended to cross wits with the two clerics, but how did one down swords in such a contest?

"Every man's future is clouded, surely?"

"No."

"No?"

Brother Bernat smiled with the benevolent tolerance of the very old for the very young. "Come and talk with us this evening. You are an interesting young man, Tobias."

Definitely nettled now, Toby barked, "In what way?"

"Your eyes do not match your eyebrows. No, I do not mock. Your strength lies uneasy upon you. You have the bones of a fighter and the soul of someone else."

Was that only a lucky guess, or was the monk detecting the hob in him? Demons could do that, but he did not think any unaided mortal could. It was Father Guillem who was the acolyte, an acolyte being a sort of adept. But anyone could be a hexer, even a friar.

"I don't think I know how to answer that remark, Brother. I'll take your little girl for a walk."

Toby strode off, cursing himself for a dimwitted boor. He seemed to be putting up every back he met. His ill temper was soon dispelled, for Pepita twisted his helmet, drummed her heels on his chest, and shouted, "Faster, faster!"

"Faster? Who do you think I am, Thunderbolt?"

"You're bigger than Thunderbolt."

And more stupid. He hadn't made many friends so far. There were only two more pilgrims to meet, and they had halted about thirty paces ahead. The don must have told them to wait there, because he was some distance out in front, heading for a rocky knoll.

Toby stopped to let Hamish and Francisco catch up. "You realize that you have to carry me on the way back, don't you?"

That made her laugh. "Which of you? The one inside or the one outside?"

He caught his breath. "Pepita, what do you mean?" She was only fantasizing, surely.

"Nothing," said the piping voice overhead. "Just, when I was looking at you, I could sort of see two of you. I can't from up here. That's very curious, isn't it? I'll ask Brother Bernat. He'll know what it means."

As long as she didn't ask the Inquisition! He

wished he could look at her and judge how serious
she was, but all he could see of her was little brown
feet in shabby sandals. "Do you often see two of
people?"

"No," she said airily. "Just you and Brother
Bernat."

The sensible thing to do would be to gather
Gracia and go. These pilgrims were nothing to him.
Traveling in company was more pleasant and nor-
mally safer, but it would not be safer for him if
Pepita started babbling her fancies to everyone else.
The slightest whisper of demonic possession led
straight to the Inquisition.

The chubby squire and his pony arrived, accompanied by Hamish, who gave Toby a reproachful
look, which he had certainly earned. Even
Francisco seemed a little less convivial.

"The last members of our company, senores—or
should I say first, since they travel at the front?—are
the esteemed Senores Brusi. The father, Salvador
Brusi i Urpia, is a man of much importance in
Barcelona, a silk merchant." Francisco dropped his
voice to a squeak. "Very wealthy! And his son,
Josep Brusi i Casas."

"They saved their hides by running away when
the rebels came?"

Francisco cleared his throat, although his eyes
had started to twinkle again. "I expect they had
urgent business in Granada or Seville."

Brusi Senior had found himself a low wall to sit
on while he waited; it appeared to be a relic of an
ancient sheepfold. He was a shriveled raisin of a
man, small and bent, but his eyes were sharp
enough and his little prune mouth screwed up in

disapproval as he watched the strangers approach. If he was rich, his garments were plain enough not to show it. His horse was a roan mare of quality, though, with smart trappings, and his two pack-horses were worth plenty in these troubled times. All three of them needed a good grooming.

The boy holding the mare's reins was about Hamish's age, but sallow and gawky, with the list-less air of a humble, bookish clerk, and already showing some of his father's stoop. He wore a knife in a sheath on his belt, but no sword. The Brusis were not fighters.

But they were wealthy, and Senora Collel might be. Why had they not obtained better protection? Had they underestimated the perils of the journey or been misled by the don?

Francisco made the usual introductions.

"More guards?" Salvador Brusi snarled. "At whose expense? I shall hold the don to our agree-ment, to the last *dinero*."

"The don is a man of his word, senor," Francisco said smoothly.

"Bah! And what does he know of these two, hm? Rogues! A pair of footpads who will cut our throats in the night and steal our horses!"

"I wouldn't want them," Toby said. "Not in that condition. Why don't you look after them better, old man? They're walking gorse bushes."

Brusi bristled. "Insolence!"

"I give what I get. If we did want to steal them, we could knock your brains out this instant and let Don Ramon ride his hack into the ground trying to catch us." Toby's Catalan was far from fluent, but he had obviously put over the gist of what he had tried to say, for Brusi was scarlet and spluttering. "Tonight my friend Jaume and I will curry your mounts for you—for a suitable fee, of course—and get those ticks out of their coats before they go sick and die on you."

He turned to Francisco, whose eyes were rather wide, but whose pudgy face otherwise bore a studied lack of expression. "Let's go and talk to the don about our order of march. Senor Brusi, you may start moving again when Miguel and Raphael catch up."

"You don't give me orders!" the old man screeched, lurching to his feet.

"I just did."

It was unfortunate that Pepita chose that moment to snigger. As Toby strode forward, he glanced at the younger Josep, and was surprised to see traces of a grin. He winked. Josep twitched in surprise and then winked back.

Don Ramon had completed his survey of the terrain from the knoll, and was now returning. Hamish fell into step at Toby's right, and a moment later Francisco's pony arrived on his left.

The old man coughed meaningfully. "Senor Longdirk, while I have greatly enjoyed your progress, I do hope you realize that here men of humble station are expected to observe a certain tact when addressing the gentry? Of course I have no intention of criticizing how things may be done in your fair homeland of Scotland, but this is Spain."

"In Scotland they would hang me for it. You think they may hold back my wages?"

The squire sighed. "I'm certain you won't ever see a dinero of them." He chuckled. "But, please, senor, I implore you, do not try such tactics on Don Ramon!"

"I have no intention of doing so."

"Shade his honor in any way and one of you will die, senor, I swear it."

"I shall be as prim as a princess."

How long could he hold to that resolve? Did he even want to try? A dozen adults and a child, and only one of them a real fighter—and even that was giving the don the benefit of a very considerable doubt. His fighting might be as muddled as his thinking. However nimble he was at getting on and off his horse, had he ever swung that broadsword in his life? Apart from him, only Miguel, Rafael, and Father Guillem were likely to put up any defense at all, and none of them could have any training or experience. With Hamish and himself aboard, the company would certainly have a better chance of surviving any trouble it might encounter. Under any normal circumstances, there would be no question—the newcomers would ask to join the band and place themselves under the hired guard's orders. When the hired guard was a raving aristocratic maniac, was that such a good idea?

Toby turned for another look at the pilgrims, which required him to walk backward, making Pepita laugh and drum her fists on his helmet. Then he turned the right way round and said in Gaelic, "Hamish? You want to serve the noble lord?"

Hamish jumped, as if his mind had been a long way away. "You're not serious? You can't be serious! You couldn't even take orders from Sergeant Mulliez! You think you can keep your temper with that snooty lunatic?"

"I might. I wonder whether he's as crazy as he pretends to be. Senor Francisco, is the Senora's packhorse carrying gold?"

The squire choked. "Gold, senor? Whatever . . . Why would you think such a thing?" His horrified expression said that it did, or at least he suspected that it did. He could have seen how the bags were handled when it was loaded and unloaded.

"There doesn't seem much on its back, and yet it walks as if it had a heavy burden. Doesn't matter." Toby must make his decision soon. "The don has to ride at the front of course."

"Of course!" Even Francisco could not imagine any other arrangement, and Don Ramon himself believed he was leading a train of a hundred—knights in livery, beautiful ladies on white horses, banners flying, band playing. It was a beautiful picture, but it wasn't real.

Nevertheless, Miguel and Rafael were the nearest thing he had to fighting men, so he had put them at the rear. The horses wouldn't like the mule, anyway. The only other man who might strike a blow, Father Guillem, he had set in the middle. And himself at the front.

"I suppose Senor Brusi is paying most of the fee, so he insists on being as close to his guard as he can be?"

"Only the king might insist with Don Ramon, senor. It is by his command that the senor travels there."

A command that conveniently forestalled argument. So the order of march made good sense, but might be mere luck. If Toby were to take charge now, what would he do? Move the two peasants to the center and put the new men at the rear? No, probably send one man on ahead to scout for trouble and have the other patrol back and forth along the line, herding the sheep.

Don Ramon had reined in to await the deputation.

"Senor?" Francisco whispered. "He would really like you and your companions to join our troupe, although I admit his way of expressing himself is a little strange. We should all like it. What do I tell him?"

"That we pray to be considered worthy of entering his service."

The squire beamed, but only briefly. "You will be careful, both of you? His honor is all he has left in the world."

"It will be safe with us," Toby said. "I am not at liberty to explain this, senor, but I have a deep respect for Don Ramon. To serve him will be a privilege."

Surprise, suspicion, then recollection . . . "You knew his name!"

"And I honor it. Pepita, you have to dismount now. This mule needs a rest." Toby reached up to lift the girl down, then discarded his pack and staff. He accompanied Francisco over to the boy on the big horse. The don stared down at them with his customary arrogance.

The squire dismounted and doffed his cap in a low bow. "Senor, Captain Longdirk entreats you to accept him and his troop into your service."

"Of course. Did you expect him to pass up the opportunity of a lifetime?" Don Ramon looked expectantly at the new recruit and bent just enough to offer a hand, palm down.

Toby bowed, unsure what was expected of him

and not entirely certain of his own intentions even yet. He looked up at the sea-blue eyes and the utter contempt in them. He was, said those eyes, dirt. But the don had looked at him like that—exactly like that—when he was on the scaffold, facing the headsman's ax. Any man capable of such defiance at the lintel of death was a man indeed.

"Senor, my company and I will be honored to serve you." *Until I cut off your head.* He kissed the pale fingers. He stepped back, bowing three times, as he had seen the don himself do.

The don showed no sign of emotion at the touching ceremony, other than a sneer which said that of course the stupid foreigner had done it all wrong but his ignorance would be overlooked this time. "Now, Captain Whatever-your-name-is, send some troopers to scout ahead. They are to keep their eyes peeled at all times for possible ambush. I want no heroics—at the slightest hint of trouble they are to run back like rabbits and report to me personally, is that clear? And set some others to patrolling the column, to make the stragglers keep up. Look lively!"

"As the *caballero* commands." Toby saluted and went back to issue the necessary orders to his company.

Hamish had heard all that, and his expression was rarer than diamonds.

"Look lively now, Sergeant Jaume!" Toby said. "Take a dozen of our best men and escort Senorita Pepita back to Brother Bernat. After that, ride herd on the civilians and make sure they keep moving along."

"Aye, aye, sir!"

"And brush up your Catalan. Your accent's terrible."

Hamish said something in breathy Catalan, too quick to catch. It did not sound respectful, and the grin that followed it certainly wasn't.

5

Scouting was an easy thing to do badly, a hard one for a lone man to do well. By rights Toby ought to zigzag back and forth across the entire width of the valley, from height of land to height of land, while investigating every bush or rock in between, but there were limits to how much ground even his legs could cover and still keep him a reasonable distance in front of the main band. Fortunately his pack was lighter than it had been.

Unfortunately, it was growing ominously light, and his solitary wandering gave him time to brood over a very grim-looking future. One of the rules of field craft he had picked up in his mongrel career as soldier, peddlar, teamster, smuggler, and most often fugitive, was that a man on foot could rarely carry more than ten days' rations. While he was unusually strong and not much encumbered with other gear, he had an appetite to match his size and bore Gracia's share on his back as well as his own. He estimated they had only seven days' supplies left. Hamish's pack was mostly filled with books, of course. They would not reach Barcelona in seven days. When they did, they would not find it built of gingerbread.

When he wasn't worrying about food, he worried about Oreste and himself chopping off Hamish's head.

Around noon he came to a burned-out *casa*.

Nothing remained of the main house except fire-blackened two-story walls with secretive little window openings, and the destroyers had gone to a great deal of trouble to waste the surrounding crops, vines, and olive trees. Only the weeds prospered, already moving in to conceal evidence—a table leg, an anonymous charred bone, half a child's doll—but the ruins were deserted and there was water in the well, so it would be a good place to make the midday halt. He signaled to Don Ramon, receiving a wave from Francisco in acknowledgment. Then he placed his pack on top of a thick, head-high wall. As a picnic site it lacked shade, but it commanded a good view of the countryside.

By the time the pilgrims arrived, he had filled the water trough. Hamish quickly began assisting Senora Collel's party, probably so he could stay close to Eulalia. Old Salvador Brusi made straight for the nearest patch of shade, leaving Josep to tend the horses, although he was obviously unskilled with them. Toby went to help him unload.

Clumsy the youngster might be, but he spoke Castilian and could understand Toby's polyglot jabber. "I apologize for my father's rudeness earlier, senor," he said diffidently.

"I am sorry I barked back at him. How far have you come?"

"With the don? From Toledo. How long will it take us to reach Barcelona?"

"At this rate about a hundred years. The mule slows us. It is overburdened."

"Yes. Often has the don told them so and made them carry half its load themselves, but as soon as his back is turned they put it all on the mule again."

"Your horses could carry more. Will you consent to take some of their goods?"

Josep glanced anxiously in his father's direction. "I shall ask, senor."

"Without trying to charge a fee, of course."

The young man smiled wanly. "That will certainly be the problem."

"It is to your advantage that we make better time."

Having established to his own satisfaction that the Brusi baggage included substantially more than seven days' food and several suspiciously heavy bags that might well contain gold, Toby returned to his pack. Hamish was already there, perched on the wall and unwrapping some of the inevitable beans. Gracia had been invited to dine with Senora Collel, who must either have ample provisions or else did not understand the danger of starvation.

The overall picture was dismal—the three women under an orange tree that had somehow survived the devastation, the two clerics and Pepita near the well, the Rafael-Miguel foursome in another corner, the Brusis also by themselves. He looked around for the don and his squire, but they had ridden off to the nearest hillock.

"A friendly lot," he observed.

"They're frightened," Hamish said, chewing. "Senora Collel is furious because she has to sleep in the open. She brought no tent. She expected comfortable inns, because that was what she enjoyed when she went south. She says it was most inconsiderate of the invaders to burn the inns."

"Fear ought to make them unite. Or the don should. That's what a leader is for."

"He's crazy! Mad as a wet cat."

"So is Gracia. It's the war, I think. I'm not even sure of old Brusi, if he's trying to carry gold without a proper escort. And I'm crazier than any of them." Toby did not really think he was crazy, but he suspected the hob was. "We all should get along famously."

Hamish grinned. "It's lonely being the only sane man in the world. You're right about Brusi. Senora Collel says he got such a good price from the don that he couldn't resist the bargain."

"Oh? And what's her excuse?"

The grin widened. "She heard about Brusi and thought he was shrewd enough to know what he was doing, so she signed up too. None of them had any idea how bad the devastation was." He tugged a weighty book from his pack.

"What's that one about?" Toby asked.

"Hmm? Catalan verse. You did tell me to brush up my Catalan."

"You planning to quote poetry to Eulalia?"

Hamish looked up, wide-eyed with hope. "Would that work?"

"I've heard it can be quite effective. And if you think it will help, you can tell her that Gracia and I are lovers."

Hamish turned faintly pink. "I already did." He began to read with great concentration.

Poor Hamish! Since the evening of the day his voice broke, he had been making advances to pretty girls. Even now that his beard had grown in—a little scanty in spots, but an honest beard—they still seemed to think of him as only a boy. He had no trade or land or family prospects. Possibly he was too intellectual, all head and no heart, and probably too solemn and serious, although he was witty enough with men. It was definitely time to send him home to the glen to wed some bonnie lass and raise another generation of schoolteachers.

And poor Toby! He had the opposite problem. Since Mezquiriz, he dared not even think about women in case he reminded the hob of Jeanne.

Oh, Jeanne!

Hamish yawned. They were both worn threadbare by too many broken nights.

"If you drop off up here," Toby said, "then you will drop off. Take a nap." He would not. The don must not catch them both sleeping on duty.

Hamish peered at him blearily. "Half and half? Wake me in an hour?"

"Promise."

Hamish closed his book and jumped down. He stretched out on the grass and was snoring in seconds.

Toby retrieved the sword from his pack and fashioned a loop of rope as a baldric for it, thinking the sight of it might make the pilgrims more inclined to accept him as a guard. Worried he might go to sleep in the heat, he clambered down and walked around to see to the others. They were all doing what Hamish was. There was no sign of Don Ramon or Francisco.

The landscape baked in silence, nothing moving under the sun, not a bird in the empty blue sky. He went off to the remains of the vineyard to see if the birds and insects had overlooked any grapes. The vines were grown on the ground, not on trellises, and he waded knee-high through rustling brown leaves, pushing branches aside with his sword. He found only a few moldy raisins to eat, but it passed the time.

Help soon arrived in the person of Eulalia, slender and slyly smiling, who had no doubt feigned sleep to evade her mistress and was now elated to have the big young stranger to herself. That he would be equally pleased she would not doubt, nor should she—her shapeless servant garb could not completely deny the lure of the body within. Her robe was of coarse brown fabric, long-sleeved to cover everything except face and hands, decorated crudely with strips of yellow and orange, probably by herself. A darker cloth covered her head, but the casing on her braid hung to her waist, and nothing could disguise the magic of the dark eyes, the sculptured perfection of features, the complexion like aged ivory. Dress her as a princess and she would be one. Small wonder Hamish had lost his wits already.

She had as few words of Castilian as Toby of Catalan. Speech could help little, but shiny red lips and dark eyes said everything.

"Are you finding any, senor?"

"No. A few."

She knelt to search among the leaves. In a moment she said something excited and beckoned him. When he squatted to see, she popped a raisin in his mouth. Her eyes again, the smile, her hand on his thigh . . .

He stood up and shook his head. "Not me, senorita. Try Jaume."

She glared at him and caught his wrist, trying to pull him down beside her. He walked away, conscious of sweat, the oppressive heat, the pounding of his heart. He despised himself for them and the lingering tingle in his loins. Were all men so easily tempted, or was he a weakling? How did other men keep their self-control in such situations?

Many didn't, he supposed. He was not the only bastard in the world.

He paced around, afraid to settle. Guard duty was more interesting at night, when a single cracking twig might be the only warning. Here, the empty landscape made it too easy. There was no sign of the don—had he left his new deputy in charge, or did he hope to catch him neglecting his duty? What disaster had brought a *hidalgo* to such penury that he could afford no better arms than discards and no squire except an old man with crippled feet?

Seeing that Eulalia had returned to the senora, he went back to the vineyard and scavenged some more. Later he saw a chicken in the undergrowth and spent time stalking it. It would not have survived so long had it not learned to be wary, and it eluded him. He did not waken Hamish. He had never intended to keep his promise.

When he went to the well for a drink, he found Gracia there in her widow's weeds, still wearing the bottle that proclaimed her delusions. She was not as tall as Eulalia, and her face was less striking, but lovely enough. So fragile! She was delicate, she had suffered, she was not perfectly sane by the world's standards. One look at her and her sheer vulnerability made him want to clasp her in his arms and swear to defend her against anything for ever. She was much more dangerous than Eulalia.

Just one kiss? There need be no seduction, no

false promises, just a moment of mutual tenderness in a world unbearably harsh.

No, not one.

"Senor, a favor?"

"If I can, senora."

She clutched the absurd bottle in both hands. "This brings questions."

How surprising! "Yes?"

She raised her chin as she did when she spoke of her mission to the dead. "My voices tell me that it will be safe with you, senor. Will you put it in your pack and carry it for me?"

It couldn't weigh much, one empty bottle. "Of course. I am honored to be trusted with it, because I know how much you value it."

She smiled again and lifted the cord over her head. He took it and hung it around his.

Fortunately he had very good reflexes. He caught the bottle before it hit the ground. Then he straightened up to face dismay that became astonishment that instantly turned to fear. She backed away, staring at him like a cornered fawn. The knots had untied themselves? No, the hob had untied them. Why should the hob object to an empty bottle?

Because it *wasn't* empty? He felt the hairs on his nape lift.

There was no use trying to think up some prosaic explanation. "It would seem, senora, that the wraiths do not approve of me as a guardian." He thrust the bottle at her quickly, lest it wriggle snake-like out of his hands. "Come with me and put it in Diego's pack. It will be safe with him."

"But . . . ? But why? How did that happen?"

"You saw what I saw." He shrugged. "I have a sort of curse on me, senora. The wraiths may not approve of me, but I am sure that they will not find fault with my friend."

"Curse?"

"Senora, what would happen if I told the Inquisition that you hear voices and gather the ghosts of the dead?"

Her lips curled back from her teeth in terror. "You will not!"

"Of course I will not. And you will not tell them about my curse! We are companions, friends. Now we share each other's secrets." After all, they were both crazy. She collected the dead, he had visions. Lunatics should stick together.

"What is this curse?" she asked uncertainly.

"It is a long story, and painful. It is why I go on pilgrimage."

She thought he meant the tutelary at Montserrat, of course. He was thinking of Oreste's relentless pursuit. He reassured her, pointing out that no evil had come to her in the last few days while she was in his company. He took her over to the place where Hamish was still snoring, and together they wrapped the bottle securely in Hamish's blanket and put it in his pack with the books.

6

When he saw the don and his squire riding down from their knoll, Toby went around the camp and wakened the pilgrims. Pepita was already alert, combing her hair; she jumped up and followed him, all big bright eyes and serious.

"Senor . . ." She tried to say "Longdirk" and stumbled over it.

"Call me Toby."

"Senor Toby." She spoke very solemnly. "I asked Brother Bernat why I saw two of you and he said that that was a very bad thing to say about anyone and I must tell you I was sorry and promise you I would never tell anyone else."

He smiled down at her—a long way down, for the top of her head barely reached his ribs. "Then I thank you and accept your promise. Did he tell you why you see two of me, though?"

She pouted. "No. He said I will understand later, and perhaps you could see two of me."

"No, just one. But it's a very pretty one."

She liked that. He wanted to ask more questions, but it seemed unfair to interrogate a child. He would have a talk with her sharp-eyed guardian.

"Are you going to catch the horses, Senor Toby? I can help! I'm very good with horses."

She certainly was. She walked up to each of Senora Collel's three in turn, took hold of its halter, then led it to Toby. He was certain they would not have been so cooperative for him. She demonstrated how the chairs and their footboards were secured to the pack saddles and explained earnestly how important it was that the folding stepladder be the last thing loaded on the packhorse, so that it would be available for the ladies to mount and dismount.

Then the two of them went to help Josep, whose bumbling efforts to catch the Brusi horses had put them to flight. He had gone around behind them and was driving them back toward the *casa*, but they were still at liberty, staying well ahead of him.

Pepita walked out to meet them and they surrendered to her with no arguments.

Josep arrived after them, hot and ashamed. He was not only inexperienced, he was obviously nervous of the big teeth and feet. Pepita's complete lack of fear could not be helping his feelings, although he thanked her graciously enough.

"I am better with ledgers, Captain," he muttered, red-faced.

"Each to his own. Figures terrify me. Let's go and steal some of the mule's load."

"Oh . . . I have not yet asked my father's permission, Captain."

"Call me Toby. If he doesn't like it, he'll have to take care of the matter himself. I need you to interpret for me. Pepita, you go back to Brother Bernat now."

"Why?"

Because there might be trouble.

"Because you need to put your hair up."

Pepita flounced off angrily. Toby led one of the packhorse over to the Rafael-and-Miguel group, who had just managed to drive Thunderbolt into a corner, where he was being difficult, with hooves flying. Josep explained their intentions in a rapid stream of Catalan, and the peasants grew difficult also. Their surly faces dark with suspicion, they shouted that they did not trust offers of free transportation, they did not trust Senor Brusi or foreigners. They did not trust anyone. The tall one with the big nose was Rafael, the burly one with the long black beard was Miguel. The women were still unnamed.

Handing Josep the horse's bridle while the argument continued to rage, Toby pushed his way in and soothed the mule. Thunderbolt was not quite willing to be friends but reserved judgment on being an enemy, since the stranger had not yet piled any mountains on him. He let Toby lead him over to the waiting heap of goods. The onlookers were impressed. The men stopped carping to watch and the women switched from strident to grumble.

Inspecting the pile, Toby saw that the problem was simpler than he had realized. A bundle of ash-wood staves would no doubt prove very useful when these poor folk were struggling to reestablish their living, but carrying such a load through this dangerous countryside was sheer insanity. The same went for three empty wineskins.

"Josep, did they start out with all this clutter, or have they been doing a little selective looting?"

The youngster grinned. "A bit of both. The barrel appeared two days ago."

"Well, will you explain to them that we must make all possible speed, that we are running short of food, that every day on the road increases our danger of being set upon by brigands, and that brig-ands, if any do attack us, will strip us of everything and either kill us or leave us naked?"

While the translation was in progress, Toby selected a weighty bundle of tools and implements and loaded that on the Brusi horse. He added a bag of meal and a bulky sack that smelled of onions. Rafael tried to stop the food being taken, Toby jos-tled him aside with a warning glare.

That, he decided, was enough ransom to put into the avaricious grasp of Salvador Brusi, but there was still too much left. He picked up the oaken bar-rel. Even empty, it was weighty.

"Ask them why they need this."

All four responded with shrill protests that it was valuable.

Toby lifted it overhead, smashed it down on a rock, and then it wasn't.

He halted Rafael's attack by placing a very large fist in front of his nose. Rafael backed off, but Miguel tried to lash at him with a whip. Toby jabbed him in the belly—gently by his standards, but enough to put him down. With shrieks that were probably audible in Barcelona, the women sprang forward, claws out, so he drew his sword. That restored order for a moment; but when he slashed the three wineskins and cut the rope around the bundle of staves, all four of them came for him, and he had to threaten them with it. Even young Brusi looked totally appalled at this method of doing business.

"Josep, tell them that all this junk must stay where it is. The rest they can load, but if their mule won't keep up, I will cut its throat and roast it for supper."

He led off the packhorse, leaving the argument still raging. As he was loading the Brusi chattels, the old man came wandering over to watch, making no effort to help. He had been watching.

"You expect me to transport those goods, senor?"

"I do."

"At what price?"

"None whatsoever."

The merchant frowned. "I do not see that their trouble is my concern."

Toby paused to wipe sweat from his forehead. "It is my concern because I am trying to get you all safely to Barcelona. Speed is vital. It is your concern for the same reason. If I can't make you cooperate, then we are probably not going to arrive before we starve. The country is barren, senor. All this gold you carry won't buy you one dried fig."

Brusi's eyes narrowed at the mention of gold. When spoken by a man with a sword in a lawless land, the remark was close to a threat. Toby gave him a cryptic smile and went back to work, while the old man watched with his wrinkles scrunched down in a glare.

As Josep approached, his father said, "I could use a man like you in my business."

Astonished, Toby took another look at him. "You are gracious, senor. What have I done to merit such praise?"

The withered lips curled in a sneer. "It is not what you have done I value, it is the breadth of your shoulders. You are as strong as two ordinary men. Good porters are hard to find."

"The senor is very kind!" Toby snapped. "You can finish up here."

He stalked away, seething. It wasn't just that people saw him as a chunk of brawn that annoyed him, it was the knowledge that porters' work was all he was good for. Or bullying destitute peasants, and he could not have managed that so easily if he were a normal size.

Heading to waken Hamish and tell him that he was now custodian of the bottle, he was intercepted by the don on his destrier. He saluted. The arrogant eyes surveyed his sweat-soaked condition.

"You show promise, Captain."

That was an improvement! "I only seek to do my duty, senor."

"Of course. We shall move out in five minutes. Have the band start playing." The don wheeled his horse and rode off.

Toby resisted a strong temptation to make an obscene gesture at his retreating back. But he did get them all moving in five minutes, with a rather bleary-eyed Hamish trotting out in front as scout and Toby himself at the rear to make sure the wrecked barrel and other debris were left where they belonged. He was pleased to see that the mule was now in a better mood, which was certainly not true of its owners. As they showed no signs of wanting to chat with him and help him improve his Catalan, he went by them and caught up with the women. The train was moving faster than before, although everyone was now rested, so the improvement might not last.

Gracia was still riding the little piebald, and thus Eulalia was walking, seeming somewhat footsore already. She turned her head so she need not look at the despicable foreigner. Another improvement!

Swaying in her horse-borne throne, Senora Collel appraised him as if she were considering buying him but found the asking price ridiculous. "Come round this side," she said sternly. "Senora de Gomez, you ride on ahead. Go with her, Eulalia. I wish to speak with this man."

Toby moved into position alongside her skirts and well-shod feet. Bent under his pack, he had trouble looking up at her face, but then it was not a face he wanted to spend much time on, all sagging flesh and ingrained paint. Tiny dewdrops of perspiration glistened in her mustache. She carried a red silk fan, which she wielded vigorously every few minutes, causing her palfrey to flicker its ears in alarm.

"You speak French, monsieur?"

Surprised, he said. "A little, madame."

"Your young friend told me of your travels. I, too, have visited Aquitaine."

"You are a lady of culture, madame."

"I am a very nosy one. I want to know why that Gomez woman was carrying that bottle and what she has done with it. She will not discuss it, and neither will the boy."

"Jaume has it in his pack now. Her tale is a sad one, madame."

Senora Collel evidenced satisfaction. "Then you may tell it at length."

Toby racked his brains. Hamish would be better at this than he would—why had he not invented some useful fiction?

"The lady was married very young."

"Obviously. Come to the point."

"Her husband was killed in the war, and her infant sons also."

"That does not explain why she wears a bottle around her neck."

Keep it simple. "Ah, but it does. It was the last gift her husband gave her, on the night they bade farewell. She has sworn never to be parted from it, as a memorial of him."

"That is all?"

"That is all, madame."

"How ridiculous! Foolish child. She will find another man soon enough, or one will find her. She is charming is she not?"

Toby risked an upward glance at the formidable senora. He had known sergeants-at-arms who would have looked prettier in her fancy gown. "Very."

"You did not sleep during the siesta break, Monsieur Longdirk?"

"The don left me on guard, madame."

"The don is a madman. We are safer now we have you. Eulalia slipped away, thinking I would not notice. She returned in a very brief time and in a very petulant mood."

"May it be that the mademoiselle suffers from constipation?"

The reply was a bark of coarse laughter that almost spooked the horse and made Gracia look around in alarm. "I don't think her problem was anything like that in the least. You and Madame Gomez are lovers?"

"No, madame." He accompanied the words with a warning scowl, but scowls bounced off Senora Collel like sleet off a limestone gargoyle.

Her eyes gleamed. "Why not? From the way she looks at you, she is yours for the taking."

That deserved no answer. He peered behind him at the mule and its mulish guardians, then forward, all the way to the don at the front. The company was moving well and staying together. He could trust Hamish to do a good job of scouting.

"Now it is my turn to ask some questions, madame, yes? Tell me about Monsieur Brusi."

She waved her fan dismissively. "Very rich, very powerful in Barcelona, a member of the Council of One Hundred. A dangerous enemy, Tobias."

"I seek no enemies, madame."

"You may have made one already in that man. He sucks life from other people. His wife hanged herself seventeen years ago. If that son of his does not escape from his father's shadow soon, he will never blossom."

Nothing surprising there. Toby had already reached the same opinion of Josep. "Father Guillem?"

The senora glanced down at him warily. "A preacher, an acolyte in the greatest sanctuary in Catalonia, indeed in all Aragon, and probably a senior one. So a pious man and probably a very learned one."

Had the renowned gossip learned no more than that?

"I think I knew that, madame, and I think he does."

She chuckled, an ominous sound. "Very likely."

"And Brother Bernat?"

Surprisingly, this time there was a longer pause, a glance even more guarded. She frowned. She glanced around, although there was no one within earshot and they were still speaking French.

"I have only suspicions, Tobias."

He did not like her use of his given name; here it implied an intimacy he had no wish for. But he did want to hear her suspicions. "Tell me those, Madame Collel, and I shall remember that they are only suspicions."

Her smile of broken, yellow fangs would strike dread into the bravest. "Why is an old man traveling with a tender child, hmm? Tell me that!"

"I cannot. There may be good reasons."

"There may be very evil reasons, also!" she said triumphantly.

"He is a friar, madame, a pious teacher of ethics."

She lowered her voice. "That is what a friar is supposed to be, yes. But is he what he says he is? I think he is an—" she paused dramatically, "—*alumbrado!*"

"I am not familiar with that term, madame."

She pouted, curling her mustache. "It is a foul heresy. There are ill-disposed people who travel the wild lands, Tobias, seeking out elemental spirits."

"Hexers. They harvest the elementals and turn them into demons. I know of this evil, but—"

"Not only hexers! Worse! You have never heard of the *alumbrados?*"

He hitched his pack higher on his shoulders, wondering what could possibly be worse than the gramarye he had met in Lady Valda or foreseen in Baron Oreste. "No."

"*Alumbradismo* is the worst form of gramarye, Tobias! These abominable persons do not worship good spirits and tutelaries, as honest folk do, but the wild elementals themselves!"

"Why should that be worse than hexing? It sounds dangerous, for elementals are unpredictable, but they are not evil in the way demons—"

She dismissed his ignorance with a wave of her fan. "These heretics sacrifice children to the elementals!"

Oh, that was ridiculous! What interest would a wild elemental have in human sacrifice? They just wanted to be left alone.

"I never heard of this terrible thing, madame. For what purpose do they do it?"

She rolled her eyes. "For power, of course! It is said that they make themselves immortal."

This was not even gossip—it was pure malice. He did not believe a word of it. "That is a most serious charge, madame. Have you any evidence?"

Senora Collel resented his doubts and scowled at him. "I told you I only had suspicions! But there is something very strange about that Brother Bernat and his sweet little ward. You speak with him and then come and tell me if you do not sense something very strange about him."

"I confess I already have sensed that he is an unusual man."

"There! What did I tell you!"

Hamish had never mentioned *alumbradismo*, and if Hamish did not know of it, then it had never been written in any book. Perhaps it was some sort of local superstition.

"I shall keep your warning in mind," Toby said. "Now tell me of the most interesting person in this company."

"The don, you mean?"

"Of course not. Madame Collel."

She laughed raucously. "So you can flatter? Ah, the woman is a terrible harridan! She was born very poor and married a man much older than herself, disgustingly rich. She has outlived three husbands. It is a well-known scandal that her household always includes a well-built young steward, whom she pays well to keep her servants in line and herself content. It is said she usually tires of these staunch youngsters after a year or so, but dismisses them with a generous requital. Have you employment in mind when you reach Barcelona, Tobias?"

He gaped at her brazen smirk. He had no idea how much she was mocking him, or if her monstrous suggestion could be at least partly serious. "Monsieur Brusi has already offered to make me a porter in his warehouse."

"I pay better, but the work might be harder."

It would indeed! "I shall keep this generous offer in mind, madame."

She chuckled. "But I do not roll in the under-growth like Eulalia. If you wish to try out for the post, you will have to wait until we arrive. What do you think of the don?"

"He puzzles me. Is he as deluded as he pretends?"

"How can he be, unless he lost his wits in battle? He is reputed to be a good fighter." From her that was probably significant praise, but she said no more about Don Ramon. She frowned. "There is something very odd about his squire, also. He bothers me more."

7

By sunset they were almost out of the hills. Hamish had located an excellent campsite, sheltered by cypress trees and furnished with a small pool trapped behind an earthen dam. The water was slime-covered and bad-smelling, but it would serve to wash off the sweat and dust of the day. When Toby tried to borrow the Brusi bucket, he was reminded of his promise to curry the horses and informed that his fee for that could be the rent of the bucket. The better one came to know Brusi Senior, the nastier the old prune seemed, but the only other bucket belonged to Rafael and Miguel and the price of that one would be the captain's heart on a stick. What a jolly lot they all were!

While Hamish was building a communal fire, therefore, Toby gave Josep a lesson in caring for horses. Eulalia attended to Senora Collel's and obviously knew what she was doing—a farmer's daughter, no doubt. Each little group sat under its own tree, well apart from the others. Pepita wandered around being friends with everyone, but she was a notable exception, because there was still no sign of the adults cooperating. Rafael and Miguel had marched up to the Brusi camp and carted away their possessions without a word of thanks to anyone.

Even the two clerics remained aloof. Toby had talked with them on the march, receiving a severe lecture from Father Guillem on the virtue of peaceable methods and the iniquity of drawing a sword on unarmed peasants. Toby refrained from pointing out that the procession had moved a lot faster since his bullying.

Brother Bernat was courteous, inquisitive, and inscrutable. At times his talk rambled and he seemed almost senile, but his questions were sharp enough. Anything he said about himself was trivial, as when Toby congratulated him on keeping up with youngsters like him.

"I am a friar, Tobias. I have been walking all my life. I would take you on any day and walk your feet off. But you have walked all the way from Scotland? By what route did you come?" Yes, Brother Bernat was much more likeable than the monk, and not as feeble and feathery as he pretended.

When the horses were seen to, Toby collected the bucket and headed for the pool. The sky was darkening already, and the long day had left him bone weary. It was not over yet, of course. He was accosted by the don, on foot but still wearing his cuirass and now bearing his great broadsword as well. He held out two wooden whistles hung on thongs.

"You will post the order of the watch, Captain."

Toby accepted the whistles and made a rapid calculation. Two would be the minimum to guard so many horses, and he was surprised the don had not ordered him to post twenty. How many men could he call on, though?

Then Don Ramon added: "Leave orders for my personal staff to be awakened two hours before dawn, so they can prepare my bath and so on."

"As the *hidalgo* commands," Toby answered gratefully. He assumed that meant the don and Francisco would take the final watch, so the night could be divided into five, which would be a great deal easier than the last few nights had been. He would not trust Rafael and Miguel together, though, and probably not the two Brusis, either. It would take some thought. . . .

"We must assume, Captain, that the Fiend has learned from his demons that I have taken the field against him. He will undoubtedly hasten here in strength to oppose me. You should anticipate a surprise attack before dawn."

Toby drew a quick breath and said, "This is serious news, senor. I shall pass it on to the officers and take the necessary precautions."

That was easier than trying to explain to the madman that he himself, Toby Longdirk—pauper, smuggler, mercenary, and habitual odd-job man— had been the reason King Nevil had invaded Spain the first time. . . .

He filled the bucket and went off into the dark trees to clean up. He had barely removed his doublet and shirt when he heard a quiet rustle behind him and a high-pitched voice murmured:

"Captain?"

He stayed where he was, on his knees, annoyed at this intrusion. "You need the bucket, Senor Francisco? I shall be only a few moments."

"Oh. No. Or not yet." The old squire cleared his throat and shuffled his feet. "I was wondering . . . That is, I propose . . ."

Toby sat back on his heels with an inward sigh. "Whatever it is, I shan't tell the don."

"Ah, you are understanding. I should like to buy some provisions, if you have some to spare. You see— you will recall—Ramon invited Doña Gracia to dine with him this evening. He has ordered me to prepare a banquet in her honor, but this will leave me a little shorter of supplies than . . . He does not realize . . ."

Toby's mind jumped back to the siesta break. Those two had ridden off alone. He turned to stare at the old man.

"Have you anything left at all?"

"Oh, yes! I mean . . . Well, not a great deal. . . ."

"Nothing?"

"Nothing," Francisco admitted sadly.

"When did you last eat?"

"We had a little yesterday."

Great spirits! "You can't go all the way to Montserrat without eating!"

"No, senor. But the don . . . He is a proud man and—"

"He still has to eat." Toby had expected that his own group would be the first to run out, or possibly the clerics, whose packs seemed skimpy, but not for a few days, and he had been hoping that by then he might have thumped these stubborn individualists into more of a team and taught them the need to share.

"I am offering payment!" Francisco whispered despondently. He held out a hand. "This ring is very pure gold."

Tony took it and peered at it in the fading light. It was a plain wedding band and could be gold for all he could tell. Returning it, he caught hold of Francisco's hand. It was a small hand, very delicate. He looked up at the plump, aged face.

"Francisca?"

She drew in her breath and snatched her fingers from his grasp. For a moment she seemed about to flee, and then her shoulders slumped. She groaned. "You are perceptive, senor! I don't think any of the others have guessed."

Toby laughed gently. "I'm sure you're right, because Senora Collel does not know. Sit down and tell me about it. As one seasoned campaigner with another, you will not object to watching me wash?"

"We can talk later, senor." She sounded close to tears.

"No, sit down! Turn your back if you wish." Toby scooped water in both hands and soaked his face, his odd-seeming, naked face. He was glad to be rid of the beard, because he hated it, but it would return fast enough. He owned no razor. "Tell me the story. I won't repeat it. I promise, but I do want to hear. Think of it as my day's pay."

The old woman settled to the ground stiffly, not turning her back but not facing him either. She sighed. "I am his mother."

Who else could she be? He might have guessed grandmother, but she seemed younger as a woman than she had as a man. The pitch of her voice had lost its strangeness, of course.

"He is of the *limpieza de sangre*, the pure blood. Look at the veins in his wrists—blue as the sky! His family is very old, very distinguished, but it was never wealthy. In his grandfather's time . . . You do not care about that. Suffice it, senor, that when his father died, two years ago, and then the bankers called in their notes, he was left with only one tiny holding. Four sheep wide and ten sheep long, he called it, but he was still a *hidalgo* with land and a roof over his head. When the rebels came, he had not even that."

Toby was starting to wish he had not asked. He slopped water over himself and said nothing. In the camp behind him Pepita trilled with laughter and a horse whinnied.

"He answered King Pedro's call, of course. He fought very bravely! You may doubt a mother speaking of her son, but I tell you much less than the truth. Many persons commented on how he distinguished himself on his first day in battle. At the end his horse was killed under him and his arm was broken. He was taken prisoner. His armor was forfeit, of course, his weapons, everything."

Toby shivered. "He was extremely lucky not to be butchered most horribly."

"I know that, senor. He killed a guard and escaped back to the Castilian lines."

"With a broken arm?"

"Yes. Alone."

That was an incredible feat. If true it deserved an epic, and somehow he did not doubt a word of it— fiction would have been made more believable. "How old is he?"

She evaded the question. "He was a man when he

was fourteen. But he could fight no more. By the time the bone had knitted, the war was over."

"And you had nothing."

"We were out in the streets. He did not even have clothes in which to go to court to seek recognition of his services." She sighed. "I doubt he would have gone anyway. He comes of proud stock. His father . . . No matter. I heard of certain persons who wished to return to Barcelona and wanted to hire a guard. I found others like them. I made the arrangements, senor. Then I went and told him what I had done."

Proud stock could not be a hired guard. Toby did not ask the obvious question, but she told him anyway.

"He was enraged! Furious! He turned the color of the dead and would not speak. I asked him if he would watch his mother starve. Or if he would make a thief out of me, for I had naturally taken some of the fee in advance to buy weapons and armor and horses. He could not answer. He would say nothing. He walked the streets for days. He did not sleep or eat. I almost wished he would strike me for betraying him so. On the morning we were due to leave, I dressed in these clothes and went and told him I was his squire and his retinue was waiting. He smiled for the first time since the war came. He ordered me to have the bugles sounded."

The knot in Toby's throat made speech impossible. He bent forward and emptied the last of the water over his hair, then rubbed it vigorously with his shirt.

"We have kept up the pretense ever since," she said, sounding proud of that. "I have told you the truth, senor."

She knew it was pretense, but how much of it did the boy believe? Was he just honoring his mother's courage or had his mind snapped?

"I do not doubt it, Doña Francisca. You are as brave as your son. We have some provisions to spare. We shall divide them with you, so that when we run out, we all run out together, and who can say what may happen before then? No," he insisted when she held out the ring again. "I will not take it. You may pay me when you collect your fee in Barcelona." He pulled on his wet shirt and his doublet over it.

"Please, senor! Let me pay with this, now."

"Never!" He could even laugh a little at her stubbornness—the son had not taken it all from his father. "Your wedding ring for a bag of beans? Even barbarous Scotsmen are not without honor."

"You do not understand," she said miserably. "They say that in Barcelona now this would be a fair exchange, gold for beans. I was a fool, I knew I was outbidding many seasoned soldiers, so I did not ask nearly enough. I had no idea of prices. . . . I did not even leave enough for food, so we have run out already. Do you think those peasants will honor their pledge? Or old Brusi? That woman? They will laugh at me when I ask for the rest. My son will not recognize the problem. And even if they pay, it will not be enough to take us home again."

That would not be a problem. Toby had a very clear image of a head rolling across bloody planks. Her son was going to die in Barcelona, and he would be the executioner. He choked down a surge of nausea and jumped to his feet. He held out a hand to help her rise.

FOUR

More Questions and Some Answers

1

They had two more clear days before death claimed the first of them. Two days were not long enough to turn the pilgrims into a team, but Toby and the don between them did effect some improvements.

"Captain," the *caballero* proclaimed as camp was being struck the first morning, "the terrain has changed. The enemy may conceal his forces anywhere. We should need a hundred men to reconnoiter our advance effectively." He was fully armed, holding his horse's reins and ready to mount, but then he had been awake for the last two hours, so his blue eyes and arrogant red mustache were bright and perky respectively.

Toby was still a little blurred by sleep. "This is true, senor." Certainly the plains offered far more opportunity for ambushes. The coastal trails wound through trees and overgrown fields.

"Reserve all pikemen for defense. Close up the ranks. The foe will direct his attacks upon our commissary."

"Um . . ." He probably meant the packhorses, and that was a reasonable analysis when the most probable foe was a starving rabble of refugees. "Yes, senor."

"Divide the infantry between the van and the rear guard."

"And the cavalry in the center? As the *hidalgo* commands."

"Excellent. Carry on, Captain. You may have the buglers sound the advance."

The don's commands always made good sense when properly interpreted. Either he had been given a sound military education or he had a natural soldierly instinct—perhaps it came from the *limpieza de sangre*—but translating his whimsies into real-world instructions required an understanding that the siege train was Thunderbolt because he carried axes and shovels, the artillery was Brusi Senior with his flintlock pistol, and Hamish's predilection for books had made him the corps of surveyors.

Other than the hired guard, there were six potential fighting men in the band: Toby, Father Guillem, Rafael, Miguel, Josep, and Hamish. Toby inflicted quarterstaff lessons on all of them whenever an opportunity presented itself. Young Josep was willing enough, but his weapons of choice would always remain the quill and ledger. Father Guillem—unlike many Galilean clerics—conceded that a man had the right of self-defense; he was surprisingly good—not quick, but powerful and devious. Rafael and Miguel were straightforward sloggers and deadly, because they saw every practice session as an opportunity to kill the big foreigner. When failure discouraged them, he let them inflict a few bruises on him to spur them to greater efforts. Of

course Hamish was better than any of them except
Toby himself, and they both had swords to use if the
game need be played for serious stakes.

He insisted the women carry weapons. Eulalia
settled for a sickle, and Gracia a knife, although he
could not imagine her ever using it. Senora Collel
accepted a stout cudgel and promised to crack the
skull of anyone who tried to steal her mount, but she
and whoever she allowed to ride the other horse—
Gracia or Eulalia by turns—were perched so high
that they were horribly vulnerable to snipers or low
branches. Salvador Brusi agreed to carry his flintlock pistol in his belt instead of his saddle bag. The
hob's reaction to gunfire was usually tumultuous.

The new order mixed up the groups to some
extent and promoted a little more friendliness.
Senora Collel and Eulalia were seen talking with
the wives of Miguel and Rafael, both of whom were
named Elinor. Brother Bernat rarely sought out conversation but would respond to anyone who
addressed him, and even a ferocious argument on
the ethics of trade between Salvador Brusi and
Father Guillem could be regarded as an improvement. The don remained aloof, locked away in his
own grandiose world.

Other, less conspicuous, relationships had developed also. Hamish became much given to quoting
Catalan poetry and noticeably goggle-eyed in the
presence of Eulalia, but his eyes goggled so easily
that Toby thought nothing of it until the second
morning, when he was striding along the line and
Senora Collel snapped at him.

"Monsieur Longdirk!" She glared down from the
giddy height of her horse-borne throne.

He knew to expect trouble when she spoke French. "Madame?"

"Your companion Jaume is debauching my servant!"

"He is?" Toby shot a glance back at Eulalia, whose turn it was to ride on the other *silla*. She tossed her head disdainfully at him, but there was certainly a hint of triumph there also. Perhaps she understood more French than her mistress suspected. It was quite similar to Catalan.

"You are not much of a sentry if you did not see them sharing a blanket in the night!" the senora sneered.

"A sentry's job is not to spy on his friends, madame. Besides, I am quite certain my young friend has never progressed beyond holding hands in the past, so who is debauching whom? Can you say the same of her?"

And bully for Hamish! Toby would not grudge him his good fortune.

"He is taking advantage of her. The girl is simple."

"I really find that hard to credit, madame."

"Then what of Madame Gomez?"

Toby's heart skipped a beat. The senora must have seen his reaction, for she curled her hairy lip at him. "You did not know about her either?"

"I am sure that you slander the lady, madame. Besides, her tragic experiences have left her in a highly disturbed emotional state, and if you are implying that I would exploit—"

"Not you. The don."

That snotty aristocratic pervert! How dare he! "I cannot believe that they are more than friends! How

can you doubt her virtue or his honor?" But Toby
had wondered what the two of them found to talk
about—the prospect made his mind reel. Imaginary
armies or imaginary ghosts?

"They, too, share a blanket," Senora Collel
announced triumphantly. Her pleasure came from
seeing Toby's anger, not from outraged morality.
"Gentry like him think casual seduction is a game,
yes? That they have the right to defile any woman
they fancy?"

"Madame Gomez is a grown woman and I am not
an abbess. Nor, if I may say so, are you, madame!"
Feeling his face burning under her scorn, he length-
ened his stride and stalked away.

Poor, foolish Gracia! All she needed was affection
to support her in her bereavement, and she was not
likely to find it in the fantasy world of Don Ramon.
If Toby himself developed ambitions toward her, he
could do nothing about them. So why this furious
urge to punch a certain arrogant stuck-up nose until
it sprayed blue blood all over its ridiculous mustache?

Yes, the company was coming together, if slowly,
and on that fourth morning he had some reason for
optimism as he strode along the column. He also had
serious worries, because the last of his food had vanished the previous evening. Father Guillem admitted
that the clerics were down to their last crumbs. The
devastation of the Valencian countryside had been
rumored in Toledo, but none of the pilgrims had
comprehended the scale of it. There were no inhabitants to offer charity, no markets in which to shop,

no crops to pillage. At noon Toby would have to propose that the haves start sharing with the have-nots, but he was hard put to see the four peasants doing that, while Salvador Brusi would expect to be recompensed liberally for every lentil they wrung out of him.

The don paraded in front with his squire, followed by Josep and Father Guillem, Pepita and Brother Bernat and Gracia, then old man Brusi and his horses, Senora Collel and Eulalia riding, and the two Elinors and Thunderbolt. Hamish, Rafael, and Miguel brought up the rear. Toby mostly patrolled back and forth, exhorting, encouraging, and keeping watch for stragglers—usually Pepita, who kept running off to search for berries or butterflies. Although he approved in general of the don's disposition of forces, he always tended to loiter near the center of the group, uneasy about that vulnerable midriff.

The sun still scorched as if it were summer. The country was a melange of overgrown pasture, weed-covered fields, burned hamlets, and groves of mutilated trees, a landscape broken up by walls and hedges and imperceptible ridges, a paradise for ambushers. It seemed deserted, but that was illusion. A sharp eye could gather evidence that people had used the road recently, and at sundown thin columns of smoke wrote warnings in the sky. Distant dogs barked in the night. Whoever the inhabitants might be, they were likely to be lawless and desperate. The calm was deceptive.

Around mid-morning, catching up with Brusi, Toby said, "Senor? Have you any idea of where we are? How many days to go?"

"No." The old man was hunched in the saddle like a bundle of sticks. "We still have not crossed the Ebro. It is utterly shameful to destroy olive trees like that. It takes many, many years to grow an olive tree. The destruction of wealth is mindless criminality."

"It is more shameful to destroy people, surely."

"People can run away, olive trees cannot. How will the cities prosper when the countryside has been blighted? The Fiend has destroyed what he has won. I do not see how he hopes to drive the Tartars out of Europe when he is worse than they ever were. He must be crazy."

"His purpose is not to liberate Europe. It is to inflict as much pain and suffering as possible." Toby knew he would not be believed, but the rich man's indifference to the plight of the poor enraged him. "He enjoys tormenting his own people as much as the enemy. I doubt he would accept the Khan's surrender were it offered. He is a demon incarnate—literally. I have that on very good authority."

The prune face wrinkled up in scorn. "Good authority? You? Some drunk in a tavern, I do not doubt. And you are privy to Nevil's secret strategy? I did not realize I was in the company of an international statesman. You are a worthy flunky for the don."

Toby shrugged and scanned the trees that had provoked the discussion. "It is not easy to kill an olive, senor. They will not burn. It is hard to uproot them. Most of these will recover sooner than the people will, for it takes twenty years to make a citizen. And the ash trees have not suffered."

He pointed to the coppice on the other side of the

trail, a forest of massive, shoulder-high stumps, each of which bore a crown of high vertical shoots. Coppices provided tool handles and staves for many purposes, and the rebels had been able to inflict no more damage than a normal harvesting would.

Brusi looked where he gestured, and thus both of them were facing the trap when it was sprung. Weedy undergrowth had concealed the shallow stream bed that flanked the track and also concealed the dozen or so men hiding in it. They had planned their ambush well, letting the armed vanguard go past before they leaped up, yelling to panic the horses. They charged, brandishing cudgels and a few swords, screaming as loud as they could.

The horses did panic, naturally. Brusi's roan reared, toppling him back into the confusion of the pack animals he led. By that time Toby had already dropped his bundle and dived under the flailing hooves. He cut his sword free from its rope baldric and thrust the point into an assailant even before he himself was fully upright. He tugged it from the falling body and somehow managed to dodge a whirling club wielded by a skinny youth who reeled off-balance before him, staring eyes and open mouth in a stark white face, both hands struggling to swing the cudgel up for a second blow. Toby stabbed at his neck and connected again—*blood!*— only vaguely aware of the screaming women and horses behind him, the crash of bodies and animals meeting branches. He parried a slash and riposted. A man with white hair . . . *blood!*

The odds were impossible, because he was facing the whole assault singlehanded. His supporters at either end of the line needed time to arrive, and their progress was blocked by the melee of fallen horses and baggage. He lashed out with a foot, parried a sword, thrust his blade into a leg, and reconciled himself to dying at any second.

Then help arrived on Atropos. Ancient the warhorse might be, but he remembered his days of glory and for a few seconds made the ground tremble beneath mighty hooves. With a piercing war cry of, "King Pedro and Castile!" Don Ramon thundered down the line like a fusillade of cannon. His lance impaled a man and nailed him to another before it broke. Atropos bowled over two more and then went by, riderless. His shield still slung on his back, the ever-agile don hit the ground with his feet and a foe with his broadsword, cleaving helmet and head both. Oh, magnificent!

As the enemy faltered before this nemesis, Toby claimed another victim. The don cut yet another in half with a mighty two-handed stroke. Hamish, Rafael, and Miguel arrived from the rear, Josep and Father Guillem from the van, but by then the fight was finished and the survivors were crashing away through the coppice. The road was a litter of baggage and bodies—some dead, some wounded, not all strangers—and one injured horse. Eulalia sat in the weeds screaming hysterically. The rest of the horses had vanished into the olive grove, leaving a trail of sacks and garments. Toby bounded across the track to where Brusi's roan had entangled its reins on a branch and caught it before it broke free. He squirmed onto the saddle and prepared to go after the runaways. His last glimpse of the battlefield was of Hamish lifting Eulalia bodily to her feet and kissing her. Her screams choked off into silence.

Full gallop through an olive grove was an exciting exercise, because he had not yet managed to find the stirrups. Fortunately the rows of trees had been set wide apart so that the ground between them could be planted in grain, but branches still slashed along his back. Lying prone, he clung grimly to his mount's neck, concentrating on not dropping his sword. It was highly probable that the enemy would have posted men to catch the fleeing horses.

In moments he was through the grove and into open pasture, where the missing animals were bucking and milling, turning away from a line of people. He sat up, slid his feet into the stirrups, and put the roan into a charge at the foe. They had not expected this attack, but he saw with dismay that they were women. One of them was already wrestling with a horse, clinging to the reins and being lifted off her feet by its struggles. Howling the don's war cry— for he had none of his own—he headed straight for her, waving his sword, wondering if he could ever bring himself to cut a woman down in cold blood. She saw him coming and lost her grip on the horse. It ran free, she fell headlong, and Toby could ignore her. The others had already taken to their heels.

He rounded up the little herd, being aided by a timely whinny from the don's warhorse, which drew them in the right direction. Doña Francisca appeared on her pony and waved cheerfully. Between them, the two riders drove the stock back to the trail.

The emergency was over. A victory, he supposed. His greatest relief was that the hob had stayed out of it.

•   •   •

He had not been away for long, and the scene on the road had changed very little. The ground was still littered with baggage, and someone had put Senora Collel's packhorse out of its misery, but it was the litter of human corpses that appalled him. Only then did he understand how he had come to be so splattered with blood, his right arm especially, soaked to the elbow. His eyes shied away from counting the bodies and fixed instead on the circle of pilgrims. They were kneeling before Father Guillem as he declaimed words of comfort. Brother Bernat stood in the background with his head bowed.

Toby slid from his saddle and hitched the roan to a tree. His legs were curiously shaky. He stalked over to the group, arriving as the brief ceremony ended and the mourners rose to their feet. He stared in disbelief at the body, was conscious of everybody's eyes turning to look at him and odd murmurs that he could not take time to understand.

"How did that happen?" he said stupidly. He could not recall any of the enemy getting past him.

It was Josep who answered, a chalk-faced Josep with water on his cheeks and eyes like festering wounds. "He was thrown, senor."

Broken neck? Heart failure? The Council of One Hundred was down to ninety-nine. The rich man was a dead man, and all his wealth could not save him from that.

"I . . . Oh friend, I'm sorry!" Toby transferred his sword to his left hand and had started to offer his right before he realized that it was bright red and still sticky. He pulled it back hastily.

Josep nodded, smiled faintly in acknowledgment, and walked away as if he wanted to be alone.

"Captain!"

Toby jumped and turned to the don. He faced a man almost as blood-soaked as himself, but one who looked inches taller and years younger than usual. The blue eyes blazed with triumph and boyish glee. "A redoubtable passage of arms, Captain! Give me your sword!"

"What?" How many bodies? Eight? Nine? Spirits, but most of them were only boys, younger than himself. Three were silver-haired oldsters. The starving, desperate survivors of some community bereft of its fighting men.

A hand tried to take his sword, and Toby swung it away defensively. "What?"

"Kneel!" proclaimed the don.

"What?"

"Give me your sword and kneel! Here on this glorious field, I shall gird thee with the belt of knighthood, Sir Tobias! Such feats of valor and prowess as we have rarely seen shall not—"

Toby's temper exploded like a peal of thunder. "Don't play your stupid games with me!" he roared. "This wasn't valor and prowess, it was bloody murder! Look at them! They weren't soldiers. Half of them were only kids. Brusi's dead, Josep's father. You promised. You took his—"

He stopped himself just in time, seeing the instant change in the *caballero's* face, the coiling surge of madness. No, the don had not taken Brusi's money. His mother had, and he refused to know that. In any case, the old man's death had been an accident, so Toby was being unfair. But gleeful boy had become furious man already, reaching for his sword, and that would be a fight Toby could never win.

He bowed curtly. "Your pardon, senor. When we arrive at our destination there will be time enough for honors. Now we must . . . With respect, senor, the baggage must be collected and redistributed on the horses. The enemy may return. If the *caballero* will excuse me, I shall make arrangements for the burial and reorganize the train." He turned his back on the don's quivering rage and looked around the pale faces. "Anyone injured?"

"Senora de Gomez," Hamish said. What was wrong with Hamish? He'd seen violent death before, so why did he look like that? "She was badly shaken by her fall, but . . . but Brother Bernat healed her, Toby." His face was saying more than his words were. "Nobody else. Just bruises and scratches."

"Healed her? Oh. Well, that's good." Something else to think about. Meanwhile they must bury the old man, gather up their litter, and move on, although he doubted there would be any reprisals after such a massacre. The survivors would come and bury their own dead. "Manuel, Rafael—either of you know anything about butchering?"

They both shook their heads, but that meant little, and he could do it himself if necessary. The food problem had been solved for the time being. They could eat horse today and tomorrow and every day until it began to rot.

2

"We owe our lives to you, Senor Toby," Josep said solemnly. He was walking, leading his two pack-horses, because he had given his father's roan to

Senora Collel to replace hers. "Without you we should have lost all the livestock, and then none of us could ever reach Barcelona."

"That is nonsense!" Toby had explained this four times already to other people and apparently had to explain it again. "It was the don who saved the day, not me. Without him, I was about to die. Without me, he would still have beaten them. He is the finest fighting man I have ever seen—he put a destrier at full gallop through a riot like a seamstress sliding a needle through cloth."

"You killed more men than he did."

"I had more time."

"He had a horse and a lance."

"Honestly, that made very little difference. He is a fighter, I'm just a big lad. Josep, this I swear—if you matched up the two us with the same arms, he would skin me as nimbly as he skinned the horse!"

The don had attended to the butchery, asserting that the dead animal was the handsomest ten-point stag he had seen in years and explaining all the time to his helpers, the two Elinors, the joys of hunting boar. Fortunately, they would have understood little of his Castilian. Mad or not, he was as skilled with a skinning knife as he was with a broadsword.

Josep smiled disbelievingly. "I do not know on what terms Don Ramon hired you that morning we met, senor, but when I pay him off at my door, I shall give you the same amount I give him, and gladly. My father's death is not to be laid to the fault of either of you."

Toby swallowed a twinge of pride he could not afford and thanked him for this unwarranted generosity. He and Hamish might not starve in the gutters of Barcelona after all, or not immediately.

Josep shot another thin smile at him. "You think the spendthrift boy will soon fritter away the Brusi fortune. You may be right, Tobias, but I am convinced that the most valuable aid a man of business can have—apart from a reputation for honesty, of course—is a team of trustworthy employees. If you will be seeking work in Barcelona, I shall outbid anyone else for your services."

"The senor requires a strong porter?"

The thin boyish face flushed scarlet. "That was not what I meant! Many of our workers have fled or were slain in the fighting and must be replaced. I will make you foreman in our warehouse without a moment's hesitation. Do you wish to discuss wages now?"

"No, senor, but I am even more grateful than I realized."

Brusi's offer was certainly better than his father's had been, and much more appealing than Senora Collel's lascivious hints. The oak tree had fallen. Josep had escaped from his father's shadow and was starting to flourish already.

He was not alone—unexpected death had given the whole band new life, a sense of comradeship. The men had shared in the digging, laying Salvador Brusi to rest by the roadside in an unmarked grave. Toby had put Hamish in charge of reloading the pack animals, and when he called a halt and announced that everything remaining must be left where it was or manhandled, there had not been one word of protest, even from Manuel and Rafael. Now everyone was chattering excitedly to everyone else. Long might it last!

They did not go far that day, for they came upon a deserted *casa*. The unroofed walls still enclosed a courtyard that would hold both people and horses and could be defended if necessary. Toby proposed that they spend the night there, although the hour was not far past noon. The don frowned and then conceded that some of the auxiliaries might need time to reorganize.

They built a fire and feasted together on horse-flesh, tough, stringy, and delicious. Toby could not recall the last time he had eaten roast meat and tried not to recall the last time he had smelled it, in the orange grove. The ensuing luxury of just relaxing for a few hours was almost as welcome as the feast—his suggestion of a break from travel had been a good one for both people and horses. He had pickets to think about, of course, and he must insist on some more lessons in using quarter staffs . . . later.

In the lazy heat of late afternoon, he had two curious conversations.

The first was when he was summoned by the don, who was sitting on a sawhorse stripped to his shirt so his squire could shave him.

"Captain," he announced grandly, "I have decided to appoint you *campeador* of Nuñez y Pardo. Henceforth you will receive a one-twentieth share of the rewards. You may divide this with your own men or not, as you please."

Toby thought he might feel very honored if he knew what a *campeador* was. He exchanged astonished glances with Doña Francisca, expressed humble thanks, and said, "What rewards, senor?"

Mild surprise. "Plunder from the cities we sack, of course. And ransoms, when we grant quarter to persons of quality."

"The *hidalgo* is most generous."

"Not at all. You and your minions fought with distinction today." Don Roman shrugged, which almost caused his mother to cut his throat. "The musketry was perhaps not up to my usual standards. See that it improves."

"Yes, senor." Was that madness in the blue eyes or mockery?

"I have also," the don continued, "been considering our future campaigns when the Barcelona operation is completed. You are an Englishman?"

"According to the English I am, senor. In Scotland we disagree on the matter."

"But you do speak English?"

What Toby called English the English called Scots, but the don was not waiting to know that. "Little better than I speak Castilian, senor."

"That bad? But you are not a supporter of King Nevil?" The copper eyebrows rose inquiringly. Behind his shoulder, Doña Francisca was gaping. Whatever her son had in mind had not been shared with her.

"No, senor. I despise him and detest him."

"Ah." That was apparently welcome news. "But Barcelona is his."

"I am only a landless freeman, senor. I cannot depose the master of half of Europe. Affairs of kings are not mine to question." The Earl of Argyll would not concede that he was even a freeman.

"Hmm. Nevil's viceroy rules in Barcelona, the notorious Oreste." The don stared away at the bright courtyard and the blue sky overhead. "My own position is problematic. My estates lie in that part of La Mancha that King Pedro was forced to cede to the rebels. It would seem that my fealty now lies with King Nevil."

Toby exchanged more puzzled glances with Doña Francisca.

"I cannot presume to advise the honored *hidalgo*."

The young man chuckled as if that were a ludicrous suggestion. He continued to study the skies, perhaps watching the lonely kites that had been passing overhead ever since the massacre. "Of course not. But tell me, *Campeador* . . . You are a brave man, even if you are of insignificant birth. Have you ever considered the purpose of life? I realize that you cannot have the sense of honor and duty that your betters have, but you appear to have some sort of perception of . . . well, manhood."

"You flatter me, senor." *You also confuse the blazes out of me.*

"And you must have a rudimentary concept of ethical principles."

"I hope I do."

"Have you ever contemplated the possibility of striking a great blow for righteousness?" The mad gaze turned back to Toby. "Of making some demonstration of your, um, manhood, that would make your life remembered, even at the cost of making it short? Of offering yourself as a sacrifice to a noble cause, in other words?"

Could even Don Ramon imagine that he stood a chance against a paramount hexer like Oreste, with his demonic bodyguards? A bloody head rolled across the boards of the scaffold. . . .

Toby took a moment to rein in stampeding thoughts. "If the cause were great enough and the chances of success reasonable, then any man should see it as his duty, senor."

The don sneered and turned his head away, almost losing an ear to the razor. "Reasonable? What sort of quibble is that? *Reasonable?* Any slight possibility that it not be impossible should suffice. I see I misjudged you, *Campeador*. You may go."

Toby was very glad to go. The don was not merely mad, he was dangerously mad.

And so, perhaps, were certain others in the party. Hamish had been babbling strange nonsense about Gracia's injuries and recovery. Gracia herself had apparently accepted Don Ramon's view of the world, because she now spoke breathlessly of his vast estates and the high honor in which his friend the king held him—which confirmed that the noble lord's honor was distressingly malleable where women were concerned.

And then there was Brother Bernat.

It was time for a serious talk with Brother Bernat.

Toby found him in a shaded corner behind a shed, sitting on the ground with his back turned, so that only his pink scalp with its downy fringe was visible—that and the gray cowl covering his narrow shoulders. In front of him lay a block of building stone like a low table, with Pepita on the far side of it, facing Toby but too engrossed to notice him. They were both very intent on something. It could only be some sort of child's game, yet their concentration was so intense that he hesitated to interrupt.

Then he saw that the girl rested her hand on the stone with a crumb held in her tiny fingers. The minute brown speck creeping toward it over the gray stone was a mouse. Or perhaps it was a vole or a dormouse or something exclusively Spanish. It looked like a mouse, but it was displaying unmouselike courage, inching forward, nose and tail twitching. Toby, too, held his breath.

The mouse came to a halt and stretched out like dough until its nose could inspect the crumb. Satisfied, it took a few more steps, and gently lifted the crumb from the child's fingertips, then sat up on its haunches to nibble at it. With agonizing slowness, she slid a finger around and stroked its back. Toby stared in disbelief.

The spell broke. Mouse and crumb flashed away and were gone. An immense grin split Pepita's little elfin face from side to side. Her tiny fists clenched with glee and drummed on the stone. It had certainly been a remarkable trick.

"I did it!" she whispered excitedly.

"You did indeed," answered the old friar. "Very well done!"

She looked up and gasped in dismay. Fear! Guilt!

"It is only Captain Tobias," Brother Bernat said without turning. "He can be trusted."

Toby stepped forward and sat down at the end of the big stone. He stared into those strangely clear eyes, dark agates in a face of ancient marble. "And how did you know it was me, Brother?"

"I knew you would be at the corner, and I could see the angle of her head. No one else is so tall."

An unlikely explanation. There was much secret

amusement in the old man's smile, but Pepita was staring anxiously at the big stranger.

He said, "I should like to have a word with you if I may."

"Have as many as you wish, my son. Don't mind Pepita. She doesn't gossip either." His voice was as soft as gossamer.

"Some do." Toby cursed himself as soon as he said the words.

A twinge of sorrow flashed over Bernat's face. "Whatever the senora said about me, she does not understand the truth of the situation." He had been put on the defensive, though, and that was disturbing.

But Toby was feeling defensive, also. To hint at gossip was even worse than repeating it.

"I put no stock in her babbling. What brings me is something that Hamish . . . Jaume, that is . . . Jaume insists that Senora de Gomez was seriously hurt when she fell from her horse today. This is not surprising, considering how high those seats are. He says she was unconscious, her face was flushed, her eyes were open and the pupils dilated. Her breath was harsh and irregular, her pulse very slow. He says these symptoms exactly match some that he once read about, so he knew she was very likely to die and he could nothing for her. He went to assist Senora Collel and found that she had escaped with a twisted ankle. The next time he looked at Senora de Gomez, you were helping to her feet. She was a little shaken but not badly hurt."

Brother Bernat smiled again. How could anyone so old endure these long marches, these hardships, the alarms of today's battle, all without at least looking tired? But he never looked tired. He never ran around like a puppy either, but he was no fresher in the mornings than he was at night. And he rarely bore any expression other than a tolerant smile. He made Toby feel like an obstreperous, bad-mannered child.

"Sergeant Jaume must have made an error, you mean? This disturbs you. Is he prone to errors?" The smile widened, displaying very white teeth— apparently a complete set, too.

"He is not prone to errors. I am disinclined to believe he made one today."

The friar looked at Pepita, who returned his smile hesitantly. When he spoke, though, he was plainly addressing Toby.

"And you decided it was time for a serious chat with the old man?"

Suppressing a bad-mannered, obstreperous desire to growl, Toby said, "Yes I did, Brother."

Brother Bernat turned to him again, but this time he was not smiling. "I am sorry if my manners annoy you, my son. I have had them so long that they are hard to change, but I know that I tend to counter questions with other questions. I have wandered the world a long time, and it is a dangerous place. One learns discretion or one stops wandering."

"I have no wish to pry!" That was a lie.

"You have a right to pry, because the security of all of us rests on your judgment. I think I can help you with your problem, Tobias."

Toby flinched. "*My* problem?"

The smile crept back, but there was no mirth in it. An attempt at reassurance, perhaps. Sympathy, possibly. "I have no problem except my manners. But you do. You ask questions, I answer with other questions, and you don't answer at all, which is your right. But it gets us nowhere. I think I can help you, but only if you will tell me the whole story. Everything." There was Toledo steel inside that cobwebby exterior.

"I—"

"You are not ready to do that, so it will have to wait. But don't wait too long, please. The sands will run out quickly once they start to go." He lifted a pale and slender hand to indicate he had not finished. His eyes bore their disturbing stare again, as if he were looking inside Toby's head. "Just answer me one thing, my son. How long has it been?"

"I don't have the faintest idea what . . . Three years, Brother."

The friar winced as if that news was disastrous. "So you were what, sixteen? Seventeen?"

"Eighteen." They were talking about the hob, although Toby had no idea how that had come into the conversation. It was the last thing he ever discussed.

Brother Bernat shook his head in dismay. "You have done very well to last as long as you have, then. Don't wait much longer, Tobias, please!"

He was crazier than the don, that was all.

"Wait for what? What do you mean about doing well to last?"

The clear dark eyes told him his denials did not convince.

"You are going to go insane very shortly. I think you know that, and know what will follow. It is amazing that you have lasted so long. I am surprised it did not happen today in the turmoil of the fight. You must have nerves like granite, my son."

Toby made half a move to rise and then hesitated. "I don't know what you mean, Brother."

"Fear, Tobias. Or rage. Hatred." The dark eyes widened. "Any sort of strong passion. You must avoid them. Great remorse, also."

Mezquiriz? He could *not* know about Mezquiriz! He *must* not know about Mezquiriz!

Toby jumped up and strode away, and if that was not rage he was feeling, it was fear.

3

The room was dim, with walls and floor of dark stone and a heavy-beamed ceiling high enough to be lost in shadow. Its stifling heat came from a fireplace at one end, which provided almost as much light as the two small, high-set windows at the other. Three men garbed in the simple brown hose and doublets of common workers waited patiently at the cool end. They were all burly and muscular, but nothing else could be known about them, for their heads were concealed in black bags. Once in a while one of them would move so that a glitter of eyes showed behind the eye holes.

A table along one side bore two tall candlesticks and a green crucifix inlaid with colored jewels, too large to be anything but colored glass. Behind the table sat three elderly men in the white supplicars and black robes of Dominicans, the Black Friars, all with their hoods back to display their tonsures, all sweating profusely. The one on the left fumbled endlessly through a pile of papers and parchments. The one on the right kept scribbling in a large book, recording the proceedings with a quill pen that he dipped from time to time in a silver inkwell. Two shaven-head novices stood at the door opposite.

In the exact center of the room hung a rope.

On one side of it stood a soldier holding a musket erect beside him, and he must be the most uncomfortable person present, because he wore a thickly-padded blue doublet, black breeches, and a polished wide-brimmed helmet, and was burdened with sword, ramrod, slow match, powder horn, shot bag, and the other paraphernalia of the professional military. He looked utterly miserable, as if this was one of the worst days of his life, and perhaps more than the heat was responsible for that.

On the other side of the rope stood Toby, stinking of his jail cell. He was trying to hold up his head with a show of courage he did not feel while he glared stubbornly at the friar in the center, the one in charge, the inquisitor.

His name was Father Vespianaso. He was a frail-seeming, elderly man, with a thin white tonsure, thick black eyebrows, and a close-trimmed, piebald beard. His eyes were red-rimmed and droopy, full of such sadness that they must have viewed all the sorrows of the world. A sagging blister of flesh under each of them was the only padding on his face, which otherwise was only a skull wrapped in skin so dry that it seemed ready to crack and flake away completely.

He looked up from the document he had been reading for the last ten minutes.

"Is the accused now ready to disavow his demon and reveal its name so that it may be cast out?"

Toby understood most of the proceedings and

knew that particular question by heart, but the
Inquisition had its rules, and the presence of an
interpreter during the examination of foreigners was
one of them. He waited until the soldier translated.

"The inquisitor asks if the accused is now ready to
disavow his demon and reveal its name so that it
may be cast out." His English was not much easier
to understand than the original Castilian. His vivid
blue eyes stared fixedly ahead, as if trying to see
through the prisoner's chest.

"Tell him I do not have a demon."

The friar had heard that familiar protest many
times during the last four days. "Tobias, Tobias!"
He shook his head sadly. "If the accused will not
confess, he must be put to the Question."

Toby understood that only too well. Examination
of a suspect went through clearly defined stages.
They had begun three days ago in a cheerful, airy
room upstairs. The questioning had grown steadily
harsher and more menacing until, at the end of yesterday's session, they had brought him down to this
cellar and shown him the whips and branding irons,
the pulleys in the ceiling, the funnels for water torture, and the ladder-like grid to which the victim
would be tied during their use. Today they had
brought him straight to this chamber, where the fire
was already lit and the three tormentors waited.
That had been at least two hours ago. So far the tormentors had done nothing more than stoke the fire.

What was the question this time? Didn't matter.

"I do not have a demon. If I did, how could I possibly cast it out? Does he think I would voluntarily
harbor a demon? Does he think such a demon
would tell me its name? I do not have a demon!"

No demon, no name. Of course the hob would count as a demon in the inquisitors' eyes—at times Toby himself found the distinction fuzzy.

There was no way out of this trap. They had explained it to him many times, being patient, aggressive, understanding, and menacing by turns. A demon could only be controlled by its name, so the accused must reveal it. If he refused, he must be forced to comply. If he still would not talk or did not know the demon's name, then the demon must be driven out of him by making it suffer. That, unfortunately, meant making the accused suffer, but suffering was better than possession, wasn't it? Supposedly an incarnate would keep its husk alive, or at least operational, indefinitely. The only way a man could prove that he was not possessed was to die.

Another question.

Same answer: "I do not have a demon!" He must keep to the same answer. How much did they know? How sure were they? Demons could detect the hob in him, so was the inquisitor himself possessed? A demon looking for employment would find nothing more congenial to its tastes than being an officer of the Inquisition. But it didn't matter whether they were guessing or certain or had just chosen him at random. Once they started asking questions, they could never admit they had picked on the wrong man. There was no escape.

The inquisitor held out a paper.

Carrying his musket, the soldier marched three paces to the table to take it, then brought it back and held it up in front of the prisoner. "The inquisitor asks if the accused recognizes this notice."

The accused did, and his sweat turned cold in the
heat. The paper was a smudged and tattered poster
dated October 1519. The woodcut it bore was a
crude drawing of himself as a youth, but a good
likeness considering that it had been done from
memory. The inscription in both Scots and Gaelic
outlined the Parliamentary act of attainder that
declared him to be possessed by a demon. It also
proclaimed a reward of five thousand marks for
anyone who brought in his corpse with a blade
through the heart.

How had they gotten ahold of that? They had not
produced that poster before, or even mentioned it.
He found his voice, although it sounded strange to
him.

"It lies."

The inquisitor did not wait for the translation.
"But the accused does recognize it?"

The soldier translated the question and Toby's
reply: "I have never seen it before. I was told about
it. It lies. Whoever wrote it was lying."

Other people had been lying also, members of the
pilgrim band, but he had not been told which. They
had all been interrogated at the roadblock—questioned separately, most of them several times.
Whatever slanders might have been spoken could
be only their word against his, but that poster was
damning. Who could argue against an act of
Parliament? The one person who might have passed
that paper to the Inquisition was Baron Oreste,
because he had been responsible for it in the first
place.

The interpreter returned the paper to the table and
came back to thump the butt of his musket on the

floor beside the prisoner and deliver the next translation.

"The inquisitor says that the evidence is strong enough to force a confession. This is the accused's last chance to repent. If the accused does not name his demon, he will now be put to the Question."

The soldier still did not meet Toby's eyes. He might be a decent enough fellow when off-duty, perhaps popular with his mates, a good singer, or skilled with women, homesick for England, planning to buy a freehold with his loot, if he ever laid his hands on any, if the war would ever end . . . any or all of those things. But now he was very much on duty and would do what he was told to do whether he liked it or not. He had no choice; this was not his fault. If he disobeyed an order he would be hanged or whipped to shreds, or his fate might be worse than either of those, because to argue with the Inquisition was itself evidence of possession.

Sweat streamed down Toby's face and ribs although there was a huge icy rock in his belly. "Tell him I do not have a demon. He is making a terrible mistake. He is going to torture an innocent man."

Even as the soldier was translating the prisoner's answer into a Castilian little better than Toby's own, the inquisitor beckoned to the three black-hooded tormentors who had been standing silently under the windows with brawny arms folded, waiting out the interminable preliminaries. The prospect of action at last must seem welcome to them, because they strode forward eagerly, crowding in close around the accused. He struggled to relax, to enjoy these last few moments without pain, but he knew he had passed up one faint chance. He should have run to the far end and grabbed up a branding iron or something and tried to break out. He would not have succeeded, but perhaps a misjudged blow would have broken his neck. Now he was hemmed in, and it was too late.

"The accused will remove all his garments."

Was this it, or just a bluff? Toby glanced at the menacing black hoods closing in, and their sinister dark eye holes. Three to one. They were all smaller men than he, but they might well be faster. Resistance would only bring violence and increase his suffering, although he suspected he did not know what real suffering was yet—the inquisitor was about to teach him.

Unless it was only a bluff. The interrogation had advanced in slow stages, so they would probably just frighten him today and start the real hurting tomorrow. He shrugged and reached for the laces of his doublet.

When he had stripped, one of the novices took away his clothes. The tormentors roped his wrists behind him and clamped fetters on his ankles. The pulley overhead jangled. Calloused hands fumbled at his back, fastening the rope to his bonds.

It did not feel like a bluff. They were going to begin with the *strappado*. Oh, spirits!

How long would the hob make him endure? It had never cared how much he suffered—it had done nothing on the two occasions he had been whipped and had once let him be beaten to a pulp in a fight so vicious that his opponent had died under his fists. It had not interfered at all, except possibly to keep him alive, and if it did start to intervene now, that would merely prove to the friars that they had been right all along.

"Tobias," the inquisitor sighed. He spoke again through the English soldier. "The accused is a strong man, but a heavy one. This will hurt the accused and may do him permanent damage. The brothers do not wish to make the accused suffer. They have his interests at heart, and they will persevere for however long it takes. The accused must tell them the name of his demon so they may cast it out and he will be a free man again."

The soldier's pink face was streaming sweat as he fumbled through to the end of that speech. He still did not look at the accused's eyes.

Toby bit back a savage desire to tell the venerable cleric to stuff his own head into a certain dark place—they would merely see abuse as confirmation of his possession. He blinked the sweat away and looked at the other two friars, who stared back sympathetically. But neither was going to help him. They mourned his plight. They thought that they knew the only way to save him from it. He was not a person any more, he was only *the accused*.

He tried to speak calmly, but the words came out as a shriek: "I do not have a demon!"

The inquisitor shook his head wearily and gestured. The tormentors pulled on the rope. The rope lifted Toby's wrists. He bent forward, but the pull continued. His arms rose inexorably, curling him over until his head was level with his waist, and then his shoulders could flex no more. He rose on his toes. The friar said a word, and the men stopped hauling. There Toby was held, gasping with the strain. He would not scream. He would not cry out.

He must not admit anything at all. Nothing but
denial.

The friar spoke again. "The inquisitor asks—"

He cut off the translation with a yell. "I do not
have a demon!"

He waited.

So did they.

They had all day, and tomorrow and next week
and forever. His toes were weakening. His toes were
about all he could see—his legs, his toes on the
flagstones, and little splashes in the dust as sweat
dripped from his hair. His toes were failing, setting
more and more of his weight on his twisted shoulders. Hot knives of pain dug in, twisting joints in
ways they were not supposed to move, prying liga-
ments awry.

Head down, he could not see the gestures, so it
was a surprise when the rope suddenly slackened.
Somehow he retained his balance on his bound feet
and let his arms down. The relief was so intense that
he gasped aloud and felt that he had failed his manhood by doing so. Panting hard, he straightened up
to face the inquisitor.

He croaked, "I do not have a demon!"

The friar smiled sadly and nodded to the two
novices at the door. They came forward and wiped
Toby's face with a white cloth, then held a pewter
cup to his lips. He drank eagerly of the tepid water.
It was refilled and he emptied it again.

The inquisitor said, "The accused has barely
tasted what will happen. He must reveal the name
of his demon or his sufferings will be a thousand
times worse than what he has just experienced."

Toby stared into those droopy, bleary eyes, so full

of sympathy and understanding. He spoke to them with all the sincerity he could muster and a mouth that was dry as salt again already. "Tell the venerable father that I know that. Tell him I am more terrified than I have ever been in my life. Tell him I will do anything he wants, anything at all, but I cannot reveal the name of a demon that does not exist."

The soldier translated. The brother with the quill scribbled busily, periodically dipping his pen in the inkwell with fast little strokes like a chicken pecking dirt. He turned a page, dipped again, wrote more.

The inquisitor nodded unhappily as if the answer had been exactly what he expected. He looked past the prisoner, to the waiting tormentors.

"Take me to a sanctuary!" Toby yelled. "The spirit will tell you that I don't have a demon!"

Maybe it wouldn't, but that was what an innocent man would say. It might not work in his case, but it would delay the torture. An hour's reprieve would be worth anything he could imagine, even ten minutes. He knew it would not work, of course. He had made the suggestion many times in the previous, more gentle interrogations. The Dominicans did not trust the spirits, or spirits would not cooperate with the Dominicans—whatever the reason, the request was always refused.

The inquisitor ignored the suggestion. The rope tightened again, bringing instant protests from Toby's shoulders. His arms rose, and so did the pain. Soon he was up on cramped, bleeding toes again. And higher still. His feet left the floor, leaving all his weight hung on his cruelly twisted arms. The strain bent his spine, crushed his shoulder blades together, wrenched wrists and elbows, but it was in his shoulders that the real agony blazed. He would *not* cry out. Oh, spirits, spirits! He had made no sound when he was chained to Sergeant Mulliez's whipping post, and he would make none now. He gasped for breath, but he would not cry out. Never!

He spun slowly, seeing the flagstones rotate below his toes. They pulled him higher, every heave and jolt a greater agony. He was going to lose control of his bladder soon. When they had raised him until his face was at head height—so they could watch his expression, perhaps—they tied the rope to a bracket, leaving him there.

How long, spirits, how long would they keep him up here?

Pain, pain, pain! This was much worse than any flogging. It was worse than his prizefight against Randal, much, much worse. How long had that lasted? An hour? Probably less, and yet it had seemed like a lifetime. Then he had at least been able to fight back, draw strength from anger, even cling to a faint hope of surviving and winning. Enduring the floggings had been only a matter of counting, knowing that each lash was one less to come. Here there was no hope at all. This would go on forever, hob versus friars. Their patience was inexhaustible and the hob immortal. The longer he survived, the more obvious his guilt.

He did not see the command given to release the knot. He fell to the stone, striking feet and toppling onto his face, uttering a startled yell. Oh, the relief! The agony was still intense, fire in his bones, but not as bad. Nothing could be that bad.

Really? They had barely started.

The young novices lifted him to his knees. Murmuring solicitously, they wiped the sweat and dirt from his face and dabbed blood from his bitten lip. They gave him water. He was shaking so hard he could barely drink, his teeth chattering on the cup.

"The inquisitor asks if the accused is ready to reveal—"

He had nothing to lose now. "He is a pig-faced, shit-eating son of a thousand fathers! All the rest of you are cowardly, dog-fornicating—"

A wooden bar was dragged between his teeth, ending his speech before he had even warmed up. The tormentors must have been standing behind him with the bit ready, so they had known exactly how he would react at this point in the proceedings, and that was a dismal reminder of how expert they were at their job. They stretched his mouth as wide as it would go and tied the rod in place with a knot behind his head. His arms began to rise again, bringing instant pain. He lurched to his feet, but the relief was momentary. Soon he was back where he had been, twirling around giddily, suffering more of the excruciating agony.

Silence.

Terrible, unendurable silence as the nine pairs of eyes watched him, waited for him to nod, to scream, to do anything. He just hung there, turning. *He would not scream!*

Silence. Pain.

Pain. Silence. It was very, very hard not to whimper. He drooled, because he could not swallow. How long must this go on?

Forever. It seemed like hours, days, weeks, but it could have been only ten or fifteen minutes.

"The inquisitor says that if the accused is ready to reveal the name of his demon, he should nod his head."

The accused ignored the invitation.

The friars rose to their feet, gathered up their papers, and marched solemnly out from behind the table, past the prisoner, over to the door. The novices followed them out, and the door shut with a heavy thud. Only the prisoner remained with the interpreter and the three tormentors. There was nothing more to do until he had been made to see reason.

One of the tormentors said something and the others laughed. He gave Toby a push, making him spin faster.

"This one is strong. He will give us many days' work."

"But he should be screaming by now," said another, who sounded young. "Let's beat him on his *cojones*." He pushed, sending Toby swinging.

"That's against the rules," said the third, shoving him back like a child on a swing.

"Father Vespianaso is not here to see."

"No, we save that for later, when he is jaded and can appreciate it."

They kept this up for a while, shoving him, spinning him, thumping him on the back to jar his shoulders. Little of their mockery reached through to Toby, locked away in his furnace of agony, but what he did hear turned some of his terror to anger and so gave him strength. Swine! Contemptible cowards!

"It is ridiculous that he is not screaming."

"This is true. Why should the friars enjoy their *tapas* in peace when we have to keep working?"

Two of them took hold of the rope and began pulling and letting go, bouncing him up and down. That was the worst yet, every jerk sending waves of agony through his shoulders. He tried to concentrate on counting the jolts: five, six, seven . . . but he soon lost track. Every breath came out as a groan. Despite everything he could do to keep still, his feet flailed in their fetters, jangling chain, tearing skin.

The bouncing stopped.

"Why does the man not scream?" the young one said. "He insults us."

"You are right," said the leader. "We will not wait for the friars. Foreigner! Tell him again."

The soldier said, "The accused may nod if he is ready to reveal the name of his demon-I-can't-do-nothing-mate."

That helped. It wasn't much, but somehow that tiny hint that someone appreciated his efforts did help a little. Toby shook his head to show the soldier that he understood. He could lie, of course, and he might get away with it once, because they would have to take the gag out for a moment to hear what he wanted to say, but to start lying would be a confession that they had broken him. The hob had no name.

Without untying the rope from the bracket, all three tormentors began hauling together, raising him higher. Round and round he turned, looking down now at the vacant table with its two candles and its crucifix, the three strong men straining to support his weight, their knuckles white on the rope, eyes shining through the eye holes of their hoods as they waited for the right moment.

Wait for it. *Wait for it!*

He was *not* going to cry out. He knew what was coming, but he would *not* cry out.

They were making him wait for it, another last chance to repent. He could nod his head and escape what was coming. He didn't.

Wait for it.

The tormentors let go. He dropped to the end of his tether. He heard things tearing in his shoulders and a universe of pain exploded through him.

He screamed.

No, he had not known what pain was. He screamed and screamed, swinging on dislocated shoulders, turning faster than before, barely able to suck in enough air around the gag to scream again. He soiled himself. Blood dribbled from his mouth. He continued to scream.

Why had he ever been born?

No! No! They were raising him again. How many times? As many times as it took to make him tell what he could not tell. As many times as it took to tear every ligament, break the joints, make his arms completely useless. He had been stupidly proud of his strength and now he would not be able to lift a crust to his lips. Then they would start on his hips, or his toes, or his fingers. Or bring out the hot irons.

They dropped him again.

He heard something break, but he could scream no louder.

The soldier had withdrawn to the window end of the room and was leaning his face against the wall, unwilling or unable to watch any more. The tormentors stood chatting among themselves, as men did when they worked together—discussing women, the price of wine, the bullfight. Whenever the prisoner's screams began to fade, they pulled him up again and dropped him, each time a little farther than before. *Agony!* More cracking and tearing. How could the pain be even greater when it had already been more than he could stand or have ever imagined?

And again.

And again.

He was stretched out on the stone floor, staring up at the black hoods with their evil eye holes. Unclear how that had happened . . . perhaps fainted? There was no false gentleness now. Two of the tormentors were leaning on his broken shoulders, pressing him down on his bound arms while the third emptied a jar of water on his face. Some of it went in around the gag, making him choke and writhe. The soldier knelt at his side. The friars were back, peering down sadly at the wreckage.

"The inquisitor says that if the accused is ready to reveal the name of his demon, he should nod his head."

They would have to take the gag out, if only for a moment. He would be able to swallow at least once. They might even leave it out if he behaved, although he should not count on that mercy. But then they would all know that he was broken. After that he would be only warm meat. That tiny defiance was all that was left of Toby Longdirk, of him, of the person who was more than a lump of meat. He shook his head.

"The inquisitor warns the accused that the pain will be increased."

One tormentor held the prisoner immobile by pressing on the ends of the bar in his mouth while the others lashed stone weights to his ankles.

4

His arms were free. The gag was gone. "Senor, what is the matter?" Wasn't that Eulalia's voice? Grass? Horrified faces against the sky: Josep, Miguel . . . Hamish shouting, "Demons, Toby, what's wrong?"

"What is going on? Stand aside!" ordered Don Ramon.

Everyone scrambled out of the way, leaving only Hamish kneeling there, holding the leather water bottle to Toby's mouth.

He choked and spluttered and spat out blood. He was flat on his back on the grass and could not even think of rising—to do so would mean moving his arms. His throat was so raw with screaming that he could not speak, but he could laugh, a pathetic little animal whimper of laughter to celebrate his escape from the Inquisition. It might not work this way when the events really happened, sometime in the future, but it was real now. What he had just endured had been only another vision. He was safely back with the pilgrims and could worry about the Dominicans another day. Life was worth living again.

"We do not know what happened, senor!" That was Josep, his voice shrill with worry. "We were rounding up the horses and the captain cried out and fell. We ran over at once. He seems to be injured."

Now there was a massive understatement! Would

he ever lift his arms again? Both shoulders burned and throbbed savagely, but the left was worse than the right, not just more painful but distorted, as if the bone was out of its socket. What sort of protector was he now? Two days since Salvador Brusi died, two days of being a hero to them, and now he was a useless cripple. How long would the pain be this bad?

"I was only a few paces from him, senor." That was Gracia. "He just dropped."

"Well, sit him up."

Toby made croaking noises and shook his head violently.

"It may well be that a demon has cursed him!" the don announced, and his audience moaned fearfully. "Bring Father Guillem."

Hamish laid a hand on the patient's forehead. "I believe it may be a sudden fever, senor. Perhaps Brother Bernat could be summoned? He is skilled at healing."

The chorus backed away, for memories of the plague were still strong in Aragon.

"We shall send both," said the don. "Collect the horses. Strike camp. We cannot wait here all day. Load the wounded into the hospital wagons."

The pilgrims ran. In a moment there was only Hamish kneeling there in the field, his face pallid with worry under his deep tan, lank hair dangling over his eyes. "Another vision?"

Toby grunted and nodded.

"It could only have lasted a couple of seconds. I saw you."

"No! Longer." He had spent at least three nights in the stinking cell. The torture had started on the fourth day of questioning—and lasted about a hundred years. Couple of seconds?

"Your beard's thicker!"

Toby started to raise a hand and stopped instantly, grimacing. "Uh?"

Hamish produced a smile that looked as if it had been slept in. "Remember we agreed we'd know it was the hob doing it if your beard came back? Well, you've got a lot more stubble than you had ten minutes ago. Several days? A week? Can't say. Don't know if anyone else will notice. If they do, they just won't believe their eyes, so it won't matter."

Did that mean anything? Was it part of the warning, a hint that he had a few days or at most a week until the torture began? A man could grow a beard and shave it off every month for years. He did not know *when* the vision had been, nor *where*. In a town, yes, because he had heard city noises from his cell window, but Barcelona or some other?

Hamish rose. "Here comes Brother Bernat. Do I tell him?"

"Just him," Toby whispered. He closed his eyes for a moment, ignoring voices. It was hard to think through the pain. He could probably walk if he was on his feet and had both arms in slings—it would be getting there that would be the problem.

What he needed to know was how the Inquisition was going to catch him and how to avoid that fate, but all he had were his memories of that hour or so in the torture chamber—plus a few vaguer memories of memories. When he was shown the poster, he had been thinking that someone betrayed him . . . pilgrims, these pilgrims. There had been other interrogations . . . in a tent? Recalling those moments of

dread and defeat when he had stripped naked before
the watching tormentors and inquisitors, he realized
that he had been removing the same shabby hose
and doublet he wore now. The future he had foreseen was not very far off. Less than a week's beard.
This was the same beard, grown longer, not next
month's beard or next year's beard.

None of this made sense! His shoulders were
going to take months to heal—if they ever would
heal properly—and yet there had been nothing
wrong with them until the thugs began systemati-
cally wrecking him. His vision of the future seemed
to have made itself impossible. Madness!

Last night, around the campfire, the pilgrims had
agreed that it could not be long now, a day or two at
the most, until they reached the Ebro, the greatest
river in Spain, and the only one of any size between
Valencia and Barcelona. They would have to cross
it on the bridge at Tortosa, which was a large town.
Large enough to have an office of the Inquisition,
perhaps. And where better to apprehend a suspect
you have a picture of than on a bridge he must
cross?

A shadow fell over his face. He opened his eyes
to see the emaciated old friar kneeling beside him.
He sensed that Pepita was there, inevitably, but
Hamish had been sent away.

"This gramarye has injured you, my son—
where?"

"Shoulders," Toby whispered. *"Strappado."*

Brother Bernat drew in his breath in surprise.
"Who did this?"

"The Inquisition, Brother."

"Ah, a great evil! And your speech? Sore throat!

Let me tend that first. Relax as much as you can and do not be afraid."

Dry, cool fingers clasped Toby's neck. He felt a tingle, then a strange sensation like ice water soaking through his flesh. The fires died away to a lingering ache. Even his torn mouth stopped hurting. Spirits! This was gramarye as potent as any he had ever met.

"Is that better?"

"Much better, Brother! Thank you. Thank you very much. How do you do that?"

The old man shook his head impatiently. "We have much to talk about. Ah, your wrists! But your arms must be the worst, yes? Can you sit up?"

Toby shuddered. He took a deep breath, released it, and then performed the fastest sit-up of his life, letting his hands trail in the dirt. His shoulders exploded in thunderbolts. He did not cry out, not quite, but that was only because he knew the child was there.

"Ah, fool that I am!" said Brother Bernat, clasping Toby's head between his hands. "Peace, my son!" The agony subsided a little. "Now I have to open your jerkin. Pepita, your fingers are faster than mine. Unlace this for the captain."

At once Pepita was there, kneeling on his other side, looking very solemn. Her hands fluttered like butterflies: jerkin, doublet, shirt—and then she chuckled gleefully. "Look, he has hairs on his chest! And a locket! Can I see?" She reached for the little leather packet Toby wore around his neck.

"No!" The amethyst was the thing he prized most in all the world, Granny Nan's farewell gift to him, but if this child were to try and take it, he could not lift a finger to stop her.

"Pepita, your manners!" Brother Bernat said sharply. "That is the captain's. Leave it." With delicate, careful movements, he stripped off Toby's loose garments until he was bare to the waist. Pepita sat back and stared, but even Toby could see that his shoulders and arms were puffed out like red melons, the left one worse than the right. He had a better view of his hideously discolored elbows, his bruised and bloody wrists. His ankles felt as if they were scraped raw again inside his buskins.

The friar muttered angrily. "This arm is out of place, my son. It may hurt when I put it back. Wait." He laid his hands on the fiery swelling, and his touch produced the same icy relief as before. "Ready?" He pushed.

That gentle pressure should have had no effect at all on a dislocated shoulder, but Toby heard a crunch and a thud as the bone slid back into place. Despite all he could do, a whimper escaped him, then it was over. The coolness returned. Gramarye!

After a few moments the friar switched his attention to the other arm. "Pepita? Put your hand here. See if you can feel what I am doing." He placed his long, slender fingers over her tiny ones.

She frowned at first, then smiled delightedly. "Yes! Yes! Can I try?"

"By all means. Take it slowly, calmly. You work on his elbow."

Toby had always thought that gramarye was pure evil—like the houses in Mezquiriz bursting into pillars of flame. This was pure goodness, the most blessed relief he could imagine. He did not understand, but his gratitude was infinite. He would never doubt Brother Bernat again. And although Pepita was not producing any detectable results in her efforts to copy what the old man was doing, he did not believe now that her trick with the mouse had been a trick.

Sounds in the distance told of the pilgrims mounting and preparing to move off, then he felt the ground shake and knew the tread of Don Ramon's horse.

"What are you doing, Brother?" demanded the arrogant voice. "And what is that child doing? Why is that man indecently exposed?"

Exposed? Had the noble lord never seen the poor toiling in the summer fields?

The gray-robed friar looked up, frowning. "We are invoking the good spirits of this country to heal him, senor. He injured himself when he fell."

Still being considerate of his arms, Toby twisted around to look up at the *caballero*. "It is as he says, senor." His voice was hoarse, but it was a voice again.

The don raised his eyebrows in surprise at this miraculous recovery. "Indeed? From the look of you, you fell a long way, Captain. Can you catch up to us? I mean, if I leave a wagon to carry you, you will follow soon?"

"We shall catch up," said the friar. "Pray proceed."

Not Hamish. He would refuse to leave without Toby.

"If your honor would be so kind as to inform Sergeant Jaume that this is my wish, senor? The password is, 'Strath Fillan.' "

Don Ramon nodded and tried to repeat that, although his Castilian tongue stumbled over the consonants. Looking uncharacteristically doubtful, he turned his horse and rode off without another word. The three of them were left sitting on the grass.

"Wagon?" Toby muttered. "Is he truly crazy or just deceiving us?"

"Attend to his actions, not what he says, my son." Unlike several other members of the company, Brother Bernat was not a gossip. "Pepita, you are doing very well. Let me finish the elbow, and you try his wrist."

The gentle laying-on of those ancient hands brought relief from pain, the most welcome thing in the world, and yet it also brought its own shadow in the knowledge that the respite could only be temporary. A few days from now Toby would have to meet it again, and then there would be no magical escape. His flesh cringed, his courage wavered. Could he bear to remain with the pilgrims after this warning?

"Can you walk now, my son?"

"I think so, Brother. But my ankles . . ."

He reached down and the friar intervened, removing his buskins and then hauling his tattered hose up his shins. He clucked when he found the lacerated skin, but again his touch worked its healing magic, and this time the effects were more visible. Eventually he sat back with a sigh, looking weary for the first time in Toby's experience. The parchment face was paler than ever, the dark eyes more deeply sunk.

"That will have to do for now, Tobias. It is not enough. I am sorry."

"It is enough. It is wonderful. I am so grateful that I cannot find words." He was still very sore, but he was not a cripple.

A trace of the familiar smile crept back. "You must find a lot of words."

"I shall tell you everything, Brother, and gladly. And now I do believe that you can help me. I am very sorry I ever doubted you. Can you rid me of the hob?"

"Hob? What is a hob?"

Dismayed, Toby paused halfway into his shirt. "A spirit, an untrained one. Not quite an elemental but one that knows something of people. It was the spirit of the glen where I was born."

"Ah! I understand. We call them imps." The inscrutable dark eyes studied him. "Then your problem is even worse than I suspected. No, I cannot rid you of it. I may be able to help you deal with it, though. I wish to rest here a little while, but you must tell me the whole story. And then we shall rejoin the others."

"I shall tell you gladly, but I do not know that I wish to rejoin the others. I am sure that someone in the party betrayed me."

Brother Bernat sighed. "I expect so, but you must not think badly of them for that, Tobias. The Inquisition is very skilled in its questioning and never betrays those who tell tales. Even an account of what happened to you here this morning would be enough to condemn you, and many people saw you fall. You are not the only person who fears the inquisitors."

"You have endangered yourself by helping me!"

"Don't worry about me. I have survived a long time." The old man smiled his cryptic little smile. "Now tell me everything, or I cannot advise you."

"I shall. Now?" Where to begin? "Let's see. I was

an orphan in a very small village in the hills of Scotland. The woman who raised me was what we called the witchwife. . . ."

It was a very long tale. When he came to tell how he had fled Scotland to escape Baron Oreste, the old friar heaved himself up.

"We must start moving. You can talk on the way."

Toby was shaky, but he could walk. There was nothing wrong with his legs, although the tormentors would doubtless have gotten to them soon enough. He tucked his hands inside the front of his jerkin, thinking that would help support the weight of his arms and ease the jarring on his shoulders. He would not want to be carrying his pack, or even his sword. Hamish would have taken care of those for him—capable, dependable Hamish. That was why he had to go on to Barcelona, to see Hamish safely on a ship. He continued with his history.

Even the brief rest had restored Brother Bernat, for he set off at his usual distance-eating pace which so belied his frail appearance. His haggard features were intent, but he displayed no reaction to the improbable story, other than an occasional penetrating half smile. Pepita hurried along at his side, looking worried or shocked or puzzled by turns, but saying nothing.

The pilgrims could not be very far ahead, because once Hamish came trotting into sight and stopped when he saw the stragglers. He waved. The friar waved back, and Hamish disappeared again. Then Brother Bernat slowed down a little, as if unwilling to catch up with the group before the discussion was ended.

Toby concluded with the visions that had begun

about two weeks earlier, a total of five of them now—a man in Valencia he had never met, the ghoul in the orange grove, Oreste's dungeon, the executions in Barcelona, and finally the Inquisition. There seemed to be no logic to them, no pattern, no rationality.

"Are these prophecies, Brother, or are they madness? If they are madness, why do they injure me? If they show the future, they contradict each other. Once the Inquisition has demolished me, how can I ever become Baron Oreste's headsman?"

"Perhaps your meeting with the Inquisition will happen later."

"No, I was wearing these clothes, I am sure of it."

The friar nodded. "The visions are not madness, Tobias, although they may drive you mad. They happened but did not happen. They are real and not real. They may be true or false. All they show is that you are in fearful danger. If the Inquisition may be looking out for you at Tortosa, then we shall have to scout the town very carefully before we enter it." He smiled wanly. "You are not alone in having reason to be wary of the inquisitors."

"They are friars too."

The old man thrust out a bony jaw. "Not of my order!"

"I am sorry, I should not—"

"No you shouldn't. To rid the world of demons is commendable, but if those who seek to do so use methods as evil as the demons themselves, then where is the benefit? And if the methods do not work, then the total evil is worse than before. But peace, Tobias! Let me think on what you have said." Brother Bernat fell silent.

5

As they were walking past the remains of an orchard, the friar began to talk again, gazing at the road ahead and speaking so softly that he seemed to be musing aloud.

"Like you, Tobias, I can see elementals. That is not a birthright but a knack one gains from dealing with them. You were a witchwife's child, and I have studied the spirits all my life. I don't know how old I am—ninety, perhaps more. It is too long to remain ignorant, but that is what I am. Spirits are still mysteries to me, and especially I do not know where they come from. They do not procreate as mortals do, but they must be replenished somehow, else the hexers would have stripped the world clean of them long ago. I like to think they are spontaneous manifestations of nature, outpourings of the power of life and beauty. Anywhere I have ever encountered a sprite was a place of beauty—a grove of willows, a grotto, a bend in a stream. But I don't know if the elemental is attracted to the beauty, or creates it, or is created by it."

He smiled his patient, gentle smile, which Toby now thought was more effective than a castle wall at preserving secrets.

"I have gathered a little lore in my time, though, and I shall share it with you if you promise not to ask any questions until I am done."

"I should gladly promise more than that, Brother."

"That will suffice. Most people know of only three types of spirit, although they are all varieties of the same, of course—the wild elementals, the benevolent tutelaries, and demons. It does seem unfair, doesn't it, that the evil ones are able to move around while the tutelaries remain always in their own domains? Their mobility is bought at a terrible price. Whatever the Inquisition did to you, Tobias, or would have done to you, could be nothing compared to the tortures an adept applies to a spirit to make a demon of it. And the spirit cannot even hope to die, as I am sure you did . . . would, I mean. Small wonder they are so malevolent!

"Your hob, though, or imp as we call them, is not bound as a demon is. It has free will, and undoubtedly it is responsible for your visions. Those are very unusual and very dangerous. Think of them not as prophecies but as warnings. No hob nor spirit can foretell the future, not in any detail. A great tutelary may recognize a sickness in a man and know that he will die soon. It may have knowledge beyond mortals' ken and be privy to great secrets, but it cannot write a history of the future. The hob knows less of what is going to happen to you than you do, because it lives only for the moment."

The pause seemed to invite comment, so Toby said, "Yes, Brother." Whatever this long introduction was leading up to must obviously be bad news.

"You, for example, are deeply concerned by the problem of finding enough food for us, but that is completely beyond its comprehension. Mostly the hob just watches the world unfolding around you, satisfying its childish curiosity. If it becomes excited, then it may do foolish things, but otherwise it is only an observer, I think. You agree?"

"Yes, Brother."

"It takes no heed for the morrow, until suddenly it realizes you are in serious trouble. Then it will react to save you, because you are valuable to it. It is undoubtedly fond of you in its way, and if it cannot understand what pain is, that is not its fault. Suffering it ignores, but your death matters to it. If it can use its powers to save your life, then it will. But supposing it cannot?"

"When it is blocked by other demons?" Toby had promised not to ask questions, but the friar either did not notice that lapse or did not care.

"Baron Oreste's demons, perchance. And the Inquisition undoubtedly uses demons of its own, although the brothers probably do not think of them as that. Once in a while they must pick on a genuine creature, and if they did not restrain it by some sort of gramarye it would blast them. When they disincarnate an incarnate it would merely take over one of their own number unless they had some means of preventing that."

"By 'disincarnate' you mean—"

"I mean kill its host, Tobias. When the husk dies, or soon after, the demon is freed. Suppose . . . Let us suppose that a few days from now you meet the Inquisition. They may be looking out for you, or someone in our party denounces you, or they just pick on a foreigner. It doesn't matter which, although that poster you mentioned suggests that they are specifically looking for you. Also, the Inquisition is normally extremely patient, absurdly so. It will keep people in jail for years while it prepares its case. For it to put you to the Question so quickly is very unusual. But you say they will begin to torture you almost right away."

"And I cannot tell them what they want to know."

"Of course. And so, eventually, you will die. Even

a strong man can only endure so much. Then, and only then, the hob realizes the problem."

"*Then?* Not until then?"

"Probably not until you are dead or near death. It realizes its mistake, but it cannot just heal you and blow a hole through your cell walls, because it is blocked by some sort of gramarye. So what does it do?"

Toby blinked in sudden sunshine as they emerged from the shade of the trees. "I don't know, Brother."

"I suspect it does what we want to do when we make a mistake. You know that terrible feeling when you have done something wrong and wish you could undo it? A thoughtless word, an error of judgment, hitting your thumb with a hammer? For us, what's done is done, but that may not be true for the hob. Suppose it jumps back in time—taking you with it, of course—and lets the world unfold again? The next time events may turn out differently."

"Spirits! I did not know that was possible!"

"I find it hard to credit myself, but I heard such a procedure mentioned as a theory once, many, many years ago. I shall discuss it with Father Guillem, if you will let me take him into our confidence. But see how well it fits the facts! Especially it fits the hob. An elemental has no need to violate the order of nature so brutally. A tutelary never would, because to change the past for one person would change it for many and might introduce other evils worse than the first. A demon cannot, because it is bound by conjuration. I have only scant knowledge of such vile hexing, but I do believe that it binds the demon in time as well as in space. The hob, though, is free to do as it likes. I expect it tried this trick once in desperation and it worked, so now it does it more often."

Usually Toby thought of himself as a horse and the hob as the rider. Brother Bernat was saying that this rider gave the horse its head—which might not be true always but could be most of the time—but when the horse wandered into trouble, the rider took it back to . . . "I find this hard to visualize, Brother."

"So do I, my son, so do I! Imagine that you are dying from the inquisitors' cruelty, say a month or two from now. The hob wakes up to the situation and flips you back to this morning. If it does this properly, then everything that has happened is wiped out. The slate is clean. You proceed more or less as you did before."

"Then I should fall into the same trap again."

The narrow gray shoulders shrugged. "Not necessarily. Life is a series of choices, of chance happenings, of little events producing large results. Small hooks catch big fish. A seed blows in the wind and a tree grows. Things may not work out exactly as they did the first time."

"The ghoul in the orange grove! The first time I tripped over Hamish and . . ." Toby rephrased a question into a statement. "You think I died, that the creature killed me!"

"It would seem so. The hob would not die unless the sword went through your heart. It mourns its friend Tobias. It finds its house growing cold, if you will forgive a cruel expression. It jumps him back a few days and lets him try again."

"But—"

"But why do you come back damaged so often? Why do you remember anything at all of the lost days?" The friar smiled his little smile. "Those are good questions, my son, so I shall ask them for you. Alas, I don't have good answers, but I suspect that the hob is going crazy. It is an immortal trying to cope with mortality.

"For us what's done is done. For the hob, what's done can be tried again. It certainly seems logical that neither it nor you should retain any memory of what hasn't happened yet and may never happen." He sighed. "This could give a man a headache. Do you understand this, Pepita?"

"No, Brother," said the child solemnly.

"Well, you are not alone."

"Déjà vu!" Toby said. "That feeling that you've been here before!"

Brother Bernat beamed. "You often have that feeling?"

"Quite often. I remember it very strongly in Brittany once and a couple of times in Navarre. And at other places, less marked."

"So! So perhaps the hob has been at this for years and you did not know. But now . . . Now, perhaps, it is going mad, so its powers are not working properly. Or other demons are interfering with it, somewhere in your future. Either way, you are coming back damaged and remembering some of what happened. Not all of it, I'm sure. You just retain fragments, of course."

Here was the bad news. "You mean I could have been—I mean I will remain—longer in the hands of the Inquisition?"

"And in the baron's clutches, too. I don't think you recall the end of the story in any of those cases."

They walked on for a while in silence. At last

Toby put it into words. "And when you said these happenings were dangerous, what you meant was that one day the hob may mess things up completely. Is that possible? Could it tie the two of us into a circle, a never-ending loop in time?"

"I am certainly concerned about that possibility."

And so was Toby Longdirk. There could be no worse fate in the universe than being tortured by the Inquisition throughout all eternity.

"The dangers facing you are uncountable, my son. The Inquisition is the most immediate, of course. I shall be most surprised if your vision turns out to be false and the inquisitors are not watching for you at Tortosa. Assuming you can pass them safely and survive all the other perils of this road as well, then Baron Oreste waits in Barcelona. If he tries to strip the hob from you, he will almost certainly take parts of your mind with it. If he doesn't, then in time the hob will inevitably go completely insane, which means you will. If you were not the man you are, that would have happened long since. Tobias, I do not envy you your future!"

"There they are!" Pepita said, pointing a straw-thin finger. The pilgrims were in sight in the distance, going slowly across a wide pasture.

"So they are," said Brother Bernat, "and we have not yet finished our business." He turned aside from the track and strode over to a thicket where many of the trees still bore bright green leaves. There, as if he had planned it, he went straight to a mossy stump in the leafy gloom and seated himself like a king on a throne. The air was cool and deliciously fragrant. "Oleanders," he explained, waving a slender hand at the foliage.

Pepita promptly discovered a trail of ants and dropped on all fours to study it. Toby sank down cross-legged on the ground before the old man, resting his throbbing arms on his knees. For a moment neither spoke.

The friar glanced at the child, who had now tracked the ants to their nest at the base of a tree and was lying there with her nose almost inside it.

"Tobias," he said softly, "you can tell me the rest now."

"Father, I told you everything!" Pause. "Everything I believed was relevant." But not Mezquiriz! He had not mentioned Mezquiriz. Must he bare even that secret sorrow? He had never told anyone. Even Hamish did not know the awful truth.

"There is more, Tobias, unless I am sadly misinformed about the human race. You are a man of considerable will, but do you tell me you have never once succumbed to the temptations of the flesh? I have watched the effect you have on our companions. You draw women's eyes like flies to honey."

"That is the hob's doing! Yes, I did let it learn about . . . about what men and women do, Brother. It wants to experience that again, and it lures women to me."

The old man laughed. "Does it? I think you underestimate yourself. But tell me what happened. I shall not condemn you for being human."

Toby bent his head so he need not see that gaunt old face with its knowing smile. He clenched his fists until his bruised wrists throbbed. "Just once, Brother. Only once! I did not know what would happen." He waited to hear the forgiveness he wanted, but nothing came. "It was at Mezquiriz, a tiny place in Navarre, near Roncevalles. It was not a casual thing, Brother. We could not dream of marriage, but we were very much in love, both of us."

"Knowing you, I am sure you were. You would not deceive a girl for momentary pleasure. You did not know, but did you not suspect?"

Toby looked up angrily. "How could I?" The penetrating dark eyes seared him. He looked away quickly.

Yes, he must have suspected, even then, for he had fled from similar situations in the past. His doubts had been more than the normal anxiety of a young man about to embark on his first lovemaking. He remembered the words spoken outside the cottage, when the ice-bound night was a soaring choir of stars and snow glimmered on the peaks. He remembered Jeanne in his arms, her sweet fragrance, the taste of her kisses on his mouth. He remembered his terrified excuses: *I am nothing but a hunted fugitive, a deserter. I have no land, no friends with influence, no money.*

Her whispered reply: *Life is short and love is shorter. If you care for me, do not deprive me of the happiness I ask.*

I love you too much to love you.

If I knew you were leaving forever at dawn, I should still want this.

"We were members of a band of smugglers, Brother. Hamish and I needed to escape from Nevil's domains, and that was the only way. We joined them. Jeanne was one of them. I loved her. By all the spirits, I loved her!"

He stared at the dead leaves under the old man's feet. Tears ran into his stubble, but he did not wipe them away. "One night we . . . we exchanged solemn promises of love. And then . . . we went to her room."

Even as they lay together on the tiny bed with starlight peeking through cracks in the shutter, even in the frantic, clumsy fumbling with each other's garments—even then he had tried to talk her out of it. She had kissed his words away. And now he could not find words. He sat in silence with the tears flowing.

"She died, my son?"

Yes! Yes! Will you make me say it? He nodded, not looking up. "Not only her, Brother. Houses collapsed or burst into flames. Hamish barely escaped. They thought it was an artillery barrage."

Brother Bernat sighed. "It does not surprise me. Passion such as that would have been far beyond the hob's imagining. So you have avoided women ever since?"

Now Toby did look up, glaring furiously. "What do you think I am?"

The friar smiled as if he accepted the rebuke. "A most unfortunate young man who deserves better of life than the curse he bears. But answer my question. Look me in the eyes and tell me the truth."

"I have never as much as kissed another woman. Not even when they ask me outright!"

"Good!" the friar said. "Then there is hope that I may be able to help you." He looked around to see where Pepita had gone, but she was out of earshot, stalking a squirrel. "And even if you did suspect that there might be trouble that night in Mezquiriz, no one could condemn you for what happened. You carry more remorse than you need. Tobias, I am truly sorry, believe me. I can teach you how to tame the hob, within limits. I can show you how to make it behave itself, so you will not go crazy and it will not thrash around damaging other people as it has done in the past. Do you want this?"

"Very much, Brother. More, I think, than anything in the world."

"There is a price to pay, though. Two prices. One is that you will no longer be able to count on the hob to defend you. Basically, I will show you how to lull it to sleep, and a sleeping watchdog does not bark."

"I would rather die than go crazy. If I do go crazy, then I will run wild like a demon, won't I? Killing, destroying?"

Brother Bernat nodded. "It is probable. The other price is that I cannot give you back what you lost that night in Mezquiriz. I know of no way to make the hob proof against ecstasy. You will remain condemned to a life of celibacy."

Toby rubbed his eyes with a knuckle. He realized that he felt bitter, which was absurd, for none of his troubles were the old friar's fault. "I am twenty-one. How old will I be when that stops worrying me?"

"About a hundred."

"I see." No, the smile was not mockery, it was sympathy. He returned it as well as he could. "Half a life is better than none. I shall be very grateful for whatever assistance you can give me, Brother. It is wonderful news that you can help me at all!" It was also very surprising. Where did such a technique come from? What was it used for? He had promised not to ask questions.

Brother Bernat studied him solemnly for a moment. "It will not be easy. You are old to start learning. Fortunately, you are a very brave young man. Nerves like granite, I said, didn't I? All you have to do is slow down your heartbeat."

Toby stared at him blankly until the old man chuckled.

"Pepita can do it! Shall I call her over to demonstrate?"

"Why should Pepita . . . ?" Now he knew why he was not to ask questions. Brother Bernat himself must know the same trick and for the same reason, whatever that might be. "No, Brother, I believe you."

"The slower the beat, the quieter the hob, like a hibernating hedgehog. It lives in your heart, remember, so when you get excited and the house gets noisy, then the hob is alarmed. You probably have a naturally slow beat, which has helped preserve you from it. The secret is calmness, serenity of mind, and you do not lose your head. Most people would have been howling maniacs this morning after what you had been through, but you recovered almost immediately."

"I am flattered that you thought so," Toby said grimly. Somewhere deep inside he was still screaming. How many days until he was back on the rope? How many nights until he could sleep without dreaming of it?

The friar's fond little smile returned. "You underestimate yourself, Tobias. It is part of your charm, if you will forgive me for insulting a virile young man by telling him he has charm. You do, though. It is emotion in you that speeds your heart and rouses the hob." He waited as if inviting comment.

"Suppose I want to run, or work hard?"

"Exercise does not matter, only emotion. I don't know why."

"Gunfire rouses it, Brother. Or thunder. Or loud music."

"Do they? Those things might annoy an elemental, but your hob should be used to them by now. Are you sure it is not you who is alarmed? If you are frightened that the hob may be frightened, then it may be your fear that rouses it. Fear, anger—those you will have to learn to control even better than you control them now, which is much better than most men do. You understand now why the passions of love must be avoided. I shall teach you the methods and leave you to practice them. You will have to devote every spare minute to it."

"Will this get me past the Inquisition?"

Brother Bernat shook his head. "I think the poster will be their real reason for detaining you. Even if I am wrong, they will detect the hob in you. Pepita did. I confess that I did, also. You may never be skilled enough to hide it completely, and you certainly cannot hope to learn the knack in a couple of days. To become even reasonably proficient will take you months."

"Then I had better begin, just in case I live that long."

"Very well. First, you must learn how to breathe. Can you breathe without moving your shoulders, only your abdomen?"

Apparently he was serious.

"I have been doing so all morning! Like this?"

"It would help if you were to remove your upper garments again," Brother Bernat said apologetically. "I shall perform another healing on you after this, which should remove the rest of your pain. You are still in pain?"

"A little," Toby admitted, easing out of his jerkin.

"More than a little, I suspect." The friar waited until the shirt came off. "Stand. Now show me. Here." He poked a finger at Toby's solar plexus. "Out. In. Out. In. Good. Now, can you do the reverse—breathe in just using the upper part of your chest?"

At the moment that hurt, of course, but it would have been difficult at any time.

"Very good! Now, start a very long breath, very slowly, beginning down here at the base of your lungs and filling them all the way to the top. Good. Hold that. Now let it out from the top down. . . ." He chuckled as he watched Toby's contortions. "Wait a moment. Now do it again. Good! Very good indeed! Let me give you the timing. Too fast and you will make yourself giddy."

In a few moments the old man nodded, looking pleased. "That is the first part. You may sit down again." He stood up. "Sit on this, and I shall work on your shoulders. Make yourself as comfortable as you can." He began to soothe more of the fire from Toby's injuries with his mysterious gramarye.

All gramarye was evil by definition, because it was wrested from demons by torture—so Toby had always believed. But this wondrous healing could never be evil. His definitions would have to be revised.

"The second part," the friar said, "is to clear your mind, and that is best done by thinking of some very peaceful scene you know well. Something from your childhood may be best. What shall it be?"

Toby pondered, calling up memories of the glen.
"There is a little lake called Lochan na Bi. I remember watching a swan swimming on it." White
plumage, dark peaty water, the hills with rain drifting down them. Reflections.

"Very good, let it be that. Some find it helpful to
have a mantra also, a phrase to repeat in your mind.
'Lochan na Bi' itself would do very well, it has a
gentle sound. So think of the swan and say, 'Lochan
na Bi,' to yourself."

Swan. Lochan na Bi. Swan. Lochan na Bi. Swan.
Lochan na Bi.

"That's all?"

Brother Bernat laughed. "That is the beginning.
Repeat it about a million times! Yes, that is all. If
you can breathe as I showed you, very slowly, see
the swan, repeat the mantra—this is called
dejamiento, Tobias. Done properly, it produces a
very deep serenity. Your heart will stay at a slow,
steady beat, and the hob will remain serene also.
Eventually you could hope to deceive even the
Inquisition."

It seemed too simple, far too simple. "If they tie
weights to my feet and haul me up again?"

The friar shrugged. "I have known men who
remained serene when the tormentors got to the red-
hot pincers. You will not achieve that level of control for many years and perhaps never."

"I shall try, Brother."

Try he did. Tricky! The breathing alone seemed to
take all his attention, leaving none for mental pictures. Swan . . . Lochan na Bi . . . He was also distracted by the cool touch of the friar's hands. After
a few moments, he peered around at the old man

and saw in his face the same weariness that it had
shown before. Healing was obviously a strain.

"I thank you, Brother. Should we not go and join
the others now?"

"As you wish." Brother Bernat sank down on the
stump as Toby relinquished it to take up his clothes.
"How far is it to Tortosa?"

Pulling on his shirt, Toby said, "How should I
know? I've never . . ." He stared in dismay at the
gentle smile. "But I have, haven't I?"

The friar nodded. "Yes, my son, you have been
here before. This is at least the fourth time you have
walked this road. For all we know, it may be the
twelfth time, or the twentieth. It may not be the
last."

6

Setting off along the trail again, they saw Francisca
in the distance, coming on her pony, and they
waved. She responded but did not turn back, so she
must have something to tell them. It was a reminder
that privacy was about to be lost, that Toby had better think up an explanation for his peculiar behavior,
and that there were still mysteries lurking on the
edges.

"May I ask you a question now, Brother?"

"No, because I have more to tell you, so I have not
finished." The old man chuckled at his expression.
"You see? Even we Franciscans can be devious! But
we give fair value. What have you there, child?" He
examined Pepita's collection of leaves and began
lecturing her on herbs.

Only gramarye could have healed Toby's injuries.

The kindly old man was certainly not an incarnate, so he must be an adept and have a bottled demon concealed somewhere about his person. But if Toby could carry the soul of the true king of England around with him in a locket, a friar could transport a demon. Granted that the initial process of capturing and enslaving an elemental was vicious, the resulting demon was still immortal. If it and its conjuration later fell into innocent hands and were applied to benevolent purposes, that was a worthy practice surely. It would have to be a secret one, though, because hexing was not merely illegal but so detested that suspects were frequently torn apart by a mob before the authorities could even arrest them. He could see no connection between what Brother Bernat was doing and Senora Collel's confused mutterings about *alumbradismo*. Nor could he see where Pepita might fit in—Pepita, whose strange rapport for horses extended even to mice.

The Inquisition disapproved of hexers almost as much as it disapproved of the possessed. Should it learn of Brother Bernat's actions, it would confiscate his demon and impose a severe penance on him, although few of the customary penalties could be applied to a ninety-year old mendicant preacher. Forfeiture of all his worldly goods would be impossible, because he had none. Flogging or a term in the galleys would kill him. But he would certainly lose Pepita, whom he obviously loved dearly, so he had as much cause to fear the Inquisition as Toby did. He was not the only one. Gracia was another, whether or not she was achieving anything with her voices and her bottles, and the don himself might be judged possessed if he babbled about his imaginary army.

Francisca arrived on her wheezing little pony and beamed delightedly at Toby. "*Campeador*, you are recovered!"

"Thanks to Brother Bernat. I had a bad fall, but his skilled massage has eased my bruises."

The old lady blinked in disbelief. "Indeed? Praise to all good spirits! But I came to urge you to greater speed, for we have seen a mounted band approaching, and Don Ramon is preparing our defenses. Perhaps you could go faster if the child rode with me?"

"I think she can manage as well on her own feet, senor," the friar said, eyeing the sweating pony dubiously.

Toby decided he could swing his sword now, although not as nimbly as usual, but he did not have it with him. "I shall go ahead, then, Senor Francisco, and let you all follow." He set off at a lope, and even that hardly jarred his shoulders.

As soon as he crested the rise he saw the pilgrims assembled amid some broken walls and tall cypresses a bowshot from the trail. It was not the fortress of Toledo, but it was the most defensible position in sight, and confirmation of Brother Bernat's view that one should heed what the don did, not what he said.

The mounted band Francisca had mentioned comprised at least a dozen riders and about ten wagons, coming at a leisurely pace. It might be no more than a trading party with armed guards, or it might be the Inquisition. It did not look much like a gang of highwaymen, but sunlight flashed on helmets and blades, and the lead man carried a pennant. If there was to be a fight, it would be a brief one.

Toby cranked up to a sprint and arrived in the shade of the cypress trees damp and breathless. Hamish offered him his sword and helmet and a look of welcome almost embarrassing in its intensity.

He went to where the don was standing beside his warhorse and saluted, conscious of all the others' wondering stares. "Your *campeador* reports for duty, senor."

The arrogant blue eyes scanned him from his head to his toes and back again. "Submit a full report in writing, *Campeador*." He turned away to study the newcomers' approach.

"Well?" Hamish demanded eagerly.

"Very well, thank you." Quickly, Toby outlined the friar's explanation for the visions and the danger of a roadblock at Tortosa. He spoke in Gaelic, which doubtless annoyed Senora Collel excessively.

Hamish pulled a face. "I have never read anything about spirits moving back in time!"

"Not everything can be found in books. The old man healed my injuries—have you ever read of gramarye being used for such a purpose?"

"No," Hamish admitted reluctantly. "Only tutelaries do such things. Or hexers, and he is no hexer."

The wagon train came to a halt. Suspicion worked both ways, and its escort would naturally wonder whether the few men and women they could see in the open were all of the don's party. The man bearing the pennant rode forward across the field with two others at his back, coming slowly.

"Campeador!" said the don. "You will present me." He vaulted with his lance into Atropos' saddle and rode off without a backward glance.

Toby could see no signs of anyone in friars' robes, which was a relief. He said, "Hamish?" and the two of them followed Don Ramon to the parley.

The horsemen dismounted. They were armed with muskets and swords and garbed like soldiers. Their pennant was unfamiliar to him.

No it wasn't! The pennant was vaguely familiar, the men were vaguely familiar, the whole situation screamed at him that he had been here before. He just couldn't remember when. Even—now that he looked at it—the scenery, the valley looming ahead, lay tantalizingly just outside the edges of his memory. *Déjà vu!*

Had it started, then?

The don reined in a dozen paces from the strangers and glanced at his aide-de-camp. "*Campeador*, inquire what manner of men these be and by what right they contest our progress."

Toby marched forward and saluted. "Senor, the noble Don Ramon de Nuñez y Pardo, traveling on pilgrimage to Montserrat with his train, bids me question what manner of persons you be."

The lead soldier was a large man, almost as tall as Toby himself, and not much older. He undoubtedly looked much more ferocious, being slung around with arms of all kinds and sporting both a broken nose and a jet-black beard as big as a pillow. Toby was certain he knew him from somewhere, he just couldn't quite place him. How could such a face be forgotten?

The man scowled, considered the question for a long moment, and then unexpectedly grinned. "As honest a party of merchants as ever sold the Sassenachs a herd by day and drove it back across the border by night." He spoke in Scots.

"Demons, we are lost!" Toby replied. "Toby Longdirk of Tyndrum."

"Graham Johnson of Girvan!" Hands were clasped in a grip that rapidly tightened until it would have crushed marble. Grins widened.

"One moment," Toby said when the brutal greeting had been mutually accepted as a draw. He went back to the don. "Merely merchants, senor, with mercenary guards."

Don Ramon shrugged contemptuously. "Question them about the enemy's dispositions and let them pass." He turned Atropos and rode away as if disappointed by the lack of opportunity for honorable bloodshed.

By that time Hamish was in full gabble with Master Johnson, while the latter's two Spanish subordinates looked on in silent disdain. Scottish mercenaries were prized all over Europe, so it was little surprise to find one here. But it was good fortune, because whatever Master Johnson's politics might be, he would have small sympathy for the Inquisition. Thus when Toby had described the condition of the lands south to Valencia and warned about the would-be horse thieves who had attacked the pilgrims, and had similarly been advised about the state of affairs in Tortosa and Catalonia as far as Barcelona itself, he could bring up the delicate subject without having to hedge.

The mercenary spat in disgust. "There's black robes and gray robes and white robes all over the place, and they have no liking for foreigners, but they didna' bother me nor Ian nor Gavin. There's a toll on the bridge at Tortosa. I dinna' recall seeing any friars there. I'd expect that don of yours to ride across wi' his nose in the air and not having to pay a groat, him being a noble and all."

That was good news. Indeed, all his news was good. Catalonia had suffered less than Valencia in the fighting, he said, and was already recovering, although still risky for travelers. There was food to be had in Tortosa, which was a major port, although prices were exorbitant. They ought to reach the town by the next day, and Master Johnson recommended the best inns for food, vermin-free bedding, and plump women respectively—no one establishment qualifying on all counts. And they were already more or less out of danger, he said, because the governor in Tortosa sent out patrols to keep order, and their reach extended almost this far south of the city. Gavin's troop had not seen a soul since the previous afternoon.

He must have told Toby the same news before, though, perhaps more than once. It all sounded vaguely familiar.

FIVE

AMBUSH

1

"Toby!" Hamish howled. "You have the brains of a trout! You are crazy! A gibbering, blithering maniac!" He was crimson with fury and disbelief.

"I expect so. Blame the hob."

Pepita, Francisca, and Brother Bernat had arrived. Everyone had heard the mercenary's news and was ready to move out—everyone, that is, except Senor Campbell, who seemed more inclined to nail Toby to a tree with a sword through his chest. The Hamish who had so adamantly rejected prophecy was apparently quite willing to believe in the hob's fresh starts, and in this case he felt very strongly that the fresh start should be aimed due south.

"To your post, Sergeant Jaume," Toby said patiently. "Demons! I'll promote you and double your pay. Consider yourself Captain Jaume from now on." Seldom had a joke been greeted with less amusement. Oh, well! "Laddie, we can talk about this when we've got everyone moving." He stalked over to salute the don, who was already mounted. "Ready to move out, senor."

Surprisingly, the response was not an order to have the band play, or the buglers sound, or the cavalry lead in column of four. Don Ramon just said, "About time. Stay close, I have questions." He urged old Atropos to a gentle amble. Francisca moved Petals into place alongside.

Seeing that Acting Captain Jaume had postponed his mutiny and was attending to the final prodding and urging, Toby heaved his pack onto his shoulders—ignoring spiteful stabs of agony from his remaining bruises—and took up position, striding along at the don's left stirrup. "Senor?"

"This valley we are entering disturbs me. What other routes are available?"

"None, senor. I asked the mercenary, and he said this is the only way to Tortosa, and Tortosa is the only place we may cross the Ebro, unless we continue upriver a very long way. Behind that ridge to the right is the sea, and beyond it you end up in the swamps of the delta. We could go west of this other hill, but we come out on the river at the same place, about four leagues south of the city. That road is much harder, he said."

Receiving no response, he glanced up and was surprised to see a grin on the don's face. It disappeared instantly. Just for that moment he had looked very young and very normal, yet when he spoke he was back in his paradise of delusion:

"And what do you conclude about the enemy's plans and probable disposition, *Campeador?*"

His enemies were figments of delusion, but Toby's were not. One man's make-believe could be another man's reality.

"Senor, if the enemy wants to contest our

progress, the bridge at Tortosa is the obvious place to do it, and the mercenary did mention soldiers there. I shall breathe more freely when we are safely across the Ebro." Or he might not be breathing at all. As he put the situation into words, he saw that Hamish was right; he was crazy not to go back while he had the chance. He should say his farewells to the don right now and head south. "But perhaps the bridge is too obvious? If I were the . . ." he almost said, "Inquisition," and changed it hastily, ". . . foe, senor, I think I would lie in wait at the north end of that mountain west of us."

"The Sierra Grossa. The one on our right is the Sierra del Montsia."

"The *hidalgo* has been here before?"

"Never. I have studied military history. Continue with your analysis."

"This deserted valley bothers me. I questioned the mercenary closely about it. He said they had met with no trouble since leaving Tortosa yesterday. He said that the governor there has pacified this area, but he admitted he saw no patrols and no civilians for the last few leagues, which I find odd."

"So what do procedure do you recommend, *Campeador?*"

"That we advance in stages, halting the main party every hour or so and sending scouts ahead."

The don twirled the points on his mustache. "Not bad for a commoner! This is traditional ambush country, and you recognized that. You have had military experience?"

Since Toby had decided to leave the don's company now—at least, he thought he had—he could ease himself out of the make-believe. A taste of reality might make the parting smoother. "A little, but I learned more while I was an apprentice in the Navarrian smuggling industry."

He expected to see shock and disapproval, but Don Ramon accepted the news calmly. "I saw the scars of the lash on your back this morning. You are a felon?"

"No, senor. The lash was part of my military experience. I told my sergeant he had the brains of a louse."

That admission was taken much more seriously, provoking a dangerous aristocratic scowl. "You should have been hanged. You are a deserter, of course. From what army?"

"From several. I give my loyalty voluntarily or not at all. It cannot be bought with force, senor."

"Yes, they should have hanged you. Trouble-makers like you are best used as examples to the others. Now tell me what really happened to you while you were rounding up the horses this morning."

"I slipped and—"

"You take me for a fool?" The crazy blue eyes glared down at him. "I have seen men fresh from the *strappado* before." Don Ramon might be a maniac, but he had packed some rough-edged experience into his tender years.

"I am not familiar with that term, senor. I am a big man. I fall hard."

"Liar! Your arms were crippled. Now you carry a pack." The kid's curled mustache seemed to flame brighter than ever against the pallor of his anger. "Hold out your hands. Your wrists were swollen and bloody; they had fresh rope burns on them. Now they don't. What happened to you, and what did that friar do to make it right?"

Toby walked on for a while in defiant silence, keeping his neck craned to watch the horseman's face. He would not be surprised to see that broadsword drawn against him any minute, and if that happened he was as good as dead. He wondered what Doña Francisca was making of the conversation, but she was on the other side of Atropos and hence not visible.

"Senor, I can add nothing to what I have already told you. If you wish to dismiss me from your service, then Jaume and I will head south at once and seek to enlist with that company we just passed. I shall regret that, but I will go without ill feelings. Senora de Gomez will, of course, make her own choice. Any questions about Brother Bernat you must address to him."

"Demons! You'd been tortured." The don seemed to be making a strenuous effort to control himself, but the outcome still hung in the balance.

"When, senor? By whom? I fell down in clear view of the others."

The don chewed his lip. "I don't know. I should very much like to know, though. If I give you my oath not to repeat what you tell me to anyone, will you explain?"

"Does that 'anyone' include the Inquisition, senor?"

Don Ramon's glare slowly changed to a smile, an uncomfortably knowing and menacing smile. "Did you tell them what they wanted to know?"

That was not the question Toby had expected, but it was an encouraging one.

"Not as far as I can remember." That felt good; it felt very good.

"Then you are a brave man."

"If the stories I have heard about Don Ramon de Nuñez y Pardo are even partly true, senor, then so are you."

Pause. Calculation. The mood had changed now.

"Are you trying to bargain with me?"

"I require certain guarantees, senor."

"Very well, I shall include the Inquisition in my oath, but you will tell me how your companion recognized me that first day we met." The don had never commented on that miracle before. Obviously he had not forgotten it.

"That is part of the same story." Toby smiled without meaning to. Whatever had happened to his intention of heading south? "Tonight, when we camp, I shall tell you everything. I warn you, senor, that it is a very strange tale, but you come into it, and therefore I am eager to share it with you."

To Toby's astonishment, the don laughed and leaned down to offer a hand. This time he did not want it kissed. His grip was almost as brutal as Graham Johnson's.

"For courage, then, Senor Longdirk." He even managed to pronounce the outlandish name reasonably well. "Tonight."

"Tonight, senor. You have my promise."

"Sworn on the honor of a smuggler, mutineer, and deserter? In exchange I offer the sacred word of a *hidalgo* of Castile." Don Ramon straightened in his saddle and glanced back along the line. "The siege train is lagging, *Campeador*. Go and find out who is responsible and have them flogged."

Toby saluted and stepped aside. As soon as Atropos had gone by him, he wiped sweat from his forehead. Had he just put his head in a noose—or his wrists, perhaps?

Nevertheless, Baron Oreste's macabre executions were starting to make more sense. That possible future supported Toby's instinct that the lunatic don could be trusted.

Hamish would burst blood vessels when he heard of this development.

2

It was Toby's intention to drop back to the rear of the column and have his promised chat with Hamish, but every group forced him to tarry and discuss the mercenaries' news. Most of them also interrogated him closely on exactly what had happened to him that morning. He kept repeating the same story until he almost believed it himself, but none of them seemed truly convinced. Perhaps he didn't look like the sort of person who would trip over his own feet in a meadow and knock himself out. He wondered what they did make of the episode, and what they would say if some Dominican friars appeared and began asking questions about him.

Eventually he found himself trudging along beside Hamish, a few paces behind Thunderbolt. There were clouds building ahead, to the north. Was that an omen or just a sign that the weather was going to break at last?

Hamish's mood had improved. He seemed quite cheerful as he said, "I still think you're crazy." He often thought that.

"You believe in my visions now?"

"I think the friar's explanation makes sense, although I see a weakness in it. If he's right, you're heading right back to the torture chamber. For spirits' sake, turn around while you still have a chance! You should get out of here like a racing camel on skates."

"I do get to Barcelona eventually, somehow. The other visions prove that. I'll try not to cut off your—"

"No, they don't!" When Hamish smirked like that he thought he was being clever. He usually was.

"They don't?"

"Listen!" He pondered for a moment, probably breaking his mental processes into small pieces that lesser minds could digest. "If the hob is jerking you back in time, then you shouldn't know anything at all about the future that won't happen, although something very similar may. Or very different. The fragments you do remember are a . . . never mind that for now. The only thing you can count on is the timing of the vision. That's the moment when you come back from the future and start over."

Toby heaved his pack higher—there was no comfortable position for it now. "I suppose you're right. Obviously what seems like hours or days to me lasts no time at all for anyone else. One minute you see me walking along happily whistling 'The Lass up the Glen' and the next I'm lying flat and howling. From then on I'm in reality again."

"It may only be reality temporarily, until it gets wiped out the next time," Hamish said gloomily. "You've seen two visions of Barcelona."

"Possibly two visions of one future."

"No, two separate futures. You came back twice."

Um! Good point. "All right. I got there twice, and I will have to arrive there eventually."

"No! That's what I'm trying to tell you. Those visions came *before* the one of the Inquisition. That means you got to Barcelona twice—at least twice, because we don't know how many times the hob had played this trick without leaving you a vision. Let's ignore that tangle. First you ended up chained in a dungeon and the hob rescued you eventually—we don't know when. The second time you were Oreste's executioner, and it pulled you back again. It was on the *next* try that you met the Inquisition. This is the fourth time, at least, that you've passed this way. You may never get to Barcelona now."

That took some thought. Too much thought. "I don't see why."

"Because," Hamish said in the same dealing-with-an-idiot tone that his father had used on young Toby Strangerson just before he lost his temper, "if the Inquisition episode came first, and then you got to Barcelona and were yanked back again, the Inquisition vision would be wiped out, because you saw that later than the Barcelona vision, even though you think the Inquisition thing happens in Tortosa, which you get to first. Clear?"

Toby groaned. "I'll have to take your word for it."

"Am I ever wrong? You foresaw the demons before Valencia, but we went through Valencia before we met the demons. We can never know what happened the first time in Valencia that didn't happen the second, except that it must have been bad. Nothing happened the second time—the time we remember—but if you had actually died there the second time, you would never have met the demons, vision or not. Yes, you apparently got past Tortosa twice, but the third time you didn't. You may never get to Barcelona!"

"Not on this try, you mean." But how many times did he want to be tortured? Suppose the hob's rescue didn't work the next time? What of that endless loop he had discussed with Brother Bernat?

"That's why we must turn back right away," Hamish concluded triumphantly. "There's no other sane course. When the going gets tough, the smart get lost."

Toby walked on.

"You don't owe these people anything, Longdirk! In fact, you're a danger to them. Brother Bernat can look after himself. Gracia is probably safer with the don than she is with you."

"But there isn't any other road to Barcelona."

"You don't have to go to Barcelona!"

"I want to go to Barcelona."

"Idiot!" Hamish shouted. He had lost his temper now and sounded just like his father. "Turn back and join Johnson's party. We can catch up to them. We could be useful as guides. They'll let us go south with them."

"I got to Barcelona twice in three tries. Or will get."

"Oh, you stupid lunk! You don't know what was different about the third time. I think I do, though. I think it's the don and the others."

"Take me through this one slowly."

"If I go any slower I'll grow roots. Something was different the third time, some choice or chance event. I think the first two times we didn't join the don and his party. We went on by ourselves, with or without Gracia."

"But I knew the don when I cut his head off."

Hamish scowled harder than ever and then conceded that much. "So you'd met him. That doesn't mean you traveled with him. I was really surprised when you agreed to. You never accept a master unless you absolutely have to. Why did you?"

"Hmm. I'm not sure." But Toby was beginning to see where the logic was leading him, and he didn't like it. It was as ominously familiar as the scenery.

"Was it because you'd just seen yourself cutting off his head?"

"Maybe."

Hamish said, "Yes it was! It made you curious. But you couldn't have seen that the first two times, because it hadn't happened yet. So that was what was different the third time—you became Ramon's *campeador*, and when we got to Tortosa someone in this group betrayed you to the Inquisition. Now you're following that same route again."

"You don't know that. You're guessing." But it was a nastily convincing theory—Toby had surprised even himself when he'd kissed the don's hand. Now he'd promised to confide in him. Fortunately Hamish didn't know that yet. "If Oreste has set the Inquisition on me and given them that poster, they don't need informers."

"You and me could slip by on our own. We could swim the river if we had to. Probably that's what we did the first two times."

"We still can, I suppose. Join up again on the other side."

"And how do you explain that to Senora Collel? If

inquisitors start questioning her, she's liable to accuse everyone of every sort of hexing ever imagined. If you've disappeared, she'll suspect the worst and set the dogs on you for certain."

Toby couldn't fault the logic, but it wasn't convincing him. He wasn't going to turn back. He was going on to Barcelona. Just brute stubbornness, maybe—he had said he would, so he would—or a show of courage, like shaking his head at the tormentors to prove to himself that he wasn't broken yet. Perhaps Hamish was right and the hob had driven him crazy, for what sane man would risk the Inquisition?

"I'll ask Brother Bernat's advice," he said. "I suggested to the don that we scout ahead before we advance in force."

"Force?" Hamish sneered. "He'll call for bombardment with cannon followed by a cavalry charge. Then ask your clever friend why your visions are so appropriate."

"Huh?"

The teacher's son was smirking again. "How many days were you in the hands of the Inquisition?"

Toby shrugged and winced at the results. "No way of telling. I have clear memories of an hour or two in the torture chamber, but Bernat thinks they might have worked on me for longer than that." Until they killed him. "And I can remember remembering a few days earlier—being questioned, being shut up in a stinking little cell."

"I could smell it on you when you came back. I still can. So why did the hob pick that particular hour or two? Why didn't you have a vision of the time you were shut up in the cell instead? The same with Barcelona. The hob is very choosy in what it lets you remember, isn't it?"

To that, also, Toby had no answer. Everything Hamish said made sense, even when he went on to call him a brainless mule, a goat butting an oak tree, and several other things less complimentary.

"We'll talk about it tonight," he promised, and set off up the line again.

Miguel and Rafael and the two Elinors were in even worse spirits than usual, taking their spite out on Thunderbolt with unnecessary whacks. Toby tried his faltering Catalan on them to find out why.

Rafael said, "Where is everybody?" He gestured at the valley they were traversing. Sierra del Montsia was steep and wooded, but Sierra Grossa displayed a gentle and obviously fertile slope. Although houses had been burned, the overall damage was much less conspicuous than it had been farther south. "You said the war was all gone from here. Why have the people not returned?" He glowered with deep suspicion.

Toby had been wondering the same and had no answer.

He went on to converse with the women, and the first he came to was Gracia, strolling along by herself but apparently happy in her daydreams. When she noticed him walking at her side, her contentment turned to doubt.

"You are recovered from your misadventure, senor?"

"A little bruised still. A guard with two left feet is not a convincing guardian, I am afraid."

"Don Ramon would never do such a thing."

"No, I'm sure he wouldn't."

She sighed blissfully. "He is wonderful, is he not? So handsome, so strong! My voices are very happy that he has taken me under his protection."

"You have told him about your voices?"

"Oh yes! He says it is a sign that I am especially favored by the spirits, a tribute to the purity of my soul."

The don's motives in saying so cast doubt on the purity of his own soul, Toby decided, and then wondered if he was merely jealous. Of course he was jealous! The Gracias of the world were forever forbidden to him, but he should not grudge her this romantic delusion, however brief it might turn out to be. It was better than brooding about ghosts. Leaving the lady to her fantasies of noble romance, he went on to the horsewomen. High on her perch, Eulalia ignored him conspicuously. Senora Collel regarded him with open suspicion.

"How exactly did Brother Bernat heal you, *Campeador?*"

"He did almost nothing, senora," he said, remembering Hamish's perceptive prediction about her gossiping to the Inquisition. "I was dazed from striking my head, and from that I recovered by myself. I had also sprained my shoulder. He is skilled in massage. That is all. I should not be so clumsy."

"Senor Campbell is not at all clumsy!" Eulalia said loftily.

"You should know, child!" snapped the senora.

Toby found the remark exceedingly humorous and bellowed with laughter. When he saw that the slut was blushing, he realized that he was being jealous again, and spiteful as well. He escaped from the presence of the formidable pair as soon as he decently could. He had never understood women, and according to Brother Bernat he could never hope to.

Next in line were the Brusi packhorses, with Josep leading them while chatting with Father Guillem. The stringy, unassertive youth and massive, forceful cleric were an odd but fortunate pairing for a necessary discussion:

"Father, Josep, may we have a word about provisions? The mercenaries inform us that there is food to be bought in Tortosa."

"As I am excessively tired of horseflesh," the monk declaimed in his rumbling voice, "that is good news. Brother Bernat carries no money, of course, but I shall provide for him and the child."

Josep caught Toby's eye briefly and looked away with a quiet smile. "I expect the prices will be exorbitant. Would an advance upon your fee come in useful, *Campeador?*"

"Very much so, senor. And while I should never dare inquire, I suspect the don may also be running a little low on ready cash."

"That would not surprise me."

As a person, the boy was twice the man his father had been. Whether he could be ruthless enough to run the family business, only time would tell.

"Would you be so generous as to have a word with Squire Francisco on the matter?"

"Ah yes, the squire." Josep smiled gently at the landscape. "I shall certainly speak with the old warrior."

There was no overt hint there, but the choice of

words suggested that Josep had guessed the lady's secret. Toby wondered who else had. Certainly not Senora Collel, or she would have told everyone by now.

So the food problem was solved. The senora and the Thunderbolt contingent both seemed to have adequate supplies left, as did Josep himself. That left the Inquisition. The domineering monk was more practical than Brother Bernat, although much less likeable. Guillem still believed that Toby should have put his fighting skills at the disposal of his rightful feudal overlord, whoever that might be. The two of them had come to a wary truce, though, and the cleric might be a valuable advisor on strategy. A little tactical bending of the truth could be justified:

"Father, the mercenary we met mentioned the possibility of the Inquisition examining travelers crossing the bridge at Tortosa." Johnson had discussed the subject, after all, even if he had not brought it up himself. "Do you suppose that Jaume and myself, being foreigners, may be harassed there?"

Father Guillem uttered a deep rumble like distant thunder. "That is very bad news! The Inquisition is notoriously self-willed and answerable to no one. If the inquisitors so choose, they could hold us up for days or even weeks. They are very skilled at asking the questions that will obtain the sort of answers they want. Before you know it, you find you have accused somebody of something, or even confessed to it yourself. It may be wise for me to pass the word around about this, *Campeador*. You will not mind?"

"I should be very grateful if you would, Father."

"The main thing is to keep your answers short and absolutely truthful." The monk peered around Josep to fix his penetrating stare on Toby. "For example, this morning you fell and twisted your shoulder. Brother Bernat massaged it for you. There is no harm in that. But add some speculation, and it could become something the Inquisition would feel bound to investigate at length. They might devote years to it. You understand what I am saying, my son?"

He was saying that he knew a lot more about Brother Bernat than Toby did. He must know all about Toby and the hob, too, for the friar had been going to tell him the story.

"I understand very well, Father."

"For my part," Josep said cheerfully to no one in particular, "on this journey I have neither heard nor seen anything worth bothering any learned inquisitors with."

"Good!" Father Guillem boomed. "But if they tell you that others have said they did and ask why you are not confirming this testimony, what do you say?"

Josep looked at him in surprise, then at Toby. He frowned, less sure of himself now. "That isn't very nice, is it? I stick to my original statement, of course."

"And if you are told that you yourself have been accused of demonic practices?"

"I deny it vehemently."

"And you stick to your original story?" Father Guillem demanded.

"Like glue," Josep said nervously. "What of Senora de Gomez?"

The monk frowned. "I shall speak with the women at once, if you will excuse me."

He stopped to wait for them. The others walked on.

"What about Gracia?" Toby inquired cautiously.

"She has strange fancies, poor girl. You understand," Josep said apologetically, "that I am much concerned about my father. It is a bad thing when a man must be buried in unconsecrated ground, far from the domain of a spirit to nurture his soul. Father Guillem has been of much consolation to me. But on the night after my father's death—we had not gone far, you will recall—Senora de Gomez came and told me that she had seen his wraith and had taken it into her care! She is going to transport it to Montserrat, she said. Naturally, I pretended to believe her and to be comforted by her words. I fear the loss of her husband and children has addled her wits, Senor Toby."

"I think you are right. It is very sad. There is no harm in her delusions, except when they upset other persons, such as yourself."

"The Inquisition might disagree with you," Josep said softly.

"It might indeed. Let us hope she will be discreet if we meet the inquisitors. But may I ask what solace Father Guillem offered you?"

"Ah." The boy smiled as if to imply he did not really believe what he was about to say. "He admits that when the rebels ravaged the land, their hexers also plundered all the shrines and sanctuaries of the guardians, but he insists that other spirits will eventually replace them, and that they will then gather any wandering wraiths to them, so the souls of the dead will be comforted. He has almost persuaded

me to continue to Montserrat with him, so that the
tutelary may confirm what he says. He is an acolyte
there, after all."

"And a learned one." Very odd! Where were these
new spirits to come from? His hob plight had made
Toby curious about the ways of the immortals, but
this doctrine was new to him. He would not ask
more, for it seemed unkind to scratch at Josep's
emotional scars. He would query Father Guillem or
Brother Bernat some time. "That is good news, for
how else can this land ever recover? Who would
live in a town without a tutelary?"

After a few more minutes, he left Josep and
caught up with Pepita and the friar. The old man
eyed him with a tolerant smile.

"How is your breathing coming, my son?"

"I find I need my lungs too much for talking,
Father, but tonight I will practice very earnestly, I
promise you."

"I still see two of you!" Pepita said mischie-
vously.

"Little demon!" The friar tweaked her ear fondly.
"She will not say such things to any strangers we
may meet."

Could a child resist the Inquisition's cunning
interrogation?

"Father, I know I promised not to ask questions."
Toby presumed that the questions he was not to ask
concerned Brother Bernat himself and his strange
little ward. (Why and how did the child see two of
him? There was a real mystery there.) He hoped
that queries concerning his own problem would be
permitted. "My friend Jaume has asked one that I
cannot answer. May I report his doubts to you, on

the understanding that you are not required to comment?"

The old man guffawed in a way Toby had not heard from him before. "Report it, then."

"He wonders why the visions I see are so apt. Out of what may be many days or weeks, the hob lets me remember each time only a few hours or even minutes. He points out that it seems to choose intervals that are especially significant. Most of them have been very dramatic warnings."

Brother Bernat nodded approvingly. "He is a perceptive young man. It even chooses episodes that are of particular concern to you—like you cutting off Jaume's head, for example—and ignores what should be of importance to itself. You do not recall the baron exorcizing it, or the moment at which it realizes the tormentors are killing you."

"Exactly! Neither of us believes that the hob is smart enough to be so selective."

The friar walked on in silence for several minutes, wielding his staff, staring at the ground. Eventually he said, "My son, I am not quite ready to answer that. You will have to be patient and trust me."

Toby made some polite response, nettled but trying not to show it. The question seemed simple enough; the answer should be. Whatever the old man was hiding from him could only be more bad news. Hamish might suggest that there was no answer and the backward-in-time theory was all moonlight and mirrors. Toby decided he would not agree. The friar was being cagy, but he did have an explanation in mind.

"Tell me about your homeland, my son, for it is one place I have never visited. Your countrymen have a reputation for valor."

"We are a pugnacious people, you mean? This is true, but you must realize that we have the English for neighbors. . . ."

Eventually Toby realized that it was almost noon and they were not far from the end of the valley, which he had identified as a possible ambush site. If the don was going to accept his suggestion that they scout ahead for trouble, then it was time to call a halt and do so. Excusing himself, he strode forward to join Atropos and Petals and their riders. As he came level with the don, he said, "Senor . . ."

But then a horseman rode from behind the trees just ahead, with a file of pikemen trotting behind him. In moments they had blocked the road, and a backward glance confirmed that a second squad was closing the trap in that direction—not so many, but armed with arquebuses. The ambush had come a little sooner than he expected.

3

They were German mercenaries, the *landsknechte* the Spanish called *lansquenets*—mostly big, bearded men who seemed even bigger in their heavily padded doublets and hose. A man unfamiliar with them might laugh at those grandiose multicolored velours and velvets and satins, with piping and padding and pleats, all elaborately slashed to reveal linings of contrasting hues and set off by wide, flat caps with trailing plumes and, in many cases, gold chains around their necks. He would not laugh twice, for *landsknechte* were tough as anvils, the elite shock troops of the Fiend's army.

Their leader was grizzled and leather-faced as if

he had seen many hard campaigns, but he was
bedecked in crimson and chartreuse as splendid as
any of the younger armored butterflies behind him.
While he rode up on a magnificent, skittish black
even bigger than Atropos, he seemed to be looking
more at Toby than at the don. Or was that only
Toby's guilty conscience saying so?

The don halted to let this upstart challenger
approach, while the pallor of his anger made the
copper mustache burn even brighter than usual. Toby
edged in close to his stirrup like a child seeking
comfort from its mother. Neither of them had anticipated the ruthless efficiency of *landsknechte*, who
had cleared the entire valley so that there would be
no residents to warn northbound travelers about the
ambush and yet allowed southbound traffic like
Johnson's party to pass undisturbed—clever!

Toby himself should not have underestimated the
Inquisition. There was not a friar in sight so far, but
he did not doubt that they were close. What a deadly
combination! The baron and the Inquisition were an
obscene partnership in the first place. It was no surprise that Oreste was willing to pay any price to
gain possession of Granny Nan's pretty amethyst,
even the indignity of dealing with the Inquisition
and assigning it some of his best troops; and perhaps no more unexpected was that the Dominicans
would stoop to cooperating with the notorious hexer
if it let them snare a nefarious international monster
such as Tobias Longdirk had been made out to be.
Why, it was a good deal all round! The amethyst
would go to the viceroy in Barcelona, and the
Inquisition would get the infamous Longdirk as
payment for services rendered.

Doña Francisca urged her pony forward a few paces. "Captain, you are in the presence of the illustrious Don Ramon de Nuñez y Pardo, a *hidalgo* of Castile! By what right do you dispute his progress?"

The mercenary ignored her, directing his answer to the don himself, with frequent sidelong glances at Toby. His men were already closing in on other members of the party, disarming them and taking charge of the horses.

"I bear authority from the Holy Office, senor. The venerable friars have asked for your assistance in answering a few questions. You will dismount now and surrender your weapons, which will be returned to you when—"

"It is outrageous! The viceroy himself will hear of this insult to—"

"You refuse to assist the Holy Office, senor? On what grounds?"

Even Don Ramon could not find an answer to that, but he was shaking with fury. To avoid straining his self-control any longer, Toby removed his baldric and surrendered his sword to a fresh-faced boy as tall as himself, a human maypole of mulberry, sulphur yellow, and cerulean blue, but too young to have earned any gold chains yet. Another man confiscated his staff. As the pilgrims were escorted off along a track through the trees, he was somewhat flattered to note that although the don merited two guards and nobody else more than one, he had a personal escort of six. Six *landsknechte* were the equivalent of at least a dozen ordinary soldiers.

•   •   •

The concealed camp was no makeshift affair, for its tents were well staked, the privies decently screened, the livestock paddocks built of stout rails. Prisoners and their baggage were delivered to an empty space at the edge of the clearing, where a dense growth of thorns would provide some shade—and also block off one possible direction of escape, of course. Their mounts were led away to a corral. Half a dozen guards remained, leaning on their pikes and saying nothing.

The ground was overgrazed and fouled by horses, but reasonably comfortable for sitting, certainly better than being shut up in a tent. Three black-robed friars came and made notes of all the names. One departed but two stayed, standing in silence. As they and the *landsknechte* could overhear anything that might be said, no one spoke at all. The waiting had begun.

Toby had not yet seen any faces he recognized, but he felt a stabbing case of *déjà vu*. Everything he looked at echoed inside his head as if he should have been expecting exactly that. It was only a few hours since his last vision, his last starting-over, and events had not had time to diverge very far. He was sliding down the same drain again. He might even be into an endless loop already, fated to repeat the next week or two over and over for ever.

He leaned back on his elbows with Hamish on one side of him and Gracia on the other, all of them silent. He began counting: five tents, three wagons, six mules, four chained wolfhounds, stacks of animal fodder, a field kitchen, two flagpoles—one bearing the green banner of the Inquisition and the other the Fiend's yellow diamond on black—

twenty-five horses, at least a score of soldiers beyond the six he had seen ride out on patrol, at least half a dozen friars, and two or three nondescript civilians. Say thirty or thirty-five in all, which matched the accommodation and the commissary reasonably well. The most incongruous object was a cage of steel bars standing in one of the wagons. It was the sort of cage in which bears were carried to bear baitings, but why should the Inquisition transport wild animals? No bets that that cage was warded against demons.

After a delay of about twenty minutes, when the anxiety level had presumably risen enough, a soldier and one of the mousy clerks came over to the prisoners and led Guillem away to one of the tents.

Obviously the interrogation was going to take all day, but when Toby Longdirk had nothing to do, there was one thing he could always do. He chose a clean spot to lay his head and went to sleep.

He came awake suddenly, and long training made him remain absolutely still, eyes closed, until he had worked out where he was and what had disturbed him . . . the *landsknechte* camp . . . voices. But several times before he had vaguely registered voices as his companions were led one by one to the tents, and each time he had merely drifted back to sleep again.

This time there was something different.

A voice he knew!

Like Hamish turning back the pages of a book, he dug for it: "You now, child. Yes, you. And stop that bawling, or I'll kick your pretty little ass. Come on! Move!"

Toby opened his eyes and raised his head. Pepita was being led away by one ear, and the man taking her was one of the clerks. He was stocky more than heavy-set, with a rolling gait that in itself now seemed familiar. But it was his voice that had set bugles a-blowing, for it was the voice of the young tormentor in the vision, the one who had made threats about *cojones*, the one with the deft line in kidney punches. Oh, yes!

Revenge? Why not? Worth a try . . .

Toby cursed as he realized that he was the last. How long had poor Pepita been sitting there in terror with her only remaining companion snoring his stupid head off instead of offering comfort? He yawned, rubbed his eyes, and sat up.

Sunset had turned the sky bloody and set a cool wind to trailing dust clouds across the camp and flapping tents. The horses whinnied restlessly in their corral; once in a while a hound bayed. Thunder rumbled faintly to the north—now that might turn out interesting! The hob liked to play with thunderstorms. He had been knocked off his feet by lightning bolts more often than he could remember.

Just he and two *landsknechte* remained, one in red, one in green, leaning on their pikes and staring at him with wary interest. They were far enough away to be out of reach, but close enough that any aggressive move against one would get him stunned or hamstrung by the other's pike. Everyone else had gone, and their baggage also.

He located his companions, sitting in a row at the far side of the camp. They were still guarded and apparently forbidden to speak.

So he would be the next. They had saved the best

for last. Moving with deliberation, he rose to his feet.

"Sit!" barked Red.

Toby turned to face the hedge and unfastened his codpiece. "Boys do it standing up." After a moment's satisfaction he pretended to be surprised that they were still watching him. "This interests you?" he inquired of Green. The man flushed, but he did not stop staring.

Making himself respectable again, Toby moved to a dry spot and sat down, wishing he dared do some limbering-up exercises. When he got his chance at that pretend-clerk, if he did get a chance, he would have to move very quickly. Revenge! He would not think of it as a murder, although it would be treated as one. That did not matter, because he was going to die anyway. Undoubtedly he would still be taken to Tortosa and tortured, but one of the actors in that sordid drama would be replaced by an understudy. Yes, yes! And there was always the chance that he might win a quick and easy death in the resulting fracas.

Time passed. Fires in the kitchen area streamed banners of flame in the wind. Thunder again, closer. It felt like rain. Red and Green moved a little nearer to the prisoner as the light faded, never taking their eyes off him.

Even in a fair fight he wouldn't bet very much on himself against either of these two, for they were both almost as big as he was and the padding in those foppish-seeming garments was actually linen armor that would block any but the surest sword strokes. Behind him was a dense wood, with thick, thorny undergrowth, so the only way he could make

a run for it would be straight through the camp.
They had horses, they had dogs. Escape was impossible, submission unthinkable, so only revenge
remained, right?

Thunder rumbled again. The wind had died away,
but the air was suddenly cold. For the first time in
months Toby wished he had a warm cloak—or was
his shivering triggered by fear? Fear might rouse the
hob, Brother Bernat had said. So might thunder.
Rousing the hob might be exactly what was needed
under the circumstances. Even if it became too
engrossed in the storm to pay much heed to him or
recognize that he was in danger, a hob rampage
would be a welcome distraction.

The troop of six *landsknechte* that he had seen
depart earlier came riding into the camp. That must
be all of them, and the day's patrolling was over.

A soldier led Pepita out of the tent and took her
over to the others.

More waiting.

Then, at last, the clerk emerged with another
landsknecht and came strutting across to the last
prisoner.

"Stand up!" said the guard in guttural Castilian.
"Bring your belongings and come with us."

Toby rose reluctantly. The clerk had not come
within reach. He was standing a pace back from the
landsknecht and coldbloodedly assessing Toby—
perhaps measuring him for the rack or judging his
capacity for the water torture. Smiling!

"You're not going to hurt me, are you?"

Eagerness gleamed in the tormentor's eye. "Why
do you ask, senor? Have you committed some crime
worthy of punishment?"

Not yet, sonny, not yet! But I will.

Lightning flashed.

Toby strode over to the inquisitors' tent with his bundle on his shoulder and the guards at his heels. As he reached it, thunder rolled overhead.

4

Déjà vu! The tent was about three spans square, with a familiar smell, stale and sour. Lanterns hung on the ridgepole cast a pale light on a floor of elaborately patterned carpets, whose beauty stood in strange contrast to the starkness of the only furniture, a trestle table facing the door. It held two plain wooden candlesticks and the same green crucifix he had seen in his vision. The soldier went to stand at one end, and the stocky tormentor to the other.

Three Dominicans sat on stools behind the table. He remembered none of them from the torture chamber vision, but they were all vaguely familiar, memories of memory. The one in the center was a plump-faced, slug-shaped man in his forties who looked weary, as well he might after so many hours of interrogation. To his right sat an older man, gaunt and ascetic; he would go till he dropped. The one to his left was younger with freckles and a red tonsure. Those two each had a thick book and an inkwell with a quill standing in it, so they must take turns at recording the proceedings, and it was the younger man's turn now, because his book was open. (Was that, just possibly, a change from last time?) Another *landsknecht* came in and stood behind Toby, meaning he now had two armed and capable fighters to evade, but he still thought he would be able to kill the tormentor when the moment came. He must not show any interest in him until then.

Silence. A flash gleamed through the striped linen of the walls. More silence. Thunder, not so near as last time. Horses whinnied in fright and the hounds began baying, until men shouted at them. More silence. The friars stared steadily at the prisoner, but he recognized the intention to disconcert him and ignored it. He knew many ways to slay a man with his bare hands, especially one he outweighed by half. At the first distraction he would kill the little bugger and hope one of the *landsknechte* would panic and shove a sword through his heart.

Still more silence.

He returned the inquisitor's gaze as calmly as he could and thought he was doing quite well at that, although one of the lanterns was uncomfortably close, illuminating his face clearly but also dazzling him. The crucifix was worrisome, because any of those colored-glass jewels on it might harbor a demon, and Brother Bernat had said that the Inquisition must use gramarye of some sort. So it was possible that the hob was helpless already, or could be quickly curbed if it started anything.

Flash!

Rumble.

"Does the witness understand Castilian?" asked the slug. The redhead reached for his quill to record the question.

"I know some Castilian."

"Does the witness agree to be questioned in Castilian?"

"I do."

"The witness will state his name and birth date and place of birth."

"Tobias Longdirk." That was not the name on the poster, but they weren't going to mention the poster. "The seventh day of September, 1501. I was born at Tyndrum, in Scotland."

The recorder did not ask to have the names repeated; he must have heard them several times already.

"The witness is traveling with certain other persons. The witness must list their names."

And so on. Where had the witness come from? Where was the witness going? Why? "I am a retainer of Don Ramon." Was the witness a deserter? This was how they had managed to waste a whole afternoon and half an evening. More trivia—what was the witness going to do in Barcelona? "Senor Brusi has offered me employment if the don does not wish to extend my service." Thunder, much closer, so close that he had to ask for a question to be repeated. *Hob! Come on, hob! Do something!* What languages did the witness know? (*Why should that matter?*) Why had the witness come to Spain? Could the witness read and write? Among the feints, a sudden punch: "What gramarye has the witness seen on his journey?"

"None."

"The witness states categorically that he has never observed evidence of hexing or demonic possession?"

"He does. I mean, I do."

"Never? Anywhere?"

"None whatsoever."

"Other members of the party have reported seeing

flagrant displays of gramarye within the last few days. The witness may wish to amend his statement."

"I am telling the truth."

"He was present during these displays."

"If I was, I saw nothing unnatural. Tell me when—"

"Has the witness ever observed evidence of necromancy?"

Toby asked to have that word explained. Conjuring the dead.

"No."

"Or discussed it?"

"No. I never heard of it until just now."

The pasty-faced inquisitor reached down and brought up Gracia's bottle to set it on the table. Toby's heart went to a fast trot.

Fortunately a deafening crack of thunder interposed to explain any reaction he showed. That bottle had been inside Hamish's pack! Did they search everyone's baggage or had Hamish admitted to having books, which the inquisitors would certainly demand to see? How many lies had Hamish told about Gracia? What had she said about her voices, the wraiths she claimed to see? What had he said about Toby, hobs, demons, amethysts, Wanted posters . . . ? Lying to the Inquisition was a major crime, evidence of possession or gramarye. And what would happen to Gracia herself? The Inquisition tortured women, too. Not Gracia! Had Toby brought disaster to all of them? Fury burned like acid in his throat.

"Has the witness ever seen the bottle he is now being shown?"

"Yes. It belongs to Senora de Gomez. Or she has one just like—"

"What else does the witness know about the bottle?"

Shrug. "It seems to have great sentimental value for her. She asked Senor Campbell to carry it. As far as I know, there's nothing in it."

"How does the witness know that?"

Demons! "He . . . I don't. I just assumed it was empty. Perhaps I asked her, I don't recall. I'm sure she can tell you if—"

Father Guillem had warned him to keep his answers short.

"Does the witness possess any jewelry?"

Toby laughed. "Me? I'm as poor as beggars' lice."

"The witness must answer the question."

"The answer is no."

"Does the witness wear a locket?"

"No."

Thunder! Very close.

Come on hob! Do something. Distract them so I can kill that tormentor and make a break for it!

The hob did nothing.

"Other persons have stated that the witness wears a leather locket around his neck."

Pepita? "The other persons are mistaken."

"The witness will remove his doublet and shirt."

An order to strip was the traditional preliminary to torture. He did not expect that here—unless this time was to be different from the vision, which it might be—but they could not suspect how much he already knew of their procedures. His heartbeat surged again as he realized that this might provide the distraction he needed, but he pretended to be alarmed. "Why? I've told you you're mistaken."

"The witness will obey or he will be forced to obey."

He glanced around to locate the two *landsknechte*, one at the end of the table to his right, the other at his back, guarding the door. They both met his gaze with cheerful smiles, as if to say a little exercise would be a welcome relief from boredom. He shrugged and removed his jerkin, dropping it at his feet. He unlaced his doublet, and did the same with that, being glad that his Onda hose were so loose that he had taken to wearing a rope tied around his waist. Finally he stripped off his shirt and balled it up tightly in both hands.

No locket.

The inquisitor's eyes narrowed. He peered around Toby to address the *landsknecht* by the tent flap. "Go and bring the two men who were set to guard this witness." He was guessing that Toby had hidden the locket somewhere.

The flap flapped. So now there was only one of the Germans present, and there would be four very shortly. Lightning dimmed the lanterns for a moment. Thunder rocked the world. *Come on hob! Wake up!*

"Search the witness," said the inquisitor.

The tormentor strode forward with a contemptuous sneer and snatched the shirt from Toby's hands. He pawed at it and found nothing, of course. Toby drew a deep breath, readying his move.

Flash! Very bright, very near.

The clerk bent over to pick up the doublet. Toby grabbed his head in both hands and wrenched it around. Bones in the neck snapped with an audible *crack. Cojones to you, friend!* He swung around to the *landsknecht*, who had already drawn his sword but did not manage to wield it before he received a fast-moving foot exactly where it would do the most good. The padding absorbed some of the impact, but even a cannonade of thunder did not drown out his scream. He crashed back into one of the poles, the wall buckled, the roof sagged.

The slug-shaped inquisitor started to rise, grabbing for the crucifix. Toby snatched it away from him, caught up the bottle in his other hand, and overturned the table with his knee, tipping it onto the friars. He spun around and dived out through the flap.

The night was pitch black. He had not expected that. Two seconds took four hours to pass, then his eyes adjusted and the streaming fires in the kitchen enclosure emerged from darkness to give him some bearings. The world flashed white and roared as lightning struck a tree not fifty paces away. In that split-second brilliance he saw three *landsknechte* coming straight for him, two with pikes and the third with drawn sword. He turned to run, and there was another, about six feet in front of him, with sword drawn.

Hob!

The world went white again almost at his heels. The explosion took his head off, smashed every bone in his body, and hurled him into the tent. He broke another pole and brought down the whole structure, which cushioned his fall a little, but for a few moments he was too stunned to move. The air was filled with strange odors, his head rang like an iron bell, and he could see nothing except puzzling green afterimages, which he eventually identified as the thunderbolt reflected on the fourth *landsknecht's* sword and gold chains.

The night was illuminated by blazing trees. *Boom!*—another fiery candle came to life. The leather tent billowed and surged beneath him as the friars tried to extricate themselves from the wreckage. Through the clamor in his own head he could make out their wails and screams, horses shrilling, dogs howling, men yelling. . . . He was holding Gracia's bottle, but he had lost the crucifix. He would die here if he didn't move. He sat up.

The three *landsknechte* had been charred. One of them was still burning. In the other direction, the fourth was starting to show signs of life, but he had his hands to his eyes—he had been facing the thunderbolt. Toby lurched to his feet. The German tried to, but he wasn't quick enough. Toby swung a foot and kicked his chin, hurling him prone again.

Then he stamped on the man's throat. There were no rules in this fight.

Boom! The hob lit another candle in the woods.

Snatching up the *landsknecht's* sword, he stumbled in the direction of the pilgrims. Before he took ten steps their guards identified him as a problem and four pikes came charging toward him. He pointed the sword at them and covered his eyes with his left hand. *Hob! There!* The flash shone red through his flesh, and thunder struck him like a flying anvil. There were real things flying, too, nasty hot wet things. The wind stank of roast meat. He was wielding the lightnings.

Boom! The hob was in full rampage now, methodically blasting the surrounding forest. He ran to join the pilgrims with his ears singing.

Count up the score . . . one and three and one and four . . . nine, meaning about eighteen *landsknechte* left to go. Still not good odds. *Boom!*

The pilgrims were all on their feet and shouting, although he could not make out their words. They must be as deaf and dazzled as he was, but some had run to save the baggage, which lay close to one of the hob's giant candles. Here came another *landsknecht*.

Toby parried a downward cut and instantly the damned blade came at him from the left—demons, this one was fast! He jumped back, parrying frantically, and the tall German came right after him, blade flashing like a dragonfly. Then Hamish kicked him in the kidneys, which distracted him enough to let Toby's sword into his right eye. Ten down. Sixteen or seventeen to go. Another *Boom!* from the hob.

Gracia was standing with her mouth open in an endless scream. Toby thrust the bottle at her. "This is yours. Take care of it." She probably did not hear, but she clutched it to her. "Hamish! Get the horses. Get lots of horses." He could barely hear his own voice.

No. The horses were churning in frenzy. So far they had not broken out, but they could never be saddled up in that condition, so flight was out of the question. The *landsknechte* would give no quarter now, no matter what the Inquisition told them. It was a fight to the death.

Two more of them coming. If they were as good as the last one, he was finished. Then a maze of multiple shadows rushed in from the side and became Don Ramon, who tossed a sword at

Hamish's feet and waded into both the advancing *landsknechte* with his broadsword whistling. While he had them distracted, Toby circled around and stabbed one in the back. The don showed no signs of being offended at this breach of chivalry, for he yelled in delight.

By then Hamish had taken on the second, driving his opponent like a herd of sheep—although the German was a much larger, heavier man—and all the time screaming curses in Gaelic. His Campbell blood was up. The brief struggle was no courtly ballet of rapiers but a two-handed slugfest, and the more experienced *landsknecht* was probably just summing up his man and biding his time. Unfortunately he backed into a thorn bush, and Hamish's blade went right through him. The victor barely had time to pull it free before Eulalia hurled herself upon him. If the good folk back in Tyndrum could see the lad now . . .

Fourteen to go.

Everyone was shouting, but Toby could not make out a word over the singing in his ears and all the other noises of horses and dogs and burning trees.

This was taking too long. If the *landsknechte* had time to organize, they would wipe the table clear in minutes. Six of them had lined up near the kitchen fires and were going through the cumbersome drill of loading their arquebuses. Toby pointed again. *Hob!* This time there was no lightning stroke but a wild explosion as the powder horns blew up. Shattered corpses flew apart in a black mist and billows of white smoke rushed away on the wind.

The collapsed tent was on fire. Friars in roiling black gowns were trying to extricate the occupants, aided by a couple of *landsknechte*. The dangerous crucifix was in there somewhere. Why should the Dominicans be spared? They were murdering, merciless swine. *Hob! There! Kill!*

Boom! The blast of another bolt of ligtning hurled bodies aside and sent flames leaping to the next tent.

A solitary *landsknecht* ran across Toby's field of vision. He pointed his sword and blasted the man out of existence. It was as easy as stamping bugs.

The captain had rallied the last of his men into a squad, and the rest of the friars and civilians had gone to them for protection. The first heavy spots of rain splattered on Toby's bare shoulders. He started forward, and hands grabbed his arm. It was Brother Bernat, wailing or shouting inaudibly, looking aghast.

"Can't hear you!" Toby bellowed.

The old man pulled closer, straining up to reach his ear. "Tobias! You must stop! What are you doing?"

"Administering justice, Brother. Let me go."

His words might not be audible, for the Franciscan's haggard face remained distraught. "No, no! Don't you see what's happening to you?"

"I know what was going to happen to me. It still may, but this time I'm going to earn it. Out of my way!"

Toby pushed the old man aside roughly. With Hamish and the don at his heels, he started to run toward the assembled *landsknechte*. Then he realized that they had turned themselves into one big target, friars and all. Fools! He stopped and pointed his deadly lightning-bringing sword. *Hob!*

Nothing happened. Demons! There were still
enough armed mercenaries there to chop the pilgrim
band into mincemeat, and they would show no
mercy. Besides, there must be no witnesses. Only
one side could have survivors now. He felt a stab of
cold panic. Rain pattered faster on his skin.

"Hob!" he screamed. "Blast them! Them! There!"

Flash! Boom! Bodies flying.

That should be it, everyone accounted for. The
skies fell in a flood of icy water, beating on him like
freezing whips. Roaring flames sputtered, dwin-
dled, and died; blackness swallowed the world. The
hob swatted some more trees but failed to start fires.

"Don Ramon, Hamish! Get them under cover!
That tent!" He must have made himself understood,
because the other two ran to collect the pilgrims.

Toby walked all around the camp, hunting for survivors. One of the dogs had slipped its collar and disappeared. The others were howling madly, fighting
their chains, and he killed them. He found two men
badly burned but still showing signs of life, so he
slaughtered them also, and later he made certain of a
few who showed no visible injuries. By that time the
ground was a morass of puddles and mud, and the
storm was moving on. He owned the camp. Its original owners were all dead, and good riddance. The
only thing he could not locate was the sword he had
brought with him. He found several so similar he
could not tell if one of them was his demon sword.
Well, whoever had need of a demon sword?

As the last drops of the rain spattered on his bare
chest and shoulders, he shivered in the night and felt
the glory of omnipotence turn sour. The taste of
revenge was never as appealing as its smell.

He went to the heap of baggage and found the don's tattered old saddle. He retrieved the locket he had slipped in through some torn stitching when he first saw the *landsknechte*.

Now he had time to ponder Brother Bernat's question: What had he become?

5

A tent designed to sleep four men along each side was a tight fit for fifteen people. No fancy carpets here—the pilgrims sat or sprawled on a litter of straw bedding in the uncertain glimmer of a single lantern, with the odor of wet people almost masking a basic reek of barracks. Toby left his sword outside and went down on his knees as soon as he entered, so he would not tower over them all. They must be terrified of him, a half naked giant, soaked, streaked with watery blood, possessed by a demon, a monster who had called down thunderbolts to destroy a troop of the finest fighters in Europe.

"I mean you no harm, none of you!"

Silence. He located Hamish in the corner to his right, but even Hamish's expression was grim, surprisingly so, considering he had an arm around Eulalia. Was he wondering whether this was the Toby he knew?

"Here, catch!" Hamish wadded up a shirt and tossed it over with his free hand.

"Thanks." Toby put it on. It would not close around his chest, but it helped. He had slept half the day, and yet he felt as if his limbs were made of stone, utterly exhausted.

Brother Bernat and Father Guillem sat together in the center of the tent, holding a sleeping Pepita, and both were frowning at the newcomer as if he had betrayed them, which in a sense he had. In a far corner the don was cuddling Gracia and either whispering secrets in her ear or chewing it. Gracia sat like a white-faced doll in his arms, immobilized by shock and apparently unaware of him. Doña Francisca looked so much like a very frightened old lady that it seemed incredible anyone could still be taken in by her masquerade.

Speaking to all of them, Toby said, "You have known me for several days. You know I mean you well."

"Did you leave any survivors?" Father Guillem demanded harshly.

"No. We are out of danger for the time being." That might be true of him, but they would feel otherwise. "I am not possessed by a demon, however it may seem to you. There is a spirit that protects me. It rarely interferes, but tonight it came to my defense. I can't control it or call it at will." Was that still the case? He had certainly been directing it tonight, pointing out targets. "It won't harm any of you if you are still my friends, as I hope you are." And he could never guarantee that, either.

"Friends?" the acolyte boomed in sonorous sarcasm. "You murder thirty men and expect us to be your friends?"

"He saved you all when Senor Brusi was killed!" Hamish snapped.

"We should have seen then that his fighting powers were more than human."

"As far as I know, they were merely human that

day," Toby protested. "Then I was fighting to protect your horses. These mercenaries were my own enemies. All I wanted was to proceed in peace along the highway, yet they would have locked me in that cage and taken me away to be tortured to death. Have I no right to defend myself?"

"Not if you are guilty and condemned by law."

"I do not consider myself guilty." What sort of defense was that?

"Did they use violence on you?"

"They were going to, as you well know, Father." But it had been Toby himself who began the violence, avenging a crime that might never be committed.

He sighed and wiped his face with a sleeve. In spite of his sleep earlier he felt deathly weary, and his shoulders still ached from the *strappado*. "The moon is rising. I will leave as soon as I can. You may come with me or remain here, as you please."

Their decision would make a lot of difference. There must be many more *landsknechte* where these had come from, and they would be after him like hounds when they heard the news. So would the Inquisition. On the other hand, this checkpoint had been a well-kept secret. Tortosa might not learn of the massacre for several days, so if he could pass by the town before dawn, he should have a sizable head start on any pursuit—provided everyone else came with him. If even one of the pilgrims remained behind to tattle, he would be in very serious trouble. He glanced over at the don, hoping for support, but the don was ignoring the proceedings altogether.

"If you do come with me, then you will have to ride. I checked out the commissary. There is ample food there. I fully intend to steal provisions and horses, and probably also a few of those gold chains the Germans wear."

That possibility produced a ripple of interest among Rafael, Miguel, and the two Elinors.

"You are trying to bribe us!" Father Guillem sneered. "You want to make us your accomplices."

He was absolutely right, and he held the moral high ground, but Toby wanted to strangle him. The moral high ground might become a killing field for all of them. Could he make the monk see that?

"In the eyes of the Inquisition, you are my accomplices already. Nothing I can do or say will change that. Furthermore, you are all in considerable danger—not from me, from others. You have two choices. You can come with me, or you can go to Tortosa and report to the authorities. If you do that, though, you must beware of revenge from other *landsknechte*. They will not be easily convinced that I accomplished the slaughter singlehandedly. At the least, the Inquisition will throw you in jail as witnesses, and it may be years before you are released."

Senora Collel wailed and clasped both hands to her mouth. The Rafael-Miguel foursome muttered nervously among themselves. The don was still paying no attention, and neither was Gracia. Josep's face was unreadable.

"Father Guillem, am I right about that?" Toby asked.

The monk glared at him. "We shall certainly be interrogated, and I admit I fear those German barbarians. Where are you planning to go?"

"If you come with me, then we can go on to Montserrat. If you do not choose to come, then naturally I cannot reveal my intentions. Once we reach the monastery and Barcelona and split up, there will be no evidence against any of you. The records were burned in the tent. No one else knows what happened. No one knows who was here."

He looked around the group. It was hopeless. Why should they trust him? He should leave now, either with Hamish or alone. Would even Hamish trust him now?

"Suppose all but one of us decide to accompany you," asked Father Guillem with a return to his earlier sneer. "What will you do to that one?"

"Nothing. Jaume and I will go alone. It must be all of you or none."

That statement brought a slow chill as each one worked it out—they must either trust him by accepting his offer or trust him not to dispose of those who refused it. In the ensuing silence, all eyes turned to Don Ramon, but he was still intent on Gracia.

"The Fiend's army never attacked Montserrat," Father Guillem said. "That was a condition when Barcelona opened its gates to him. If you go there, the *landsknechte* may follow you in. You are a marked man."

Toby had been a marked man for years, but the monk had made a good point. Furthermore, the hob had a virulent dislike of tutelaries. "Agreed. I have no wish to cause more trouble. I shall deliver you to the safe area and leave you there."

"I hate those German brutes!" shouted Senora Collel. "It was they who slaughtered the people, raping and burning. They deserved what happened to them. And I have no sympathy for the Inquisition either! Some evil person brought false charges against my second husband, and he died in their cells. I was not allowed to see his body, but I know they tortured him. They admitted he must have been innocent because he died! I think Senor Longdirk did us all a favor tonight. I trust him."

Surprised, Toby nodded his thanks to her. He wondered who had started the tales about her husband and reproached himself for being unfair.

"Can we keep the horses?" one of the Elinors asked slyly.

"I don't see why not. Say you found them. There are stray horses all over the place." Toby could see the lines forming now, friends and non-friends. "Josep?"

Josep glared at him angrily. "I have no wish to be racked."

"You may get racked anyway," Toby snarled. "I thought you were my friend." He was being unfair. Young Brusi was a rich man who could be tracked down by his name alone, whereas the four peasants would vanish into anonymity in the countryside somewhere.

The tent was stuffy and he was exhausted. He ought to walk out, saddle a horse, and ride away before he fell asleep right here on his knees. He owed these people nothing.

"It is our moral duty to report this man for murder and the use of demons," Father Guillem proclaimed. "If we accompany him, then we become accomplices in his crimes."

Brother Bernat stirred and said something. Father Guillem objected in an urgent whisper. The old man shook his head, insisting. Reluctantly, the monk scooped up the sleeping Pepita and took her onto his own lap. She did not awaken. Brother Bernat clambered painfully to his knees. He looked twenty years older than usual, bent and withered.

"Come here, Tobias."

Toby did not stand. He scrabbled forward until he knelt before the friar. "Brother?"

"Will you trust me, Tobias?" Bernat's dark eyes were somber and yet somehow menacing.

"Trust you? To do what?"

"To look into your soul."

Toby felt a chill of alarm. He did not know the source or the limits of the friar's strange powers, and who would dare let his soul be examined? Everyone has secrets.

"Is this necessary?"

"It is vital for all of us, especially for you. You trusted me to heal your body, my son."

"You mean you can heal my soul now?"

"No. But I may be able to tell how badly it has been damaged."

"Then look wherever you can."

"Relax. Do not resist." The friar clasped Toby's shoulders in his bony hands. For a moment he just stared into his eyes. Then, inexplicably, he was staring *inside* him.

Toby could feel that needle-sharp gaze peering, probing, slipping gently past his defenses, bypassing all the walls he had raised against a pitiless world, prying into corners he had walled off even from himself, uncovering secrets he had tried to forget and things he did not want to know. Physically he seemed to be frozen, unable to move a finger in that frail grasp, and yet he felt himself balling mental fists, preparing to smash the intruder and drive him out before he could steal away his soul. He fought against the impulse. He forced himself to retreat, to submit as layer after layer was stripped away. His body shook with effort, his face streamed with sweat. He was being violated. He could not tell what odious truths were being uncovered, only that the innermost cavities of his being were being opened and inspected, that he was naked, flayed, dissected. Then, finally, in the deepest, darkest cellar of his mind, something else stirred. Something unknown roused and began opening a last door, preparing to emerge and meet the intruder. He had no idea what shame it might be, but he sensed the friar's alarm, his efforts to repel this horror and keep it caged. Bernat's eyes burned with effort, but it was not enough. Shuddering, Toby threw his own will and weight into the struggle, and the two of them forced the door closed together.

Brother Bernat sighed and released him.

Toby sank back on his heels, shaking and only now aware that he was sobbing, tears cascading down his cheeks. He wondered what everyone else must think of him.

The old friar sat down again, steadied by a hand from Father Guillem. He rubbed his eyes as if they ached.

"Well?" barked the monk.

"He is not guiltless. Yet the choice he had to make tonight was a very hard one. It may be that he chose the lesser way, but I cannot judge him, because I have never had to make that same choice. He means what he has been telling us." The friar looked at Pepita, but she was still sleeping soundly and he did not try to take her back.

"What did you see?" Toby cried.

The old man regarded him sadly. "I saw that you are still who you think you are, my son, but only just. You came close tonight to becoming something else, and if you ever travel that road again, you must not expect to return."

The tent was very quiet.

Toby pulled himself together as well as he could, although his skin crawled. He could see Hamish nodding as if the old friar had merely confirmed his own suspicions.

Guillem muttered something about "taking a crazy risk," and Bernat smiled wearily.

Now where did they stand? This had gone on too long.

"So you will come with me, Brother?"

The friar nodded. "That seems to offer the path of least violence. I will not willingly provoke a blood feud, and I dread what may happen if the Germans send more men after you."

"Father Guillem?"

The monk scowled. "It violates everything I believe in to condone such a crime and let the perpetrator escape, but the alternative may bring more trouble, and to innocent people, too. Yes, if everyone agrees to accompany you, then I will not refuse."

"I will not be the only holdout either," Josep said quietly.

Toby gave him a grateful smile. But what of the don? He was the hired guard, he had even helped fight the *landsknechte*, so why was he remaining aloof from the debate? His attentions to Senora de Gomez were becoming perilously close to indecent.

These people depended on their *hidalgo* for leadership. If he and Brother Bernat both supported Toby, surely the rest would follow.

"Senor? Don Ramon?"

"Ah!" The don looked up and beamed. "Finished your pep talk to the troops, *Campeador?* Good." He released his companion and sprang to his feet to address the company. "At ease. Tonight we won a signal victory against greatly superior forces, and *Campeador* Longdirk in particular distinguished himself and deserves all our thanks. We are indeed fortunate to have an officer of his talents and courage fighting alongside us. This was a noble engagement in which we inflicted heavy losses at no cost whatsoever to ourselves and took significant quantities of booty, which will be distributed in the customary fashion. Alas, the enemy still outnumbers us. We shall outflank him by going upriver to Lerida and circling around to strike a decisive blow from the north. Now that our supply and transportation difficulties have been overcome, I anticipate that our progress will be greatly expedited. I rely on your continued enthusiastic and brave service in the future as I have in the past. That's all. Carry on, *Campeador.*"

Apparently it was to be unanimous. Bewildered, Toby looked to Hamish, who shook his head disbelievingly and then managed to smile.

SIX

ALUMBRADISMO

1

Over the gray scrub uplands of La Mancha, stretched out to the bottom of the somber, clouded sky, trotted a line of twenty horses, fourteen of them with riders, the rest bearing baggage.

Ah, they were a fine sight! Blisters and aches were healing, even Josep rarely fell off these days, and the pilgrims believed in themselves. Watching them come in the low light of evening, Toby could relish a niggle of pride that he knew would appall Father Guillem. They were traveling in far better style now than they had when they first met Toby Longdirk, and he had a shameful inclination to give himself some credit for that, even if he would never mention it to anyone else. Admittedly, his success had been bought at the price of some three dozen lives, but if kings and generals could be praised for victories and booty, then why shouldn't he? The *landsknechte* had gained their wealth by looting, so he had merely returned some of it to Spanish ownership. Father Guillem did not approve of such views, but most of the others did.

They had passed Tortosa in the night and carried
on up the valley of the Ebro. The interior had not
suffered from the war as badly as the coast had.
Already houses were being rebuilt and there was
traffic on the byways, the life of the land thrusting
out shoots as men plowed and pruned and herded.
Having ample provisions, the pilgrims had ridden
by the scattered settlements without stopping, and
in four days no one had contested their passage,
no pursuers had come howling for their blood.
Now they could truly believe they had escaped.
Even if the massacre had been discovered, the
delay should block any efforts by the governor,
the *landsknechte*, or even the Inquisition to learn
who had been seen traveling when, to where, on
what road. The future could become interesting
again. Horses made a huge difference, eating up
the leagues.

The weather had broken, bringing cold and
squalls. He pulled his cloak tighter around him as he
waited for the others to arrive, cursing a bitter wind
he would have welcomed with rapture only days
ago, grateful for the clothes he had looted. His doublet was indigo with scarlet lining showing through
the slashes, and his hose were a shocking mismatch
in yellow and blue. The grandiose *landsknechte*
costume was distinctive, but both Josep and Doña
Francisca assured him that stylish Spanish gentle-
men had begun to adopt the mercenaries' custom of
a heavily padded doublet worn without a jerkin. So
as long as he kept the cloak around him and did not
flaunt a plumed cap, he could pass as a civilian with
more money than taste.

He had ridden ahead on Smeòrach to locate a

campsite. Smeòrach was a fine young gelding, strong and eager, named after the thrush because of his speckled coat. Even after a long day of carrying his oversized new owner, he fretted at being made to stand. He wanted to stretch out and run.

The don arrived, still wearing his motley armor and carrying his lance but mounted now on the *landsknechte* captain's showy black stallion, which he had chosen because it had a vicious temper and thus presented an interesting challenge. Doña Francisca was following some ways behind on her piebald mare, both Petals and Atropos having been released to fend for themselves in honorable retirement.

Smeòrach whinnied a welcome. Toby saluted and gestured apologetically at the dusty gully behind him, which offered nothing but a puddle of rainwater and some shelter from the eternal wind.

"This is the best I can find, senor."

The don regarded the prospect without enthusiasm. "It must suffice. We may do better tomorrow, when we reach the valley of the Segre. We shall follow it to Lerida, but once we turn east, the country is more settled." Although his mother confirmed that he had never visited these parts before, he had not been wrong yet.

"Senor, I am worried about the friar. He has never ridden in his life before, and he is very old. He cannot endure this pace for long."

"You'll think of something, *Campeador*." The don had no patience for unwelcome realities. "By the way, just before that honorable exchange with the foreigners, you promised to tell me your story. You have not yet done so." He frowned as if this were rank mutiny, but in fact Toby had just not had a free minute. He had not even contrived any private chats with Brother Bernat, who still had much to tell him.

"I shall be honored to do so this evening, senor, to both you and Senor Francisco, if he wishes to attend. After supper, if that will be convenient?"

"Yes. And why don't you and Sergeant Jaume dine with us in our pavilion, hmm?"

Toby thanked him solemnly, although the entire company now ate together around a communal fire. Nor did the expedition have even one tent, although that had begun to seem like a foolish oversight.

The don went off to choose a sleeping place. His mother rode by with a tired smile, followed by the other women, all chattering like starlings at sunset. Gracia and Senora Collel had insisted on retaining their previous mounts and the awkward *silla* sidesaddles. Eulalia and the two Elinors managed surprisingly well, although none of them would ever be described as a stylish rider. Pepita thought riding was tremendous fun. Toby had expected her to double up with one of the adults, but she had selected a high-stepping gelding, calmed him with a touch, and ridden him from then on as if she had been weaned on mares' milk.

Rafael and Miguel actually smiled at Toby as they passed—oh, what a change that was! Of course they were rich men now, by their standards. They and their wives had scavenged through the *landsknechte* camp like jackdaws, gathering all the valuables. As far as Toby knew, no one else had collected as much as one gold link.

Hamish was next, leading the pack train and garbed even more garishly than Toby was, in purple and gold and lime green. He bowed graciously in the saddle as he went by.

Finally came Josep and Father Guillem, the worst riders. The monk had fallen off several times and Josep been thrown twice, although neither had broken any bones. They were leading Brother Bernat's horse.

"What happened? Where is he?"

"He is coming," Father Guillem said with the disapproving scowl he wore anywhere close to Toby. "He prefers to walk."

Toby gave Smeòrach a kick and had his head jerked back as the gelding took off like a crossbow quarrel. This, in his horse's opinion, was more like it! After about a mile, just when he was working up a good sweat, the irritating man on his back annoyed him thoroughly by reining him in again.

The gray-robed friar was trudging along at his usual pace, apparently not in distress. Toby dismounted and fell into step on the windward side, leading Smeòrach. "Are you all right, Brother?"

Obviously Bernat was not all right. He could walk any of them off their feet, but he had looked drawn and exhausted ever since they first put him on a horse. At the moment he had his hood up, so his face was not clearly visible; yet he seemed better than he had at noon, and he greeted the question with a dry, tolerant chuckle.

"There is nothing wrong with me that you can help, not unless you can somehow lift sixty years or so from me, and I doubt even your hob can manage that."

"We should not have come so far today. I am sorry."

The old man shook his head. "You have good reason, many good reasons. I will not hold you up. I am better with my feet on Mother Earth, that is all. You must not worry about me."

"But—" Toby realized he was in danger of clucking and remembered how he hated to be mothered by Hamish. "I will worry, but I will try not to nag." He busied himself loosening Smeòrach's girths as they walked.

"There is one thing you may do for me, Tobias. Keep your eyes open for some pleasant little town that has not been ravaged too badly. I have a need to find a shrine in the near future, a small sanctuary."

Toby tried to catch a better view of the old man's face. How urgent was this need? "The don says we'll reach Lerida tomorrow."

"No, I want a smaller place."

"I am sure the Lerida tutelary will be skilled at healing, Brother."

"Healing is not what I need," Brother Bernat explained patiently.

"Oh! Then why . . . ? But most of the lesser shrines are empty. The spirits were raped away by the Fiend's hexers."

"Yes, I know that."

Completely fuddled now, Toby gave up trying to understand. "The don says we will soon be in country more populated than this."

"That will do. I have a few days yet. How is your meditating going?"

"I keep trying. Every night on my watch. And even when I'm riding."

The friar laughed faintly. "I had no idea that it was possible to meditate and ride at the same time."

"I'm not sure it is," Toby admitted. "But I do try whenever I have time."

"It will come. There is a right way and a wrong way to put a horse in a stall, isn't there?"

"Huh? Well, they like to have their eating end next the manger."

"And lying on their backs with their feet in the air would count as a wrong way?"

"I've seen them try it." Where was this conversation leading?

"Then I picked a poor analogy. What I mean to say, Tobias, is that there is more than one way to put a spirit inside a person. A hexer has a special way of inserting a demon into a husk to make a creature. A free demon will possess a man in another way."

"And the hob?"

"Seems to have found a third position. From what you have told me of your experiences, it may have tried several times before it got comfortable. Father Guillem thinks that is why the Inquisition failed to conjure it, although he is guessing. There is yet another—"

"Is that why you say it cannot be exorcized?"

"No." The old man walked on for a moment with his head down, his face hidden by his hood. "I must tell you this now, Tobias, although I would have preferred to keep it for later. The reason you cannot ever be rid of the hob is that it is too late."

"I guessed that. It's put down roots, hasn't it?"

"You have grown together, and you will continue to grow together. To remove the hob now would leave very little of you. That is how you bring back such useful memories from the future. Warnings, you called them, and you said the hob wasn't smart enough to be so selective, but you certainly are. It used your intelligence to choose the warnings, manipulating you. And manipulation seems to work both ways—doesn't it, Tobias?"

Toby squirmed like a worm on a hook. "Well, maybe a little. Maybe once . . ."

"Which of you destroyed the *landsknechte* and the Inquisition?"

Murderer! "I did, Brother. I told the hob where to strike. It was the storm that roused it, and I've been wondering if that was what was different from the time before, when it jerked me back to start over—this time the storm came. The storm was just luck, but once the hob began rampaging, I found I could direct some of the thunderbolts. I've never felt anything like that before, and I had trouble directing it at the end. Whatever power I had didn't last long."

The friar sighed but did not comment.

"Doesn't a man have the right to defend himself, Brother? They were going to torture me to death!"

"Because they thought you had a demon. They weren't so far wrong were they? No, I don't really blame you for fighting back. I believe you would have chosen another way to escape if there had been one. But you and the hob are growing together, and eventually there will be no difference between you. Which of you is going to be master? I warn you, if it can ever gain control of you, then it will. It will take you over completely."

"And I will go crazy?"

"You will be its creature, my son. The hob may not be as malicious as a demon, but it has no conscience, not yet. You know what happened at Mezquiriz."

Toby shivered, for his worst fears were being confirmed. "Is this inevitable, Brother? Because if it is, then I must try to kill myself now."

"No, it is not inevitable. You still have a chance. You were not a child when it happened, but you were not fully adult, either, so there is hope. Time will work on your side. Through you the hob must learn what it is to be mortal, what is right, what is wrong, what suffering means. We teach the spirits these things, my son. It takes centuries to train an elemental to be a tutelary, and you do not have centuries."

"Is there no quicker way?" Toby asked

Apparently the old man did not hear that impertinent question. "Keep practicing your meditation, for that keeps the hob quiescent and you in control. The two of you will gradually merge into one, but it will take many years, and you must emerge as the dominant partner. Rush the process, as you were doing the other night, and the hob will be the survivor."

They were almost at the campsite.

"That's all I can do—breathe funny, think about swans, mumble 'Lochan na Bi' over and over?"

"That is quite enough to keep you busy!" Brother Bernat said sharply. "The safest thing would be to enter a monastery, for there you would have no distractions. I just cannot see you ever becoming a monk, though. I think you would go out of your mind with boredom, and then you would be no better off.

But do try and stay away from battles and women, from strong drink and hair-raising escapades."

"And if I do? If I am the survivor, what will I be then?"

The friar walked on for a long while before he answered. "Whatever you deserve to be."

"What does that mean?"

"Ah. You promised not to ask questions until I had finished, Tobias. I have not finished yet. Not quite."

2

The men unloaded and groomed the horses, watered them and set them free to graze, hobbling a couple so that they could be caught in the morning and used to round up the rest. The women gathered firewood, ground grain, made biscuits of dough to bake under the ashes. Those persons who chose to do so washed themselves. By the time the meal was ready, darkness had fallen, and the company gathered around the fire in no especial order to eat and share stories.

Some nights now they had singing after their meal, for Don Ramon had liberated a vihuela from the *landsknechte* camp. He had not only a gentleman's skill at playing it but also a fine tenor voice—there seemed to be nothing he was not good at, except facing reality. He could pick up the melody when the Catalans sang their songs, and even manage to accompany Hamish in Scottish ballads, although Hamish's memory for lyrics was much better than his ability to stay in key. Father Guillem had a powerful bass and a repertoire of monastic chants from many lands.

After that evening's meal, though, Toby took Hamish aside and asked him to organize a second campfire some distance from the first, where he and the don could have a private chat.

Hamish disapproved, naturally. "How can you possibly trust him? He's as batty as a bell tower! His head's full of eels."

"And I have foreseen his death. It may not happen, but I owe him a warning, at least." For some reason he could not identify, Toby felt he *ought* to trust the don, that it might be important.

Hamish went off muttering but did what he had been asked, as usual.

Toby invited Doña Francisca to attend also and then decided to include Josep, who had supported him steadfastly and deserved recognition for it. The inquisitive Senora Collel tried to gatecrash, bringing Gracia with her, and the don peremptorily ordered them away, insisting that women could not attend a council of war.

The five huddled around the little flames that danced on their nest of twigs and streamed ribbons of smoke into the night wind. Pale light flickered on intent faces.

"This is a strange tale," Toby began, "perhaps the strangest you will have ever heard, but Brother Bernat believes it, and I suspect no lie would ever deceive him. I must warn you that it involves truths that are dangerous to know. The Fiend has decreed that anyone who learns these things must die, so you may prefer not to listen. Whether that will reduce your peril, I cannot say. Just by associating with you, I have put you all at risk."

"A dramatic preamble!" proclaimed the don. "Let us hope that the gravamen is worthy of it."

No one departed. So there, in the cool night breezes, Toby told his whole improbable story once again. Hamish just scowled in silence at the starlit hills, for he knew it all. Josep and Doña Francisca grew more and more worried as it progressed, but Don Ramon seemed to find it dull. Perhaps his internal fantasies were too vivid for him to appreciate anyone else's adventures, no matter how bizarre. He yawned frequently, although he beamed approval when Toby described how calmly he had laid his head on the block to have it chopped off. His mother wailed in horror.

"That's all," Toby concluded. "Have I left out anything, Jaume?"

Hamish blinked himself back to the present. "What? Sorry. Wasn't listening."

Toby chuckled. "You weren't even here! You left us at Glen Shira and Loch Fyne."

Hamish smiled, half abashed, half wistful. "I was thinking about girls."

"This Baron Oreste," asked Doña Francisca, "did he not lead the army that sacked Zaragoza? Then he is a monster!"

Toby nodded. "Most true, Senor Francisco. He is one of the Fiend's bosom friends."

"Does a demon have friends?" asked Hamish. "Or a bosom?"

Ignore that. "General, courtier, advisor, potent hexer. A monster for all seasons."

"And you say he is viceroy in Barcelona?" the old lady persisted.

"That was what my vision told me."

"And what the *landsknechte* told me," said the don, "when I demanded to see their authority." He smiled and twirled up his mustache. He had lost his air of boredom. In fact the firelight sparkled in his blue eyes with a strange excitement.

"So he is after you and this amethyst?" asked Josep, appalled.

"Mostly the amethyst. I am of no real interest to him, except that I have tweaked his pride too often."

"Then you must not go near Barcelona! Surely so great a hexer will track you down at once."

"Honored Senor Brusi," Hamish said, "were you to write that advice on my friend's forehead with a stonemason's mallet and chisel, he would still not notice. I have been telling him the same thing every chime of the clock for weeks."

"I suppose I shouldn't," Toby conceded.

"Spirits preserve us! The earth moves!"

"Conditions have changed," Toby said, a little nettled. His main reason for going to Barcelona had been to see Hamish aboard ship and homeward bound, but Josep could arrange that much better then he could and would certainly be willing to do so. "I was hoping that the baron would rid me of the hob, but it was never a very plausible plan, and Brother Bernat fears that it would cripple me. I'll decide what to do when we reach Montserrat. I may go on to France."

"Or Florence?" said Josep. "Or Majorca, or Salerno? I have . . . my house has branches in all those places, and my offer of employment still stands." He chuckled, detecting Toby's astonishment. "Barcelona is a great trading city, Senor. Not so

very long ago it ruled half the Mediterranean. It is
still cosmopolitan, a center of the arts, a—"

"Yucch!" snarled the don. "Trade? You insult the
man. You insult all of us by even mentioning it. A
true man's ambition is the accomplishment of great
deeds of valor. Still, I suppose he is only a peasant
and would not understand that. Perhaps trade is all
he is good for, after all." He turned to the peasant in
question. "Is Baron Oreste a creature like his master?"

"No, he is human," Toby said. "Although he is a
hexer, he himself is bound to absolute obedience. I
was told once that the demon that controls him is
immured in a beryl set in one of the many rings he
wears. He cannot remove the ring and so escape
beyond the demon's reach."

"He is mortal, then." Don Ramon twirled up the
points of his mustache with apparent satisfaction. "I
ask merely out of curiosity, you understand. I shall
be paying my respects to the noble lord when we
reach Barcelona."

"*What?*" shrieked Doña Francisca.

They were all staring at the don. Had he taken
leave of his senses? Well, yes. Some time ago. But
where was his confused mind wandering now?

"I warned you, senor," Toby protested, "that by
associating with you I have put you in peril. You
know of Rhym, and that is a capital offense. The
baron can find any number of executioners apart
from me."

The *caballero* shrugged with superb disdain. "My
estates lie in lands ceded to Aragon under the treaty,
so my rightful liege is now the . . . King Nevil himself. It is fitting that I call upon his deputy when I

arrive in Barcelona." His mad eyes scanned them all, daring them to argue.

"No!" His mother had both hands to her mouth and looked ghastly in the firelight.

He dismissed her protest with a sneer. "*Campeador?* Francisco is well past his best. I need a younger squire. If you are seeking employment, I can offer you a career with prospects greater than anything your haberdasher friend there may dream of. Of course you will require training, but you seem to have some capacity beyond brute brawn."

Did the don really think he could kill Oreste, a hexer protected by innumerable demons? For a moment Toby was tempted to say that he would rather apply his brute brawn in Josep's warehouse or even Senora Collel's bedroom—but discretion prevailed.

"You honor me greatly, senor. I beg you to let me have time to weigh your splendid offer against certain other obligations I am not at liberty to reveal."

"As you will. I am confident we shall reach Barcelona within the week, if we continue at our present pace."

But the present pace was liable to kill Brother Bernat. There lay Toby's other obligation.

3

Oddly enough, the rain didn't help at all. The countryside had become greener and gentler, little rolling hills that a man could *almost* imagine were somewhere in the Scottish Lowlands, and that just made the ache worse. Some people are never satisfied. Hamish was astride Liath near the head of the

line, right behind the don and his squire, and it was
his turn to lead the pack train again. At least that
kept his mind occupied, so he had less time for
brooding.

Not that he couldn't work in a bit of brooding if
he wanted to. They would be in Barcelona in a few
more days. Toby wanted to send him home. He
wanted to go. Josep said he could arrange it for him
quite easily, although winter sailing was erratic, so
he might have to lay over for a few months in
Seville or Lisbon. But he didn't want to desert
Toby. Not that the big man needed him, except for
friendship, but going home was going to feel a lot
like running away. There could be no second
thoughts—once they parted, Toby would vanish
into a war-torn continent and they could never hope
to meet again. Life back in the glen would seem
dull as mud after the last three years' adventuring.
There were a lot of interesting places he hadn't
seen yet. What to do?

Rain was running down his neck. That *really*
made him homesick!

There was Toby now, coming back on that big
spotted gelding of his. Ever since they passed
Lerida he'd been zigging and zagging all over the
landscape, investigating every little hilltop village
they passed—looking for somewhere for Brother
Bernat to lay up and rest, he said, although he was
probably hoping to find a spirit willing to heal whatever was wrong with the old man. If his problem
was just old age, not even a spirit could do much
about that. Many tutelaries refused to heal strangers
anyway.

Somewhere back along the line, Eulalia laughed.

She was a problem much worse than homesickness! One night they'd gone off into the bushes together, and she hadn't protested when he kissed her—she'd started unlacing his hose. She had shown him what to do next when he wasn't sure, and in no time at all he'd achieved what he'd been wanting to do for years. He'd thought of it as a great victory. But it wasn't. It had turned out to be a terrible defeat, because now he kept wanting to do it again.

He did not like Eulalia, and she did not like him, and they had told each other so several times. But they both enjoyed what they did with each other. Not that she admitted it. If he did not ask her, she would not ask him. No, she would just tease him until she had him begging and promising anything she wanted. She was very good at that. He knew he was taking a terrible risk of getting her with child, if he hadn't already. Or she would say he had whether he had or not, and when they arrived in Barcelona Senora Collel would throw her out in the gutter. Then Hamish Campbell would find himself having to marry a woman he didn't want. Every morning he swore he would not succumb again, and at sunset she would melt all the lumps out of him with one glance from her sultry Spanish eyes. Why was he so weak? Why did women have this awful power over men?

Why couldn't he be like Toby and not need women?

A shout from the rear turned his head. Something was wrong. The don wheeled his horse and went charging back to see, followed slowly by Francisco. Everyone else was stopping. Hamish directed Liath around a patch of bushes, watching to make sure the train followed without any stupid quadruped trying to take a shortcut, and then led the way back. By the time he arrived at the group he could guess that the problem was Brother Bernat.

He dismounted. "What happened?"

Josep said, "The Franciscan. He reined in and said he felt faint. We helped him down . . ."

Hauled back almost on his haunches, Smeòrach skidded to a halt in a shower of mud. Toby flung himself from the saddle and plunged into the group, hurling Manuel and Rafael and others aside. Hamish sighed to himself and waited. Toby was fond of the old man and grateful for that strange healing he had gained from him. He was going to be upset if this was the end.

"How bad?"

Josep shrugged. He said, "Can't tell," but his face said very bad.

Hamish surveyed the countryside. The village Toby had just visited was only a mile or so off, on a low hill, but even from here it was obvious that the roofs had fallen in and the walls were blackened. The tower of the sanctuary was a stump, so there would be no spirit there and probably no people either. The town was just one more casualty of the terrible war, and he wondered why Toby had even bothered going to investigate it.

Then Toby's head rose above the others again. The watchers parted for him, and he emerged with Brother Bernat cradled in his arms. The old man's face, the color of skim milk, nestled against Toby's shoulder. His lips were blue, and his eyes not merely closed but sunk back into his skull. Toby went past Hamish without a word and set off along the road with huge strides. If he was looking for a place to dig a grave, why so much hurry?

Father Guillem and Pepita scurried after, running to try and catch him. Apparently they were heading for the village, but Toby's sword was hung on Smeòrach's saddle, so they had gone unarmed. Hamish detached his own blade from Liath, slung the baldric over his head, and thrust the reins at Josep.

"Look after them."

Josep's protests that he couldn't handle the train faded away as Hamish went racing after the others.

Toby was running up the hill, setting a fearful pace in spite of his burden. The monk flapped along behind him like a giant bat, holding Pepita's hand. Glancing back, Hamish saw that the others were following, but at a leisurely pace. The don would probably make them wait outside the gates, because the horses might break legs in the ruins, even if there were no thieves lurking there.

He caught up with Father Guillem, whose face was as red as a furnace door. Pepita would obviously be weeping if she had any breath to do so. What was all the burning hurry?

"There can't possibly be a spirit up here!" Hamish panted.

The monk said, "No," and kept right on going.

Hamish ran past them, slipped on a patch of mud, caught his scabbard between his legs, and fell flat on his face. Cursing in a mixture of Gaelic and Catalan, he scrambled to his feet and discovered he had wrenched an ankle. He switched to Breton and Castilian and began to run again in a wild, painful hobble.

He went by the child and Father Guillem a second
time. Toby had almost reached the shattered town
gate, and a couple of men had appeared, watching
his approach. Hamish drove himself even faster,
steadying his sword with one hand so he didn't
make a fool of himself again. Why were they doing
this? Did the old man just want to die in a shrine,
even if it had no tutelary? Was this some Franciscan
custom?

Toby slowed to a fast walk and went through the
gateway with the two men following and Hamish at
their heels. They glanced around and then ignored
Hamish, following a few paces behind Toby. They
were making no move to molest him and did not
seem to be armed, but Hamish decided to stay at
their backs and keep an eye on them.

The road was narrow and dim in the rain, but it
was not obstructed by debris and gruesome bodies as the streets of Onda had been. Although
most of the buildings were unroofed and stank of
burned timber, the village was inhabited, and the
residents had made a start on cleaning up and
rebuilding. People began emerging from alleys
and doorways, men and women both, even a few
ragged children. Toby seemed to know where he
was leading this procession, crossing a couple of
tiny plazas without hesitation and apparently
heading for the stump of a tower that marked the
sanctuary.

When he reached it he ran up the steps and turned
around. His face was red with effort and his chest
heaved. The old man in his arms was showing no
signs of life, but Toby nodded approval and went
into the sanctuary. There couldn't be a spirit in

there, or the hob would have stopped him, so what was he doing?

Hamish followed with the crowd at his heels. The building was open to the sky, a burned shell, but the floor had been swept clear. Most of the tracery had gone from the windows, the little that remained still holding a few pathetic fragments of stained glass. Throne, candles, images, pictures had all gone. Only the carved altar on the dais at the far end survived, its cracked and blackened stonework showing traces of gilt and paint.

Toby advanced almost to the altar steps and halted, still holding Brother Bernat in his arms. The spectators gathered in silence behind him, watching intently. Hamish wished he knew what was going on, because everybody else seemed to. He went forward to see if he could help. He could hear the old man breathing in a faint rattle that made him want to cough.

Toby knelt. Hamish took off his wet cloak and spread it on the flagstones so he could lay the old man down. One of the villagers spread another cloak over him. Then they all just waited in the rain, Toby on his knees, everyone else standing. If the spirit was still present, it was ignoring them. There must be many more comfortable places to die.

More people were drifting in. Father Guillem arrived, pushing forward to the front with Pepita in tow. The child knelt and took the dying man's hand, sobbing, not saying anything. For a moment he seemed to rouse. His eyelids flickered but did not open.

"Brother," Toby said. "We are here. It is a good

place." His voice cracked. "It will be all right now, Brother."

Pepita bent close and whispered urgently. The slack mouth twitched as if he were trying to speak, or even smile. He gasped a few harsh, rattling breaths . . . stopped . . . a couple more . . . then a long silence. His eyelids opened slightly, showing only whites. Toby reached down and closed them. They stayed closed. The watchers sighed.

Toby stood up and looked around—at the monk, at Hamish. He nodded and pulled a wry face. There was more than rain wetting his cheeks.

"Well done, my son." Father Guillem patted his shoulder. Surprisingly, Toby did not react angrily to this patronizing.

"Pepita?" The monk raised her and tried to scoop her up in his arms. She struggled free and went to Toby instead. He lifted her and held her. She sobbed on his shoulder.

There must be fifty people there now, but what were they all waiting for? Even Toby seemed to be expecting something.

A boy stepped forward from the crowd and walked past Hamish, moving in an oddly stiff gait and wafting a strong odor of goat. He was no more than twelve or thirteen, dirty, clad in rags, thin as canes. He climbed the steps and turned to look over the assembly with a strangely unfocused stare. There was a faint glow around him! So there *was* a spirit after all, and it was responding at last, too late to help.

Everyone was kneeling now.

"You will be our children," the boy said loudly. Some of the women cried out in joy. "If we may have your love, we will cherish you in return. The man's name was Bernat. Bury him where he lies now and honor his memory. He taught us well and carried us long."

The childish treble rang out again. "Tobias and Guillem and Jaume, we thank you for your help and give you our blessing. Pepita, dear child, weep no more. We told you, we warned you, and we love you still. Why should you weep now that your friend's task is ended? He has completed what he gave his life to. He is with us and will always be with us."

Pepita pulled loose from Toby's embrace and knelt down beside him, choking with her efforts not to sob. The big man put an arm around her.

"Some of you still doubt," the boy said. "We will give you a sign to comfort you. Eduardo, what happened to your eyes?"

"I was hit by a sword, holiness," responded a voice from the crowd.

"Domènech, help Eduardo come forward."

The crowd seemed to rustle. A tall young man with a bandage over his face rose up in their midst and then helped an older, white-haired man to his feet. People cleared a path for them as they shuffled to the front, the old man leading the younger by the hand.

"You may remove the wrapping, Eduardo," the boy said. "Can you see now?"

"Yes! Yes!" The young man threw away the cloth and fell to his knees. "Praise to the spirit! Praise to Saint Bernat!"

Voices picked up the refrain. Hamish, like everyone else, lowered his face to the floor in acknowledgment of the miracle.

"Joaquim has some good years left in him," the

tutelary said with a dry chuckle so like Brother
Bernat's that it brought a lump to Hamish's throat.
"Fetch Joaquim here. We will cure his legs and he
will be keeper of our sanctuary. You may have
Sancho back now, Joanna. Give him our thanks for
lending us his voice."

Hamish looked up just in time to see the glow
fade from the boy and his blank expression change
to one of horror as he realized where he was. He
sprinted down from the dais, red-faced and bewildered, only to be grabbed in a fierce hug by a short,
fat woman, probably his mother. The building
buzzed with excited chatter.

The town had a tutelary again, it would live. And
even Toby had been expecting this! How had he
known? Why had he not discussed it? Could it be
that Hamish had been so tied up in his problems
with Eulalia that he had not been paying attention to
what was going on?

"Our work here is done," Father Guillem said, rising. "Are you consoled now, Pepita? That is not
Brother Bernat lying there, so you need say no more
farewells."

He put an arm around her to lead her away, but at
once the strangers were mobbed by the excited,
grateful villagers offering food, shelter, hospitality—
anything. Toby and the monk declined as graciously
as possible, explaining that they were on a pilgrimage
and must rejoin their friends.

A little later, as they were leaving the town,
Hamish said: "I don't understand. I never read anything about this!"

Toby smiled, although his eyes were still rimmed
with red. "You can't find everything in books. It is

called *alumbradismo*." He was amused at being able to lecture Hamish for a change, curse him! "There is more than one way to put a spirit into a person. Or into a town, apparently."

"But . . . not a hob?"

Shadows darkened Toby's face. "No, just an elemental, and a lifetime of example. I expect Pepita will explain it to you, if you ask her nicely."

He was not going to, obviously.

SEVEN

MONTSERRAT

1

Two days of steady rain had left everyone grumpy, miserable, and soaked. Father Guillem, coming trudging back along the trail to rejoin the pilgrims, looked like a bedraggled black beetle, and the way he was wielding his staff suggested that he was a beetle in a very foul temper. But why was he so obviously ignoring the man on a donkey following a few paces behind him?

Toby was no more cheerful than anyone else. He ought to be practicing his meditation exercises and cultivating serenity of mind, but he had his hands full with Smeòrach, whose simple mind was anything but serene. He kept trying to stamp on Toby's feet and jerking his head to try and pull his bridle loose from Toby's grasp. He hated the rain just as much as people did, and standing still was never his strong point anyway. As a *landsknecht* horse he associated a village like that one with nice dry stables, perhaps even oats or hot bran mash, so please could they go there now?

Evidently not. There were men with guns and pikes at the gate, and Father Guillem's efforts to negotiate had obviously not prospered. He was wearing a very unpious scowl as he returned to report.

"We are not welcome?" Toby asked.

The monk shook his head, shaking water from his cowl. "They refused absolutely."

"Did you explain that I am a Castilian nobleman?" the don demanded incredulously.

"I did, my son. And also that I am a senior official of the abbey. I even mentioned they were turning away women and a child, but it made no difference."

"Did you offer to pay?" Josep asked. His lips were blue and his teeth chattered. Most of the others looked just as distressed.

"Even that." Father Guillem shrugged and made an effort to be charitable. "They have their reasons. The Fiend's forces withdrew a few weeks ago— they did not despoil the countryside here, because of the truce that had been agreed, but a company of *landsknechte* was billeted in the village and caused all the usual troubles. Now that they have gone, there are lawless bands marauding, preying on innocent travelers or anyone else they can catch. They warned me we must be on our guard."

"But there are no troops around?" Toby said. "No garrison around Montserrat?" For him, that was very welcome news.

"They know of none." The monk looked around his dispirited companions and raised his voice. "Be cheerful, my children! There is a fine campsite half a league farther on. Tomorrow is the last day. By nightfall tomorrow we shall be safe and comfortable in the monastery."

"It can't be too soon. Your companion, Father?"

Everyone turned to look at the other man, who was just sitting on his donkey and smiling in patient silence at nobody in particular. He was clean shaven, fortyish, bareheaded. His jerkin and hose were plain but well made, shabby from long wear yet still serviceable. Apparently he enjoyed being wet, because the hood of his brown woollen cloak lay unused on his sodden shoulders.

Father Guillem frowned. "His name is Jacques. He is a servant of the monastery—a gardener, cleaner, porter, anything of that sort. He says he was sent to meet Senor Longdirk."

Everyone now looked at Toby.

"I am Senor Longdirk."

The man smiled uncertainly at him.

"You have a message for me?"

"No, senor."

"Then who sent you to meet me?"

The smile faltered. "Don't know, senor."

All eyes switched back to Father Guillem. "He is simple. I know him and know of him, but I have never spoken with him, except to order him to fetch something or clean somewhere. The villagers say he arrived last night and was refused admittance. He must have slept under a tree. He was still there this morning, waiting for Senor Longdirk. Frankly, I don't think you'll get any more out of him."

Toby glanced hopefully at Hamish, but he seemed as bereft of ideas as everyone else.

"The tutelary must know I am coming, though."

"Obviously!" the monk growled. "But what does

it wish to tell you and why pick so useless a messenger?"

"Would the spirit itself have sent him, or the abbot, or who?"

"I have absolutely no idea." Bad-tempered black beetles disliked mysteries just as much as Hamish did. "I wouldn't trust Jacques to find his left hand with his right. The fact that he found you at all suggests that the spirit guided him." With a little more grace the monk conceded, "There is no harm in him."

"Did you search him for a letter? His pockets?"

"Of course. He has nothing, absolutely nothing except a razor, a thimble, and some shiny buttons. I don't think he's eaten since he left Montserrat."

Toby tried not to smile at the cleric's annoyance. "So all we can do is feed him and take him back with us?"

"Apparently."

Strange! Why send a moron when there must be dozens of eager young novices who would enjoy such a break in routine? It was something to think about. Toby looked to the don. "Your orders, senor?"

The don pouted across the field at the guardians of the village. "Artillery is rarely reliable in weather like this." He twirled up his mustache. "Lead the troops out, *Campeador*. I shall join you shortly."

"Um . . ." Telling Don Ramon to be careful would be a futile exercise. Besides, Toby approved of what he thought the young maniac had in mind. "Just let me get the others out of range, senor. Mount up, everyone!"

By the time the procession was moving in some

sort of order, the don was cantering Midnight around in a wide circle, warming him up. Then he swung his shield into place, couched his lance, and charged the villagers at the gate.

He had been right about the arquebuses, for not a shot was fired. Three of the defenders displayed military training, swinging their pikes forward in the standard drill to oppose cavalry. The rest just screamed and fled back through the archway. Seeing themselves deserted and the madman still coming, the pikemen chose discretion over posthumous honor and followed. The gate slammed shut just in time, although the don could certainly have come faster and ridden them down had he wanted to. Yelling his war cry in scorn, he set Midnight to prancing and cavorting on their doorstep for a moment, before coming after the pilgrims. As he galloped by them, heading for his place in the van, they all cheered him mightily, even—Toby was amused to notice—the normally humorless Father Guillem. The mysterious Jacques merely smiled, not understanding the joke.

"Sometimes yon laddie is not as daft as he lets on," Hamish remarked with glee.

"You don't think that was daft?"

"No, I mean he didn't wait around until they found a dry arquebus!"

"True." Toby shivered as more water trickled down his neck. "We'll have to keep our eyes peeled for rustlers tonight. Some young hotheads may try to redeem their honor."

"Not to mention the brigands. Um . . . you won't mind if I trade with the monk and take second watch?"

"Not if he has no objection." Toby eyed his young friend inquiringly.

"He said he wouldn't mind." Hamish was looking elsewhere.

It was standard procedure now for him to share first watch with Josep. It was also standard procedure for him to spend second watch with Eulalia, although presumably not watching anything. Quite often he was still off in the shrubbery with her when Toby was awakened to take third watch. Although Toby was careful not to pry, he had overheard enough angry words to know that their romance was not all honey and rose petals. Remembering how he had seen Hamish in earnest conversation with the acolyte that afternoon, he wondered if Father Guillem himself had suggested the switch.

"I don't mind. Just don't turn your back on Rafael tonight."

"I never do," Hamish said sharply. "Why not tonight especially?"

"Because tomorrow's our last day as a group. First thing in the morning, I plan to bring up the matter of the *landsknechte*'s gold. I think there should be a friendly sharing-out of the loot."

"They know that?"

"They may guess."

"I agree about the sharing-out," Hamish said. "But you're dreaming if you expect it to be friendly."

The campsite, when they reached it, was a dense grove of cypress, but even there the ground was waterlogged. The pilgrims muttered and grumbled and made the best of it. Their fire smoked, people banged their heads on low branches, and the horses had to be hobbled to keep them from wandering in search of better grazing. No one was in a mood for singing.

The inexplicable Jacques ate as if he was starved. He spoke to no one unless he was addressed and even then provided no information. He could tell Toby nothing about the road he had come or people he had met on the way; indeed he had forgotten that he had been sent to meet Senor Longdirk. It had been the villagers who told Father Guillem that much. When he was not admitting that he could not answer a question, he just stayed in one place and smiled, but when Toby asked him to chop firewood he worked hard until he was told to stop.

Surprisingly, Pepita disliked him. She seemed frightened of him, and this was very unlike her. When Toby asked her why, she pouted.

"He is broken."

"He's not very clever. Do you think he may hurt you?"

She shook her head. "But he is broken." She seemed unable to explain what she meant.

Hamish found him an intriguing problem. "He's French, originally! Speak to him in Catalan and he answers in Catalan. But speak to him in langue d'oc and he answers in langue d'oc! He knows some German too. He must've traveled a lot. How did he manage that with no wits?"

"Pepita says he's been broken."

"What does that mean?"

"I wish I knew," Toby said soberly.

The night was black as pitch. Everyone retired as soon as the meal was over. Toby, having given the sentries' whistles to Josep and Father Guillem,

rolled himself up in his wet blanket to sleep.
Hamish was already curled up shivering in his, so
he really had turned over a new leaf. Amazing! How
long would it take Eulalia to turn it back again?

2

A white swan drifting across dark water, trailing a
soft vee of ripple, one dark foot just visible
below . . . Lochan na Bi, Lochan na Bi.

The swan was swimming in the back of Toby's
mind, and it seemed to be working. He could not
judge his heartbeat, but he felt no fear or even anger,
no sweat or dry throat. Of course he always tended
to stay cool when there was a fight coming, so perhaps this was not a fair test of Brother Bernat's technique. He could not hope to win against the don, so
he must try and talk his way out of his predicament.

He said, "I am at fault also, senor. I should have
wakened at the proper time, as you did."

About the hour he should have been coming off
watch, the don's foot in his ribs had awakened him
and not gently either. Hamish and Rafael should
have called Toby and Miguel; they in turn should
have called the don and his squire. They had not.
Don Ramon had demanded an explanation. In the
ensuing search, it had been Doña Francisca who
found Hamish lying in the weeds, bound and
gagged, one side of his face caked with dried
blood. Now Don Ramon was demanding Hamish's
head.

From the way Hamish was holding it with both
hands, he might be very glad to be rid of it. He was
barely conscious even yet, sitting there huddled

under a blanket in the first glimmers of a very rainy dawn while nine people he had been supposed to guard stared down at him with expressions ranging from Pepita's sympathy to the don's homicidal fury.

Nine. Once the pilgrims had numbered sixteen. Now they were only ten, not counting Jacques who was still asleep in his cloak, and that was assuming Hamish and Toby survived the next few minutes.

"It was his job to call you, not yours to wake yourself," Don Ramon repeated. "He failed in that duty. He failed to sound the alarm. The penalty for failing on guard duty is death."

"Not in this case, senor," Toby said with the best blend of deference and stubbornness he could muster. "He was set to guard against intruders, not against treachery from his friends." *Liar!* He had warned Hamish not to turn his back on Rafael.

Hamish peered up at him blearily. He did not speak—fortunately so, because he was confused enough to say almost anything, even the truth.

"A sentry taken unaware," said the don, "is put to death. I expect he was fornicating in the bushes with the whore."

Hamish closed his eyes in abject misery.

"Were you?" Toby asked. He was taking a risk, but he was almost certain that the answer was no.

Hamish whispered, "No."

"I believe him, senor. Granted, the fire she lit in his belly has melted most of his brains, but he would not betray us when he was supposed to be on watch. Josep? You've shared watch with him more than any of us."

Josep's anger twisted into a grin. "No, *Campeador*. Sometimes he lay with her before and sometimes after, sometimes even both, but never during."

Hamish's great romance was common knowledge. He opened his mouth as if about to speak, then turned his head and vomited. Had he done that five minutes ago, he would have suffocated behind his gag and this inquiry would be a post mortem. He might easily have frozen to death. Feeling a rush of hatred for the people who had treated his friend so, Toby reached again for calm. Lochan na Bi!

He scowled at Eulalia, who was wearing what she might think was an expression of wounded innocence. "But the whore may have been an accomplice. I cannot imagine Jaume being taken like a broody hen unless he was distracted somehow. Did she come and talk with you?"

Hamish tried to shake his head and winced. "Don't remember," he croaked.

"Then they must have bribed her!" the don decided. "If we search her, we shall find some gold chains, I expect."

Eulalia screeched at this outrage to her honor and appealed to Senora Collel. The senora told her to shut her face. Gracia, who had been standing beside her, pointedly moved away.

"That wouldn't prove much," Toby said. "She may have looted some from the *landsknechte*." He had a strong suspicion that Eulalia had been helping both Manuel and Raphael enjoy their newfound wealth behind their wives' backs, but he would not say so in front of Hamish.

Again Eulalia erupted in torrents of Catalan. The senora silenced her with a slap as loud as a gunshot.

Hamish's eyes had opened wide. He turned to

look at Eulalia and suddenly produced a strange sound, somewhere between a laugh and a choke. "I do remember! She came and told me she's with child."

"She is lying," Senora Collel declaimed. "I know it."

True or false, that assertion would certainly have been a potent distraction, and for a moment even the don looked amused. Then he found his anger again. "Very well, *Campeador*, we shall let Jaume live. See that he is thoroughly thrashed. We are wasting time. We must hunt down the traitors."

"No, senor."

Icy silence.

"Do I hear you correctly?" the don said very quietly.

Lochan na Bi . . . "Yes, senor. They will travel at least as fast as we can, and they have several hours' start on us. To chase them would be folly. They have stolen some horses from us, but we stole them in the first place. They do not seem to have taken much else that did not belong to them."

He waited for contradiction from Josep or Senora Collel, who used their moneybags as pillows, but neither disagreed. Whatever balance Miguel and Rafael still owed on Don Ramon's wages was a debt that must not be mentioned, and his mother had always known that her chances of collecting from them were slim.

But not all wealth was beneath a *caballero*'s dignity. "You forget the rest of the booty!" the don snapped. "That belongs to all of us. You, especially, earned your share. They did not."

A penniless fugitive fleeing from the long arm of Baron Oreste would certainly find a few gold chains

useful, but Toby could not accept that he had earned
a link of them. It had been the hob who destroyed
the *landsknechte*, not he. The fight had not been
honorable, so the prize was tainted and he would
shed no tears over losing it. He was probably being
stupid again, but that was how he felt.

"We cannot ride down the fugitives without their
seeing us coming, senor. They will have ample time
to make the evidence disappear before we reach
them."

"We can make them tell where it is!"

"Not I, senor."

The don's hand was on his sword hilt. The blue
eyes flamed madness. "You are refusing my
orders?"

"I am advising the noble *hidalgo* that to pursue
those worthless peasants would be folly. We can
reach Montserrat by evening."

"This a matter of honor you cannot comprehend.
We shall pursue the thieves."

"Not I, senor."

Day by day Toby had been taking over the leadership of the group. Spirits knew he had not planned to
and had done everything he could to preserve the fiction that the hired guard was still in charge, but no
one was deceived. Now he had thrown down the
gauntlet. It had been inevitable, probably, because he
could never tolerate authority for long and was especially incapable of obeying nonsensical orders, but to
upstage the deranged *caballero* was to die for insolence. As the don's great sword slid from its scabbard, his mother caught hold of his arm with both
hands.

"Ramon, he is right!"

He froze. He could not have looked more shocked had she stabbed him.

Gracia stepped in front of him. "Senor, please!" she whispered.

"I agree with the *campeador* and your noble squire, my son," Father Guillem boomed. He rolled forward to clap a hairy paw on the don's shoulder. "What good will be served by a long chase and then bloodshed? As Tobias says, we should merely be trying to steal back stolen goods, and some of us might be hurt in the fight. It will be you and he against the two of them."

Toby waited, arms folded, doing his breathing exercises. The don just continued to glare at his mother, and she glared right back at him—truly, there was a most admirable lady! At last he opened his hand, the sword dropped back in its scabbard, and death flew away.

He was still insanely furious, though, and he would never forget this insult. "We must be guided by the counsel of the holy scholar in matters of righteousness. The woman will remain behind, though. She has forfeited any claim on us."

Eulalia cried out and threw herself on her knees. "Senores! Senoras! You will not abandon me!"

Hamish opened his mouth—

"No!" Toby barked. "You owe her nothing. She didn't tell you her lies earlier, did she? She came to distract you when you were on guard. She was in on the plot, Hamish. She set you up so Rafael could cosh you."

Hamish groaned and buried his face in his arms.

"Senoras!" the don proclaimed. "Take this harlot over there and strip her. Find out what—"

Instantly Eulalia was gone through the trees, arms and legs flying. Only Toby or the don could run her down and catch her, but that would be beneath the don's dignity, and Toby was glad to see the last of her.

Pepita moved over to Hamish and clasped his head between her hands. "Let me try to ease your pain, senor." Everyone else was suddenly made uneasy by this suggestion of gramarye.

"Prepare to move out, *Campeador*!" The don spun on his heel and stalked away. The others dispersed, and Toby began to consider the problem of catching the remaining horses, because the deserters had removed their hobbles to delay pursuit. Fortunately Smeòrach would usually come to his whistle.

Montserrat lay somewhere in these forbidding hills. This was the last day.

3

The last day was likely to be the worst. At times Toby could barely see two horses ahead of him, either because the trail was winding through forest or because the fog had closed in like gray bed curtains—and frequently both. The rain varied from annoying to drenching. Once in a while terrain and weather would open up to reveal a breathtaking, unreal landscape, towering almost vertically overhead in bright green slopes and spectacular beetling cliffs whose tops were lost in cloud. It was perfect ambush country.

Father Guillem insisted that there was only one road up this valley and hence no chance of getting lost, but Toby was far less worried about losing his way than he was about the reports of bandits molesting travelers. To send scouts out ahead would be useless in these conditions, even if he had any to send.

One way or another, the pilgrimage was ending. If he could deliver his charges safely to Montserrat, then Pepita, Gracia, and Father Guillem would remain at the monastery, while the others would resume their journey to Barcelona in a day or two. Toby himself would carry on alone, toward France, but here he was very close to Baron Oreste, who must be hunting for him with gramarye.

All day the don rode a few lengths ahead, bearing his lance and shield ready for use. Toby mostly stayed at the rear with the rest of the men, but from time to time he would ride along the line, trying to raise people's spirits. It was hard to keep up a cheerful front in such weather. When he asked Senora Collel to take a turn at leading the packhorses, she refused vehemently.

"I did not entrust myself to the don's protection," she snapped, "in order to serve as a mule skinner. Furthermore, I contracted to be escorted directly to Barcelona, not dragged up into these wild hills "

She was probably looking for an excuse to refuse further payment, and she was undoubtedly annoyed at no longer having a servant to nag and bully. But she had not mentioned hiring Toby as her resident Pretty Boy since she learned he was possessed, and that was an improvement.

Even the normally sparkly Pepita seemed glum, although that was partly because she still mourned Brother Bernat. She perched on her horse like a sodden bundle of laundry, her tiny, pinched face peering out from a cocoon comprised of every spare garment the pilgrims possessed. "You are my friend. I do not want you to go away and leave me."

"I do not want to leave you either, Senorita Pepita. I have enjoyed traveling with you, but life is full of sorrows, and parting from friends is one of them."

"You sound just like Brother Bernat! Why cannot I teach my spirit friend about happiness, instead of just about sorrow?"

"You have taught it about friendship by being my friend. Friendship is a great happiness, perhaps the very best of all."

"I shall not forget Brother Bernat, because he was my friend, and I shall not forget you."

"And I shall always remember you. You have taught me many things about carrying the burden of a spirit."

She wagged a minute finger at him. "You must not let it throw thunderbolts at people again! That was a bad thing you let it do."

"No, I never shall. I promise." He would at least try.

Even Doña Francisca was not quite her usual indomitable self. "I will pray to Montserrat for you, Senor Toby. I am very grateful for all your help. We should not be here now had it not been for you."

"Oh, that isn't true. In fact, I put you all in danger. You would have done better without me. Your son would have managed perfectly well."

She smiled disbelievingly. "I only wish we had money to reward you, for you have served us all loyally without a hope of—"

"I wish you had money, too, senora, for then I

could refuse it. Journeying with you has been its own reward."

Gracia was better company, foreseeing the end of her strange mission. Either she did not comprehend the pervasive danger, or she had faith in her voices.

"These mountains must be very splendid when the sun shines, must they not?"

"Indeed they must," Toby agreed. "Brother Bernat said that spirits choose beautiful places for their domains, so I suppose very great spirits should have very wonderful scenery."

"My sons will be happy here, and all those other wraiths also." Her hand closed around the bottle. She had not been parted from it since he rescued it from the Inquisition.

"I am sure Montserrat will cherish them. And what of yourself? You will enter the nunnery?"

She hesitated. "I swore I would not mention . . . But this is our farewell, yes? We shall never meet again, and I owe you so much that I cannot bear not to tell you. . . . You will not betray my confidence, senor?"

"Of course not."

"Don Ramon and I are pledged to be married! He wishes his saintly mother to be first to hear the news, and she is presently at home, running his great estates, so we are to say nothing until he has a chance to write to her."

He looked down at the stars of happiness sparkling in Gracia's eyes and could say nothing except to offer his congratulations and best wishes. The don was a man of honor as he defined honor. Deceiving pretty girls did not count. It was a gentleman's privilege.

Jacques rode in silence, smiling blissfully at the fog, except when he was answering a question with a worried, "I don't know, senor." He claimed he could not remember how long he had lived at Montserrat, where he had come from before that, or even if he had ever been married. Once he burst into song and sang to himself a long romantic lament in French without ever hitting a wrong note or stumbling over the words; and another time, as Toby came by, he was shaving while still riding on his donkey. He did an excellent job, too, without a single nick. Toby was tempted to borrow the razor and try the same feat just to see if he could do it, but his courage failed him. Jacques was a total mystery.

Josep was so muffled under a sodden fur hat that little of his face was visible. He smiled with blue lips, though, and held out a purse. "Your fee, *Campeador*."

It clinked. It was weighty.

"Senor Brusi!" Toby protested, without even opening it. "This is too much! And the journey isn't over yet."

"Too much for my life? No, you have earned every *blanca* of it. I included an open letter to my agents in other cities. If you can find your way to any of them, they will give you employment."

Toby thanked him sincerely, but he untied the purse and removed the letter. "This will be incriminating evidence if I fall into the Inquisition's clutches, senor."

"Then read it and destroy it, but memorize the names. I shall write and tell them to look out for you."

"You are very kind," Toby said awkwardly. Kindness was a phenomenon he had met so rarely that he hardly knew how to handle it.

Father Guillem, who normally wore a solid frown, was beaming cheerfully because he was almost home. That did not stop him from giving Toby several stern lectures on the importance of keeping the hob under firm control in the future.

"Had it not been for Brother Bernat's testimony," he concluded, "I should certainly have reported you to the Inquisition in Tortosa. By all the customary criteria, you are possessed by a demon. Your watch-word from now on must be eternal vigilance!"

It must be Lochan na Bi. Toby assured the learned acolyte that he was aware of the dangers.

And Hamish.

Hamish looked like a three-day corpse, very different from his usual merry self. The bandage round his head failed to hide all of the bruise swelling like a slice of raw liver on his temple. Unless the spirit was willing to heal him, he would need a week in bed to recover from that injury. He spoke little, which was an ominous sign, and he was visibly weakening as the day dragged on.

Under the pall of cloud, darkness seemed to come hours earlier than it should. The road entered a dense pine forest and grew steeper and steeper until it was zigzagging up a precipitous hillside. The horses found it hard going, although wagons obviously used the trail, for the stony surface was deeply rutted, running rivulets of reddish-brown water.

"Are you all right?" Toby asked anxiously, several times.

Usually Hamish just nodded, although the answer

was obviously, *No*. Once he asked, "How much farther now?"

"An hour or so, Father Guillem says. Maybe less.
He isn't sure where the safe zone begins, but he
expects there will be a checkpoint soon. Look, if
you want to hear some *good* news, I'm not having
any feelings of *déjà vu*. None at all! I've never come
this way before, I'm certain."

Hamish squinted at him blearily, his face a white
blur in the gloom. "But when we get to the checkpoint it's goodbye?"

"Father Guillem will show me the trail out to the
north. Josep has promised to find you a ship, has he
not?"

Hamish nodded, looking even more miserable.

"I wish you safe voyage," Toby said awkwardly.
Life without him was a dismal prospect. "Don't
bother giving my love to the glen. I'll miss you,
friend. We've had good times in among the tough
ones."

"And you don't want me around after what happened last night."

"That has nothing at all to do with it. I have made
blunders of my own often enough, and you have
pulled me through them."

"Not on that scale. I wish I could be strong like
you. You don't let women bother you."

Could he really believe that? Sometimes the
bookworm was as blind as an earthworm.

Toby tried repeatedly to cheer him up. "Look on
the bright side—you're going home! It's just your
sore head that's making you feel this way. Did
Pepita help your headache? You want me to ask her
to try again?"

"She did no good at all. Why don't you try instead?"

"Me?"

Hamish scowled. "This *alumbradismo* . . . When you called down the lightning on the *landsknechte*, that was gramarye, sort of. Like Brother Bernat's healing."

"I suppose there's a resemblance, but frying people is a strange way to cure what ails them."

"Very funny. He had an incarnate spirit, you have the hob. So why can't you learn to control it the way he could?"

"I don't think he could control it. He could ask, that's all—like praying to a tutelary. I wouldn't know how to start. He said I mustn't even try to control it, or it will end up controlling me. Maybe in thirty or forty years, he said, I will be able to risk asking favors of it, in small ways. I'm no saint, Hamish, and I'm sure I never will be. The hob isn't an elemental, and it isn't 'sitting right,' whatever that means. I was too old when I started. The best I can hope for is to keep it from interfering."

He suspected his chances of doing even that were slender as gossamer. He was bound for disaster, sooner or later. That was another reason to go on alone.

Hamish sighed. He liked the world to be more logical. "You're not planning anything foolish, are you? You're not going to go off with the don to try and kill Oreste? Or try to buy him off with the amethyst?"

"Never. Strangling that monster would be a very good idea, yes. I would dearly love to squeeze his throat until his eyes pop and his tongue sticks out and his face turns purple, but I know it's impossible. I just want to keep well away from him, and the Inquisition, and the Fiend. A quiet life for me and the hob, nothing exciting. A job as a woodcutter, perhaps, or a stonemason—something I can put my muscles to work on." Then he lied. "Perhaps someday a wife and children, if I can ever be quite sure that—"

"Demons, Toby! I don't want to go! Not yet. Please?"

Toby sighed. "Let's get you to Montserrat. If the spirit will cure your cracked head, then you'll be able to think straight again."

Hamish managed a smile. "Thanks! But I know what I'll—"

They peered into the murk.

"Toby? Isn't that the don shouting?"

Toby urged Smeòrach forward.

4

There could be no better site for an ambush. Overhanging foliage made the trail into a tunnel, gloomy and foggy. The slopes on either hand were impassable for horses, overgrown and much too steep. Don Ramon, in the lead as always, had just gone round the next bend and now came cantering back into view, his warning shouts growing clearer. Only one word mattered: *Barricade!*

For an instant Toby wondered if the man had panicked at the sight of the expected checkpoint, then discarded the notion. Other men might make such an error, but not the don, and the odds must be overwhelmingly bad for him to have turned tail.

Roadblock ahead meant danger at the rear, of course. Cliff down on one side, cliff up on the other. A perfect trap, lobsters in the pot.

The only hope was to turn tail and hope to break out downhill. As Toby reined Smeòrach in, he saw the women start to turn their mounts, but then Josep knotted up the pack train like kelp on a beach and blocked the don's path completely. Worse!

He spun Smeòrach around, back toward the last bend, shouting warnings to Father Guillem and Hamish. He drew his sword and reined in with an oath as the brigands came around the corner. There were at least a score of them, a ragtag band of pirates, all on foot and clad in a motley collection of garments and armor, but spread out in good order, not all clustered in an easy target. Someone knew his job well. Pikes, swords, no arquebuses—the don had proved the previous night that firearms were useless in such weather—but also crossbows. In desperation Toby looked again at the flanking slopes and saw more men above the trail, even a couple in trees on the downhill side. Chattering to Hamish, he had missed those, but so had the don. A dozen bolts were pointed at his heart. They would have difficulty missing at that range.

It would be small comfort while dying to know that Baron Oreste was not going to get him, nor lay his fat hands on the amethyst.

Sick with despair he glanced back. Jacques had jumped from his donkey and was disentangling the pack train, apparently very expertly. The don would get by it in a moment. But even he could do nothing against this force.

Had they been *landsknechte*, Toby might have

hoped to give himself up in return for the others' freedom, but one glance at these ruffians was proof enough that they were only after loot, not him in particular. He felt mostly anger at being taken so easily . . . frustration at failing so close to his destination . . . sheer terror at what those bolts could do to his flesh . . . an urgent disinclination to die . . . the hob! Not the hob!

Swan. Lochan na Bi. Swan. Lochan na Bi. Swan. He lowered his sword and strove to breathe as he had been taught, struggling to calm his racing heart. He must not let the hob rampage! It might strike down his friends as easily as his foes.

And besides: *If you ever travel that road again, you must not expect to return.*

"Company halt!" barked the leader. He was big, although probably more blubber than muscle, with a coarse, black-bearded face. He wore a steel helmet and breastplate. Alone among the group he carried no weapon in his hand, but a gilded hilt protruded from the scabbard at his side. He regarded the catch with satisfaction. "Throw your swords over there."

His arrogant smirk made Toby's fists clench and brought sweat to his forehead even as he repeated his mantra and tried to think of the swan. "We are but poor pilgrims, senor. We have little worth stealing except our mounts."

"We'll be the judge of that. Throw away your sword, boy."

Gold did not matter now, and certainly the horses did not. Even if the pilgrims lost everything except their lives, they could walk to Montserrat from here.

Toby eased Smeòrach forward to place himself ahead of Guillem. "Will you spare our—"

Before he completed the move, the monk roared,
"Fools!" in a voice like a cannonade and kicked in
his heels. Startled, his horse leaped into motion.

Toby shouted, "Careful, Father!"

Still bellowing, the monk rode straight for the
brigands, going much too fast over the rocks and
mud. "You are within the domain of the holy tutelary of Montserrat. It will not condone such violence!"

"Take him, Jordi."

A crossbow cracked. Father Guillem and his
horse went down together in a somersault and rolled
on the muddy, rocky trail. The horse screamed, tried
to struggle to its feet, shrilling in pain, but then collapsed in a heap and fell silent. Father Guillem lay
face down, half dragged out of his robe. The bolt
must have gone right through him without hitting
bone, or the impact would have hurled him backward out of the saddle. If the shot had not killed
him, then the horse had smashed him to pulp. He
was either dead or dying.

"Seems he was wrong," said the leader. "Nice
shot, Jordi. Throw down your sword, boy, and dismount." He had summed up the group and picked
out Toby as the leader. He knew his business. He
had the same cold blooded efficiency as Arnaud
Villars the smuggler; he even looked like him.

"You will spare our lives?"

"Your lives are no use to me, sonny, but if you
don't get off that horse right now, we'll shoot you
off it."

Smeòrach was fast and nimble. Toby might get
one of them—the leader or another—before they
got him. Maybe even two. By then he would be a

hedgehog of crossbow quarrels and what would happen after that? Unless a bolt took him through the heart, his body might fight on without him. Or the hob might lash out with lightnings, destroying brigands and pilgrims and forest indiscriminately. Or it might flip him back in time to the Inquisition. Whatever it did, Brother Bernat had said, *If you ever travel that road again . . .*

He threw his sword into the trees and turned in the saddle to address the others. "Do as they say! They will spare our—"

"King Pedro and Castile!" Hooves thundered, mud sprayed, horses whinnied in alarm. Having won his way past the pack train, the don came charging down the trail with his lance couched.

It should have been obvious that Don Ramon de Nuñez y Pardo would not surrender to a common footpad, nor even forty of them. Or perhaps he thought he was leading a whole army of armored knights against the Moors. Whatever the reason, honor demanded death. Toby spun Smeòrach around and kicked him harder than the poor beast had ever been kicked. Astonished but ever willing, Smeòrach leaped forward. Toby rode him straight into the oncoming maniac.

The don held his lance in his right hand, aimed to strike an opponent approaching on his left—that was correct technique for jousting, and he was undoubtedly well practiced in the arts of chivalry. But the terrain was very treacherous, and one thing that almost never happened in the best tilting yards was a horse careering into you at high speed from the right and a young man of very large size hurling himself on top of you. Lance, shield, knight,

Longdirk, and Midnight all went over together in an
explosion of mud and stones. The outraged
Smeòrach carried on up the trail as fast as his
hooves would carry him.

The brigand leader walked over and put the crippled
Midnight to death with a single deft thrust to the
heart. He peered at the don, then wiped his sword on
the animal without bothering to administer another
coup de grâce. He took a longer, warier look at
Toby.

The world had not quite stopped spinning. He had
managed to rub most of the mud out of his eyes but
had not yet catalogued all his scrapes and bruises.
Still too sick and shocked from the impact to think
of sitting up, he returned the brigand's calculating
stare as well as he could from ground level.

Total disaster! In three years of wild adventuring,
he had never failed so hopelessly. Even in his
visions of Oreste's dungeon or the Inquisition's torture chamber he had been alone, whereas here he
must endure the reproach of friends who had
depended on him. Now he could appreciate Brother
Bernat's warning that he would no longer have the
hob to defend him. Worst of all, he had accepted the
old man's word for it that next time the hob would
take him over permanently. He might have been
wrong. It had never done so before. For the others'
sake, Toby should have risked possession. The don
had done the honorable thing, while he must live
with his guilt—Montserrat piled on Mezquiriz.

Only the monotonous hiss of the rain disturbed
the silence of the forest. Then Doña Francisca threw

herself on top of her son with a wail. His helmet had fallen off; his auburn hair trailed in the mud. He was either dead or stunned.

The surviving members of the company arrived on foot—Pepita, Josep, Gracia, Senora Collel, and Hamish leaning on Jacques's shoulder. Brigands closed in around them with drawn swords. Others had already taken charge of the horses, moving as if they had performed this operation many times.

Toby sat up—carefully and painfully.

"That's far enough, sonny!" snapped the leader. "José, keep an eye on this one. If he as much as twitches, kill him."

"With pleasure, *Caudillo*." The nearest guard took up position in front of Toby, aiming a cocked crossbow at him. He was a rangy youth with a nasty leer on his unshaven face. "It will not be a difficult shot."

Toby groaned and just sat where he was in the mud. The spinning slowed.

Night and fog were closing in. Vague shapes of horses jingled and splashed as they were led away down the road. The captives huddled together at the verge, surrounded by their grinning captors. Some of the brigands dragged Francisca off the don and began searching his body for valuables. The monk lay where he had fallen, ignored.

The *caudillo* stepped up to Gracia and leered. "You're worth keeping. You'll come with us." He raised his voice. "The rest of you take your clothes off—all of them."

"That is barbaric!" Toby roared.

"Kill him if he speaks again, José."

"You promised not to harm us—"

"I promised nothing. Shoot him at the next word, José. That's an order."

Toby stared up helplessly at José's teeth and eyes shining mockingly in the gloom.

The *caudillo* sneered down at him. "Too late for heroics, little boy. You can keep your lives if you behave, but that's all. Nothing more. The run up to the monastery will warm you. This one has a treat in store for her." He poked a finger at Gracia's bottle. "What's in this?"

She clutched it with both hands and tried to step back, but there was a tree right behind her. "Nothing, senor!" she wailed.

"Nothing?" The *caudillo* seized the bottle in one hand and her throat in the other. With a yank, he broke the thong and snatched it from her grasp.

Gracia screamed and tried to reach for it. Toby ground his teeth, horribly aware that any visible move would provoke the twitch of José's trigger finger that would end everything. At his back, his hand groped the gravel in search of a rock small enough to throw, large enough to damage . . .

The *caudillo* pulled out the stopper and tilted the bottle. Nothing emerged. He snorted and tossed it over his shoulder. It shattered. "We'll fill your flask for you tonight, senorita. I told the rest of you to take your clothes off. Do I have to kill one of you to get . . ." He turned and peered up the road. "What's that noise?"

The crossbow menacing Toby fell away as José stepped back, staring fixedly at something in the woods. His eyes seemed uncannily bright in the gloom. "Oh, no!" he wailed. "No, no!"

Toby risked a quick glance around and saw

nothing behind him except darkness and tree trunks.
What was going on?

With a shrill scream, the *caudillo* drew his sword.
"Leave me alone! Begone!" He parried like a
fencer, then began slashing and leaping as if beset
by invisible foes, gradually drawing away from the
captives.

More of the brigands cried out and started flailing pikes or swords at the fog. Their frenzy grew
wilder, their screams of terror louder. Metal
clashed against metal. The prisoners were being
totally ignored. Injuries forgotten, Toby lurched to
his feet and made a dive for a fallen sword. He
came back armed and much happier for it,
although he could see that there would soon be no
enemies left. His friends huddled in around him, as
if he could defend them from what was happening.
Gracia clutched at him, and he put an arm around
her.

"The voices!" she cried. "Oh, do you hear them,
senor? Do you hear what they are saying?"

"I hear nothing." But he could feel the hair on his
scalp stir.

Pepita's squeal sounded more like laughter than
fright. Senora Collel shrieked wordlessly and kept
on shrieking until Toby gave her a shove. "Be
quiet!" he said. "Will you draw attention to us?"
She choked into silence.

There was no escape, for the road was blocked
in both directions by cavorting weapon-wielding
madmen, whose windmill strokes were inevitably
starting to find flesh-and-blood victims. Screams of
terror were being overwhelmed by screams of
agony and mindless rage. José was still the closest;

he swung his bow like a club at a swordsman, who turned on him with a string of lurid oaths. The two of them engaged in a wild duel, bow against sword, both slashing ineptly as if they could not see each other properly, both shrieking hysterically.

"Villains! Monsters!" the *caudillo* bellowed. "I will not accept your lies!" He felled José from behind. The other man promptly reversed his sword and threw himself on it. A crossbow bolt thudded into the *caudillo's* breastplate, toppling him backward. He kicked a few times and then lay still.

It was almost over. A few vague figures still screamed and howled in the fog, battling one another without mercy or any visible reason. When they lost their weapons they went for each other with bare hands, punching and strangling, battering heads on rocks. Several hurled themselves over the edge of the track, their yells dying away in thuds and crashes among the trees on the slope below.

"Wraiths?" Hamish said. "Can you see them, senora?"

"I can hear my voices!" Gracia cried.

"Victory!" Josep cried shrilly. "Senora de Gomez has defeated them!"

The last two brigands rushed at each other in a duel, shrieking nonsensical insults, hacking wildly with no attempt to parry. One dropped, the other took a couple of paces and pitched headlong to the ground. The gurgling cries of pain died away into silence.

It was over, all over. Incredibly, the enemy had destroyed themselves in their madness, to the last man. No one would mourn them, but they might have claimed two worthy lives in their villainy, and those lay heavy on Toby's mind. He had come to like the mad don and admire him. Lately he had even come to terms with the crusty old monk. In fact, if not in name, Toby had been in charge, so their loss was on his conscience now. He also owed Gracia a profound apology for doubting her and her voices.

More screaming . . . in the distance, farther down the hill.

"Listen!" Josep shouted. "The wraiths have gone to rescue our horses." His voice cracked with fear or excitement.

Pepita laughed. "They will drive them back to us!" She was much less upset than any of the adults. "Those bad men were fighting ghosts. Did you see, Toby? Their swords went right through them!"

"I did not see, but I guessed." He saw that Doña Francisca was kneeling over her son again. "Is he alive?"

"I believe so, senor."

"I am glad."

The don was young and fit, and all he had suffered was a fall. Was there any chance that Father Guillem had survived? Stepping over corpses, picking his way through the slaughter, Toby set off down the road to where the acolyte lay beside his horse. Everyone except Francisca came after him, wanting the comfort of his presence. He was a failure and a coward, but he was all they had.

He squatted to lay fingers against the stricken man's throat. Astonishingly he found a pulse—weak but regular, not the fluttering uncertain beat of a dying heart. Although it was hard to tell in the gloom, he could see no trace of a wound, or even injuries. Another miracle? He felt anger surging and struggled to suppress it.

He rose. "Father Guillem's still alive! We must get him to the sanctuary as fast as possible."

"I do not think that will be necessary," Hamish said quietly. "Listen."

Hooves clinked and splashed on the downhill bend—apparently the horses were returning as Pepita had predicted. But there were voices from the opposite direction. Balls of brightness in the fog came into view around the corner and gradually resolved into flaming torches as they approached, a dozen or more of them.

5

The five at the front were nuns in black robes and head cloths, and although four of them held lanterns, almost nothing of their faces could be seen. They halted a few feet from the huddle of pilgrims and just stared at Toby, who had remained standing when his companions knelt. The one in the center was taller and probably younger than the others. She carried no light, but the rain around her glimmered with another sort of brightness.

Behind them came a dozen monks in the black robes of Benedictines with their hoods raised against the drizzle, so that the flicker of their torches showed only disembodied faces floating in the gathering dark. They divided into two lines and took up position like a guard of honor along either side of the road, shedding light on the battlefield. More monks without torches followed them.

"Is this not wonderful!" Gracia enthused, reaching

up to pull on Toby's arm. "After so many troubles, to find sanctuary! And the wraiths tell me that Montserrat will cherish them. . . ." She prattled on.

Toby kept his attention on the silent women and especially the one with the golden shimmer around her. So this was the famous tutelary of Montserrat! Why had it not intervened sooner to prevent so much anguish and so many deaths? He felt he had a bone or two to pick with Montserrat, but it was obviously not going to speak until he behaved like a grown-up. Angrily, he threw down his sword and sank to his knees on muddy stones that felt accursedly sharp and cold through the only pair of hose he possessed.

As if that were a signal, four novices came forward bearing a litter. In reverent silence they lifted Father Guillem onto it and then bore him away up the road. Others were similarly attending to the don. Lay servants arrived with clattering, squeaky carts to remove the dead.

So the two casualties were to be cured of their injuries, were they? But why bother with the litters? Why not perform the miracles right here? Toby's own aches had almost totally disappeared. And Hamish's, also, apparently, for he was holding his head up and smiling as much as anyone, and he had not smiled all day. And that meant . . .

He struggled to quell fury. That meant that the fight had been a hoax. Not an illusion, for those dead men seemed real enough. And dead enough. But a fraud, nevertheless. The *arrogance* of it! The *callous*, deliberate *slaughter!* A tutelary should never allow such evil things to happen within its domain! Father Guillem had known that, but

Montserrat had silenced Father Guillem before he said too much. Montserrat had been playing tricks—evil, evil tricks. Why? Something to do with Toby Longdirk, certainly. Dangerous tricks. The brigands might have provoked the hob into another rampage, putting everyone at risk. What *had* happened to the hob, which had always shunned tutelaries in the past?

The incarnation spoke, her voice clear and cold like the note of a bell, a voice to brook no argument. But she addressed the words to the night, not to anyone in particular. Her eyes were closed.

"Pepita, you would be welcome here for Brother Bernat's sake, but you are equally welcome for you own. Stay with us and be cherished."

Pepita beamed. "I like you! You make me see rainbows." She ran forward. One of the older women smiled and bent to hug the sodden bundle, then scooped her up and carried her away. As they disappeared from view, a childish voice shouted: "'Bye, Toby!"

"'Bye, Pepita," he shouted. "Spirits bless you."

"Gracia," said the spirit, "Margarita, Josep, Hamish . . . and Tobias. You may rise." It fell silent until they did so. Perhaps it spoke then in confidence to Hamish, for he suddenly pulled off his bandage and grinned at the incarnation with all the stupefied adoration of a spaniel.

The last bodies were being wheeled away; the last of the pilgrims' horses led off. The monks with the torches remained, human candlesticks to illuminate the proceedings. Somewhere higher on the hill a large wagon squeaked and rattled. And more feet, more hooves? Unless there was a freak echo at this spot, it sounded as if two minor armies were approaching, one up the hill and one down, and they were going to meet right at Toby Longdirk. That could not be coincidence.

The rain was growing heavier.

"You come seeking sanctuary," the spirit said. "But your petition has already been contested. Antonio?"

Surely a monastery wouldn't throw a man out in the hills on a night like this without even Smeòrach? Why couldn't they all go indoors and hold this meeting in front of a roaring fire of pine logs?

Many men had halted in the background, their weapons and armor glinting faint reflections of the torchlight. The Antonio the spirit had summoned marched forward out of the darkness. He saluted the incarnation, then stared at Toby with only a faint trace of curiosity in his customary granitic expression.

It felt much like an uppercut to the jaw. Toby knew Captain Diaz of the Palau Reial in Barcelona, but Captain Diaz would not recall their previous meetings, because they had never happened.

"Repeat your concerns, Antonio," the incarnation said, eyes still closed.

"Your Holiness has already seen the document. I have a warrant for the arrest of the foreigners Tobias Longdirk and Hamish Campbell."

Toby shrugged with as much unconcern as he could manage, sending numerous trickles of water racing down his back. He wished his insides felt as cool as his outside. "On what charge?"

"No charge is specified. You are to be detained by order of his Excellency the viceroy."

Toby spared a glance for Hamish—who returned a grim scowl—then addressed the incarnation. "Holiness, I appeal for sanctuary! This is gross injustice."

"We agree. Catalans cherish their ancient freedoms. Antonio, you must present a reason."

Diaz frowned, and if he had been a man who showed emotion it would probably have been surprise. Surely he had not expected the tutelary to hand over a suppliant without cause? Or had he already been assured that in this case it would? The stench of *trap* was unmistakable.

"The civil power's warrant is cause enough, Holiness, when it deems that lives are in jeopardy."

"If Oreste can be so arbitrary, then so can we. We require you to give us a specific reason."

Another voice intervened before Diaz could respond, a voice whose rasp of age did not lessen its deep authority: "I can present a reason. Captain Diaz is acting on my behalf. The man Longdirk is possessed by a demon." Out from behind the soldiers came a tall, elderly Dominican.

Randal's first punch. The first and last bout in Longdirk's brief career as a professional prizefighter had opened with a sickening lesson in just how hard a man could hit a boy. This punch felt even harder. He had been told repeatedly that tutelaries would never have dealings with the Inquisition. Why must he always turn out to be the exception to every rule?

The old man's pouched eyes inspected him, then a smile like a sword cut parted the skull face. "There can be no question that this creature belongs to the Inquisition, Holiness."

"No question?" For the first time the spirit lost a little of its inhuman calm. "There can be no question that our authority is paramount within our domain! Do you dare dispute this, Vespianaso?"

Hamish recognized the name and muttered something fiery under his breath.

The friar's bow was perfunctory. "Of course not, Holiness. But unless you plan to retain him here, then you must hand Longdirk over to the appropriate authority outside, and in all Spain that proper authority is the Inquisition." He cupped his hands and blew into them to warm them.

"This is not our concern!" Senora Collel cried. "I have no truck with demons! Holiness, I beg you—"

"Be silent, Margarita! The rest of you may be required as witnesses, depending on our decision. Tobias, do you deny the charge?"

Surprise! Perhaps there was hope after all?— if Montserrat was willing to defy both Oreste and the Inquisition. Again he wondered whose were the feet and hooves coming up the hill. It was late for anyone to be on the road, especially in such weather. Things were happening too quickly.

Still, he had no choice now but to gamble on the tutelary's honesty, no matter what tricks it had been playing earlier.

"Yes, I deny the charge."

"State your case, Vespianaso."

The friar shrugged as if that would be a waste of time. "The man was identified as a creature years ago in his native land. He has been pursued across all Europe, spreading death and destruction in his wake. He was indicted again in Castile this summer and escaped again. We set up a checkpoint to intercept him near Tortosa. It was wiped out. Thirty-four men died. I am surprised that your Holiness would even—"

"This is all hearsay. Have you witnesses?"

The rain that sizzled in the torches was driving hard in Toby's face, but more than cold was making him shiver. Yes, there were witnesses: Gracia, Josep, Collel, and the others now up at the monastery. He must not let them be dragged into the Inquisition's coils.

"I do not deny that I was there, or that the men died. But I am not possessed of a demon."

"In that case," inquired the inquisitor with heavy sarcasm, "I assume Captain Diaz is here to enlist you?"

"Tobias," the incarnation said, "you quibble about the nature of the sprite. Do you seriously expect us to release you so that you may continue your bloody course?"

He wiped his eyes. "Brother Bernat instructed me in how to control this sprite you mention."

"Did you control it at Tortosa, or did it act without your guidance?"

That fast one-two left him no defense. He had admitted that he bore the hob. Which of them was master did not matter. "I had not yet had time to master it," he mumbled. "It is behaving itself now."

"That is only because we have subdued it. Do you regret what happened?"

Both Oreste and the Inquisition had underestimated the hob in the past, but Montserrat had centuries of experience and far greater wisdom than either of them, so perhaps the hob was truly incapacitated this time. . . .

He shrugged. There was no way to deceive a spirit. "Yes, in the sense that I wish they had just left me alone. I do not enjoy killing. But put me in the same circumstances again, and I would still not submit to violence. The reverend friar reversed the truth. I am not possessed, and yet I have been hunted and hounded across all Europe. For three years I have lived in dread of being stabbed through the heart by any stranger I met, and what the Inquisition planned for me was a great deal worse than that. I have the right to defend myself, do I not?" The best method of defense, he recalled, was attack: "And who are you to judge me? You slaughtered as many or more here tonight."

"That was not our doing."

"This is your domain. You let it happen."

"They came to loot and rape and so deserved the death they met. We intervened only to save innocent lives."

"You absolve yourself very glibly!" He wished the spirit would lose its temper and shout back at him, but immortals did not do that. The icy girlish voice was slaughtering him. "I was saving innocent lives at Tortosa—my own and other people's. I don't see that my actions are any different from yours."

"We are not on trial here, Tobias. You are." Punch!

"Sauce for the gander is not sauce for the goose?"

Hamish thumped his arm with a warning growl. "Be respectful, you big oaf!"

"Why should I be respectful? If this is a trial, then the judge should be in the dock with the accused. I was being threatened with the most humiliating and painful death imaginable. Does an immortal deny a mortal the right to defend his life?"

"We do if he is deserving of death," the spirit said.
"The men you slaughtered were doing their duty,
legally and morally."

"You call torture moral?"

"Would you have submitted had the penalty been
beheading?"

Punch! Feeling as if all the breath had been
knocked out of him, Toby again wiped his face with
a sodden sleeve. He could never win a battle of wits
against one of the wisest tutelaries in all Europe. If
this went on long enough he would freeze to death.

"It wasn't!" he shouted. "It was torture. You argue
in circles. I deserve death because I defend myself
from being put to death for defending myself?"

"And what were you defending yourself from at
Mezquiriz?" the spirit persisted in the same calm
tones. "What threat to you were the sailors on the
Maid of Arran? Or the women who died in Bordeaux? Or the soldiers at Limoges . . ."

Punch, punch, punch! He would not survive much
more of this. Perhaps the tutelary was dragging all
the details from his own memory. The incarnation's
eyes were still closed, but the nuns attending her
and the monks with torches all stared at him in
wide-eyed horror.

He found his voice; it sounded strange to him.
"You know that the hob is not a demon."

"Tell that to the dead in Mezquiriz. Tell them in
Tortosa. You may not think of the sprite as a demon,
but who else can agree with you?"

"Brother Bernat did!"

"We are not bound by his conclusions," the spirit
said. "He was fallible."

"And you are not? The hob's motives—"

"The hob's motives do not matter, only its actions. Your promises to make it behave in future are not credible. You show no repentance. We judge you to be possessed."

Now he was on the ropes!

For a moment no one spoke. He caught Hamish's eye and answered the horror in it with a shrug. There was certainly some truth in what the tutelary said—the hob could be very demonic at times. If he were just given time to learn the techniques Brother Bernat had taught him . . . but he might never succeed, and every failure would risk more innocent lives. Toby Longdirk was not guilty of anything except wanting to go on living, and the hob would not have let him kill himself anyway. Could it rescue him from the Inquisition again? This time, after Tortosa, the inquisitors would be very careful.

"So you will hand the creature over to us, Holiness?" Father Vespianaso inquired, rubbing his skeletal hands. He looked pleased.

"Unless the man asks us to exorcize the demon, or sprite, or hob, or whatever he chooses to call it."

Hope pealed like thunder. Toby came out with fists flailing. "Is that possible, Holiness? I have been wanting that for years!"

"It is possible," said the incarnation. "You had time to become acquainted with Jacques?"

Oh, bloody demons! Knockout!

6

Jacques! Toby had completely forgotten the inexplicable messenger and had not seen him since the ambush, but he was inexplicable no longer, and neither was his message. This was the worst blow yet. He stared in revulsion as the gardener-cleaner-porter came shuffling in through the misty rain with a bemused smile on his empty face. Horror, horror!

"He is broken," Pepita had said.

"No, Jacques, do not kneel," said the spirit. "You are no less worthy than any of these men. Tobias, make your choice."

Desperately fighting for time to think, Toby shouted, "No! I don't understand."

"You do understand, but we will spell it out for you. We can exorcize the sprite, the hob, but much of you will come with it."

"That? You will turn me into that?"

"Something like him."

"He was possessed by a hob too?"

"An elemental. *Dejamiento* does not always work. Jacques was a very fine man in his way, but he lacked the patience and self-denial needed to become a true *alumbrado*. He succumbed to carnal temptations and the spirit ran amok, just as your hob did at Mezquiriz. When it was exorcized, much of Jacques was lost. The same will happen in your case, although perhaps not as severely, for he had been invested since childhood. You may not be as badly damaged as he is, but you will certainly lose something. You will do no more harm to others. You will be happy as he is happy and remain here, being well cared for, but you will not be the person you are now."

"You would turn him into a rabbit?" Hamish shouted. "This is barbaric!"

"Possession is worse," said the spirit. "Choose, Tobias."

In his vision of cutting off Hamish's head, he had been free of the hob. And he had been a slobbering moron. A demon had enforced his obedience to the baron, but the demon had not made him into that cringing idiot, that butt of the court's humor, that bumbling sycophant who would shamelessly take women to bed at his master's orders or cut off his friends' heads without a care.

To become a moron or be tortured to death? A long life of useless idiocy or a short one of unspeakable agony? It would not seem short. He wanted to ask Hamish to advise him, but that would be grossly unkind, for no man should be expected to make such a decision—not for himself nor for anyone else.

No, he could not subject his flesh to the inquisitors' torments again. And if he accepted what Montserrat ordered, he would at least be cheating Oreste of his triumph.

Hoarsely, he said, "If you will grant me asylum, then I accept the exorcism, Holiness."

"On that condition we grant you sanctuary for the remainder of your days."

"Wait!" Captain Diaz had been watching in grim silence. "If we cannot have the man, then I must still claim a certain purple gemstone he possesses. Sergeant Gomez!"

"The amethyst is mine!" Toby roared.

"What is this gem?" Father Vespianaso demanded angrily. "An immured demon?"

"No, it does not contain a demon," said the tutelary. "Give it up, Tobias. You have no further use for it."

"It has great sentimental value for me. My foster mother gave it to me, her last gift. It is my property.

Will you tolerate armed robbery in your realm, Montserrat?"

Diaz stepped forward with another soldier at his heels. "You have admitted to being a demonic husk, so you have no rights in law. Give me the stone."

It was another failure, but a man should know when he is beaten. Toby fumbled at his collar to pull the thong over his head; he opened the locket and rolled out the amethyst onto Diaz's waiting palm.

Surrender.

The captain walked over to the closest torch and inspected the purple crystal. "Thank you." He came and took the locket from Toby, replaced the stone in the little bag and turned to his companion, who held out an ivory casket. The locket went in the box, and then the box into a satchel, which Diaz slung over his shoulder.

"I wish I could say that you were welcome," Toby said ruefully. "Do you know why the baron wants it so badly?"

"I do not want to know." Diaz turned to the incarnation. "And the other man, Holiness? My warrant also names Hamish Campbell."

Toby had forgotten that. He stared in horror at Hamish's pale face.

"He is not possessed! He is not guilty of any crime!" He was guilty of knowing the truth about King Nevil, though. Oreste would see him dead for that.

"He has been your accomplice for three years," Father Vespianaso retorted. "It was his duty to aid the authorities in apprehending you."

"The man Campbell belongs to us!" bellowed a new voice.

They had all been too engrossed to pay attention

to the newcomers whose clattering and splashing Toby had heard earlier. Heads turned to peer in the downhill direction, where a second troop of soldiers stood in the darkness, a considerably larger force than Captain Diaz had brought. After everything that had happened already, it was not surprising that they were *landsknechte*.

The tutelary would never be surprised by anything. "Approach and state your claim, Leopold."

In marched the mercenary captain, a solid, powerful-looking young man whose russet beard failed to conceal a monstrous scar deforming his mouth. His doublet was splendid, his ermine-trimmed cloak hung open to display a wealth of gold chains adorning his chest. He saluted the incarnation respectfully, but he merely sneered at Diaz.

"The man slew our comrades!" His Castilian was almost incomprehensible under a harsh Germanic accent. "He to us belongs!"

Captain Diaz cocked one eyebrow. "I have a warrant from the viceroy."

"It is a matter of honor!"

"It is a matter of law. Your presence here violates your contract, *Hauptmann* von Münster. Why are you absent from your post at Lerida?"

"For honor, Captain. Perhaps a Catalan cannot appreciate honor?"

"My warrant names both men," Diaz said stonily, turning to the incarnation, "as your Holiness is well aware. His Excellency would be highly displeased if—"

"Are you threatening us?"

"Not at all, Holiness. I merely quote my orders."

Lightning on a dark night, claw marks in the sand—of course it was a threat! Toby should have seen the truth much sooner. The Fiend's army was supposedly excluded from Montserrat by treaty, but Diaz and Vespianaso had been waiting up at the monastery. Nevil's viceroy would never let a mere treaty stand between him and the hated Longdirk. And although Montserrat's wisdom and power were legendary, and its mountain realms immune to almost any mundane attack, it would not be able to withstand the baron's demonic legions. Oreste had sent Diaz with an ultimatum, and the spirit had yielded. The tutelary had sold out to the hexer and the Inquisition.

Von Münster was scowling at Toby with hatred and disgust. "About the creature nothing we can do, but the man is ours for justice."

"It is nice to feel wanted," Hamish remarked airily. "Shall we start the bidding at ten ducats?"

Toby shot him an admiring smile. "The fault was not his. Let him go, *Hauptmann*. Promise me a quick death, and you can take me instead."

"Fools you think us, demon? You stay here. We a witness have." The mercenary turned and barked orders in German.

Two men strutted forward as if they had been waiting for the command, hustling a woman along between them, and of course it was Eulalia, which explained how the *landsknechte* had tracked Toby into Montserrat so easily. But they must have been close on his heels even before they caught her.

"Tell the friar what you to us told!"

Although she was bedraggled and looked half frozen, her eyes flashed triumph at the sight of the prisoners. "The big one burned up the men with thunderbolts." She tossed her head defiantly and smiled as she pointed to Hamish. "I saw Jaume killing one of the foreigners with a sword."

Father Vespianaso massaged his bony fingers. "This may be more serious than we thought. Did you see evidence that he was possessed, child? Did he behave strangely, talk aloud when there was no one there, fall into trances? Did he use unnatural powers—to take advantage of you in some way, perhaps?"

Eulalia accepted the threads offered and began to embroider. "Oh yes, Father! Oh, yes! He summoned me to his bed by night, and I was unable to resist. I didn't want to go, but he had some terrible power he used that made me helpless to refuse his demands. He violated me many times, and he was supernaturally strong, strong beyond all mortal men, never tiring, never satisfied. And he would mutter strange things I couldn't understand, about foreign places and secret books and—"

"That will do for now, my daughter."

Hell hath no fury . . .

Oh, Eulalia! Her spite really should be directed at Toby, because Hamish would certainly have forgiven her by bedtime, but she must have heard enough to know that Toby was beyond her reach now. Oh, Hamish, Hamish! *See what I have brought you to in return for your loyalty and friendship?*

He wanted to scream. He wanted to blast the spirit of Montserrat and its famous monastery to ashes. And the Inquisition. And Oreste, who had won at last. And Nevil the Fiend, demon Rhym, the ultimate cause of all this evil. But he could do none of those things. He had lost everything.

"One hundred ducats?" Hamish said. "Do I hear

two hundred? I am flattered, but unfortunately she is lying. Isn't she, Holiness?"

"She was telling the truth about the sword," the spirit said. "Everything else was exaggeration and wishful thinking. Campbell is not possessed."

"Then I take him!" snapped Diaz.

"How far do you think you will get?" the *landsknecht* sneered. "Spare your men's lives and your own and give him to us."

"What an unseemly squabble!" Hamish remarked, shaking his head. "Why not just agree to let me go?"

Then it was Father Vespianaso's turn again. "We must of course accept the holy spirit's declaration that the accused is not possessed. But he has undoubtedly known for many years that his companion is, and he has done nothing about it. He bears much guilt as an accomplice and must be questioned at length. If the facts are as I have just stated, then justice will be done."

"Under torture questioned?" von Münster demanded.

"Possibly."

"Only possibly?"

"Very probably. We must make quite certain that he is telling the whole truth, you understand."

"And what his penalty will be?"

The friar shrugged as if such details were unimportant. "Assuming he is found guilty, I would expect him to be sentenced to a series of public floggings followed by some years in the galleys. At least ten years. It will depend on the evidence."

Even Hamish could not smile at that.

"One of my comrades he to slay was seen!"

"Of course, there is that, too," the friar agreed.
"Then, Leopold, my son, I can assure you that the
man Campbell will ultimately be handed over to
the civil authorities for execution—to be hanged
for murder or burned at the stake for consorting
with demons. Do you agree with my opinion,
Antonio?"

"I am no lawyer, Father." Captain Diaz was much
too wily to get caught in that mill. "My orders were
to arrest these two men, take them to Barcelona,
and deliver them to you for examination. His
Excellency reserved only the right to ask them a
few questions if he so wishes. *Before* you ask any,
that is." His emphasis implied that *after* the
Inquisition began its interrogation would be too
late to obtain useful answers. "Longdirk has been
granted asylum here, but I shall take Campbell and
deliver him to the Inquisition. Does that satisfy
you, von Münster? Have I your word that you will
return your troop at once to Lerida and make no
attempt to interfere with the transportation of these
prisoners?"

The mercenary displayed his gargoyle smile
again. "I so promise."

Father Vespianaso rubbed his hands in undis-
guised pleasure. "You will also take the witness into
custody, Captain. And these other witnesses also."

Senora Collel wailed like a trampled cat.

"No!" Hamish snapped. "I confess to the killing.
There is no need to arrest anyone else, Captain."

Toby moaned. Hamish was headed to torture and
death, and he was to live on, growing old pottering
contentedly around the monastery herb garden? It
was intolerable. Everyone else here was bargaining

madly—couldn't he? He was the one Oreste and
Vespianaso really wanted. Could he buy back
Hamish's life with his own?

"Your confession is recorded," the inquisitor said
with a macabre smile. "But there is another matter
that must be investigated. The massacre here
tonight—was that also the demon's doing? Or do
we have another demon to hunt down?" He peered
at Josep, Senora Collel, and Gracia. "I still think we
need to interrogate these witnesses."

Gracia uttered a shrill cry of alarm.

And Senora Collel opened her mouth. . . .

"Yes!" Toby yelled. "The brigands' deaths were
my doing also! My demon slew them and I gloried in
it. If I change my mind and refuse the exorcism, will
you release all these others, including Campbell, and
swear not to molest them in future?"

Would the tutelary expose his lie? Or had it
planned this to fulfil its agreement with Diaz?

Father Vespianaso considered his confession with
sly calculation. "Whom are you protecting? Only
Campbell?"

"We accept those terms for the others," Diaz said.
"But not Campbell. The two of you come and the
rest can go."

Toby's mouth was incredibly dry in marked contrast to the rest of him. He knew what was in store,
and *strappado* would be the least of it. But he could
not let the inquisitors get their claws in Gracia. And
he could not betray Josep, either. Hamish was
beyond saving, thanks to Eulalia.

"And what happens then?" demanded von
Münster. "A sword through the monster's heart? It
is too good for him."

Father Vespianaso continued chafing his fingers. "He will be taken to Barcelona for examination."

"Examination?" barked the mercenary. "What is this examination? Has he not confessed? What need is there of examination? He slew our friends, and justice we seek."

The friar shook his head regretfully. "It is revenge you seek, my son, and we cannot countenance that. The Holy Office is guided by mercy and does not put men to death. It seeks only to drive out their demons. As the accused is refusing exorcism, it will be necessary to use harsher means."

"You mean you will torture him until the demon he expels?"

"Regrettably, we will have no choice. But we are moved by compassion, not a craving for vengeance."

"So he will suffer, suffer a long time?"

"He is a strong man and apparently a very determined one."

"That means yes?"

"I fear this may well be so." The friar blew on his hands again.

The scar made *Hauptmann* von Münster's smile particularly horrible. "Then I am satisfied. Will it be possible to view the body?"

"No. It would be too distressing for those who do not understand the need for—"

"That is enough!" said the spirit. "Antonio will take the two men named in the warrant. Leopold and his men will return peaceably to their post. And Vespianaso renounces any further proceedings against the rest. Is this your decision, Tobias?"

Unable to speak, he nodded, not looking at Gracia

or Josep. He wouldn't mind taking Senora Collel and Eulalia by the scruff of their necks and banging their heads together, but that was not possible. The Inquisition would have him.

"So be it," said Montserrat.

The audience was over. When the golden shimmer vanished, the abandoned incarnation staggered. Her companions steadied her, whispering inquiries. She nodded reassuringly, and they all walked away with their heads down. One of the torchbearers went with them to light their path. Josep and the three women were hustled after them by more monks before anyone could think of suitable farewells.

Failure, despair, cold, exhaustion . . .

"Sorry, friend," Toby said. "This looks like the end."

"Ah, you're as daft as I am." Despite his pallor, Hamish managed to produce a faint smile. "We never died before, did we?" He widened the smile into a reasonable facsimile of his favorite grin. "I hate ships, anyway! I didn't really want to go home. Life around you is never dull."

"You may wish it was before long."

"Trust the hob!"

Too late. Toby would be damned if the hob intervened and damned if it did not, but he must not let Hamish outdo him in courage. "Of course. We must be as strong as the rocks in the hills."

"Strong as a billy goat's third horn," said Hamish.

Horses clattered and snorted. Men were hurrying around: Captain Diaz taking over the torches from the departing monks, von Münster mounting up and preparing to move out. The wagon Toby had heard earlier had been waiting in the background and now began squeaking forward. He was not at all surprised to see that it carried a bear cage.

"Longdirk!"

Toby looked down. "What can I do for you, Captain Diaz?"

The soldier studied the prisoner for a moment. "You're a cool one."

"I'm a very cold one at the moment. We're also hungry."

"I'll see what I can do. You are going to come quietly?"

Father Vespianaso and three other friars were standing guard around them, all four holding jeweled crucifixes. A circle of a dozen armed men backed them up. The cage would certainly be warded. It was almost flattering to inspire such precautions.

Toby managed a hollow laugh. "I know when I'm beaten."

The captain nodded. "Hands in front of him, sergeant." The last remark was addressed to a man standing beside him holding chains, and it was a welcome concession, a surprising one. It produced a frown of disapproval from Father Vespianaso.

Toby held out his wrists for the manacles.

EIGHT

BARCELONA

1

Anyone but the Inquisition would have classed
that journey as torture in itself. Even Hamish could
not stand erect in the cage, while to sit down was to
be bounced unmercifully as the wagon racketted
over the rough trail. Just as it began to move out,
Captain Diaz appeared with some stale bread and
peppery sausage for the captives. They ate it greedily after their long day, but he had either overlooked
drinking water or had none to give, so they soon
found themselves racked by thirst while rain buck-
eted down on them. Chained hand and foot, they
spent the night crouching or squatting, clinging to
the bars for support and trying not to batter into each
other as they were thrown about.

Dawn found them on the plain, although the road
was hardly less rough and the weather little better.
Other traffic appeared: peasants heading for the
fields or driving animals to market, traders with
wagons, a few fellow travelers hastening by on
horseback. They stared apprehensively at the sight
of two caged men being conducted by Dominicans,

knowing them to be possessed. Fear might easily
have turned to rage, but Diaz and his troopers were
able to deter violence.

Toby felt no relief when the flat-topped towers of
Barcelona came into view at last. They were
impressive, no doubt, but they reminded him of
tombstones. When the wagon rumbled through the
north gate, he thought of prison. The fine buildings
with their grand arches and stairways made him
wonder which was Josep's and what it would have
been like to be born rich, to have grown up with a
family and servants, never being cold or hungry.

Morning crowds in the street cleared hastily out
of the troopers' path and gaped at the ominous captives in their iron crate. A few children screamed
insults and daringly threw filth, but there was no
riot. The wagon rumbled unmolested along the
Portal Nou to the center of the city and the Palau
Reial. There, in the courtyard, the cage was
unlocked. Toby emerged first to make the awkward
descent from the wagon, but he was so cold,
bruised, and exhausted that he hardly cared where
he was or what was happening. He wondered if
Baron Oreste was watching his prize being delivered and gloating over the precious amethyst.

An escort of soldiers, friars, and anonymous lay-
men urged him forward. Head down, he shuffled
and jingled along in his chains, going where he was
directed, doing what he was told. Soon he was
struggling down steps and the air was foul with the
fumes of candles and rushlights. He assumed he
would never see daylight again.

Déjà vu arrived only when he staggered into the
crypt itself. The thick pillars and slimy walls were

at once familiar: stench of rot, writhing shadows, instruments of torture, the great rack halfway along on the right . . . He was returning to a place he had been before, although never in this reality. So certain was he that he knew where to go that he blundered straight ahead when he was supposed to turn, and the guards jostled him hard enough that he almost fell. They led him to some moldy straw, and he sank down on it with a sensation of infinite relief. Just to sit on rotting straw and lean back against wet stonework was pure heaven after so many hours of being churned in a metal box, and much better than being spread-eagled on the wall like a tapestry. A rusty iron collar was locked around his neck and chained to a shackle.

He could not stop shivering; if he was really lucky, he would die of pneumonia. The soldiers went marching out, but the place was not dark yet— Father Vespianaso and four other friars remained, watching him. He wished they would go away and give him some peace so he could sleep. With a sigh he reached deep inside himself to find some remnants of defiance.

"Gloating, are you?"

The old man shook his head sadly. "No, my son. Any servant of the Inquisition who gloats is dismissed instantly. I am feeling sorrow for your obduracy and the sad pass the demon has brought you to. I am wondering how I may best aid you in driving it out."

"That sounds like gloating to me." He was alone! "Where is my friend? Where is Jaume?"

"He has been confined elsewhere."

Toby's spirits sank a notch lower—he would

never see Hamish again! He had been counting on having company to support him in his ordeal and hoping he might be able to comfort Hamish in his. They had guessed that and would not allow it. Obviously this crypt must be warded against demons; they need not take such precautions with Hamish

"We have sent for dry clothes," Father Vespianaso said. "If you cause trouble we shall leave you as you are, but we have no wish to ruin your health."

"You have every intention of ruining my health. You just intend to do it personally, that's all."

"It is the demon that makes you think that. Believe me, my son, you will come to thank us for what we do. You will beg us to increase our efforts to aid you. Meanwhile, do you want the garments or not?"

Dry clothes? What did they feel like? It was hard to remember. To accept such a favor would probably put him deeper into his captors' power, but the temptation was too strong to resist. Angry at his own weakness, Toby said, "Yes, please."

He was very nearly asleep when servants arrived with the garments. His wrists and ankles were unshackled, but they left the collar on his neck. He stripped and was given a coarse towel to use, then a shirt, hose, doublet, no jerkin, and all the time the friars stood and stared at him like black owls until they could chain his limbs again. Yet to be dry in the torture chamber was better than being in a cage in the rain. He would soon learn to be satisfied with even lesser pleasures.

"Food? Water?"

"Water. No food."

At long last they went away and let him sleep. His last conscious thought was that they were passing up a wonderful opportunity. If they began their tormenting while he was in this tumbledown state they would soon have him weeping like a baby. The only reason they were not doing so, he assumed, was that Baron Oreste had reserved first crack at him.

2

He had no way of knowing how long he slept, but it could only have been an hour or two. Many times he jerked awake, or partly awake—wondering where he was, why it was so dark, who was on watch, why he was so sore and so cold, what had just run over his feet. Once or twice he heard faint noises, probably just rats, although there was no reason why there might not be other captives in this dungeon. Poor devils.

Lanterns being hung on sconces shocked him to alertness and instant terror. They were about to start! He sat up in a clatter of chains, scraping neck and wrists on rusty metal, finding only a soldier laying a pitcher and a bowl within his reach; and then, as his eyes adjusted to the painful dazzle, Captain Diaz standing farther back, regarding him impassively. The other man marched away, leaving just the two of them.

"Good morning," Toby mumbled. "Or is it evening?"

"Eat. Eat quickly."

Must keep the victim's strength up. Busy day ahead? Toby reached for the bowl. It contained a sour, coarse gruel, but even that was welcome, and

he began to scoop handfuls into his mouth. He was
stiff with cold and ached all over from his battering
in the cage.

"Where is my friend Jaume?"

Diaz shrugged. "He needn't worry for a while yet.
It takes them months to prepare a case like his."

"How about my case?"

The captain shrugged again. "The viceroy is coming to see you. That's why you haven't got long to
eat."

Toby scooped faster. "When are they going to
start on me?" he mumbled with his mouth full.

"You really want to know that?" Diaz was probably breaking major regulations by speaking with a
convicted husk like this. There was a decent man
behind that dour expression.

"Yes. Yes, even if you tell me they're on their way,
I'd like to know."

"As soon as they can. As soon as the baron gives
them leave. In a hour or so, probably."

Toby almost choked and had to gulp down some
water. Very bad news! "What's their hurry?" He
filled his mouth again, although fear had knotted up
his gut.

"You want to know that too?"

"Mm."

"They summoned their two best tormentors from
Toledo. They've been waiting here for a week."

"I'm honored."

"I'm not." Diaz turned on his heel and headed for
the door. Give him his due, the captain disliked his
duties and was not afraid to show it.

Toby peered around the dungeon, realizing he
had been tethered where he had a clear view across

at the rack. The rack was said to be even worse than the *strappado*, although he found that hard to believe. Off to his right stood a horizontal beam on four legs. The Spanish horse, they called that—sit a man on it and tie weights to his feet. Braziers, metal chairs, thumbscrews. Life would not lack for variety. Perhaps he should have settled for the exorcism. No. Better him here than Gracia. Better to die as a man than live as a sheep. But how long would he remain a man? What would they turn him into with their unending . . . ? And there was one of the horrors now, a black-robed figure walking in silence on the far side of the rack. His hood was up, and he seemed to be inspecting the equipment, because he was not looking at the prisoner. Toby wondered if he could throw his bowl accurately enough to hit the bugger and reluctantly decided that he could not. It was worth more as breakfast than a missile, anyway. He ate every scrap of the slop and sucked his fingers. They would be hand-feeding him soon.

Two men arrived carrying a table and set it down a couple of paces in front of the prisoner. One of them was Oreste's valet, the silent blond Ludwig. They left without as much as a glance at him.

Why a table?

Gramarye? *Déjà vu*: another table in another dungeon. Valda had used a table to hold her equipment on that long-ago night when she tried to conjure Nevil's soul into Toby Strangerson and so began all his present troubles. Then he had been staked out on the floor while her four creatures stood around him holding candles. The hob had rescued him then and the hob had escaped from this crypt before—or had it? He didn't know the answer to that question, because he had not seen the end of the story; he did not know when the hob had made its move to reverse history. It could have happened days or weeks later.

Footsteps coming, but in a rhythmic military stride, not the shuffle of the friars. He had never thought he would ever be glad to see Oreste or Oreste's men, but anyone would be better than the black-robed horrors. It was not Oreste, though, not yet. It was Diaz back with three soldiers.

Toby said, "My compliments to the cook, Captain. Traditionally the condemned man should eat a hearty breakfast. That wasn't it, though." Was humor in such a situation courage or cowardice? Was he just babbling to hide the terror gnawing at his soul?

Diaz certainly saw nothing to laugh at, but then he probably never would. "We have to move you. Will you cooperate or make us use force?"

"Oh, I'll cooperate," Toby said. "I bruise easily, you know. I have a very tender skin." Pride would not let him ask where they were going to move him. To the rack? Oreste might be planning to engage in a little torture himself, but a hexer should scorn such primitive methods. It would be out of character for the effete baron to stoop to personal violence, wouldn't it? Even if he had ordered the babies burned in Zaragoza.

Diaz remained unamused. "Take off the collar, free his hands."

As two men attended to that, the third moved the water pitcher and slop bucket out of harm's way and put the empty bowl on the table. Ludwig appeared in silence and laid a small ironbound chest beside it, then withdrew as quietly as he had come.

"Stand up," Diaz said. "Take off your shirt."

Toby bit his lip and obeyed. While he was unfastening his doublet, he discovered that he was out of witticisms. All the signs were pointing to major gramarye ahead, and he had not anticipated that. Was this where he was turned into the devoted slave who had chopped off Hamish's head? No, he must not rely on his visions as guides to what to expect. They were not prophetic. Conditions had changed this time. Tortosa was different. Going to Montserrat was different. Both he and Hamish were prisoners of the Inquisition this time, and even Oreste could not extract them from that situation—except by major gramarye, of course.

Wait and see.

His arms and chest were covered with bruises. He threw away his shirt, expecting to be told to lie down, but he was made to stand against the wall and spread his feet as wide as he could. They threaded the chains from his wrists over pulleys and hauled his arms out sideways and overhead until the manacles bit into his flesh. When they had finished he was spread-eagled against the icy, slimy stonework. It was worse than he had foreseen in his vision, for this time he had no freedom of movement at all.

Suddenly he realized that the hexer himself was standing beside the table, watching the procedure with slitted eyes. *Déjà vu* again: red velvet cloak, puffed and slashed jerkin of blue and gold, crimson tights—that must be his dungeon-visiting costume—jewel-headed cane, golden hair net, wide, flat hat shadowing the lardy face, torso grotesquely inflated by the overstuffed costume, scarlet lips. The second most evil man in Europe. Or the most evil, if one remembered that Nevil was not human.

Diaz must have seen something change in Toby's face, because he turned. He saluted. "Your Excellency, the prisoner has been secured as you instructed."

"Good. Go. Lock the door. I am not to be disturbed until I knock, Captain. Not by anyone. Not for any reason whatsoever. Is that clear?"

"Yes, your Excellency."

The soldiers left without waiting for orders, moving with a haste that suggested they were terrified of the viceroy. The captain followed at a regulation pace. He had gone only a few paces when Oreste picked up the dirty bowl that had been left on his table and threw it after him. It missed, hit the floor, shattered in an echoing crash. Even the impassive Diaz jumped and reached for his sword. The soldiers spun around. Two of them were hidden from Toby by a pillar, but he saw the expression of sick terror that came over the third one's face as he realized what had happened. Someone would have to be flogged for that oversight.

"Out!" roared the baron. His Excellency was in a very bad temper.

Any faster and their march would have been a run.

Oreste scowled after them until the great door shut with a crash that echoed in waves around and around the crypt. When it had faded into silence, he raised his left hand to his mouth. *"Rigomage per nominem tuum . . ."* He turned around to his right. *". . . igne et tempestate impero . . ."* He turned to his left.

" . . . *fiat lux.*" And again to his left. At once the blocks of the barrel-vaulted ceiling began to glow with the pale gentle lavender light that Toby remembered from the vision, growing rapidly brighter until the entire crypt was clearly illuminated and he had to screw up his eyes until they could adjust to the glare.

The hexer was taking a risk, surely, in letting his victim hear the name of one of his demons? Did that mean that Toby would not live to repeat it to anyone, or just that Oreste knew he did not understand Latin? Oh, if only Hamish were there! He would have been able to tell the conjuration controlling the demon from the command it had been given. But if he were there he would undoubtedly be chained to the wall, too, and hence unable to perform the actions that were required by the ritual.

Oreste minced around the end of the table and peered up at his captive with a plump smile. "I am, of course, Karl Fischart, Baron Oreste of Utrecht, currently his Universal Majesty's viceroy for Aragon." He bowed.

"I am Longdirk."

"Yes. I knew that already, actually. You are even bigger than I expected. You don't look as frightened as you should be."

"I'm quite stupid. I expect you will educate me."

The baron stared at him for a moment and then uttered a childish titter. He turned to lay his cane on the table. "No, you are not stupid, Tobias. You are the wiliest and most resourceful opponent I have ever encountered. Oh, I suppose a few others like the late and unlamented Lady Valda have held me at bay for longer, but she had infinitely greater resources than you. You had only your native wits and an

astonishing resilience. I truly regret that our long
contest must end so tragically for you." He opened
the chest on the table. "I have long dreamed of con-
scripting you as an ally—with gramarye, of course.
I would not insult you by suggesting you would ever
aid me voluntarily, but any man can be hexed into
cooperation. Alas, that will not be possible."

So one outcome had been eliminated, and if it had
been the worst that Toby had feared, that probably
just showed how limited his imagination was.

The baron began removing objects from the chest
and setting them on the table: a silver chalice, a
dagger, two candlesticks. "Ah, excuse me! I tend to
forget that your remarkable calm stems from
courage and not stupidity. I give you my solemn
assurance that you are not going to suffer the fate
that the odious Vespianaso is planning for you."

Toby licked dry lips. "That is welcome news,
Excellency. Will I be pleased when I hear the alternative?"

"No, but it is better. Truly, Tobias, I would spare
you if I could, but I have my orders. This is a mercy
is it not?" The baron paused in his business and
peered across the table with his tiny eyes.

"If you gave me the choice I would take that, yes."

Nodding as if reassured, the hexer continued his
preparations, laying out glass vials, a parchment
scroll, a mortar and pestle . . . the casket of carved
ivory. "You have nothing more to fear except a few
minutes' suspense while I get ready, and the trivial
indignity of having some arcane sigils drawn on
your chest."

Dignity? What need had a man tied to a slimy
stone wall with his hose settled down around his

hips to worry about dignity? And yet he was trying very hard not to jangle his chains as cold and fear made him shiver. Twenty-one was young to die. He had hoped to live twice that long. Some men even reached fifty, although that was rare.

"I shall not be sorry to cheat the Inquisition."

"Ach!" said the baron. "I disapprove of the Inquisition, I really do. I find their practices obscene. I am not an evil man by nature, you know. I never wanted to be anything more than a humble scholar. All the vast knowledge of gramarye and conjuration I gathered I never used for any wicked purposes. I had a European reputation as a man of lore and wanted only to be honored for that." But this soft-spoken, pudgy gentleman was the monster who had sacked Zaragoza, an ogre with a reputation for savagery second only to that of the Fiend himself. "Alas, I was susceptible to flattery, and when the youngest son of the king of England begged me to take him on as a student, I accepted. What an unhappy day that turned out to be!"

If the Inquisition heard that confession, it would burn him at the stake, or try to, at least—Oreste and Vespianaso must be very uneasy partners. There had been a friar snooping around earlier, who might still be there, lurking behind pillars, spying on what the viceroy was up to with a convicted incarnate. Toby could not recall seeing him leave and saw no reason to mention him.

"A bright lad, he was, young Nevil." Oreste fussed cheerfully with his vials and potions. "Now I need a lock of your hair, dear boy." He picked up the dagger and came around the table, smiling his scarlet lips.

Suspecting trickery, Toby stiffened as the blade approached, but he lost nothing more than a twist of hair. Oreste took it back to add to the concoction in the goblet.

"He was a dreamer, though. I doubt if he would have held the throne of England very long. Everyone noticed the change when Rhym took him over."

"Was it you who killed his brothers and his father?"

The baron emptied a couple of vials into the chalice. "Goodness, no! That was darling Valda. With more than a little help from Nevil himself, I dare say." He uncorked a bottle and added something that looked like fresh blood. Why so much preparation just to kill a helpless man?

Silence became oppressive very quickly. "Were you there when he and Valda tried to conjure Rhym?"

"Fortunately, I was not." Oreste chuckled. "It might have taken me instead! Now, where did I put the . . . ah! There is one thing I have been meaning to ask you, Tobias. I have tracked you very closely for years, so I know almost everything you have done and everywhere you have been." He had begun grinding something in the mortar, which left him free to look up and smile across at his victim. "The one matter that still puzzles me is just what happened at Mezquiriz."

No! He would not tell that.

The baron tut-tutted. "Come, my boy! You are about to die. I am doing you a favor. Surely you can humor an old man's curiosity, hmm?" He had only to speak a word to one of his demons and Toby would babble out the whole story in terrible detail. "It is little enough to ask."

It was very little to ask, but it took a real effort to answer. "The hob went berserk."

"Yes, yes! But why? You had eluded me at the border. You were not in danger, and there was no great spirit there to provoke it. So what ignited the hob?"

Toby turned his face away. "I lay with a woman."

"Ah!" The pestle stopped for a moment. "I never thought of that. Yes, I can see what might happen. I wondered if it had been your first attempt to control the hob."

"I can't control the hob. I was told that it would take me over and control me."

The baron began grinding away again. "That is certainly the more likely outcome. The two of you must be very intertwined by now—but you know that, because you refused the exorcism. And the girl? She died? This is sad."

He seemed quite sincere. Why was he keeping up this meaningless chitchat at all? Just to comfort his victim and keep him from brooding on his imminent end? But he was a sadistic, murdering monster. He probably knew how Toby's hips ached already, how his hands had gone numb. One thing was certain—he would not be revealing so many secrets if there was any chance of the prisoner living to repeat them to anyone.

He emptied the contents of the mortar into the chalice and then consulted the scroll, moving his lips in silence.

A condemned man could try a last request, even if there was very little hope of its being granted.

"Excellency? It does seem unfair that my friend Hamish should be put to death just for being my friend, when a skilled adept such as yourself is allowed to prosper unmolested."

"Hmm?" Oreste looked up and smiled so broadly that his eyes disappeared altogether. "Ja! It does indeed! But life is rarely just, my boy—even you have lived long enough to learn that! The Inquisition is well aware of my reputation, but there is nothing they can do about me. You don't catch lions in mousetraps. And lions have to tolerate mice. We live and let live, the Black Friars and I—with a few exceptions, that is—so don't worry about Master Campbell. He knows the truth about Rhym, and we don't want him blurting that out on the rack, now do we? I expect he will catch a fever in his cell and die quite soon. In fact, you have my word on it. Well, I am just about ready, I think. Sorry to have taken so long."

"And what happens now?" Toby asked, mouth suddenly dry.

The baron came around the table carrying the candlesticks. He placed them on the floor near Toby's feet, not looking at him. "I am going to exorcize the hob. But at the same time, I will exorcize you also." He peered up at the prisoner's face, perhaps hoping to see some appropriate signs of terror. "Ingenious, isn't it?" Chuckling, the hexer minced back to the table. "You and the hob go into the amethyst, and the soul of Nevil goes into you. When Vespianaso puts his thugs to work, they will be tormenting the wrong man!"

"So it will be Nevil who gets tortured?"

"My master finds the idea amusing."

Toby clenched his teeth and said nothing.

Oreste shrugged. "It was Rhym's idea, not mine. Nevil is a danger, so Nevil must die. This we all know. Of course I shall hex him so that he cannot reveal the great secret he alone knows, the name to conjure Rhym. He may scream all he wants that he is the rightful king of England and not Toby Longdirk, but the tormentors will not believe him. He will have to scream at them in Latin, as he knows no Spanish tongues. Rhym finds this prospect entertaining."

"What happens to me?"

The baron picked up the carved ivory casket and stroked it lovingly. "You become immortal. You and the hob will be one. Together you will make a wonderful demon."

"Don't you torture spirits to make them into demons?"

The baron shrugged regretfully. "This is true. But the worst part of torture is not the pain, dear boy, it is seeing yourself being ruined, joint by joint, muscle by muscle. It is knowing that life will never be as good again, and that you cannot grow back missing eyes or charred flesh. That doesn't apply to an immortal. A little suffering and you will learn to serve me." He laid the casket down and stared at Toby appraisingly. "Don't worry about the gramarye failing, as Valda's failed. I borrowed a couple of convicts from the city jail to practice on. I sent them home in each other's bodies, quite successfully."

"You promised I would not suffer!"

"A trivial untruth. I was being kind."

"It will be my body they are disassembling. I should prefer to remain and die with it."

"You have no option." Oreste opened the ivory casket and took out the leather locket. "It is the penalty of your own success, Tobias. Had I managed to catch you myself, then I would have spared you . . . spared your life, that is, not your will. You would have been useful as a man, too. But what you achieved at Tortosa was so extraordinary that you frightened the Black Friars out of their robes. From Gibraltar to the Pyrenees, the Inquisition was screaming for your carcass. When I saw that there was no way I could keep them away from you, I reported the problem to his Majesty, and he thought up this procedure. It is certainly ingenious."

"If the Inquisition finds out about the substitution, then Nevil will live!" Argument was useless, of course, but he could not submit to such an abomination without protest.

"The Inquisition will not find out. The inquisitors will dismiss Nevil's complaints as more evidence of his demon's cunning. Even if I told Father Vespianaso myself, he would not stop now. They are always so convinced that they are right that they accept their own conclusions as infallible evidence. So Nevil goes into you and you go into the—"

The stone he was holding was a smooth black pebble, nothing like an amethyst. He looked up at Toby, but Toby could only stare. What? Who?

"How did you do that?" the baron screamed.

"Do what, your Excellency?" There could be small pleasures, even in a torture chamber.

"Diaz swore he saw the amethyst and put it in this casket! No power could have touched it in there, not even Montserrat itself. You! The hob?"

"I didn't! I don't control the hob. Montserrat had it

warded last night, and you have it warded now, don't you?" Absurdly, Toby was suddenly more frightened than he had been by anything that had happened yet. Oreste was far more dangerous than the Inquisition. Oreste could make him suffer forever.

"I will have the truth, Longdirk!" The baron bared his teeth in fury.

Or in fear? He had obtained the soul of Nevil at last and then lost it again, and Rhym the Fiend was going to be very, very mad about that.

"I will have the truth!" He raised his left hand to his mouth and turned in his dance. "*Rigomage per nominem tuum igne et tempestate impero semper veritatem Tobias dicat.* Now, Longdirk, tell me how you switched those stones!"

"I didn't."

"Did the hob? Can you control it, talk to it?"

Perhaps if he claimed . . . Before he could think of a likely lie, the truth spilled from his mouth. "I don't know if the hob did it. I can't control it. Only at Tortosa it seemed to follow my gestures. I talk to it, but I have never seen evidence that it hears me."

A friar stepped out from behind the closest pillar and spun around in a swirl of black robe, saying very rapidly: "*Rigomage per nominem tuum igne et tempestate impero Orestes dormet.*" He took two quick steps to catch the falling baron, then lowered him gently to the floor, where he lay still and snored peacefully.

3

It had happened so fast that Toby just hung in his chains and gaped. He had apparently been saved from the baron and was now back in the power of the Inquisition, which was a very questionable improvement.

Or perhaps not, because the newcomer's all-black habit was that of a Benedictine monk, not a Dominican friar.

Certainly not, for then he straightened up and threw back his cowl, revealing not a tonsure but a mop of auburn locks. *"Campeador?"*

Spirits! "You are a most welcome sight, senor!"

Hopefully he was. Their last meeting had involved Toby's hurling him ignominiously into the mud. Apparently that was not going to be mentioned, for he twirled up the points of his mustache and grinned smugly.

"There is always a sense of satisfaction in lifting a siege." The don stepped over the prostrate baron and peered up at the prisoner's manacles. "You don't have the keys to those rusty things, do you?"

"You could use the demon. My Latin is equally rusty."

"Ah! Of course!" He went through the ritual again, this time commanding, *"Tobias liberetur!"*

The locks on Toby's wrists and ankles sprang open. He flopped down on the straw to catch his breath. Things were moving very speedily. "Thank you!" He chafed his hands, wincing as they began to throb.

"Thank Rigomagus, not me," the don said cheerily. "'By fire and storm'? It must be a very minor demon to have such a terse conjuration, don't you think? An odd-job demon? Fortunate, that! If the invocation had been longer and I'd got it wrong, we might have been in serious trouble." He chuckled, being understandably very pleased with himself.

"How did you get here?"

"Just walked in. Oh, from Montserrat, you mean? Well, when I learned what had happened, Francisco and I marched into the basilica and told the tutelary that its decision had been wrong and its actions were unacceptable. It agreed at once and begged us to come and rescue you. When we get back you will be granted sanctuary. It sends its apologies."

Alas! For a few dazzling moments Toby had seen rainbows of hope in the clouds, but obviously the spirit had done nothing to untangle the *caballero*'s wits. His story was all moonshine and dragon turds, because one thing a major tutelary would never do was reverse itself like that, and Montserrat had flatly told Toby it was infallible. He was not even out of the frying pan, let alone the fire, and the addle headed don had jumped right in beside him—a moving gesture, but a suicidal one.

"Apologies? It sells me to the Inquisition and then says it's sorry? How very touching!" Without rising from the straw, Toby reached for his shirt and doublet. Apologies, indeed!

"My attitude entirely, *Campeador!*" The don turned away to scowl at the paraphernalia on the table. "But it made amends by providing this absurd garment and another one like it for you, which I brought. They are spelled to distract attention—I just walked in here and no one saw me."

Poor deluded fool! No one questioned clerics at the best of times, and besides, Toby *had* seen him, even if he had mistaken him for a Dominican friar, which was easy enough to do. Getting in and getting out would be unlikely twins, for it was not hard to imagine Captain Diaz's reaction should two Benedictines emerge from the crypt and try to walk past the guard without explaining how they had come to be in there in the first place.

"And of course it offered us horses and some food to eat on the—"

"Us? No! You didn't involve Doña Francisca in this?"

The don spun around, blue eyes glaring madness. "What name do you profane, varlet?" He reached inside his robe, and very obviously he had a sword in there—not his great broadsword but still a lethal weapon.

Toby was on the floor, half dressed, totally vulnerable. "I meant to say . . ." He was hexed and could not lie. "I should have said 'Senor Francisco,' of course, senor!"

"It sounded as if you named my sainted mother— a lady of paramount nobility and such immaculate reputation that, were you to speak but one idle word of her, I should be forced to cut out your tongue."

"Such was never my intention. I am mortified that my clumsiness distressed you, senor."

"You will receive no other warning." The maniac released his grip on his sword reluctantly.

"Do please continue your inspiring chronicle, which surpasses the ancient tales of chivalry."

Mollified, the don preened and twirled up his mustache. "As it happened, I decided that the journey would fatigue the old man unduly, so I came alone. There is nothing much else to tell. Josep gave me a letter to his steward, so I left Smeòrach at the

House of Brusi on the Carrer Montcada and was promised fresh mounts for our return. I put on this absurd garment and walked in here."

He made it sound very easy, but probably no one ever tried to rescue prisoners from the Inquisition— most people would be as frightened of the captives as they were of the friars.

"I admit," Don Ramon said, "that I did not anticipate the baron. He was an unexpected complication, especially when I learned what he was planning."

"I am amazed. Your courage is exceeded only by your modesty, senor!"

"Of course. The first time he invoked the demon, I heard its name, but I did not see the actions. It was fortunate that he invoked it again."

Toby rose. "And how do you propose that we escape from here? There are armed men on the door." Oreste's orders to Captain Diaz had been very specific. "Can we really trust this gramarye of yours to that extent?"

"I no longer expect to escape." Don Ramon frowned down at the sleeping hexer. "By choice, I shall be struck down while battling my way out against overwhelming odds, but that is of little importance. You may take the other robe and depart, because you are only a serf. I am a *hidalgo* of Castile and must consider my honor. Since this unspeakable hexer has fallen into my power, I cannot refuse the opportunity to slay him. 'Twill be a valorous deed and well worth dying for, but of course I can't do it while he is unconscious. He must know he is going to perish, and at whose hand. As a churl you would not understand."

Toby considered the prostrate hexer and laughed

ruefully. "Senor, for years my greatest ambition has been to choke the life out of this monster with my bare hands. Yet, churl though I am, I find I am as helpless as your noble self while he is in this condition."

"Curious! But I foresee trouble when I awaken him and he regains command of his demons. Have you any suggestions, *Campeador?*"

Toby had several, of which the most important was that the two of them leave Barcelona alive and healthy and soon. How could he talk sense into the maniac while he was conjured to speak nothing except the strictest truth?

"It will not be easy, senor. Baron Oreste has many demons immured in those rings, and some of them are undoubtedly conjured to defend him. I presume that they have not interfered thus far only because he has come to no harm yet, and they may enjoy seeing him shamed like this. Demons obey specific orders only and detest those who control them, but any move to injure Oreste will trigger their compulsions. As you said, Rigomagus is undoubtedly a very weak demon, so others could override it and awaken their master at any time."

The don frowned dangerously. "I have already announced my intentions, *Campeador!*"

"I am attempting to assist, senor. Pray hear me out." With his mind flapping in frantic circles, Toby went to the baron and squatted down to study his fat hands. "He has a total of ten rings here, and the jewel on his cane may also hold a bottled demon. I was told once that he is hexed to absolute loyalty by a demon immured in a beryl. Are you familiar with jewels?"

"No. What are you proposing?"

"The baron is forbidden to remove the beryl ring, but it may be possible for us to remove it, depending on the exact terms of the conjuration." It was a very slim chance. Would Rhym have overlooked that loophole?

"Bah!" said the don and began to pace. "I do not see how that would solve anything. You would still have to take him out of the demon's range—to Montserrat, say, or even farther. Only then would he be free of it."

Toby rose and went to the table. He examined the black pebble, then replaced it in the locket and hung the locket around his neck again. There was a mystery that might haunt him till his dying day— whenever that was. He tucked the dagger inside his doublet, making a silent vow that the Inquisition would not take him alive the next time.

"This casket, senor? I have met its like before. It is warded against demons. If we put the beryl inside and shut the lid, the baron will be free of his compulsion."

"So! Ingenious!" Don Ramon came striding back, looking pleased. "But we do not know which is the correct ring, not even which is Rigomagus."

"Nor do we know which holds Rigomagus or the demons that guard his life. We shall have to remove all of them and put them all in the box."

The two men eyed each other uneasily. Would guardian demons stand for that?

Then the don twirled up his mustache again. "And he will be only a fat old man with no powers of gramarye! Very well. Let us begin!"

Gently they pulled the rings from the sleeping man's fingers, and Oreste continued to snore peacefully. Nothing catastrophic occurred, but when the last one came free Toby realized that he was almost giddy from holding his breath. He wrenched the jewel from the end of the cane and put that in the ivory casket also. They had done it!

The don said, "Put the box on the table, *Campeador*, and close it."

4

"We shan't be able to see much when the light goes out."

"Ah! Good tactical thinking! Wait." Don Ramon stalked off to inspect the furnishings of the cellar. He returned bearing a black robe, a rusty metal rod that was probably a branding iron, and a fierce scowl. The robe he tossed down on the table. "That will get you safely out of here, *Campeador*. And this bar will have to serve. Ready?"

He performed another conjuration, calling on Rigomagus to extinguish its light. Darkness surged into the crypt like a black tide—gramarye! Shapes emerged as Toby's eyes adjusted to the glimmering glow of the lanterns.

"Ready, Tobias?"

"Ready, senor."

Don Ramon reached inside his robe for his sword. "Close the lid."

Toby shut the casket. The snoring stopped.

"Mmf?" Oreste's eyes flicked open. "What happened? Longdirk!" He began to rise and then sank back, blinking in horror at the sight of his prisoner free and clothed. He did not seem to notice the don's blade in front of his nose. *"Rigomagi in nomine—"*

"No good, baron!" Toby said. "We have trimmed your claws."

Oreste lifted his hands and stared at his empty fingers. "Free? Free!" he screamed. "Free! You have released me!" With an effort astonishing for his bulk, he squirmed to his knees—almost losing an eye on the don's sword in the process—and threw himself down to grovel at Toby's feet. "Free at last! Now kill me! I am not fit to live. Kill me!" He grew louder and more frantic, babbling hysterically.

It was disgusting! Their plan had worked beyond all dreams, and they had turned the greatest hexer in Europe into a cringing, whimpering poltroon.

Don Ramon sheathed his sword and swung a foot at the ample rump so temptingly presented.

"Get up! Stand on your feet like a man!"

"Wait!" Toby could remember how he had reacted when he thought he had beheaded Hamish. "Give him time to adjust. He has been a slave for years."

The don scowled impatiently as the lamentation continued. Toby put on the robe—not that he believed that it had been hexed, but it was a good disguise and might confuse the guards when he tried to leave. Just how that was going to be done remained to be seen.

Eventually the baron's weeping choked into silence. He rose to his knees and peered around. "Longdirk?"

"Here."

"Oh. Yes. You are hard to see in that . . . How did you get that? What has been happening?" If was not a genuinely broken man, he must be the finest actor in Europe.

"We locked your demons away in the box. Whose man are you now, Oreste? Still Nevil's?"

"No, no! Yours! I don't know how you managed this, but I am eternally grateful. I will do anything for you. Oh, I deserve to die, Longdirk. I have done terrible—"

"You are going to die!" declaimed the don. "I, Don Ramon de Nuñez—"

"Any recompense I can make!" sniffed the baron, ignoring him.

Realizing that he was still wearing his robe, the don angrily stripped it off, becoming somewhat entangled in his sword and branding iron in the process.

Oreste squealed in alarm, making Toby's heart take a wild leap. Was it possible that those robes really *were* enchanted? No, that was ridiculous! Why should Montserrat reverse its judgment? The baron was confused, that was all.

"Wh-who are you?"

"As I was saying, I, Don Ramon de Nuñez y Pardo, *hidalgo* of Castile, denounce you as a monster and a disgrace to the title of nobility you profess to bear, and I do hereby challenge you to mortal combat. As we have only one sword, I offer you the choice of weapons. Stand up!" He held out the sword and the rusty rod.

The baron stared at him very hard, blinked around in search of Toby as if he couldn't see him, and then heaved himself to his feet. He bowed shakily. "As you will, senor. I do not deny your charges, but I accept your challenge gladly."

He took the branding iron.

"Don't be absurd!" yelled the don. "I have studied

under de la Naza himself! I am one of the finest swordsmen ever to wield a Toledo blade."

"You let me have the choice. Now guard!" The fat baron swung a clumsy blow.

Don Ramon caught the rod with his left hand and twisted it out of Oreste's grasp. "You deny me satisfaction! So die like the churl you are—go ahead and strangle him, *Campeador*, as you wanted."

But Toby could not kill in cold blood either, and he had begun to shiver with excitement, starting to believe he might live.

Hope is the mother of disappointment.

"The baron appears to be truly repentant, senor!" Seeing his companion's eyes starting to flash anger again, he went on quickly: "Any man can be hexed to obedience. Under the same circumstances, I chopped off your head. It is true that to slay the Fiend's premier hexer would be a wondrous and valorous deed, celebrated throughout all Europe. How much more daring and effective, though, to turn the weapon against the man—or against the demon, in this case! Oreste knows his master's darkest secrets. Why destroy him when you could use him? If I am right, he would at once become Nevil's most dangerous enemy." He would also be a passport out of the Palau Reial.

The don considered this proposal for a moment and then raised his coppery eyebrows very high. "You shame me, *Campeador*! Why, indeed, should we waste our time on this trash when we should be plotting the downfall of the monster himself?" He beamed and clapped Toby on the shoulder. "A magnificent vision! You will join me then in a crusade to overthrow the Fiend?"

It would be hard to think of a greater insanity than
that program, but this was no time for argument,
and fortunately Rigomagus was now caged, so Toby
was again capable of deceit. "Senor, nothing will
give me greater pleasure than to assist you when
you destroy Rhym and rid Europe of its atrocities.
Well, Excellency?"

"Don't call me that!" Oreste rubbed his face. "I,
also . . . I have very much to atone for. But the
Inquisition . . . May I sit, please? I am not thinking
very clearly." He was in shock.

They took the lanterns and led him to a stout iron
chair, strong enough to support his bulk. He sank
down in it gratefully, although its purpose was to
hold a man immobile while his feet were being
roasted or his fingers crushed. Toby brought him the
water pitcher, and he drank.

"Now, Baron. The first problem is, can you get
me and my friend out of here alive? Can you defend
us from the Inquisition?"

"I . . . I don't know." He wrung his fat hands. "I
am still viceroy, I suppose. In any other crime I
could just issue a pardon, but not in a case of possession. If I try to release you, even my own guard
will mutiny. The Inquisition would rouse the city.
There would be a hue and cry, a house-to-house
search for a convicted creature. There would be
riots. Nowhere in the city would be safe for you."

The don opened his mouth, and Toby held up a hand
to silence him. They waited. Either the baron was a
consummate actor, or he was genuinely trying to help.

"There are ships. But you are not easily dis-
guised. . . ."

"Montserrat!" The don's eyes glittered. "If you

are truly as penitent as you profess, then you will accompany us to Montserrat and testify to your repentance before the spirit!"

The baron's bulk shuddered like jelly. He closed his eyes, but then he managed a nod. "Yes," he muttered hoarsely. "No man has ever had more on his conscience. I cannot ever hope to atone, but I should make my confession, if it will hear me. We can go in my carriage. You will not dare go to the monastery, of course, Longdirk. . . ."

"Yes he will," the don said. "The tutelary has offered him sanctuary."

The baron ignored him. "But I could take you part of the way, smuggle you out of Barcelona, give you money." A grotesque smile writhed over his doughy face. "After all these years it is hard for me to think like an ordinary man now. I keep wanting to use gramarye."

"We are not going to open the casket," Toby said firmly, "if that's what you—"

"No! No! Never! But I can get you out of town, I am sure. Even provide an escort."

"And Jaume? We must rescue him also."

The baron sighed. "That should be easier. In his case the guards will obey my orders; they approve of anyone who slays a *landsknecht*."

Toby exchanged nods with the don. They would have to trust him. "Very well. You will knock on the door and order Diaz to summon your coach and bring the prisoner Campbell to you. Do not mention Don Ramon or myself, and we will try to pass as innocent monks."

The baron rose shakily. "I shall do my best, Longdirk, I swear it!"

Don Ramon drew his dagger. "You understand that you will lose a kidney if you do not?"

"Yes, yes! And you understand that death would be a welcome release for me? But I shall do my best to make recompense for all the harm I have done you. I wish I could do as much for all the thousands of others." Shuffling like a very old man, the baron headed for the door.

Toby went to replace the lanterns and fetch that precious casket.

Hope is the mother of disappointment. . . .

NINE

TO CATCH THE WIND

1

Hope was also much harder to handle than despair. Despair was simple, merely a matter of courage, and courage was only pride. But hope was a tease. Hope was a temptress who flaunted offers of life and safety, or even happiness, and whipped them away again. Hope was a will o' the wisp dancing over bottomless swamps.

Step by reluctant step, Toby was driven to belief. No matter how he fought against hope or chided himself for starry-eyed dreaming, the evidence grew that the baron and even the mad don were to be trusted. Over and over he warned himself that the more he let himself believe, the greater would be his pain when the trap snapped shut around him again. Yet still that seed of hope kept sprouting.

The first inkling was the way the baron tugged his cloak around himself, to hide his muddy clothes and ringless hands, after he had rapped on the door. He had not been told to do that.

Locks clattered, hinges groaned, Diaz appeared in the opening. "Your Excellency?" He did not even glance at the two shadowy monks so close to the viceroy's back.

"Summon my carriage immediately."

"At once, Excellency."

"And bring out the other prisoner—Campbell. He will accompany me."

A moment's hesitation. "He is technically the Inquisition's now, Excellency. I have your authority to insist?"

"Certainly. Use force if you must."

A gleam of satisfaction vanished instantly. Lowering his voice slightly, the captain said, "The friars are here. They are anxious to begin the interrogation."

"Not yet. Not till tomorrow at the earliest. Wait," Oreste added as Diaz began to turn away. "Longdirk is to be left undisturbed. He . . . that is, he is being stubborn. We must teach him a lesson."

The captain raised his eyebrows, which for him was equivalent to a gasp of disbelief. "Left as he is, senor? Chained like that?"

"Exactly as he is. No food, no water, no inspections, even."

"But he cannot stand indefinitely, senor! He will faint eventually, and with his arms held up in that position, then he will certainly suffocate."

"I do not ask for advice!" the baron yelled. "He is not to be disturbed by anyone, for any reason whatsoever! Until I return."

"Of course, Excellency!" Diaz saluted. His face bore the nearest thing to a smile that Toby had ever seen on it—he obviously thought the baron was planning to cheat the Inquisition by granting the prisoner a merciful death.

*   *   *

There was another hint a few moments later as the
baron and his escort walked along the arched pas-
sageway to the stair and its seductive hint of daylight. One of the soldiers who had chained Toby to
the wall an hour earlier jostled him, muttered, "Beg
pardon, Father," and seemed to forget him again
immediately.

Out in the courtyard a wan noontime sun was trying
to break through flimsy clouds without much success, but the rain had stopped. Toby clutched the
ivory casket, ignoring the wide iron gates and
thoughts of making a run for it—there was no safety
for him in the streets. He could not walk freely under
the sky like other men; he was officially certified as
not human.

The baron leaned against a pillar with his eyes
closed, pale as a corpse. Toby moved in close to him
on one side, the don on the other with his dagger concealed in his sleeve. Guards stood around, exchang-
ing puzzled glances, but no one showed any interest
in the two Benedictines, not even a group of genuine
Benedictines who wandered across the courtyard,
deep in conversation. Now followed a torment of
waiting, a time for hope to sicken and fear to thrive.

Then Diaz returned with a troop of soldiers,
escorting Hamish, who shuffled along in leg
chains. His hands were in manacles, his features
puffed and discolored by the battering he had taken
in the cage. He squinted against the light, holding
his head high and trying to look brave—he might

well be deceiving anyone who knew him less well
than Toby did. He scowled when he saw the baron,
but his gaze flickered past the two fake monks with
no sign of recognition at all. Hope surged a little
higher yet.

Eight white horses brought in the viceroy's carriage,
a gilded cottage on wheels. The steps were set down,
but then there was a delay while the prisoner was
pushed forward, looking puzzled and alarmed. Toby
squeezed past the watchers and scrambled up, into a
scented salon roomy enough for a dozen people. He
settled himself on a silk-padded cushion and held his
breath.

It was going to work! *Great spirits, you will not
betray us now?*

Hamish clambered up, one foot at a time, steadied
by soldiers' hands. His eyes widened when he saw the
luxurious interior, but he did not seem to notice that
there were was someone there already. He sat down
and scowled as he tried to make himself comfortable
in his fetters. The baron's bulk darkened the doorway,
with the don right at his back.

"Where to, your Excellency?" called Diaz from
the outside.

"To Montserrat."

The door was closed, orders were shouted, and
the viceroy's escort began mounting in a clatter of
hooves and jingling harness. The baron flopped
down on the bench beside Hamish, drooping like a
man exhausted. Hamish frowned at him distrust-
fully. Whips cracked, voices shouted, and the cumbersome machine began to roll. Eight white horses

clattered out through the arch into the street, and the great wheels rumbled behind them.

Toby threw back his hood. *"Ceud mile failte!"* A hundred-thousand welcomes.

Hamish gaped and made a croaking noise.

"I think we have just escaped, thanks to Don Ramon here, and Montserrat, and his Excellency. You know Baron Oreste, at least by sight—and by reputation of course."

The baron looked round. "Master Campbell? I am very pleased to meet you at last, and in happier circumstances than I could have anticipated." He did not look pleased. He looked like a man going mad.

"The baron," said Toby, "is now one of us."

Hamish licked his lips. "Well now!" he whispered. "Ain't that one for the books!"

The armed escort kept the population at bay, but there was booing in the streets as the freedom-loving Catalans expressed their opinion of the hated viceroy. Had they known that the coach also contained a convicted incarnate, even Captain Diaz and his troop could not have defended it. Only when it rumbled out through the city gate and began to pick up speed on the muddy highway could the flower of hope open fully.

It was going to be a strange journey. The baron relapsed into bleak silence, but from time to time he would lift his head to stare longingly at the ivory casket like a drunkard deprived of his wine. All would be lost if that lid were to open for even an instant, so Toby wrapped it securely with the girdle from one of the now-discarded robes and kept it on the bench between himself and the don.

He succeeded in breaking a rusted link in the chain on Hamish's ankles, but the manacles defeated him. Hamish contorted himself inside out so that his hands were in front of him instead of behind his back, which was an improvement. Then he had to be told the whole dramatic story. By the end of it he was grinning like his old self.

Don Ramon, as hero of the hour, was in high spirits. "Truly, *Campeador*," he proclaimed, "this is a noble crusade on which we embark! We are prepared to listen to your recommendations on how we should begin."

"Crusade, senor?"

The blue eyes glittered. "The crusade on which we agreed—to overthrow the Fiend and rid the world of Rhym."

Oh, demons! "The *caballero* is asking me about a matter of high strategy on which I am unqualified to advise him, being only a serf. Perchance the baron may be better able to discuss it."

The don scowled at that notion. Quite apart from his ghastly reputation, Oreste was an upstart, a former scholar jumped into the minor nobility by the Fiend. His lineage was nonexistent when compared to that of Nuñez y Pardo.

Even if Toby had the slightest intention of going hunting for the tyrant—which he did not—there were still too many ditches in his immediate future for him to start worrying about Nevil. Dare he trust himself again to Montserrat? It had already sold him once. Why should it defy the Inquisition on his behalf? It would be defying Nevil also, for

although Oreste was no longer a threat, the Fiend
had many other hexers at his command, not to mention his never-defeated army. Furthermore, to suc-
cor the outlaw Longdirk now, the spirit would have
to admit that it had made a mistake the first time,
and that seemed even less likely.

The robes, though . . . the robes were evidence.
With some difficulty, he roused the baron from his
lethargy and asked about the robes. Oreste confirmed that inanimate objects could be hexed.

"Not for long, though," he mumbled. "The effect
will fade in a few days or weeks at most." He
relapsed into his bitter brooding.

So perhaps Montserrat really had behaved as the
don claimed!

And the other problem was the amethyst, which
had been an amethyst when Diaz had placed it in
the warded casket and a pebble when it came out.
Neither Hamish nor Oreste could suggest a solution, and if they couldn't, Toby Longdirk need not
trouble his pretty little head over it, so he put the
matter out of his mind.

He wanted to practice his meditation exercises,
but he began sliding into sleep as soon as he
began. He was more exhausted than he could ever
remember, with the strain of the last twenty-four
hours piled on all the hard days before. Don
Ramon went to sleep, then Hamish did the same,
but Toby must keep watch on the box and the
brooding baron.

By the time they awakened, the setting sun was
shedding a ruddy glow on spectacular precipices
ahead. Now that he did not expect to die soon, Toby
could concede that the world was interesting again

and peered out at the scenery. The don had no such curiosity in rocks.

"When you find that amethyst, *Campeador*," he proclaimed, "then our duty is to deliver it to the Khan at Sarois, so that the rightful Nevil can be restored to the world of the living and reveal the conjuration."

Toby turned to the baron. "Would that be possible, Excellency? Can Nevil be reincarnated?"

"Hmm? What?" Oreste shrugged. "In theory, yes. That is what Rhym fears above all. In practice, it is more likely that the boy would emerge as a slobbering idiot or a raving madman. He would certainly not be in a cooperative frame of mind, and Nevil was no mean hexer in his own right."

"Besides, who is to provide a living body?" Toby asked. Valda had volunteered him to make that sacrifice, and the memory made his skin crawl.

"In such a cause, any chance is worth taking," Don Ramon insisted.

"But we don't know who took the amethyst."

This intrusion of reality made him pout. After a while he tried again: "Then the first step must be to rally an army. An invasion of France by the combined forces of Castile and Aragon would be a beginning. You will cooperate, of course, baron, since you are still viceroy?"

"Me?" Oreste shook his head mournfully. "You must not count on me for help. Rhym will very soon learn that I have escaped his binding. My days can be numbered on the fingers of one hand."

There might be people in the world worse off than Toby Longdirk, which he found a stunning realization. "Possibly Montserrat will defend you, Excellency."

"Me?" the baron said incredulously, and that one agonized word ended the conversation.

2

Darkness fell as the carriage was inching its way higher on the hairpin road, but even before it left the valley floor, Hamish's manacles and gyves fell off in a sudden clatter. He jumped, grinned nervously, and said, "We seem to be expected!"

"And welcome," Toby added. No one spoke a word after that, as if they were all afraid that the tutelary might be listening—an illogical reason, because it was just as capable of reading their thoughts.

Welcome, but what sort of welcome? If there was now a third option other than death or exorcism, why had it not been offered before? Or had Montserrat just concluded that exorcism was the better solution, whether Toby wanted it or not?

The weary horses took a long time to haul the great vehicle up to the monastery, but at last the track leveled off, and the wheels rumbled to a halt. Torches flamed in the darkness outside the windows, and male voices raised in anger. It sounded as if the monks wanted the honor of opening the door for the distinguished visitor, and the viceroy's guards were resisting. But the door did open eventually, and the steps were pulled down. Cumbersome and reluctant, Oreste heaved himself to his feet and descended to the courtyard.

Hamish followed, free of his chains. And then went the don and Toby in their enchanted robes. Toby walked unnoticed right in front of Diaz. The temptation to speak to him had to be resisted, for the

captain would be better off when the hue and cry
started if he did not know where the missing prisoner had gone.

Monks in black habits had already escorted the
baron away, hunched and old, a broken man. His
interview with Montserrat would be interesting, but
he was entitled to a private confession like any
lesser penitent. Toby headed in the same direction,
sure that the spirit could see him even if no one else
could. He knew his invisibility had been lifted when
he saw Hamish grinning at him. The don had disappeared in the crowd.

"Do you suppose," Toby said, "that any suppliant
has ever come to Montserrat with a hob in his heart
and eleven demons under his arm?"

"No, and never one as hungry as I am, either!"

"If the senores will allow me to guide them?" The
speaker was a genuine monk, an elderly, dignified
man with a ponderous belly extending the front of
his robe. Without waiting for a reply he set off across
the courtyard.

There was little to be seen of the buildings,
although they were larger and more numerous than
Toby had expected, huddled close together on their
high shelf, backed by more sheer cliffs. The ancient
holy place, clothed in wind and night and mystery,
was impressive even by starlight.

They entered a vast, dim hall, and there their
guide stopped and awkwardly turned his bulk. "You
are invited to share our meal, senores, in about an
hour, and the abbot will formally welcome you at
that time. Meanwhile, you will be guided to your
quarters. If there is anything you need that has not
been provided, you have only to ask."

"You are too kind," Toby said politely, thinking that a little more kindness would have been welcome the previous day. The monk waddled off.

"This is more what I was expecting yesterday," Hamish said. "Wine and roast goose? Venison, perhaps?"

"Or you could ask them to take you straight to the library."

"Hmm! One of the greatest in Europe!"

"See you next year, then."

"You going to stay here that long?"

Toby had been joking. He had no idea what the future held in store for him, not a year, nor even a day, and he hardly cared. "Perhaps. This would be a good place for me to learn how to keep the hob suppressed. You'll be back in Scotland long before that." He yawned.

"No!"

"No? Lost your homesickness?" That was surprisingly welcome news.

"After this? I'd be eating the heather in a week! What are we going to do now, Longdirk?"

"Eat, I hope. Sleep. Think again in a week or two."

Hamish's eager grin faded. "But this crusade the don—"

"Demons! You go crusading with him if you want. It's been a stressful day, but I haven't lost quite all of my wits."

"Senor?" said a childish voice near Toby's elbow.

It came from a cropped-headed novice who clutched a lantern in both hands as if he found it heavy. He could be no more than twelve and was either remarkably brave or unaware that he was

addressing a convicted incarnate. "Will you be kind
enough to follow me, senor?"

"I shall be honored. Lead the way."

Leaving Hamish staring after him with a per-
plexed frown, Toby followed his guide along a maze
of corridors, up several flights of stairs, and finally
to a low oaken door. By then he had discovered that
the boy's name was Alfonso, he was a choirboy and
would be chief soloist as soon as Felice's voice
broke. With little less confidence, Alfonso also
explained that he intended to be the abbot when he
grew up.

Toby expected a monastic cell and would be surprised if he could stand upright in it. A cot long
enough for him to sleep on would be astonishing.
What he found when he ducked under the lintel was
a chamber fit for a king, larger than Granny Nan's
cottage and four times the height. Being careful not
to laugh, he peered around so he would be able to
remember it all and share the joke with Hamish: a
fire crackling in a huge stone fireplace, candles
gleaming in silver holders on the table, velvet drapes
hanging beside real glazed casements, the walls hidden by tapestries—thick rugs on the floor, a basin
and ewer and neatly folded towel, two padded
chairs, and a four-poster big enough to take him and
several friends. He had never merited such a room in
his life and never would.

"I fear you have made an error, friend Alfonso. I
am not the viceroy."

The boy's face crumpled in worry. "No, senor!
Brother Tomas pointed you out to me himself. 'The
big one,' he said!"

"But this room?"

"Yes, senor! The royal chamber, he said. For the big man—begging your pardon, senor."

"Oh, I know I'm the big one, so don't worry about that."

"We are very cramped for space just now," the boy suggested nervously. "With so many refugees. Er, I mean no offense, senor! I am certain this is the correct place."

What game was the tutelary playing now? Such effusive hospitality must come with a monstrous bill, to be presented on the morrow. He padded over the rugs and laid the casket on the table. This would be only the fourth time in his life he had ever slept in a real bed, and last night he had been chained like a dog. Hamish was right—life in Tyndrum *would* seem very dull.

"Well, if you're quite sure . . ."

"Quite sure, senor. I shall come back later to guide you to the refectory."

Could he stay awake that long? "That is very kind of you. It is a magnificent room, but I still think there has been some mistake." He heard the door close.

"Indeed there has," said another voice, a familiar voice, clear like a silver bell.

He spun around. Alfonso had shut the door with himself on the inside and was standing there with a faint smile fixed on his face and a golden shimmer around him. Bracing himself for more treachery, Toby went down on his knees, which put their eyes at about the same level, although the boy seemed to be staring through him rather than at him.

"The mistake was ours. It has been many centuries since we had to apologize to a mortal, Tobias."

"I am grateful to you for sending the don to rescue me, Holiness." What did it want of him now?

"It should not have been necessary. We misjudged you. We have not met anyone quite like you before, you see."

"What does that mean?"

The spirit chuckled, although the boy's expression did not change. "It means that even we should not claim to be infallible. Our knowledge is confined to our experience, which is vast but not infinite, and there are exceptions to every rule. And that rule we overlooked! We have some questions to ask you."

Questions? Montserrat was as close to omniscient as it was possible to be. Toby suppressed an aching yawn. Why couldn't this wait until morning? "There are others who need you more than I do tonight—the baron, for instance."

"We are attending to him now in the basilica. Your case is urgent, too. So listen. We first heard of you when reports came of the slaughter at Tortosa, obviously the work of a demon. It did not seem to concern us, for it happened far outside our domain, but a few days ago the Inquisition appealed to us for help, something it has never done before. We do not approve of the Black Friars' methods and frequently not of their choice of victims, but they perform a service in hunting down demons as they flit from one spirit's haunt to another. This one, we were told, had escaped to the north, to Lerida, and now appeared to be heading in our direction. Furthermore, although their reports were scanty, the friars believed that it had taken hostages. So we were concerned.

"Soon it became clear that the viceroy was also

concerned. Instead of the handful of yokels the Inquisition is usually granted to aid it in making arrests, he assigned a troop of professionals under the competent Captain Diaz. He also had the insolence to demand our assistance. As it is Oreste's fault that there are so few tutelaries left in Aragon at the moment, we were even less inclined to cooperate with his men than we were with the Inquisition, but it was made plain to us that the consequences would be drastic if we refused."

All of this sounded very much as Toby had worked it out for himself. What was so urgent? Why must it be tonight?

"When you drew closer, though, we saw that you were far from a typical case of possession. Your companions seemed to be under no compulsion. They evidently accepted you as human, and that was worrying indeed, because only supremely crafty demons are capable of that deception. The most egregious such imposter is Nevil the Fiend, of course."

Toby had not foreseen that view of him. "But could I have misled Montserrat?"

It did not answer that question. "The other possibility was that you had somehow managed to gain control of your demon after the massacre, but that theory was so improbable that we did not consider it. The cooks are basting the roast geese, and you will not want to miss dinner. Go and get ready."

Disconcerted, but aware that some of his weariness came from hunger, Toby rose and went over to the stand with the basin. He would have to turn his back on the tutelary! Undress in front of it?

"This feels wrong, Holiness, disrespectful!"

The boy was still staring woodenly at the fire-place, but the spirit laughed joyfully.

"Since when have you worried about being respectful, Tobias? No, you have earned a little ease, and rules do not apply to you. We shall talk while you wash, for this is a long tale. Your arrival happened to coincide with a raid by a band of brigands. We decided to kill two birds with one arrow and regret to say that this may have been a lapse into vanity. We nudged matters a little, so that you encountered the brigands on the road just below here. We prepared to defend the hostages from harm and waited to see what would happen, fully expecting that you would deal with the villains as you had dealt with the *lands-knechte* and thus relieve us of the need to do it our-selves."

Toby tossed his shirt on the bed after his doublet. He tipped water into the basin. It was hot. There was real soap!

So the tutelary had been testing him? It had not been as mistaken as it was making out, because it had sent Jacques to meet him and show him what exorcism could do. It was not being completely honest with him even now. It wanted something of him, but what? What would be written on the bill?

If it read his doubts, it did not comment on them. "The results were surprising. You did not invoke your demon. In fact you were prepared to die rather than try to use gramarye, so you had not yet lost your humanity, and that meant there was still hope for you. This was a complication, because you would lose that chance if the Inquisition got its hands on you, and of course von Münster and his troop were also after you by then. Consequently we offered you an exorcism. Our real intention was to give you sanctuary and our guidance in dealing with the hob. The exorcism itself would have been a last resort, only to be applied if we could not help you come to terms with—"

"If you had said so—"

"If we had said so, there would have been violent objections from the Inquisition and Captain Diaz and *Hauptmann* von Münster. But you amazed us again. In the end you chose the Inquisition! We regret the ordeal you have been through, Tobias, but you did make your own choice."

He did not believe any of this, not for a moment. Montserrat had manipulated them all, and especially him. It was still doing so. Then the glowing embers under the logs on the hearth reminded him of the braziers in the crypt, and he shivered.

"You did very well to defang Baron Oreste," the spirit said.

It did not say that it was surprised, though.

"That was all the don's doing."

"Oh, was it really?"

"Yes. I am grateful to you for sending him."

"Thank his mother," the spirit said with amusement. "A most valiant lady! Not that Ramon needed much persuasion once she suggested it."

But who or what had put the idea in Doña Francisca's head? "Holiness, can you help him?"

"The don? Help him in what way?"

Toby stared across the room at the boy's blank face. Conversations with mystic voices were very frustrating. "Well . . . Untangle his wits."

"Ah. You mean he does not draw the line between fantasy and reality in the same place you do?"

"Yes."

"Who is to say which of you is right? If you gave him the choice, would not he choose to have his reality made more like his fantasies, rather than the reverse?"

"I suppose so. But . . ."

"Have you ever seen him attacking a windmill, Tobias?"

"Attacking a windmill, Holiness? Why would anyone . . . No, I haven't."

"Then he is not as mad as he might be. Does he not always behave as if he knows a windmill is a windmill, however he may choose to describe it? Ask not what we can do for Don Ramon, but rather what will you do for him!"

"Me? I'm just a big stupid—"

Again the spirit chuckled. "You're not at all stupid when you think no one is watching. We are giving you answers, but soon we shall demand answers from you. You see that silver box on the table? Go to it."

Tossing down the towel, Toby walked over to the table. The box was finely crafted but small enough to fit in his fist. He had disregarded it, assuming it was only a tinderbox, but when he opened it now he found it to be empty. He turned to frown uneasily at the incarnation.

"This would hold a ring, perhaps? It is warded?"

"Very good! Yes. The demon that controlled Baron Oreste is named Avernus, and it is immured in a beryl. He describes it as a square, greenish stone held by eight claws in a gold setting."

Toby began to untie the binding around the ivory casket. "How dangerous will this be?"

"There is some danger," the spirit admitted. "You must be as quick as you can. We can keep the demon from Oreste, but we may not be able to prevent it from striking at you. You may see strange visions or feel the building shake. It may even hurt you. Try not to let these things distract you."

He undid the last knot and took hold of the lid. "Hurt me how badly?"

"Perhaps quite badly. The pain may be severe."

Oh, it must be nice to be an immortal and order people around like that! Toby opened the casket and nothing terrible happened. He fingered quickly through the glittering hoard inside until he found a gold ring with a square, greenish stone. He put that in the silver box and shut both of them. Then he turned around to glare at the paralyzed Alfonso.

"Well, did I pass that test? That's all it was, wasn't it? You were testing me again!"

"Partly. And yes, you passed. Your heartbeat never changed."

Upstart, overgrown elemental! "Blast you and your sleazy tricks!"

Alfonso suddenly turned his head to look straight at him. "Not all trickery, Tobias. The demon was loose, but we were able to contain it. Now we can put it where it will do no more harm."

"Then let's talk about the amethyst. Who stole it?" He took off the locket and opened it. A purple gem rolled out into his palm. He stared at the incarnation in bewilderment.

"The locket has been hexed, Tobias. If anyone but you opens it, they just find a black pebble—a very subtle piece of gramarye!"

"You did that!"

"It was none of our doing."

"Then who? The hob isn't capable of subtlety. It doesn't care about the stone anyway. Not Oreste. Some other spirit in Barcelona?"

"No. Oreste has subverted all of them."

Toby waited for more and nothing came. He hung the locket around his neck and stalked over to the bed, where garments lay waiting. They looked large enough, plain but well cut. He began to dress. The choirboy was still frozen in place, so the audience was not over yet.

"What happens next? Will you defend me from the Inquisition?"

"We will," the spirit said. "But we think you are safe from the Black Friars now. Having lost you twice, Vespianaso will be in deep disgrace—under suspicion of collusion, even. He may well learn something about the rack himself."

"That poor old man? Dear, dear!"

"We shall assign you a penance for that remark," the spirit said, "but not a very hard one. His brethren will hesitate to meddle with you. When you leave us we can certify that you have been cleansed of your demon."

"That's assuming I can learn to keep the hob suppressed?"

"Of course. We shall help you as much as we can, but you must not remain very long with us. We cannot defend you against Nevil, whether he brings his army or sends his legions of demons. A solitary assassin may evade our attention. You must leave soon. Now, we grant you one more question and then it will be our turn to ask."

Toby took a hard look at Alfonso's face, but of

course it revealed nothing. What question was he supposed to ask? And what questions was he going to be asked?

"The locket, then. Who hexed it?"

"You did. We don't know when, but it doesn't matter. The fences are falling, Tobias. You and the hob are becoming dangerously close. You must not use it like that! If you were not aware that you were doing so, that merely shows the extent of your peril. Even an innocent little enchantment like that one may offer it an opportunity to take you over completely."

"And I must stay away from women, and danger, and try to be a saint like Brother Bernat!"

"Women, yes. Danger maybe—you are remarkably resistant to fear. Most of all stay away from demons, for they rouse the hob as nothing else does. Now we have three questions for you. First, what you are going to do about the demons in that casket?"

"Me? I give them to you! I have no need for demons."

"Nor do we. They are yours, because you won them, but they are useless without their names, and only Oreste knows those. The jewels themselves are worth a fortune, of course."

Toby had never thought of that. Riches? Before he could even start to comprehend what wealth might feel like, the melodious voice spoke again:

"Our second question: What are you going to do about the baron?"

"Me? It is you who must help him. I know what it is to be enslaved as he was."

"We have managed to bring him some comfort

already, but he needs time to heal. And he is in danger here, like you, probably danger much greater. He wants to make recompense, but without his demons he is only a tired old man. Our third question: What are you going to do about the don?"

"Me? Kiss his hand and depart. He is a fine fighter and likable in his way, but I need lunatic noblemen no more than I need bottled demons. I was hoping you could cure him."

The spirit uttered a very human-sounding sigh. "Tobias, it is almost time for Alfonso to return and take you to dinner. We need answers. You cannot just parrot, *Me, me?* We say, *Yes, you!* Now decide!"

"Decide what?" He sat down on the edge of the bed. Taken unaware by the softness of the down, he sank into it much farther than he expected and toppled back on his elbows. It felt like a swamp, and he knew he would never be able to sleep on it, tired though he was.

He stared in perplexity at the oblivious boy. The boy stared in the general direction of the fireplace. The fire crackled, wind wailed through a gap somewhere, and that was all.

"Tobias, we cannot prophesy, but we can make very good guesses. We do not know that you will master the hob, but we are prepared to gamble on it. Europe is about to fall to Nevil, the demon incarnate. The people call out for a leader, and you have more potential than any man we have met since Charlemagne called in here in 778."

"Now it's flattery, is it?" Toby sneered. "You'll find I have a large hide to butter."

"And a thin one. He who will not take orders must give them. We have helped you, have we not?"

"So now you present the bill. How much do I owe you?"

"Everything," said the spirit. "And nothing, for we did not plan to offer you our help. You have won, Tobias—won!"

He struggled up out of the bed. "I had help."

"Of course you had help!" Now the spirit sounded exasperated. "All mortals need help! There is no shame in accepting help, especially when you have earned it. Loyalty begats loyalty. You went to a terrible death to spare your friends. It was you who inspired the don to hazard his life for you, not us. That was the only way he could admit that you had saved him from the brigands. It was you who defeated Oreste, just as once you defeated Valda. The victory is yours."

It was a strange notion. He stood for a moment, letting that concept soak through his weariness. Victory? Oreste, the Inquisition, the *landsknechte*— even Montserrat itself. He had won! He squared his shoulders.

"And?"

"That is what we ask of you. What will you do with your success?"

Must he decide now, tonight? So tired. But yes, of course! "The iron is hot? The tide runs?" It *must* be tonight, before the glow of victory faded, while everyone was still here.

That was what Hamish had seen.

"The sailor sets sail when the wind is in his favor, Tobias."

He laughed. "I am not accustomed to victory, Holiness! It is a new thing." And a very sweet one.

Alfonso beamed and said, "It is time for dinner,

senor!" in his tuneful soprano. He walked across to
the table and picked up the silver box that contained
the demon Avernus. He obviously did not realize he
was doing so, or where he was going to take it. "It
is roast goose tonight, senor! I could smell it downstairs."

Silence. After a moment, he said, "Senor?"

Toby snapped out of his reverie. He grabbed up
the jerkin. "I'm ready. Lead the way, lad. Let's go
and catch the wind!"

EPILOGUE

Captain Antonio Diaz Davila liked to think of himself as a devout man—within the limits imposed by his profession—but on his previous visit to Montserrat the tutelary had refused to hear his confession. That rebuff had been a devastating shock for him. He had only been obeying orders! That the spirit did not view this excuse in the same way he did had caused him considerable anguish and self-examination.

Today's unexpected return visit was a welcome chance to make amends. Having seen the horses stabled and his men properly quartered and served at the refectory's loaded tables, he put Sergeant Gomez in charge and sent himself off duty—possibly forever.

All his life he had tried to visit Montserrat at least once a year. The great church was very large and old, and very splendid. By day its richness never failed to snatch his breath away, but it was just as impressive in near-darkness. A hundred starry candles failed to illuminate its expanse or the worshipers who came at all hours to pray in a silence so profound that it seemed to echo. There, after long

meditation on his knees, Diaz confirmed his decision and felt peace. He might die very soon, but
what really mattered was what would happen to his
soul when he did.

Even then, in the middle of the night, many of the
confessionals were occupied, but he found an empty
one and knelt on the cushion provided. He waited
apprehensively until an elderly nun came in and
took the chair before him. She said nothing, just
folded her hands in her lap, smiled over his head,
and waited. He would have preferred a monk, but
truly it did not matter. Only the spirit would hear.

He began with the least of his failings—shortness
of temper, fits of envy, ill-considered speech. He
progressed to more serious matters—excessive
severity toward a couple of recruits, his recent ten-
dency to drink too much, and a shameful incident
with a certain married lady. He listed the actions he
had already taken to set things to rights where he
could, plus a few other possible reparations that had
occurred to him during his meditation. Then he
came to the problem of his duty and hesitated.

The spirit spoke for the first time. "Antonio, you
were right to dispose of these lesser affairs before
you tell us of your greater sorrow. For all the matters you have mentioned, though, we accept your
repentance. Do as you have promised, and they will
imperil your soul no longer."

He savored that blessing for a moment. Then he
drew a deep breath. "The other problem, Holiness,
is that I am a soldier and must obey orders.
Even . . . I mean when . . . Although . . ."

"Take your time. You are in no immediate danger
of dying, and we have all Eternity."

He glanced up gratefully, although the nun had never yet looked down at him. "You told me many years ago that a boy could honorably aspire to be a soldier, although the risk of doing evil would be greater for him than for other men. When Queen Caterina left and my superiors surrendered the palace to King Nevil, I obeyed orders and stayed at my post. Soon I was promoted. I accepted that promotion, even knowing that the Fiend was a most evil tyrant. I reasoned that if I did not take the position then someone else would, and—"

"That is never an excuse. We told you so when you were sixteen."

"I remember, Holiness, I remember! I mean that I . . . that another man might not try so hard to . . . I mean. . ." Another deep breath. "Whenever I can, Holiness, I obey my orders in the least evil way possible. Barcelona groans under the viceroy's tyranny, and some of his evil comes to them through me. I have tried my best to minimize it, truly I have! During the riots, when I was ordered to fire on the crowds, I had the men load one-third charges, so that the shots would more likely wound than kill. When I was sent out to arrest twelve hostages at random, to be executed in retribution, I chose elderly persons, invalids, cripples. It did no good! The baron knew at once what I had done and sent me back for another twelve— young people. My efforts to do less evil merely produced more." His mouth was dry. His heart ached with the memory.

"Antonio," said the serene voice of the spirit, "the greatest of all tragedies is that evil cannot prosper long without the help of the good, and yet prosper it does. Though you were doing less evil than the baron wanted, you were still doing enough."

"I see that now, Holiness. You opened my eyes. I will serve him no more. I will not return to Barcelona with him tomorrow, or whenever he leaves here. If you refuse me sanctuary, then I must flee and hope that he does not track me down with his black arts. He regards anything less than perfect loyalty as treason."

Some executions for treason lasted for days, with the victims' suffering extended by demonic power beyond all normal endurance. He had no close family, but his cousins and uncles might well . . .

"A late repentance is still repentance. This is your firm decision?"

"It is, Holiness."

"Then you are forgiven. Walk in peace and do better."

Ah, what blessed relief those words brought with them! The tutelary had not yet offered sanctuary, though. Nor named a penance . . .

"Was it only our anger that opened your eyes, Antonio? Nothing else?"

"Your disapproval was enough, Holiness, when I had time to think about it. Although . . . well, later I watched a young man give himself up to the Inquisition in place of his friends. When I compared his actions with mine I was ashamed, bitterly ashamed. I saw myself rotting in evil."

"And how did you see Longdirk?"

The question disconcerted him. "An impressive young man, but a tragic one. I am surprised that his demon was able to conceal itself so well. He showed absolutely no signs of possession that

I could see, unless the brigands ... but I did not really witness what happened to them."

The tutelary sighed. "Ignore his demon for now. We believe he has mastered it, or will soon. We can discuss that another time. Without the demon, would you accept that man as a friend?"

The question stabbed to his heart. "Alas, Holiness! The boy is undoubtedly dead by now, hanging in chains that I fastened myself."

"Answer our question."

"Friend? That one would never have extended friendship readily. To have earned his trust would have made any man proud, for it would have been an anchor in the wildest storms."

"He is not dead."

"It would be better for him if he were. Are you saying you want me to go and rescue him, Holiness? A man possessed by—"

"No, we are saying he is here, beyond the reach of the tormentors. He stole away the viceroy's demons and left him bereft of his powers."

"He *did?*" Was *that* why Oreste had come hastening to Montserrat? "Longdirk did? He and his demon? Why, that is the most incredible, wonderful—"

"No help from his demon. A little aid from us and from one of his followers, but mostly just Longdirk himself. He reminds us very much of El Cid in his younger days, before he realized how good he was."

"Praise indeed, Holiness!" Diaz muttered. *El Cid!*

"Praise well earned. The baron was enchanted to obey the Fiend, you know. Now Longdirk has released him, he is truly penitent. Like you he will serve Nevil no more."

"That is marvelous news, Holiness!—for Barcelona,

for Aragon, and for me." So Diaz need not resign his commission? But he had promised to do so, and the tutelary had let him make that promise.

"It is good news. We have not yet named your penance, Antonio. First, go and meet our hero. Return here in the morning." The nun rose from her chair to end the interview. "We shall guide you to him."

Without waiting for his command, his legs raised him from the cushion and walked him out the door. Needing no light, they moved him surely through the silent, dark labyrinth of the monastery, along corridors and up stairs until he was thoroughly lost. Eventually he came to a door and his hand lifted the latch without knocking. He entered a capacious chamber, lit dimly by dying embers in the hearth and a single candle.

A large man sat by the fireplace, his head nodding. He was apparently about to retire, stripped to his doublet and hose. He looked up with a smile as Diaz closed the door.

"Welcome, Captain Diaz!" He rose and came forward to offer a hand. "So you got my message?" His grip was powerful. Even in chains he had been impressive. At liberty and close quarters he dominated, and not all of that dominance came from his size.

Message? Did this vagabond use the tutelary as a page?

"I am very happy that you escaped, Senor Longdirk, even if it was my responsibility to see that you did not. I am glad you made a fool of me."

The young outlaw's smile became a yawn, and Diaz saw that he was exhausted—which was hardly surprising in the circumstances. "I did not make a fool of you at all. You cannot be blamed, because Montserrat did it all. I regret that I cannot offer you some wine, but they drank your share also." He gestured at the table, which bore bottles and several goblets. Apparently there had been a party.

"It is of no matter," Diaz said.

"Sit, then." Longdirk waved him to a chair and sank into his own as if even his great limbs could barely support him. He leaned his head back with a sigh. "I want first to thank you, Captain. You treat your prisoners with respect, and I have been locked up, arrested, confined, manacled, fettered, and incarcerated often enough to be a good judge of jailers. I appreciated your kindness greatly."

Sensing mockery, Diaz bristled, but he could detect no guile in those dark eyes, deep-sunken under their heavy brows. Deathly fatigue, yes, and a worry that belied the man's efforts to seem relaxed. But no trace of ridicule. "That was some kindness!"

"You did what you had to do, and you did it without jeering or unnecessary humiliation. There is no better way to assess a man than to see how he treats a beaten foe."

"The orders he chooses to obey are more revealing, senor. Montserrat tells me that you have gelded the hexer. For that I thank you from the depths of my soul! All Europe will rejoice at the end of the infamous baron."

"I took his demons away from him, yes. He's not basically an evil man at all, Captain." The big mouth twisted in a weary grin. "So tonight I gave them back to him again."

"You jest?"

"No. He broke down and wept. It was very touching." The outlaw smiled through his exhaustion.

"You are more gracious to beaten foes than I have ever been, senor. Was this wise?"

"I hope so. I need his help, you see, as well as . . ." Longdirk interrupted himself with an enormous yawn. "Excuse me! As well as yours—your help. I wanted to invite you to the meeting, but Montserrat said you were busy. I'll outline the plan and let you sleep on it. It will be called Don Ramon's Company, naturally. Have you met the honored *caballero*? No? You have a treat in store. He postures a lot, but he's brilliant at working out what I want to do and then ordering me to do it. He disapproves of fighting for money, but his m . . ." Another yawn. ". . . His squire persuaded him that this was the only option open to us. I shall be his *campeador*, whatever that is—it just seems to mean that I do all the work."

Diaz was beginning to see the penance the tutelary had in mind for him.

"Senor Josep Brusi has agreed to provide the necessary financing on very generous terms. The baron . . ." Again Longdirk yawned. Muttering angrily, he heaved himself out of his chair. "No, sit still. The baron will be our hexer—he is most eager to serve and no band in Europe will be better protected. My friend Hamish—Jaume—will be in charge of intelligence, because he has more of it than he knows what to do with."

Longdirk shuffled across to the bed and returned with a quilt. "That's as far as we got. About five hundred men, I think, to start with—pikemen, arquebusiers, cavalry . . . possibly some light artillery. We're going to begin in Italy."

Some comment was required. "Start what, senor?"

The big man was spreading the quilt on the floor. He looked up, bleary with exhaustion, having trouble making his eyes focus. "Fighting, of course." His grin made his heavy-boned face seem oddly boyish.

"Fighting whom?"

Longdirk straightened up and rubbed his eyes. "The Fiend. He's unbeaten so far, but I have a few ideas. A bit of success and we can start gathering allies . . . A fighting man could not ask for a foe more worthy, or *un*worthy, I suppose. He's got to be stopped. Think it over and we'll talk again in the morning. Josep's provided some gold already, so we can start recruiting and arming right away. Sorry, Captain, I'm tuckered out. If I don't lie down I'll fall down. Can you find your way to your quarters? Any questions so far?"

More than a few! It all sounded like raving insanity, and yet . . .

Yet he was a believable leader! Young and brash . . . but believable. He had thrown himself to the Inquisition to save his friends. He had escaped the Inquisition by some incredible miracle. He was competent, indestructible, unconquerable. Men would follow him. Even Diaz himself?

But . . . But . . . But!

Was it heresy to compare him to El Cid?

"May I inquire what experience you have, senor?"

The boy changed another yawn into his big grin. "None, if you mean conventional military experience. That's why I need you as my deputy. But fighting? Oreste has chased me all the way from Scotland. It took him three years to catch me, and even then he had to call in Nevil and his army. I think I know a little bit, Captain!"

The tutelary vouched for Longdirk, so he could not be as crazy as he seemed. Not crazy at all. He could master demons and overthrow the greatest hexer in Europe.

But!

"If I may have time to consider the matter, as you suggested, senor?"

"Of course. Can you find your way out? Better still, take the bed. I can't possibly sleep on anything that soft. No, I mean it." With no hesitation, Longdirk dropped his clothes and settled himself on the quilt. His wide back was brutally netted by the white scars of the lash, but Diaz had seen those before.

With a luxurious yawn, the big man rolled himself up in a cocoon and laid his face on the rug. "I think you're going to accept, Captain. I know you better than you know me, although I can't explain that now. Take the bed, I mean it!"

"You are very generous, senor!" Diaz snuffed the candle and went over to the huge featherbed, which he had already decided was the most appealing thing he had seen in years, and infinitely better than the thin straw pallet waiting for him in the cramped cell he had expected to share with Sergeant Gomez.

He knew that the offer was a sort of bribe. It would make the other offer harder to refuse—companions in arms already, sharing quarters, sharing trust. Either Longdirk was much more devious than he seemed or he had infallible instincts for handling men. Or he was just naturally generous.

Diaz stripped and sank deep into warm softness. Bliss!

Successful mercenaries could become very rich.

"One last question, senor. Why Italy?"

"Hmm?" said a sleepy voice from the darkness. "Because Nevil's bound to strike there soon. The princes and republics are arming like crazy, hiring every mercenary they can lay hands on. The baron and Hamish agree that Italy's where the next big battles will be. Mind you, I'm not at all sure that Jaume doesn't just want to be Giacomo."

After a moment he muttered, "That was a joke, I think. Spirits keep you, Captain."

"And you also, *Campeador*."

REALITY CHECK

My geography is more or less accurate. Social customs are very similar, although the absence of monotheistic religions makes some differences inevitable—Medieval Europe without Christianity is a contradiction in terms.

A divergent cast of characters takes over the historical stage after 1241. One of the great turning points in European history occurred in December of that year, when Ogedai Khan, son and successor of Genghis Khan, drank himself to death in far-off Mongolia. The unbeatable Mongol army, which had already conquered Russia, Poland, and Hungary and was poised to advance westward, turned back and never returned. (Russia remained under Mongol suzerainty for more than two centuries.)

Alumbradismo was a transcendental heresy associated with the Franciscans and first detected by the Inquisition in 1519. It sought total submission to God through meditation and claimed healing powers for some of its practitioners.

I have not overstated the cruelty of the Spanish Inquisition.

—K.H.

Enter a New World

THE WESTERN KING • Ann Marston

BOOK TWO OF THE RUNE BLADE TRILOGY

Guarded by the tradition of the past and threatened by the danger of the present, a warrior — as beautiful as she is fierce — must struggle between two warring clans who were one people once.

Also available, *Kingmaker's Sword*

FORTRESS IN THE EYE OF TIME • C. J. Cherryh

THREE TIME HUGO-AWARD WINNING AUTHOR

Deep in an abandoned, shattered castle, an old man of the Old Magic mutters words almost forgotten. With the most wondrous of spells, he calls forth a Shaping, in the form of a young man to be sent east to right the wrongs of a long-forgotten wizard-war, and alter the destiny of a land.

THE HEDGE OF MIST • Patricia Kennealy-Morrison

THE FINAL VOLUME OF THE TALES OF ARTHUR TRILOGY

Morrison's amazing canvas of Keltia holds the great and epic themes of classic fantasy — Arthur, Gweniver, Morgan, Merlynn, the magic of Sidhe-folk, and the Sword from the Stone. Here, with Taliesin's voice and harp to tell of it, she forges a story with the timelessness of a once and future tale.   *(Hardcover)*

Fantasy from 🏰 HarperPrism

DRAGONCHARM
• Graham Edwards

IN THE EPIC TRADITION OF ANNE MCCAFFREY'S PERN NOVELS

An ancient prophecy decreed that one day dragon would battle dragon, until none were left in the world. Now it is coming true.

EYE OF THE SERPENT
• Robert N. Charrette

SECOND OF THE AELWYN CHRONICLES

When a holy war breaks out, Yan, a mere apprentice mixing herbs in a back-water town, is called upon to create a spell that can save the land . . . and the life of his beloved Teletha.

Also available, *Timespell*